CAT FIGHT

HELLBOUND BOOK TWO

GIN GRIFFITH

ISBN: 978-1-963705-13-3

Cover design: Clarissa Kezen ckbookcoverdesigns.com

Published in the United States of America by Harbor Lane Books, LLC.

www.harborlanebooks.com

To the beautiful savage inside every girl.

CHAPTER 1

*O**ut. Want out. Out NOW.*

God, her cat was driving her nuts. "Just *wait*."

Juno's snarl was quiet, but a human pedestrian still shot her a startled look as he hurried past.

Cyrus snorted beside her. "That bad, huh?"

Juno rolled her shoulders, trying to ease the prickling sensation of her jaguar pushing at the inside of her skin. "Been too long since we ran."

Cyrus hummed in agreement. He was seriously too beautiful to be running around fighting demons in the shadows—dark skin, smooth shaved head, cheekbones for days, light blue eyes that glimmered with intelligence.

And mischief. "Roof?"

She shot straight into the air, sailing past the windows of the downtown apartment building like she was riding an invisible elevator. A kid playing with action figures on his windowsill dropped one of them as she flew by, his mouth gaping and wide eyes following her ascent.

She dropped unceremoniously onto the roof, narrowly missing an air conditioning coil. Cyrus grinned when she leaned over the edge to flip him the bird, his white teeth gleaming in the dark.

Fucking telekinetics. Her lips twitched despite herself.

The rooftops of the city stretched for miles before her, dotted with utility fixtures and scaffolding, fire escapes and the occasional crappy lawn chairs, potted plants and swooping strands of string lights. Pipes and radiators belched steam and dripped condensation, their puddles reflecting the neon lights and flashing billboards of downtown Concordia.

Out NOW—

She let her jaguar explode to the forefront.

Cyrus and Rogan had asked her once what it felt like to shift into animal form. She'd groped for something they could relate to, but the two dudes didn't know how it felt to finally whip off a bra after a long day or let your hair out of a too-tight ponytail. A burst of relief, a buildup of pressure finally released.

She told them it felt like an orgasm. Which made Rogan go slightly pink, and made Cyrus's ice-blue eyes spark with interest.

Her black paws ate up the distance across the roof, and when she reached the edge, she sprang off, leaping across the alley far below and catching a hint of Cyrus's scent as she sailed overhead. Crisp and sensual, like a strong martini, with the underlying tingle of magic that tickled her nose. Comforting, familiar. They'd been squadmates for a long time.

She went airborne again, limbs stretching, muscles pumping, heart soaring.

Free.

The city was alive with smells. Food vendors with their steaming trucks, restaurants venting out the back, clouds of vape and pungent homeless people and splats of bird shit from those damned blue pigeons strutting along the sidewalks. One flapped lazily past.

Snap. Snap with teeth. Eat? Play.

Juno inwardly snorted with agreement, but her amusement died when a messenger drone came into view, rising up from beyond the edge of the building to hover close to her head. What the hell was that thing doing up this high? They usually hovered over cars and pedestrians, not up on rooftops.

Drone? Is it buzzing you? Grab it. Could be surveillance.

Cyrus's voice in her head had ceased to surprise her a long time ago. It was one of his many talents, along with being genius-smart, supermodel good-looking, and a powerful telekinetic. The whole silent communication thing only seemed to work with those he was emotionally close to. As far as Juno knew, Cyrus could only talk to her and Rogan inside their heads. She'd be shocked if he could wedge his way inside Killian's thick skull.

She snapped at the drone whirring around her. An irritated swipe of her paw brought it crashing to the rooftop, its fragile wings fluttering before going still. She picked it up with her teeth, padded to the edge of the roof, and chuffed at Cyrus before tossing it over. She didn't bother waiting to see if he caught it, kind of hoping it landed on his pretty head. Spinning from the ledge, she sprang onto a series of pipes before leaping to another rooftop.

Fun. Free.

Yes. This was what they needed, both she and her cat. This was what they'd been missing while the squad had been lying low for the past week, trying to find their footing after their world imploded.

Betrayal was a bitter bite on her tongue. She did not give her trust easily. She'd given it to Magistrate Thackeray White, ruler of the city's magical population and founder of the top-secret Demon Eradication unit. She'd trusted his kind smile, his quiet encouragement, his fucking money that kept the team in the best gear, the best room and board…and then

Rogan, their leader, fell for a half-succubus, and the Magistrate went bat-shit crazy.

Her claws gripped a scaffold and she swung herself onto the platform above in a graceful arc, trying to ignore the acid burn of shame in her belly.

She'd watched. Just watched, as her squad leader, her captain, her brother, for all intents and purposes, was stripped of everything he loved and tossed out on the street.

She'd watched and did nothing. All of them had.

It still didn't seem real.

The sick feeling had yet to totally leave her stomach. And that was nothing compared to the kill order the Magistrate issued next.

That, at least, Juno would never even consider. The rest of the squad had been just as shocked—and that was before the ceiling caved in and the Magistrate's secret lab was destroyed by demons. It turned out Jovi, the half-demon who ruined Rogan's life, was also half angel. Her father, the fallen archangel, Alistor, had appeared at the end of the battle and scared Jovi's psycho succubus mother back to hell. ARC, the Archangel Regiment in Command, had ordered the Magistrate to grant all of them safe passage when they said they weren't working for him anymore. They'd found a new home at the boarding school Rogan had helped get off the ground all those years ago, but Light House wasn't exactly a fortress of security, and the squad knew better than anyone that the Magistrate had patience, power, and spies everywhere.

The sense of a giant ticking clock was giving her major anxiety. Add that to the crippling guilt and mandatory R&R, and it was no wonder both she and her jaguar were going out of their skin.

Her paw slipped on a wet spot, and she torqued to stay upright, her muscular feline body reaching for the next foothold even as a sharp pain zinged along her shoulder blade. The electric sensation jolted her memory, taking her back to a pool of water at the base of an exploded holding tank. The Magistrate's electric orb hit the water, and all at once, she was a seizing, twitching mass of agony—

Then, black. Nothing but black.

She had no clue how long she'd been out. All she knew was that when she lifted her heavy lids, it was to find a pair of lion-yellow eyes inches from hers, a thick, muscular lap cushioning her head, and a hot, wild scent bringing her back from the brink.

The look on Killian's face...that utter terror followed by immense, sweeping relief—she had to have imagined it. Right?

Squadmates didn't look at each other like that.

Killian Diallo sure as hell didn't look at her like that.

Cyrus's voice sounded in her head. *Got a couple live ones down here.*

Paws scrabbled on the asphalt as she instantly changed direction, locating Cyrus's scent and springing off the roof with a snarl. She zigzagged her way down to the asphalt, where Cyrus faced off with a pair of skeletal wraiths. At the flick of his finger, a dumpster flew across the alley to pin one of them to the wall. Its inhuman shriek was deafening, but Juno only had eyes for the other target, who was about to launch something at her teammate. She leaped into the air and collided with the thing, a bony sack of skin that stank of sulfur and made her hackles go up. As soon as its bony back hit the ground, her claws went to work. Jaguars had the most powerful bite of any big cat, but she avoided putting her mouth on the enemy unless absolutely necessary. Demon blood tasted like battery acid.

With a final swipe, the wraith went still. Her jaguar huffed in the humid night air, sniffed to confirm the target was dead, then stepped gracefully off the corpse to check on Cyrus.

He studied his target with muscled arms folded, casually

considering the hellspawn pinned to the alley wall. "Do you work for Inara?"

The wraith writhed and screeched, trying to wrench itself free.

"Where'd you get in?"

They were always looking for hellmouths, the portals where demons entered the midrealm. You'd have thought it'd be easy to find a giant smoking hole in the middle of the city, but the squad had never found one in Concordia. The only one they'd seen had been in hyena territory a few weeks ago, the one that revealed Jovi's evil mother, Inara, was kidnapping hyena shapeshifters and sending them back to their clan, possessed by demons. The team didn't know how to close hellmouths, though John was constantly researching new rituals and techniques. The archangels could close the portals, but they had trouble hanging in the midrealm for extended periods of time. Luckily, the squad had a fallen angel on their team now, and though he'd lost a lot of his powers, he had the other archangels on speed dial.

The wraith pinned against the alley wall hissed something in a strange language. Cyrus made a face, then pulled back his palm. The dumpster flew toward him. Before the wraith could peel itself off the brick, Cyrus sent the dumpster smashing into its bony body, pinning it once again and severing its head, which toppled onto the pile of trash.

"Ooh, two points." He shot Juno a cocky grin that turned into a grimace as he lifted his arm to examine his formidable bicep. The metallic scent of blood hit her an instant before Cyrus's curse. "Damn, it got me."

Juno padded closer and saw a jagged slash splitting her teammate's flesh, shining wet in the faint glow of the city streetlights. It looked nasty.

Cyrus cursed again and checked his watch. "It's almost four. I'm gonna head back, have John or Jovi patch me up. You good on your own for a bit?"

She chuffed and gave him her back. He knew she could handle herself.

"Stay safe. And Rogan is serious about that four a.m. curfew. See you at home."

She watched his silhouette melt into the distance, excitement bubbling in her feline chest. She'd get to run a bit longer, free and on her own. After dragging the headless corpse of Cyrus's kill over to her own dispatched enemy, she used her teeth to pull a small white marble from a pocket on her watchband. Like all shapeshifters on the squad, her watchband expanded and shrunk to fit both her animal and human forms, which was necessary because their watch was what powered their lens. And their lenses were what allowed them to see the invisible hellspawn that roamed the midrealm.

The marble rolled to a stop next to the demon bodies before emitting a high-pitched whine. Juno shut her eyes against the blinding flash of light, then retrieved the marble from the now-empty spot on the asphalt. Their enemies had been poofed into thin air, leaving nothing for unassuming, demon-blind pedestrians to trip over.

She slipped the vaporizer into its pocket and trotted to a nearby fire escape, giddy with anticipation. It had only been a week, but it felt like forever since she'd gone for a run. Her muscles begged to be used. Leaping up the webbed iron stairs, she found herself once again on the rooftop, looking out over the neon-lit streets.

Silka's corporate office loomed in her periphery, along with the burnished gold of the Pyramid casino and the towering blue and white blocks of Magical Law Enforcement headquarters. The pillars of her past, each with memories heavy enough to crush her if she let them.

Lights and smells and sounds rushed past her as she ran, pushing herself higher, farther, faster. There was nothing soft about Concordia. The city was harsh and hard, from its blaring billboards to cold concrete streets. She sailed across another series of slanted roofs, paws spreading for balance. A pile of scrap metal gleamed far below as she leaped across a gap. If she fell, nothing would cushion the blow.

Good thing she never let herself fall.

The slow current of Red River glinted in the distance. She made her way toward it, sprinting over balconies, inwardly laughing at the startled cries of the few late-night revelers enjoying a drink under the stars. God, yes, this was what she needed. Loose and alive, powerful and free—

An acrid scent brought her up short. She skidded to a halt at the edge of the roof. A quick series of jumps brought her to the ground, and she followed the smell of her enemy toward the river.

The second her paws hit the gravel along the river's shoreline, there was a screech to her right. She spun and found herself facing a huge, bipedal bat-like demon, narrow mouth gaping wide as it shrieked into the night, diving at her. She crouched low, her jaguar form coiled, ready—

A massive golden body slammed into her from behind.

She stumbled, getting tangled in a warm, leathery wing, and felt a burning pain across her jaguar's shoulder blade. *Fuck.* Fury gave her claws speed as she fought her way free, wrenching loose in time to see Killian Diallo, in his enormous lion form, slamming her target to the ground.

His paws plunged into the demon's sternum. There was a wet squelch, a dry crack, and an ear-splitting scream as its rib cage was ripped apart. Something wet slapped Juno's muzzle. She shook it off and swiped at Killian's tail. The slash mark on her shoulder lit up with pain. She ignored it.

A huge lion head swung around, yellow eyes glinting in the dark.

She morphed into human form and glared at him from all fours. "What the hell are you doing, Diallo? You're not on duty—"

A shriek from the left had her whipping around, ducking under a swiping talon just in time. She dodged and rolled, grinding dirt into her open wound, and shifted into jaguar form before leaping at her target. There was a battering of sound—flapping wings, screeches of pain, her own growls. She almost had it. She just needed the right angle...

A furry golden freight train bashed into her side, knocking her clear.

Goddammit. She rolled to her feet as Killian ripped out her opponent's windpipe, his lethal fangs tearing into the demon with a savagery that made her jaguar purr.

He spat a mouthful of black blood on the ground and lifted his gaze to hers.

She morphed back into human form and rose naked from all fours. Those slashes on her back stung like hell. The fact that her teammate took her kill burned even more. "What are you doing?"

Bones rippled beneath fur. Paws elongated into thick masculine fingers. The coarse ruff of his mane lengthened into tangled strands that hung well past his broad shoulders. The lion's pelt melted into acres of muscle, and Killian Diallo stared at her from a crouch. He looked just as primal as he did in animal form. Tribal tattoos covered his arms and chest, the black lines a stark contrast to the smooth bronze of his skin. "You shouldn't be out here."

It hurt and pissed her off all at once. He was good at that. "Excuse me?"

The bones of his face were hard, carved, and animalistic. His dark blond beard did nothing to soften the granite lines of his jaw. Handsome wasn't the word for him. Raw, yes. Magnetic, yes. Dangerous, definitely. "You don't remember being electrocuted to death?"

Abruptly, she was back in a ruined lab, staring up into those lion eyes and watching the weight of the world fall from his massive naked shoulders. "I'm fine."

"You *died*, DeSilva." His deep voice, already rough as gravel, was pure animal now.

She pushed the tiny flutter of fear aside. "I didn't die. John said—"

"*John* wasn't fucking there." His nostrils flared as he breathed, fogging the air like a dragon.

She swiped at her long, dark hair, hanging loose after her shift and blowing in the fishy breeze coming off the river. A rat scurried from a pile of trash under the nearby bridge. Her pulse leapt, but she jerked herself back into focus. "He said he would've felt it." John, the squad's teleporter and healer, was a spirit walker and said there was a web that connected them all, that he could feel each one of them in it. "I didn't die, and Jovi healed me with her angelic healing powers or whatever, and Rogan cleared me for duty."

Killian scoffed.

"I'm *fine*."

His lip curled. "Yeah, that's going on your tombstone, isn't it?"

The world took on a verdant sheen, and she knew her cat's neon green eyes were flashing at him. "What the hell is your problem?"

Their watches vibrated. Four o'clock, patrol over. And a text from Rogan. *Everyone in the kitchen, stat.*

Killian read the text on his watch and shifted into lion form without another word, stalking away into the night.

The Light House Boarding School For Magical Youth was an old refurbished factory. Rogan's burly silhouette waited just inside the front doors, backlit by a rectangle of golden light. Scents bombarded Juno as she padded inside—old metal, the lingering aroma from dinner, dozens of orphaned mage kids, and the scent of magic, strong enough to make her nose tingle. Hanging with Cyrus and John for so long had helped her get used to the feeling, but being surrounded by this much magic on a daily basis was still battering to her shapeshifter senses.

It was fine, though. She could handle it.

Yeah, that's going on your tombstone, isn't it?

Rogan frowned at Killian. "What are you doing out?" Sharp green eyes scanned the black blood splattered on the lion's golden flank.

Killian shifted to human form. "Needed a fight."

Rogan's frown deepened before he turned to the wardrobe they'd stashed in the entryway and pulled out two stacks of sweats, tossing them each a pair. "Kitchen. We need to talk."

Secondhand appliances, steel countertops, and ancient-looking kitchen gadgets gleamed beneath the overhead lights of Light House's small commercial kitchen. Wolf was digging a hand into a box of cereal, his rubber ducky pajama pants riding low on lean hips, with his tight abs on display. Cyrus's blue eyes tracked a chef's knife as it flipped lazily in midair, end over end. The wound on his upper arm was puckered and pink, healing fast. John's crow familiar, Tika, watched from her perch on John's shoulder. Alistor, Jovi's fallen archangel father, loomed by the refrigerator, his black trench-coat stretched over colossal shoulders, black brows drawn. Juno had yet to see the guy smile.

Killian's big arm wedged against hers as they squeezed through the door. She pushed. So did he. They stuck. With a mutual glare, they shoved through the doorway and headed to opposite corners of the kitchen.

Settling against the doors of a double oven, she raked a hand through her hair and bit back a wince. The slash across her shoulder blade hurt like hell. The cement floor was cold, and she tucked one bare foot against her calf while Rogan made a beeline for his woman.

Rogan's woman. It was still weird to say that. Still weird

to *see* that. Jovi was perched on one of the counters in a white tank top and a pair of hot pink panties, returning Rogan's glare with a sultry smile.

"Really? No pants?"

"Oh, nobody cares." She tugged him forward by the shirt.

"*I* care—"

"I don't mind," Wolf said helpfully from the pantry, grinning when Rogan shot him a murderous look. His mop of chestnut hair, streaked with the bright white of his wolf form, flopped as he cocked his head, sniffing the air. "Who's bleeding?"

Juno deliberately ignored a certain lion's pointed stare. "Me. It's fine."

Killian snorted.

She gritted her teeth. "What's this about?"

John was already easing behind her to lift the back of her oversized sweatshirt. She bit back a curse as the fabric scraped her wound. It hurt. A lot. And it could've been completely avoided if her teammate hadn't stuck his big, furry muzzle where it didn't belong.

John made a low noise. "That's ugly."

"Oh, don't worry, it's fine. She can handle it," Killian said nastily from his corner.

She barely managed to keep her claws in. "Fuck you, Diallo."

CHAPTER 2

Well, well. He'd succeeded in pissing off the queen of cool. Killian might've been proud of himself if he wasn't so busy holding back his lion.

Want.

His beast was clawing at his insides.

The scent of her blood sent his cat into a frenzy. He gripped the edge of the counter, welcoming the bite of stainless steel into his palms.

Silence followed the curse Juno had thrown at him. Several brows popped, but Rogan's drew together as he turned away from his female. He'd tossed an apron over her head in an attempt to cover some skin, but only managed to make her look like she was wearing a sexy chef's costume. Then again, Jovi was half succubus—she always looked like a walking, talking wet dream.

Well, someone's wet dream.

He couldn't help but shoot a glance at Juno, who was staring at him like she wanted his balls for breakfast. John held up the back of her sweatshirt while he worked on her wound, revealing a tawny six pack that clenched as she breathed. Dark hair fell in a curtain around her shoulders, loose as always after she shifted. The second she could find a hair elastic, it would be back in its tight ponytail, swinging with every sway of her hips, brushing the curve of her strong back, begging to be wrapped around a male's fist—

Rogan frowned at the two of them. "What happened?"

She died in my fucking arms, that's what happened. His hands tightened on the edge of the counter.

"He kept interfering with my kills."

Killian kept his eyes pinned to the opposite wall, wishing he could staple them open—maybe then he wouldn't sleep, wouldn't dream, wouldn't fucking *blink* and see her lying lifeless in his arms, lush mouth hanging slack, chocolate eyes staring blankly as he shook her like a panicked, desperate fool.

Juno looked back to Rogan. "You cleared me, right?"

Rogan's eyes narrowed, but he nodded.

"Then, there's no reason for anyone to treat me like I'm less than a hundred. Jovi fixed me up, John looked me over, you cleared me." She pointed at each of them in turn. "I'm good to go." She moved her shoulders irritably, no doubt feeling the prickling sensation of John's healing abilities. Killian's lion settled ever so slightly, knowing she was being looked after.

Fuck.

Rogan considered her for a long moment. The big knife Cyrus had been flipping with his telekinesis hovered in midair. "Agreed."

Juno shot Killian a smug look.

"But I'm pulling you, anyway."

Shock, hurt, and anger flashed across her face before she smothered them with that mask of control that drove him out of his mind. "Why?"

"We need a lawyer."

Juno went very still. Her face revealed nothing, but he saw the way every single muscle tightened up. His own body tensed in response.

"We need to get Light House out from under the Magistrate. I'm not letting him get his hands on any more kids."

Rogan had been an orphan himself, taken under the Magistrate's wing and groomed into the perfect little soldier for his secret project, the Demon Eradication unit. Rogan had worshiped the man, considered him something like a father figure...until the bastard revealed himself to be a twisted motherfucker who'd lied to Rogan since childhood and had no problem ordering the rest of them to kill him. Evil had a lot of faces.

But what did needing a lawyer have to do with Juno?

She tugged down her sweatshirt as John moved away from her. Arms folded tight across her chest, she nodded. "I'll talk to him."

Him *who?*

"Who?" Wolf was clearly just as confused.

Cyrus watched Juno from across the kitchen. "Vasquez."

Stainless steel crunched beneath Killian's grip.

Jaguars were more solitary than most shapeshifters. They didn't have the same clan structure as lions or wolves, but they sure as shit recognized power, influence, and strength. Rafael Vasquez, owner of the Pyramid casino, its underground fighting arena, and countless other things that made him rich as hell, had it all in spades, and was as close to alpha as jaguars got.

He was also Juno's ex.

Killian held onto the counter with everything he had, feeling a tendon pop somewhere in his neck.

Wolf whistled, long and low.

"What?" Jovi said, looking around the room. "Who's Vasquez?"

"Oh, he and Juno used to..." Wolf clicked his teeth and wiggled his brows. "You know."

"Ohhhh." Jovi looked at Juno.

"It's fine." A tiny line appeared between her brows when she caught herself repeating her goddamn epithet. "I'll do it tomorrow."

His beast was tearing at the inside of his skin, desperate to claw its way out, to touch, to take, to claim—

Want.

"Thank you. I want the rest of us lying low. We keep patrolling, but stay out of sight as much as possible." Rogan's wide jaw ticked. "We're being watched."

Cyrus pulled a tiny flying drone from a pocket and directed it to the middle of the kitchen with a casual finger, where it hovered in midair. One wing was crunched. "Juno found this buzzing around the roof."

"I'm sure the Magistrate is probably spreading shit about us around MLE. We need to be careful." Rogan gave Jovi and Alistor a stern look. "You two, especially. I want you to back off on the Sip n' Spell runs and drinking in the Blender. You draw attention." His eyes heated as they traveled over Jovi's luminous skin and waterfall of bubblegum pink hair. "I don't really want to have to bust you out of MLE again."

Jovi folded her arms, sighed, and nodded before jerking her head toward her glowering father, whose own waist-length hair blended in with his black leather coat. "He doesn't really like it, anyway." Her mouth twitched. "Everyone hits on him and it makes him feel weird." She ended on a snorting laugh, and a few more echoed around the room.

Alistor's scowl deepened. "These mid-dwellers are very...handsy."

More snickers broke out, but Killian didn't feel like laughing. Maybe the idea of a giant fallen archangel being hounded at the bars would be funny if he could picture anything but Juno alone in a room with Rafael fucking Vasquez.

WANT.

"We done here?" he managed. The tendons in his neck throbbed. When Rogan nodded, he all but bolted from the room.

CHAPTER 3

Watching an angel try to shoot a gun was funny.

Juno pressed her lips together. She shouldn't laugh. But Alistor was just so ferocious and larger than life with that icy stare and big, resonant voice...and the dude couldn't fire a phaser to save his centuries-long life.

As he fumbled with the slick metal weapon, Juno's eyes slid over to Cyrus.

His voice sounded in her head. *Don't you dare look at me, I'll lose it.*

She jerked her gaze away from Cyrus to find Wolf biting his knuckles to stifle his laughter, and yanked her focus away from him—only to collide with Killian's amber stare. She looked quickly away.

Their makeshift training center was little more than a big, empty room with some weight racks and cardboard targets on the far wall, but it would do. It would have to do. They didn't have the luxury of the life-like city setting, holographic targets, and real-time weather simulator they'd had back at the Bunker. They didn't have a lot of the luxuries they'd had back at the Bunker, like 24/7 access to a state-of-the-art armory, and all the weapons they could ever want.

Luckily, Jovi apparently had friends in low places. Dimitri Zmey, notorious alpha of the reptile shifters, had supplied them with a stock of guns that weren't fingerprint-enabled. In other words, untraceable. It had cost them a pretty penny, and suddenly, that was something that mattered.

Here she was again, giving up a silver spoon for a plastic spork. And not regretting it for a second.

There was a clatter and a foreign curse as the angel fumbled the gun. His broad back flexed as he stooped to sweep it from the floor. He'd tossed his trenchcoat in a corner with a defiant glance at all of them, as if daring them to comment on his wings. If you could call them that.

Juno's gut squirmed at the sight of the translucent filaments that hung weakly from his shoulder blades, the forlorn remnants of once powerful appendages. She'd seen archangel wings before, vast and formidable, gleaming with layers of soft feathers, as strong and breathtaking as the angels themselves. The thin wisps that undulated from Alistor's muscular back were a mockery of what he once was.

"Have you *no* swords?" he demanded, black hair flaring around his torso as he whirled toward the gathered peanut gallery. His wings followed sluggishly.

Apparently, while Juno was busy almost dying, Alistor had thrown his enormous archangel longsword at Inara when she was vanishing into thin air, and the sword vanished with her. They could only hope it had caused serious damage and she'd be licking her wounds for a while. Not that it would stop her minions from finding their way to the midrealm.

"Fresh out," Wolf said, sounding strangled.

There were a few more muffled snorts of laughter. Someone coughed. The angel glared around at them, those crystal blue eyes fierce and defiant, shoulders proud.

Suddenly, it wasn't all that funny.

And suddenly, Juno was back in her father's plush office, being scoffed at for wanting martial arts training. Back at the academy, the only female and the only shapeshifter in her class, pretending she didn't hear every single snicker, every single taunt. Back in the Arena, facing off with her first ever opponent while the crowd laughed and jeered.

Their laughter hadn't lasted long, but it still made her feel like shit.

"Here." Juno stepped forward to help position the angel's hands on the phaser. "You have to remember to take the safety off."

"None of you took your *safety* off!"

Beside him, Jovi bit back a smile. She was dressed as usual in a short skirt, black combat boots, a little T-shirt showing off her tight belly, and a stack of candy necklaces around her throat. "Yeah, they did, Dadistor. They're just super fast. Show him, babe." She gestured to Rogan, who stepped forward and showed Alistor the red light on his phaser, indicating the safety was enabled. The next second, his weapon was pointed straight at the target, and there was a smoking hole in the center of its cardboard head.

The archangel blinked.

Jovi patted his arm. "I know. They're all annoyingly good at it. I don't even bother. I just do this." She launched a stream of fire at the target, which erupted into flame and fell to a pile of ash on the polished gym floor.

"Hey, that took me forever to cut out," Wolf protested.

"You need to work on your other skills." Rogan planted his hands on his hips and squared off with Jovi. "We've talked about this. Your magic burns you out fast, and you might not always have a dozen candy necklaces around your neck to refuel."

"Then, I'll just come find you." Jovi trailed a fingertip down his chest. "I point, you shoot, right?"

Something tender passed between the two of them before

Jovi stretched one of the necklaces into her mouth and bit off a candy, somehow managing to make her crunching look sexy. She rose on tiptoes to brush her lips over Rogan's. His hands didn't leave his hips, but his body softened ever so slightly, melting toward his woman like wax to a flame. Juno's cat watched, fascinated.

When Jovi lowered to the floor, Rogan didn't move an inch. But his pale green gaze pinned her to the spot. And then, he parted his lips, revealing a single hard candy between his teeth.

Jovi laughed, low and satisfied, and an answering spark flared in Rogan's eyes before he flicked the candy into his mouth and regarded her seriously. "I mean it."

The saucy smirk left Jovi's face, and she nodded.

Want.

Juno shook herself, unwilling to examine whether that thought came from her or her cat.

Rogan straightened, all business once again. "Alistor, we'll work on getting you a sword. I'm sure Zmey can make one. For a price. Meanwhile, you have healing and teleportation abilities. Don't discount those. Maybe you could even step back from combat for a while. There's no shame in that."

John, who was wearing sweatpants and nothing else, was already dipping into his primal strength and mobility movements. He halted for a split second before continuing his fluid, mesmerizing flow. He was beautifully sculpted, graceful as a dancer and strong as a gymnast, in incredible shape despite his non-combat role. Tika cawed from a rafter.

Alistor leaned in, looking down on Rogan from his towering height. "I have been in combat since the *dawn of time*, human." When Rogan folded his beefy arms and held the angel's gaze, Alistor sighed, looking away. "And I can no longer beam to a location."

Rogan's brows knit. "But that's how you got to the lab."

Yeah, apparently Juno had missed that part, too—the

fallen angel appearing in a blaze of light in the middle of the battle at the lab, making one hell of an entrance.

"That was the first time since my Fall. I was very angry when your friend, Nora, told me of your existence." Alistor speared Jovi with eyes that matched her own. "Very angry that I had not known."

While Jovi chewed her lip, looking awkward, Wolf held up a finger. "Wait, so you got mad, and then you were able to flash to her?" When Alistor nodded, Wolf rubbed his chin, then strode forward and slammed a fist into the angel's nose.

Shouts rang out as Alistor's head snapped back. He righted himself slowly, staring down at Wolf with murder on his face. A trickle of blood leaked from his nose. "You *strike* m—"

Wolf kicked him in the crotch.

Alistor let out a guttural grunt, hunching over and cupping his balls.

Wolf was already running. "Catch me if you can, big man!"

With a snarl of rage, Alistor straightened, clenched his fists, and vanished, only to reappear in a flash of light, blocking the doorway just as Wolf skidded to a stop.

"There you go!" Wolf grinned.

Alistor's punch laid him out flat.

"Saw that coming," Cyrus muttered as Wolf's back hit the polished wood floor with a smack. His groans floated across the room.

"You *can* flash!" Jovi clapped as Alistor stomped back to the group, wiping blood from his nose. "All we have to do is piss you off!"

As an earth-shuddering growl rumbled from the angel's throat, Rogan quickly placed Alistor's phaser in his hands. "Let's keep working on firearms for now." He checked his own phaser cartridge with a sigh. "I need to talk to Father Scott about getting more Holy Light."

Alistor scoffed. "Holy Light." At the resounding silence, he shook his head. "This realm's religious ideas never cease to baffle me. Do you truly believe some human chanting over a vial of light has some magical effect?"

"It certainly seems to have an effect on demons."

"The light has an effect. It has nothing to do with your priest." When they all stared at him, Alistor sighed. "The bottom-dwellers are born in darkness. They cannot withstand such concentrated light. It defies their very nature. That is why your light wounds them. You need no false blessing from humans who serve a false deity."

Everyone seemed to be holding their breath.

"Let's be clear. By false deity, you mean..." Rogan looked at Alistor expectantly.

"If a single, all-powerful being exists, I have never met them."

"Aren't archangels supposed to be God's warriors?"

"We serve ourselves." Alistor shook his head. "The early mid-dwellers were stupid. They created much false lore surrounding our existence. It astounds me how many still believe it."

Rogan didn't seem surprised, but he spoke carefully. "If you serve yourselves, how do you Fall?"

Alistor's face hardened. "We High Ones have our own code. It is binding. I broke it and paid the consequences."

Rogan heaved a breath, nodding. "None of us here are Bible followers, but I'll admit meeting the famous archangel Michael threw me."

The fallen archangel glowered. "He always has enjoyed the attention."

A few laughs echoed around the group. Rogan was right, none of them were religious, but it was still something to have a literal angel confirm that God as they knew it didn't exist.

Although, nothing changed for Juno. She could rely on herself, and she could rely on the squad. Same as ever.

She was about to suggest they get back to training when Jovi spoke. "What about the souls?"

Alistor peered at the red safety light on his phaser. "What souls?"

"The souls that get sent to hell. For torture. Because they were bad." Her face was white, her crystal gaze haunted.

"You can't torture a soul." John's low, smooth voice carried across the vast gymnasium. Everyone's head swung around to stare at him. Black brows lifted. "You can't torture a soul. It's not physical. It can't feel physical pain."

Jovi's voice took on a panicked edge. "But she said that was part of their punishment, that their soul would be made to feel pain. That's why they seemed solid and real. It was part of their punishment." She met John's gaze somewhat desperately.

Pained, he shook his head.

"So, all those people I..." Jovi's throat worked, her eyes a million miles away. "They were real people? Living people?"

Shit.

Jovi combusted.

Shouts erupted as she burst into flames. Everyone leaped back. Rogan jerked toward her, barely halting before he got incinerated.

"I knew they weren't all bad." Jovi's voice was warped within the flames.

"Jovi," Rogan said sharply, hands outstretched.

Jovi's head turned until she locked eyes with her father. Pink hair swirled. Fingers glowed like live coals. "All those people I...how did they get down there?"

The angel's face was hard as stone. "The bottom-dwellers took them."

Jesus. The squad had been fighting demons for years, but

they'd never seen hellspawn kidnap people and haul them away.

"We believe the demons keep them there to feed." The thin filaments of Alistor's wings whipped.

"Sick. Like a fucking pantry?" Even Wolf looked horrified.

News articles of missing persons flashed across Juno's mind. Unsolved kidnappings, people who disappeared without a trace. Was this what happened to them? Her stomach churned.

"That's not why Mommy Dearest wanted them." Jovi sounded eerily distant. "She had those people brought there for me. To practice on." The flames grew.

"Jovi," Rogan said again.

The flames vanished. Jovi stood shaking in the middle of the room, tears pouring down her pale, perfect face.

Without a word, Rogan swept her into his arms and strode out of the gym.

Silence throbbed.

Wolf gestured weakly to John. "Look what you did. You made the demon cry."

"She was one of us, long ago. Inara." Alistor stared at the empty doorway, his voice filled with bitterness. "She Fell for a mortal. Lost her wings. I do not know what transpired afterward except that she asked to return. But she broke the code. She could not return. We turned our backs on her."

"So Inara isn't truly a demon." Cyrus watched Alistor carefully. "She's a fallen angel. Like you."

"Whatever decency Inara had is lost. She is warped. A different being altogether. I know not what to call her other than one of the vile creatures she commands." His voice lowered to a snarl. "The day I become like her is the day I hope for my own beheading."

Long, uncomfortable seconds ticked by.

Juno needed to punch something. Or run. Or break a

sweat. Anything but sit here and stew over this series of bombshells. "Come on, let's train."

They split up, Cyrus joining the target practice, Killian heading to the weight rack, and Wolf running to one of the ropes they'd hung from the rafters, shimmying up without using his feet. The pink cupcake tattoo on his upper arm bulged with every pull.

Juno studied the makeshift stations around the space. What did she need to work on? Where was she weak?

There was a pull-up bar wedged in a doorway.

Could she pull herself out of a hole?

She jumped for the bar and did three slow, steady pull-ups.

What about with a broken arm?

She tucked one arm behind her back and slowly, excruciatingly, pulled herself up.

What about blindfolded?

She closed her eyes and did another. Sweat beaded on her forehead. After a few more variations, she dropped to the floor, chest pumping.

What if I'm trapped? Pinned?

She glanced up at the high ceiling. "Wolf. Come lay on me."

"Ooh, kinky." Wolf did a swan dive from a rafter.

Juno's heart leaped into her throat as he hit the mats, tucking into a gangly somersault at the last second and bouncing to his feet, arms wide.

"You're going to kill yourself one of these days," she muttered as he jogged over.

"Never." He stuck his tongue out with a wild grin.

Shaking her head, she dropped to her belly on the mat, grunting when his weight landed on her back. He was taller than her, his legs extending far beyond her boots. "Try to hold me down."

Wolf was lanky, but made of long, solid ropes of muscle,

and she felt the considerable strength of them as he tensed above her. She pressed her palms into the floor, shoving upright with all her power. He was heavier than he looked, but she managed to get some space between her and the mat. Triumph rushed through her.

He bore down, and her arms collapsed an inch.

Hell, no.

With a grunt, she shoved him upright, throwing his weight from her back and rolling smoothly to a crouch, ready for him. Her blood pounded from the effort, but she gave him a smug grin as he sat up, long legs sprawled on the mat, panting.

"Not bad. Next time, let me tie you up." His brows wiggled, that shock of white hair gleaming against his wild chestnut waves.

"In your dreams."

A loud bang sounded across the room as Killian practically threw his dumbbells on the rack, shirt off and chest pumping, sweat gleaming over his tattoos.

Ignoring the jolt in her belly, Juno checked her watch. "I've gotta go. Covering Israel's agility class." Israel Stroud was one of the world's most respected fighters, and he did some consulting and freelance work when he wasn't teaching Light House orphans the basics of combat. He'd asked Juno to sub for his agility class while he was off filming some training videos or something. She couldn't say she was looking forward to it. Kids weren't exactly her thing. Dusting herself off, she helped Wolf to his feet and headed for the door.

"Don't forget, they're not all invincible like you."

Her head snapped around at Killian's nasty sneer. He'd moved over to target practice, and he barely met her eye before turning to his cardboard cutout and taking aim, muscular back flaring.

Asshole. "What the hell is your problem, Diallo?"

He fired, putting a hole in his target's chest. She strode out of the room, willing her claws to stay inside her skin.

————

"Get up that rope. No telekinesis, Kyla!"

Christ, these kids were lazy. Who knew subbing for an agility class would be so lame? These little mages looked like they'd never even tried to climb a tree. Juno shook her head, trying to imagine her eight-year-old self doing anything other than vaulting through the concrete jungle, swinging from scaffolding and shimmying up cell towers. She'd been a lean, muscular weapon by age ten. Not that it did her many favors.

Her father was cooly furious whenever she came back from one of her runs around the city, flushed and windblown and more alive than she ever had been inside Silka's slick corporate walls. Juan DeSilva was so far removed from his jaguar he might as well have been human. Juno could only remember seeing his animal form a handful of times. He was far more interested in power, money, and his multi-million credit corporation. He couldn't fathom why the heiress to the Silka fortune would rather run across dirty rooftops than slink around his upper-crust world.

DeSilvas control their animals, not the other way around.

She'd often wondered if her mother, who died giving birth, had shared her love for movement, for testing her physical limits, for letting her cat out of its cage.

At fifteen, her father had forbidden her from running downtown in her animal form. At seventeen, she found out just how serious he was about his rule.

Another kid plummeted to the mats covering the polished wood floor, jolting her out of her memories just as a smoky-sweet scent tickled her nose.

Jovi sauntered across the gym and stopped beside her,

folding her arms and surveying the scene. Any trace of tears was gone. "Wow, they really suck."

Should she ask if Jovi was okay? How could someone be okay after that? "You should've seen the obstacle course."

Jovi snorted. They stood in silence, watching the kids bumble around. When a willowy blonde girl fell to the mat, landing with a sickening crack and a fire engine wail, they swore in unison.

Jovi waved the girl over. She obeyed, sniffing and cradling her hand, which was already sporting a blackening thumb.

Jovi peered at it. "Aw, that blows." As the kid blinked watery eyes at Jovi's version of sympathy, she laid her palms gently over the girl's thumb, closed her eyes, and started to glow.

The girl gulped. "Can I be done for today?"

Juno watched the bruises fade beneath Jovi's glowing hands. "Done? Nah, you'll feel better soon. Jovi's amazing."

Crystal drops clung to the girl's pale eyelashes. "But what if I fall again?"

What was this kid's name? Larissa? Juno put a hand on her small shoulder. "Then, you'll get up again. And Jovi will heal you and you'll keep going. Just like you're doing now."

Larissa's throat bobbed. "I'm scared." She gazed at her thumb. It looked almost normal, but based on that trembling lip, the girl was still seeing it swollen and black.

Juno crouched in front of her. "Hey. Sometimes we fall. Sometimes we get hurt. Sometimes we get hurt really, really bad. But that doesn't mean we don't keep trying. We get up and dust ourselves off and believe it'll be better next time."

Larissa cast a worried look at the rope. "What if it's not better next time?"

She put some steel into her voice. "Then, we try again. Because we're strong girls. And strong girls don't give up." She leaned in. "Especially when there are boys to beat."

Larissa's smile was watery, but a spark of resolve lit her face when she glanced at her classmates.

Jovi released the girl's hand. "Good to go, babe. Go kick some ass."

With a final sniff, Larissa headed back to the mat. When she swiped a hand over her cheek and grabbed the rope, a surge of pride crashed through Juno's chest.

Get it, girl.

She and Jovi shared a grin. The female's otherworldly glow had faded, but her skin was somehow still luminous under the buzzing gym lights.

A little over a week ago, Juno had been beating the shit out of that delicate skin in an interrogation cell, convinced this woman planned to ruin the only life and family she had. And less than an hour ago, she'd seen the same woman weeping with remorse over innocent people she'd been forced to hurt.

Juno reached into a pocket, pulled a butterscotch candy from the stash she'd started carrying, and handed it over.

Jovi took it with a smile. "I love the way you guys are handling your guilt." She popped the candy in her mouth and rattled it around her teeth. The woman was obsessed with sugar, partly because it helped replenish her magic, and partly because she had a relentless sweet tooth.

Juno shook her head. "It's not just that. Although, I still can't believe you're so cool with it."

She could see it clear as day, a battered Jovi shackled to a cell wall, bruised and bleeding, dark circles under her eyes from Cyrus's attempts to penetrate her mind. And a resigned, dead expression on her beautiful face as she repeated, again and again, that Rogan hadn't breached confidentiality. That she had no idea the squad were demon hunters. That he hadn't told her any of their secrets.

Lying for him, over and over, knowing he'd given her up for capture and torture and God knew what else.

What would it be like, a love like that?

Jovi watched a girl propel herself up a rope by shooting force fields beneath her own ass. "Sometimes, you just do what you have to do. And I know why you did it. You were protecting your family." Her gaze fell to the floor as she sucked her candy. "I always wanted something like that."

Juno's heart clenched. She remembered that feeling, that deep ache, that yearning for something warm and safe and soft. She hadn't found it until Rogan made her a part of the team—the family—he was building.

And she'd almost let Magistrate Thackeray White take it away from her.

She had zero experience with female friendship. The kind of females who slinked around Silka had tongues sharper than their claws. But this was Rogan's woman, and she'd basically brought Juno back from the brink of death.

Plus, she was really fucking cool. "Well, you're part of it now."

The smile Jovi shot her quickly turned crafty. "So, what's with you and the big, bad lion?"

Every muscle in her body tightened. "You mean, besides the fact that he's an asshole?"

"Mmm." Jovi's knowing blue eyes gleamed. "He didn't look like an asshole when he was holding your dead body in his lap. He looked destroyed."

"I wasn't dead," she said automatically, even as her heart sped up.

"Same difference. You guys never..."

"No."

"Why not? There's obviously a thing between you two."

Heat rushed through her before she could stifle it. "There's nothing between us except squad. Just like all the other guys."

"Uh huh. So, why are the two of you so bitey and the rest of you are totally cool?"

"Because he's a dick."

"Hmm." Jovi considered this, then shrugged. "Yeah, he kind of is. Probably needs a cuddle."

A laugh escaped her. Killian, the growliest male on the planet, needing a cuddle? Might as well snuggle up to a giant, pissed off cactus.

"Works on Rogan." Jovi grinned at Juno's incredulous look. "Tough guys need snuggles, too." She appeared to think. "And tough girls." Her gaze slid over, but Juno refused to meet it.

She did not need snuggles.

She had the squad, she had her freedom, she had a strong body and no trouble finding a willing male to take the edge off when she needed it. She was fine.

They stared at the kids for a while, but all Juno could see was big, golden Killian Diallo curled around some soft, beautiful female, nuzzling her hair, soaking up the comfort of skin on skin.

Jovi's bellow snapped her back to the present. "Hey, you buncha pussies! Quit using your powers. This is agility class, for fuck's sake!" She darted forward, scattering kids like a flock of startled pigeons, and leaped onto a rope, where she clung like a monkey and pointed at the other ropes hanging empty nearby. "Get your asses up there!"

Juno grinned. This chick was something else. No wonder Rogan fell for her. No wonder he fought for her.

Her smile fell as guilt pooled in her belly once more. *You were protecting your family.*

Yeah, she was. And she would do it again, no matter how much it sucked, because this family was all she had.

She stapled that thought to the inside of her brain. She'd need it later tonight, when she walked straight into the jaguar's den.

CHAPTER 4

The slinky black dress parted high on Juno's thigh as she climbed the Pyramid's sweeping front steps, black heels clicking on white marble. Her gaze traveled upward, tracing the bricks that rose like a golden mountain from the city streets.

Her jaguar's hackles went up. *Threat.*

It was a warm night. The ornate double doors were flung wide and flanked by tuxedoed bouncers wearing earpieces. Music, laughter, and the cacophony of slot machines poured onto the steps. A potpourri of various vapes floated above it all, making her nose twitch.

She steeled herself and nodded at the bouncers as she strode inside.

The Pyramid dripped gold. Glossy black walls and floors reflected opulent gold chandeliers and carved pillars, the vast, curving bar, its ring of velvet chairs, the staff's satin vests—all shining in some shade of the lustrous hue. A far cry from the dirt and concrete of the Arena buried far beneath their feet. She could almost smell the sweat and blood, the bleach lingering on the cement, the cloud of cigar smoke and vape. The roar of frenzied crowds echoed in her ears like it was yesterday.

Maneater. Maneater.

Juno wound her way toward the back, skirting patrons who were no doubt buzzed on her father's liquor, and headed for the door she knew was tucked into a dark corner.

Another tuxedoed bouncer watched her approach. Though her stomach squirmed with nerves, she gave him a smooth smile. "Javier."

He didn't return the smile.

"Got some gray in the beard, I see."

The flicker of amusement was quickly masked. He waited.

"I need to see him."

Javier murmured into his earpiece, waited a second, then pressed his thumb against a fingerprint scanner. The door slid soundlessly into the wall.

Juno stepped into a mirror-plated elevator and waited for the doors to swish closed. Gold buttons in the shape of a pyramid gleamed on one panel. Pressing the unmarked one at the top was automatic, muscle memory at work despite a seven-year hiatus.

Threat? Her cat tensed, on alert.

We're fine.

Her pulse thumped in her throat as the elevator rose. She could see it in her reflection, a faint flutter at her neck. She brought her hair forward to cover it. Straight, sleek, and shining like a river of dark chocolate over one shoulder, it was weird to see it out of its tight ponytail. Stranger still to see her eyes lined with smoky shadow, her lips glossy, and her cleavage on display in the deep vee of her dress.

Beauty is power, she reminded herself. *Beauty is a weapon.*

She hated these games.

The elevator slowed to a stop and the doors parted silently, revealing a black marble wall veined with gold and another security officer standing with feet braced and hands clasped. When Juno stepped out, he scanned his thumbprint, and part of the marble wall slid aside.

She walked into the room and felt the door close behind her.

It was like stepping into outer space. The top of the Pyramid was made of solid glass, a transparent triangular room floating high above the streets. City lights dazzled beyond the floor-to-ceiling windows, the stars appearing close enough to touch. A plush area rug muffled the click of her heels as she headed for the imposing black desk in the center of the room.

Rafael Vasquez leaned against it, arms folded in his exquisite suit, watching her.

Fuck.

She tilted her head, letting her lids drop and her lips curve. "Rafael."

"Don't fucking do that."

The quiet murmur sent a shiver of warning down her spine. His deep, accented voice slid over her like rough velvet, bringing thousands of memories with it. The suit did nothing to mask the powerful body beneath. He'd been keeping up with his workouts, and unlike his guard, there was no trace of gray in the inky hair that swept back from his smooth face.

He looked good. Really damn good. But then, he always did. "Do what?"

Dark eyes glittered beneath black lashes. "Don't play pretend with me, *negra*."

"Fine." She dropped some of the sex from her posture. Her pulse raced. He could probably sense it, damn him. He could always read her like a book. "How've you been?"

He pushed away from the desk and glided toward her with lethal grace, a silken predator in a thousand-credit suit.

His dark, familiar scent surrounded her as he drew near. She'd practically worn it on her own skin for years. "Why are you here?"

She wasn't short, but he stepped close enough that she had to tilt her head back ever so slightly to meet his eyes. He probably did it on purpose, knowing it would piss her off. Knowing she wouldn't back away.

Amusement gleamed as he took her in. "Ah. You need my help."

"I need a lawyer."

A brow lifted. "In trouble, *negra*?"

"Not me. Kids."

His gaze shot to her belly, and Juno rolled her eyes. "Not *my* kids. Just some we're looking out for."

Rafael contemplated her before strolling to the bar in the corner. Ice clinked into glasses. "If you want my help, I'll need details."

Danger.

Her cat obviously hadn't forgotten that this male couldn't be trusted. Not anymore. The skin between her fingers prickled, her claws begging to be unsheathed.

"It has to stay between us." She took the glass he offered, then nearly dropped it when she caught the very familiar aroma drifting up from the golden liquid.

Silka. Of course the bastard would serve her the family's liquor. She slid him a dangerous look.

His mouth lifted. "Discretion is my middle name."

"I'm serious, Raf." The nickname slipped out, and his eyes flared.

"Tell me."

He was so…much. Dark and simmering and buzzing with male energy. She walked over to one of the glass walls, staring past the neon lights and blinking billboards toward MLE headquarters, rising like a white and blue monument in the night. The top floor—the one that had imploded less than two weeks ago—looked perfectly intact. Had the Magistrate rebuilt it that quickly, or was he using a high-level concealment charm to hide the destruction? Either way, that kind of power was disturbing. Especially considering who was wielding it.

"I'm sure you know I was part of an elite team at MLE." His silence confirmed it—he'd kept tabs on her over the last seven years. She'd never expected anything less. "The squad has defected. And we burned some serious bridges with the Magistrate."

She watched in the reflection as he approached, slow and silent, easing behind her, radiating heat. They made a beautiful pair. Her, sleekly muscled in her tight dress and heels, eyes lined with kohl and hair shining over one shoulder. Him, tall and dark and deadly in designer linen.

Their eyes met in the glass. "Are you safe?"

Irritation flared, but she tamped it down, turned to face him, and spoke through her teeth. "Yes, but we need help."

She told him about the Light House, the kids who lived there, and the looming legal issues. He listened silently.

"What aren't you telling me?"

She lifted a brow. "A lot. My team's work is confidential."

"Do you have a mate?"

Her jaw tightened. "No."

The faintest hint of a purr rumbled from his chest, so quickly gone she could have imagined it. But she didn't. "I'll help."

She narrowed her eyes.

He smiled, slow and triumphant. "Three dates."

Her stomach plummeted. "No."

"That's my price."

"Why?"

His eyes smoldered. "At one point, we enjoyed each other's company."

Images bombarded her. The two of them tumbling on

satin sheets, surging against glass walls, rolling on the plush rug beneath her very feet. Her claws raking his back, her teeth sinking into his skin. Their bodies twined around each other, his eyes glowing with love…

She tore her gaze from his, shaking her head. "This was a mistake."

"Juno." His accent turned the J soft and seductive. "Three dates."

She stared at the metallic threads in the rug, her heart thumping. The kids needed this. The squad needed this.

Fine. It will be fine.

She met his gaze. "One."

"Three."

"Two."

Silence. "Agreed."

"Just dates. And I choose when."

His white teeth gleamed. "I choose where."

"Public."

He shook his head.

Goddammit. "Rafael, I'm not playing this game with you."

"Dates, *negra*. Two dates. And the kids will get their lawyer." He studied her like he was reacquainting himself with every inch of her face.

"Fine." She tossed back the liquor and shoved her empty glass into his chest on her way out.

———

The walk home did little to chill her out, especially since the summer air was sticky with humidity and her stupid high heels had chewed blisters in her ankles. Grumbling, she carried her shoes in one hand as she made her way through Light House's halls to her room. The scents of her squadmates drifted from below their doors as she passed. They'd taken over one of the wings of dormitory-style rooms, as far from the kids' sleeping area as they could get. She headed straight for the squad's communal bathroom at the end of the hall, beyond ready to scrub the makeup from her face and the lingering traces of Rafael's scent from her nose.

Cyrus exited just as she reached for the door handle, a white towel wrapped around his hips and his underwear-model body on display. But the shadows under his eyes were what caught her attention.

"You good?" There was a hickey on his neck and nail marks on his shoulders. The smell of soap was strong enough to cover anything else, but the look in his pale blue eyes told her everything she needed to know—he'd banged some female tonight and then wiped her memories before coming home alone.

His cocky smile would've fooled anyone who didn't know him better. "Very. You?"

She mimicked his fake grin. "Very. Let me in."

He stepped aside to let her pass. "Looking good, DeSilva."

"Flies and honey," she muttered, catching his quiet laugh as the door closed behind her.

The shower soothed her, warm and private and stocked with her favorite gingerbread-scented body wash. It was one of the few truly feminine things she owned. She watched the bubbles circle the drain, wishing she could rinse away her nerves just as easily.

The cement floor was smooth and cool beneath her feet as she padded back to her room. None of them had brought much with them when they defected. This space could've been anyone's, it was so blank and barren. Just a stack of clothes, a bed, and a lot of silence.

She hit the lights and slid between the sheets before turning onto her side. Her knees pulled up automatically, one fist curling against her chest. The sheets were cold, but they'd warm up eventually. Kind of. It was fine.

A few minutes later, she pulled her second pillow against her torso and threw a leg over it, squeezing it close. Her nose brushed the soft cotton as she huddled under the covers, clutching the bag of feathers and foam. It wasn't warm, and it didn't hold her in return, but it also didn't stick a knife in her back.

CHAPTER 5

Dinner wasn't what it used to be.

Back at the Bunker, the evening meal had been a fairly quiet hour of shop talk and snarky banter. Now, Killian sucked chicken out of his teeth, watching a sticky rubber ball sail across Light House's dining hall and bounce off the wall. Shrieks of laughter echoed, a mad scramble sounded behind him, and a kid bumped into the corner of the table, making his beer bottle teeter wildly. He caught it and lifted it to his lips for a swig.

"Killian! Killian, watch!"

He glanced over. A seven-year-old with thick glasses hovered near his shoulder, bouncing in his sneakers. At his questioning brow, the kid scrunched up his face, clenched his fists, and a fat, gray thundercloud appeared over his head. There was a crack, and a torrent of rain spewed from the cloud, drenching the kid and the three-foot radius surrounding him. He parted the ginger hair plastered to his forehead, beaming.

Killian tilted water off of his plate. "Cool."

The kid skipped away, his thundercloud hovering a foot above him.

"Franklin, get back here and clean this up!" Theodora Donnovan, Light House's executive director, skirted the puddle and settled across from Killian with a sigh. The dining hall was a huge room with high ceilings containing several mismatched, beat-up dining sets. The adults usually snagged the long table at the back in an attempt to find some quiet amid the chaos. It didn't work. All around, kids chattered, silverware clinked, and chairs scraped. The noise was damn near deafening.

It reminded him of home.

Theo waved a hand and the puddle evaporated into a mist, then disappeared. Must be convenient to be an aquamage. "Kids like you."

Killian grunted.

"They think you're a superhero."

Killian forked up a huge bite of chicken. Tender and juicy. Gloria was doing God's work back there in that kitchen. She'd come with them when they defected—Rogan had made sure of it. Theo was cool with it, but the Light House's former cook had taken one look at Gloria, flipped them the bird, and stormed out, spouting some nasty racial slurs that made Killian's claws twitch beneath his skin.

"Maybe you'll inspire them to work harder in the gym." Theo's amused gaze swept over his thick biceps. "You work out, right?" When he gave her a dry look, she grinned wider, then scooted over on the bench when Juno appeared with her own plate. She plunked down, flicked her ponytail over her shoulder, and started stabbing at her food like it wasn't dead yet. His lion perked up its ears, then settled with a pleased growl as she started to eat.

Safe. Fed.

Fuck's sake. He swigged his beer, realized it was empty, and was debating getting another when Cyrus, Rogan, and John sat with their own dinners.

"What about Rafael?" Cyrus asked, as if someone had mentioned the bastard's name.

Juno glared at him. "Stay out of my head."

Cyrus raised a brow. "You're projecting like a mofo."

Rogan hadn't even picked up his silverware. "Did he agree to the lawyer?"

Juno skewered a slice of meat. "After I meet his…conditions."

Something deadly sizzled to life in Killian's belly.

"What conditions?"

"Dates. Two."

Every single nerve ending in Killian's body went up in flames. His fingers curled around his fork.

MINE.

Rogan watched Juno like a hawk. "Are you okay with this?"

Her chin ticked up an inch and her eyes went cool as she put on her mask. "We need it."

"That's not what I asked."

"It's fine."

There it was again. "Thought you hated the guy." His growl drifted across the table.

She shifted that cool gaze to him. His lion wanted to crawl all over her, bite her, heat her up until any trace of that bullshit chill was gone. "It doesn't really matter, does it?" She looked back at Rogan. "It's fine. I'll get the job done." She checked her watch and cursed. "I gotta go." She pushed up from the table and swept from the room, ponytail swinging like it was as mad as she was.

There was a sharp metallic snap. Heads swiveled toward him. Killian stood, dropped the two halves of his fork onto his plate, and stalked mindlessly out, barely refraining from ripping the dining hall door off its hinges.

The streets were alive with flashing lights, friendly shouts, and honking horns. It barely registered. Everything was blurred except her.

Juno was halfway down the city block before she caught his scent. He saw it—the miniscule turn of her head, the ever-so-slight stiffening of her shoulders. But she didn't stop, and neither did he.

She was dressed in her usual black leggings, black boots, and black tank top. A far cry from the sleek, feminine dress she'd been wearing last night, and a thousand times sexier. As gorgeous as she'd been in that curve-hugging sheath, *this* was her. Powerful. Capable. Ready for action. Her ponytail brushed the small of her back as she strode down the block. Men did doubletakes. Killian's fangs threatened to punch out of his gums. His skin was too tight, his muscles swelling, hot and dangerous, like balloons hooked up to a boiling faucet.

The smell of the city was usually overwhelming. Hot pavement, food trucks, civilians crowding the sidewalks, trash and sweat, the river's fishy tang. Killian didn't smell any of it. Juno's scent cut straight to his brain. Lower. Deeper. It flipped a switch he didn't want to name. His boots pounded the asphalt, eating up the distance between them. The world took on an amber sheen, and somewhere in the back of his mind, he knew his eyes had gone lion yellow.

Something collided with his chest. Killian's hands snapped out automatically, catching the elderly human woman he'd nearly plowed into the pavement. She smelled musty, like her clothes had been tucked in a closet for decades. Fear widened her eyes when he scowled down at her.

Shit. He steadied her bony shoulders. "Sorry."

She hurried off, clutching her handbag.

He looked up to find Juno standing a foot away, hands on hips, her scent washing over him in a rush of warm spices and dark femininity.

"What?" she snapped.

She had a tiny mole at the corner of her mouth. In her human form, it was a beauty mark, slightly darker than her skin. In jaguar form, it was a miniscule white freckle. In either form, it was sexy as hell—

"What, Diallo?"

He blinked. "What?"

Her brows lifted. "What the hell are you doing?"

He met her gaze, and shit, he was right back there, kneeling in a puddle with glass cutting into his knees and her lifeless head in his lap.

Fuck. "Going downtown. Is that all right with you?"

Her dark eyes narrowed. She raked a glance over his body, making it tighten even more. A strand of hair floated across her face. He clenched his fists.

After an eternity, she stepped away. "Don't be too rough with the tail-chasers, I hear they're delicate."

He snarled at her back. "Have fun with the boyfriend."

She spun and jabbed a finger toward him, her eyes flashing. "Don't call him that. This is the last thing I want to be doing."

Fierce satisfaction burned through him at her words, and at the fact that her icy exterior had been obliterated. "Whatever you say."

Her lip curled before she turned and strode away toward the Pyramid, half a block away and reflecting the setting sun like a polished gold mirror. At the curb outside its entrance, a sleek, black car popped a door open, and she slid inside without so much as a glance in his direction.

Was Vasquez in the car with her now? Inches away from her, breathing her scent, touching her skin?

Killian spun on the spot and tried to remember how to fucking breathe. Pedestrians parted like sardines before a shark as he stalked the sidewalks, eyes down and fists tight. A nerdy mage wearing a lab coat stood on a street corner, pulling random women aside and glamoring half of their faces like a department store makeup clerk. "Sir!" He spotted Killian and gestured grandly to his latest victim. "You're a strong, virile man. Don't you think she looks—"

He snapped his jaws at the idiot, who stumbled backward and tripped off of the curb as Killian stomped past him onto the footbridge. Red River was low. It had been a dry spring, and summer wasn't looking any wetter. A whiff of fish floated up from the meager current. Killian curled his lip at the brackish water winding sluggishly through the concrete jungle. The river looked nothing like that back at home.

No, not home. Pride lands weren't home anymore.

The Blender district was alive with happy hour devotees looking to leave the work week behind in a drunken stupor. Killian bypassed the flashy clubs and the cop bars, nose twitching at the fragrant steam wafting from the Chinese restaurant on the corner. He passed a twenty-four hour tattoo parlor and palmed his way into the tavern next door.

Slash was all black inside, with giant painted claw marks cutting jagged swaths across the back wall. Pool balls clacked together, darts thunked into cork, and metal music thumped at a low volume. Shapeshifter bars catered to the delicate senses of their clientele, keeping the music quiet, the menus carnivorous, and the tech minimal. Eyes flicked over him as he entered. More than a few pairs flashed gold, amber, and orange. They could probably smell it on him, the wild, manic desperation.

A brunette slinked up to him. Curvy, with dark, hooded eyes.

"No." He looked past her and pointed at a skinny blonde arching her back against the bar. Her eyes flared as he snagged her by the waist on his way to the back. She scurried to keep up, petting him like a prize horse.

Slash's back corridor boasted four private bathrooms. The first two were occupied. Killian swung the blonde into the third, kicked the door shut behind them, and pinned her against the wall, digging a condom out of his pocket. He hated the things, but unlike female shifters who were only fertile one week out of the year, this human might be ovulating right this second, for all he knew. Her shiny skirt practically flew up to her waist all on its own. Killian ripped open his fly, rolled the condom on, and thrust into her.

The blonde gasped like a porn star and wrapped her legs around him, hanging on for dear life as he pounded her against the grimy cinder block. She smelled like hairspray, self-tanner, and perfume. And under all that fake was the real scent of her—human, and horny as hell.

One of her high heels clattered to the floor. The other bit into his ass as he hammered into her, gripping her thighs, trying not to smell her, trying not to hear her piercing yips of pleasure, trying not to notice any fucking thing at all. She gave an obscenely loud cry, and Killian drove deep, blowing his load with a grunt. His instinct was to bite—her ear, her neck—but he didn't want his mouth anywhere near this chick. Being inside her was bad enough.

His heart pounded as he eased her to her feet and tugged her skirt back down. She leaned against the wall and raked her hair back, panting.

"Wow. Lion, right?" Her eyes gleamed as they roved over him. "Always wanted to try a lion."

Fucking tail-chasers.

Killian chucked the condom in the trash, zipped up, and left without a word.

Good. But not mine.

His beast needed to get a goddamn grip.

Back at the bar, he ordered a triple whisky and slammed it down, then signaled for another.

"That was fast." The curvy brunette had appeared on the stool next to him. "She do the trick?"

He flicked his empty glass toward the bartender and glowered at the bottles lined up against the wall.

"Must not have. You don't look very relaxed. Although, maybe you're not drinking to relax. Maybe you're drinking to forget?"

What was she, a cerebromage? Just what he didn't need. Another whisky appeared in front of him. He tossed it back, wishing the burn lasted longer, and jerked his chin for another.

"I could help you forget."

Killian spared her a glance. "I don't do brunettes."

"Why, is she one?"

"Who?"

"The one you're trying to forget."

"Put it on my tab," Killian snarled at the bartender, and stalked out.

The streets were a blur, pedestrians bouncing off him as his feet hauled him back to Light House and his lion roared inside his skull.

He headed around the back of the school and climbed the grassy hill at the rear of the property. He needed air, space... he needed to destroy something.

He crested the hill, ready to rip one of the leafy trees right out of the dirt, and froze. A small figure sat at the top of the hill, knees hugged to its chest, staring out at the darkening skyline. He heard a tiny sniff.

Fuck.

Franklin's head lifted when Killian stomped over. His freckled cheeks were wet, his face flushed.

Killian plopped himself down on the grass. Franklin sniffed again. Silence stretched between them.

"Blaine was mean to me," Franklin whispered.

Killian grunted.

"He said my power is stupid."

Killian glanced above the kid's head and saw the fat thundercloud hovering over his ginger hair. "Yeah? What the fuck can Blaine do?"

"Phytomage. Plants."

"That sounds stupid."

Franklin wiped his nose. "He can make poison vines and stuff. He tripped me." He stuck out a skinny leg. Slashes of red circled his calf, swollen and rashy.

Little asshole. "So, hit him with a lightning bolt."

Franklin's lip trembled. "I can't do that. All I can do is rain." He glanced up miserably at the thundercloud.

Killian grunted again. "So far."

Franklin looked at him. The kid's glasses had to be a quarter inch thick. Behind them, hazel eyes shone with tears, but his mouth lifted in a watery smile.

Killian looked back at the streets. A few moments later, he reached out and dragged the kid against his side, leaving his arm looped over the boy's small shoulders.

They stayed like that for a long time, until footsteps sounded on the hill behind them. Rogan's scent followed closely behind.

"Franklin, they're looking for you inside."

Franklin wiped his nose and slid out from beneath Killian's arm, rising to head back into the school.

"Hey, kid." Killian waited for Franklin to turn. "Meet me in the gym in half an hour."

Franklin's face lit up. He nodded, and there was a spring in his step when he headed down the hill.

Killian turned back to the street. After a few moments, Rogan settled his muscled form on the grass a few feet away. They stared at the city in silence.

"Your lion's riding you."

Killian watched a yellow faebug float lazily across his field of vision and willed his claws to stay inside his skin. What was she doing with Vasquez, right this second?

"You almost look as bad as when I found you."

It was six years ago that Killian had stalked into the city, raw and reeling with grief. The buzz of tech, the flashing lights, the sounds and smells of Concordia had nearly pushed him over the edge, but he'd heard about the Arena, the underground fighting ring beneath the Pyramid casino, and headed straight for it. The bouncers had taken one look at him and billed him for a fight that same night. Killian had nearly shredded his opponent.

Rogan was in the stands that night. And he'd come each night after, moving closer and closer to the cage, watching Killian with eyes that missed nothing. After a week of straight victories, Killian emerged from the changing room, bloody and battered and breathing through a broken nose, and found Rogan waiting for him. The man had asked if he had any close family. Killian said no. Rogan told him he could offer a better release for all that rage.

Moving into the Bunker, training and patrolling and slaying hellspawn night after night, had pulled him back from the brink.

"Whatever you're doing to burn it off isn't working. Is it touch-hunger, or something else?"

Shapeshifters were primal, tactile creatures at their core. If a shifter went without intimate touch too long, they got twitchy and pent-up, quick to lash out. Touch-hunger, it was called. If it wasn't addressed, the shifter spiraled into aggression, surrendered to their beast, and eventually went so feral their humanity disappeared. Nothing but raw animal instinct would remain—fuck, fight, feed. He'd seen it happen once, back in the jungle. As alpha, his dad had to put down one of his own.

"I'm handling it." And he sure as shit wasn't talking about it. "Isn't your female wondering where you are?"

Rogan barked a laugh, and Killian glanced over in surprise. He could count on one hand the number of times he'd heard the man laugh. Now, as his squad leader stared into the distance, the corner of his mouth lifted like he was imagining something Killian couldn't see. "Trust me, when Jovi wants to find me, she'll find me."

Killian stared at him. "You're different."

Rogan quieted. "Everything is."

Silence lengthened between them, punctuated by the occasional car horn from the street below.

"Is it worth it?" The words tumbled out of him, and Killian instantly wanted to snatch them back.

Rogan was quiet for a long time. "She is."

The scent of torched sugar wafted toward them. Speaking of the demon...

Jovi sauntered into view and plopped into Rogan's lap, making him grunt. He shifted her around until he was comfortable. Jovi was sucking on a popsicle—cherry, from the smell of it. She poked it at Rogan's lips.

He resisted, scowling. "I don't want that garbage."

"Oh, really?" The sensual smile in Jovi's voice would've made any man's cock stir. From the corner of his eye, Killian saw the silhouette of her tongue run slowly up the length of the popsicle.

Electricity flared between them, sexual and sharp. Killian surged to his feet and stalked down the hill without a word. Stone-cold Nash Rogan's warm chuckle followed him.

CHAPTER 6

Rafael remembered all her favorite foods.

His rooftop patio overlooked a sparkling private lake, where fountains danced in the night air, their underwater lights glowing softly. A warm breeze stirred the lush plants surrounding an elegant table set for two.

"You're not eating."

Juno glanced at her untouched plate where a thick, charred venison steak, buttery escargot with fragrant garlic, and an avocado-mango salsa with jalapenos sat. It smelled divine.

"Don't tell me your tastes have changed completely."

Juno sighed and sliced off a bite of venison. It exploded with flavor and practically melted on her tongue. She couldn't stifle her moan. Whatever he was paying his private chef, it wasn't enough. Then again, knowing Rafael, it was probably plenty.

Rafael smiled and licked his fork, his black dress shirt left open at the collar to reveal his corded throat. "Tell me about your work."

She'd expected him to dig, but it was still irritating. "I told you, it's confidential."

"Even though you've defected?"

She nodded.

"Hmm." He speared a succulent escargot from his plate and held it toward her lips.

She reared back like he'd offered her a lit grenade. "Are you fucking kidding me?"

A grin flashed on his chiseled face. "I had to see it."

"What?" She barely refrained from swatting his fork away.

"That fire in your eyes." He ate the escargot himself.

Asshole. Trying to feed her from his hand, like he wanted to claim her. They'd been down that road. She folded her arms, her appetite gone. Her cat flexed its claws.

"Do you love it?" His face was suddenly serious in the flickering candlelight. "This job you can't discuss?"

This life you left me for, his eyes said.

Yes, she loved it. The family. The freedom. The acceptance of who she was, deep at her core—a fighter. She nodded.

"And Nash Rogan, does he keep you safe?"

"I don't *need* Nash Rogan to keep me safe." Chair legs scraped as she pushed up from the table. "You still don't get it." She gripped the balcony rail, staring blindly at the verdant grounds of Rafael's estate. Beyond the lake with its dancing fountains, tucked behind the evergreens lining the edge of his private woods, was the vast, extravagant obstacle course he'd built for her all those years ago.

Exquisite cuisine, luxurious living quarters, a safe place to run. Everything she could ever want, right here in this beautiful cage.

"What does he give you that I can't?"

She let him see her exasperation. "Freedom." He never did understand why that meant everything. "It's not about Rogan, anyway."

"He recruited you from the academy."

"Yeah, because I was the best." She stabbed a finger at her

chest. "*I was the best.*" She could feel it now, the fire spitting from her eyes. "And he was the only person who didn't want to lock me up."

"Not lock you up, *negra*. Take care of you."

She spoke through her teeth. "I can take care of myself. I *want* to take care of myself."

She'd been so excited to join the academy. Magical Law Enforcement might be full of mages who would turn up their noses at a shifter in their ranks, but there were no rules against other races joining. And it was the only place that would train her to be something she actually wanted to be.

Her father's disdain was expected. Rafael's betrayal was not.

Someone high up in the academy owed him a favor, and he used it to try to keep her from joining. The one person she thought really saw her, really loved her, had gone behind her back to keep her from the only life she wanted.

His jaw tightened. "I told you I was sorry. I still am sorry."

"Yeah, you're sorry it hurt me. You aren't sorry you did it."

He didn't argue.

"Why are we even talking about this?" She tightened her ponytail and let a smile slide across her face. "How's business, Raf?"

"Don't *fucking* do that." His hands were relaxed on the table, his body predator still.

"Why not? This *is* business. Don't delude yourself into thinking otherwise."

His claws shot out from between his fingers, slicing the tablecloth, leaving smears of blood on the white linen.

Her heart thundered, but she arched a brow. "Well, look at that. Dinner and a show. I'd say that counts as a date." She headed for the door, holding up a finger. "One down."

CHAPTER 7

By the time she marched onto Light House property, she was ready to pop, quivering from anger and nerves and everything she thought was dead and buried. It had taken her seven years to lock that shit away. It had taken Rafael Vasquez less than an hour to dig it all up.

She needed to run. She needed to beat the piss out of something.

A hug didn't sound too bad, either.

Scowling at the thought, she headed for the gymnasium, so wrapped up in her own head that by the time she heard the voices, it was too late.

Juno stopped short in the doorway. Killian was in the center of the room in gym shorts and nothing else, facing off with that shrimpy storm mage, Franklin. They were circling each other like wrestlers, Killian's enormous, hulking body casting shadows on the mismatched floor mats.

"I'm bigger than you. Stronger. You have to use what you got. Speed," Killian growled. He took a swipe at the kid, who dodged, tripped, and face-planted onto the mat. His glasses went flying. "Get up."

Franklin groaned, but he got to all fours and crawled to retrieve his glasses.

Killian's head snapped over.

Their eyes locked, and heat—different from the boiling anger that had carried her home—curled in her belly.

And there it was. The other thing she'd been trying to bury.

"Oh, Juno! Can you show me?" Franklin said, relieved. He slid his glasses onto his nose and shoved them up. "I don't know what I'm supposed to do." He gestured helplessly to Killian.

Killian popped his shoulder, avoiding her gaze. "The kid's getting beat up. I'm teaching him some hand-to-hand."

She was surrounded by good-looking males of every species on a daily basis. Those massive flexing muscles shouldn't be so distracting. "Isn't that what Israel's classes are for?"

"We don't learn *combat* until we're older. We just do agility and stuff now. Will you show me? Killian, do that thing you were trying to do before." A little hand snagged Juno's forearm and pulled her onto the mats. "Juno, show me how to get out of it." He scurried off to the side, nodding encouragingly.

Juno faced off with Killian's enormous bare chest. It was glistening with sweat, his tribal tattoos standing out starkly in the gym's overhead lights. The man was huge even for a lion, his body heavily muscled and impressively defined. His golden hair was loose around his shoulders, as it always was these days.

Touch.

She sank into a ready stance and gave him a *come and get it* gesture.

He came at her like a cannonball, all explosive power and strength. She leaped aside, crouching to sweep a leg beneath his bare feet. He jumped over it, but she was already somersaulting away. He swiped. She dodged. He lunged. She flipped. She evaded him time and again, ducking, contorting, leaping.

The gym melted away. Her body sang. She landed a flip—and found a thick elbow hooked around her neck.

"You're supposed to get caught," Killian growled in her ear.

A bolt of heat shot through her. *Never.*

She reached overhead and grabbed a handful of his golden hair, giving it a brutal yank. His snarl rumbled against her back, but his hold loosened just enough for her to free herself. She ducked out of his grip and hammered a kick into his diaphragm for good measure.

She didn't hold back. Never had to with Killian. And short of actually wounding her, he didn't hold back, either.

He always was her favorite to spar with. Not that she'd ever tell him that.

He grunted when her boot connected, but grabbed her ankle and tugged sharply, making her skid forward on the mat. Her groin collided with his. Their gazes met for a split second.

She jumped, wrapped her other leg around his waist, and used the momentum to spin them both to the floor. She landed on top of him, forearm at his throat, ready to crush his windpipe. Amber eyes flashed yellow, his lion staring back at her.

He smelled fucking incredible.

She leaped up as he rose to stand, and they faced off, chests heaving.

"Wow," Franklin breathed. "But…can you show me how to get out of that choking thing again?"

Juno wrenched her focus back to the kid. "Is someone *choking* you?"

"Well, no, but that was so cool!"

"What exactly are these kids doing to you?"

Franklin shrugged and looked at the floor. "Tripping me and stuff."

The red welts around the kid's leg suddenly made sense. Fucking bullies. She met Killian's gaze, then, with a sigh, turned around and braced herself.

Killian took her to the ground with a leg sweep. She hit the mat in a pushup position and looked up at Franklin. "You're here. Then what?"

Franklin's eyes were wide behind his glasses. "Uh. Vines?"

"Drag you backward?" She had a sudden, vivid recollection of one of her early fights in the Arena when she'd almost been strangled to death by a phytomage's lashing appendages.

Killian's big hand on her ankle snapped her back to the present, and then she was getting rubber burn—and a hot thrill—from being pulled across the mat. "Ow, dammit. You have a knife?"

"Me?" the kid squeaked.

Juno could practically hear Killian's eyes roll. A snort escaped her. "No knife. Okay. Are these vines poisonous?"

The kid nodded.

"Well, that sucks. But you can cure poison later. Twist around, grab them anyway and rip them off." She demonstrated, twisting onto her back, crunching up and prying Killian's thick fingers from her ankle. "Then, hit the guy, any way you can." She kicked Killian in the kneecap.

He barked a curse and leaped back. A low growl rumbled from his chest.

Juno's cat purred in response.

They drilled for another hour, teaching the kid how to land a kick, how to throw a proper punch, and how to dodge. Franklin was scrawny, weak, and had pathetic stamina. But he kept trying.

"Franklin." Theo stood in the gym's doorway, arms folded

and scarlet hair loose around her shoulders. "It's late. Get showered, and get to bed."

"Okay." Franklin shot them a tired smile. "Thanks, guys." He shoved his foggy glasses up his nose and trudged off. Theo flicked them a speculative look before following, leaving her and Killian alone.

The vast gymnasium shrank to the size of a closet.

Awareness roared to life. The air between them practically crackled with electricity. Why did it have to be like this with him? She'd just had a workout; she should be happy and relaxed. Instead, she was balancing on a dormant power line, knowing someone was about to flip the switch.

She lifted her ponytail off her shoulders and fanned her neck. "Think she's going to be pissed about this?"

"Like I give a shit."

Why did she even try? "Of course you don't."

"That kid needs to know how to take care of himself. They all do."

That stopped her short. "I agree."

Their eyes met and held. Abruptly, a look of disgust crossed his face. "You smell like him."

Her stomach gave a little jolt. Did she? They hadn't even touched. "So?"

His lip curled. "Last thing you want to be doing, huh?"

Anger blasted through her. "Fuck you, Diallo."

"Nah, I'm good. Not into sloppy seconds."

The gym went green as her jaguar boiled up inside her, ready to take a swipe at him. "Yeah, I'm sure you were that tail-chaser's one and only."

As a nasty growl rumbled from his chest, a shrill whistle rang from the doorway. She tore her gaze away from Killian to find Wolf leaning against the door jamb, munching a stick of jerky. "If you two are done hissing at each other, it's snuggle time."

So not in the mood. "Pass."

"Mandatory. Squad first."

It had become their mantra, their code. Their reminder about what they'd almost lost. Sucking in a calming breath, Juno nodded.

"See you there." Wolf sauntered away.

She and Killian parted without a word.

Half an hour later, she was curled up on a sagging couch in Light House's crappy TV room, sandwiched between Cyrus and Rogan while her freshly showered hair made damp circles on her T-shirt. Wolf and Jovi stood in front of the old TV set, arguing over which movie to watch.

"*Bite Hard.*"

"Not *Bite Hard*. That is so dumb."

"*Bite Hard* is awesome, and it's my turn to pick, anyway—"

The remote floated out of Wolf's hand to bop him in the nose. He snatched it, whirled, and chucked it viciously toward the sofa. Cyrus jerked his head out of the way just in time, snorting with mirth. The remote flew across the room and goosed Wolf on the ass, making him jump and whoop. As laughter echoed, Wolf erupted into animal form, sweatpants shredding to reveal an enormous white wolf baring mean-looking fangs.

Jovi clapped in delight, Rogan sighed, and John, reclining in a threadbare armchair, tossed a kernel of popcorn at the giant wolf. It was snatched out of the air by a swooping black crow, and Wolf spun, snapping his jaws. John threw more kernels for them to fight over, Wolf jumping, Tika diving, and Jovi loudly cheering them on.

Rogan checked his watch. "All right, come on. It's late."

He'd insisted on these nightly squad hangouts ever since they moved to Light House. They'd always trained and eaten together at the Bunker, but this was different. These sessions weren't about working out or talking shop, but relaxing, rebuilding, and healing from everything that had gone down over the past few weeks.

She watched Rogan pluck a miniscule piece of lint from his shirt. What did he give her that Rafael couldn't? A life she actually wanted. A family who understood her.

She owed him everything.

Would he have abandoned *her*, even at the Magistrate's orders? Would he have tortured someone *she* loved?

Cyrus's arresting blue gaze swiveled to her, and his voice sounded in her head. *You good?*

She latched onto that smooth, familiar voice like a lifeline and nodded, trying to refocus.

How'd it go with Rafael?

She shot him an *I'm not going there* look. No one needed to know how much that visit had thrown her. Not to mention the shit with Killian in the gym afterward. Did he actually think she slept with Rafael?

She looked directly into Cyrus's pale blue eyes and tried to project her thoughts as clearly as possible. Cyrus was the one with the ability to communicate telepathically, but if she focused enough, it was almost like a real conversation. *I didn't sleep with him.*

Cyrus's brows lifted to his smooth, shaved hairline. *Never crossed my mind.*

She nodded again, deliberately avoiding looking at a certain lion who sat on the floor in the corner. Of course, that meant she was thinking about him.

Cyrus's gaze shifted to Killian, then back to her. *You two have been extra catty lately.*

He's being an extra asshole lately. Ever since she'd almost died and been resurrected in his arms.

God, that look on his face. That staggering, naked relief...

Nope, nope, nope, not going there. *So* not going there. *Raf brought up old shit. It messes with me.*

I'd ask if you want me to kick his ass, but you'd probably do it better.

She gave Cyrus a genuine smile, and he returned it, knocking his shoulder into hers. *Just one more date, tomorrow night. Then, it's done. I'll be fine.*

Wolf melted into human form and rose from all fours, lanky and unconcernedly naked. His cupcake tattoo was a splash of bright pink on his upper arm, his eyes still the gold of his beast. Objectively speaking, he was obnoxiously cute, all sharp-featured and tousle-haired and full of the kind of lazy male confidence that brought females to their knees. He did absolutely nothing for her.

More popcorn flew as protests rang out. "Man, go get some clothes. I'm not watching the whole thing with you naked," Cyrus said.

Wolf sauntered deliberately toward the sofa and lowered his bare ass to Cyrus's lap. Cyrus gave him a hearty shove, and the two of them tumbled to the floor in a tangle of limbs. They rolled and grappled, throwing elbows and insults. Wolf was faster. Cyrus was sneakier. Both were powerful fighters practically bursting with arrogance and testosterone.

Fuck it.

Grinning, Juno dived in.

"Son of a bitch," Wolf grunted when she landed on top of him. She wrapped her leg around his and nearly managed to pin him before a sudden shooting pain in her nipple made her jerk away.

"You honked my tit!" She clapped a hand to her breast, laughing.

"You asked for it!" Wolf's cry was muffled as Cyrus slithered over him like an eel, trying to get a shoulder lock.

Juno launched on top of the pile and held on for the ride as the two males bucked and tussled. When Cyrus almost tossed her, she dug in and clung tighter.

"Ow! No claws!" Cyrus's icy glare was her only warning

before she flew backward, spine thumping against the nearest wall.

"No telekinesis!" she retorted, and went back for more.

The three of them wrestled and rolled in a tangle of arms and legs, each trying to hook an ankle or pin a shoulder to gain the top position.

"Gross, why are you so sweaty?" Juno's palm slipped off Wolf's bare skin yet again, costing her the hand position she needed to flip him.

"If the male ain't sweaty, you ain't doing it right!" He did a lightning-fast maneuver that knocked Juno aside. Cyrus was on him the next instant, his skin looking even darker against the pale flash of Wolf's naked limbs.

"Fuck off." But she was laughing again. Blowing hair from her face, she flopped back onto the couch, content to watch the two of them duke it out. Her cheeks hurt from grinning.

She looked around the room. Jovi surveyed the chaos with shining eyes. Rogan watched her with a quiet smile, and when he glanced at Juno as if he felt her stare, his lips curved further, like he knew what she was thinking, felt what she was feeling.

Squad. Family.

This was everything. This was worth fighting for. This was something she couldn't—wouldn't—jeopardize again.

She didn't have anything else. She didn't want anything else. These people knew her, understood her, and accepted her for who she was, and they didn't try to turn her into anything else.

Her heart squeezed. She tilted her head until it rested on Rogan's broad shoulder. Beneath the ever-present coffee and mint, his scent was like rain-dampened stone, clean and mineral-like and solid as a rock. She allowed herself a few seconds to soak it up before lifting her head.

Rogan wasn't a touchy person, so when his broad palm patted her knee, it nearly brought tears to her eyes. She blinked hard, her gaze bouncing around the room before it landed on the corner.

Killian sat on the floor with his back against the wall, his presence looming even as he sat apart. She could've sworn she saw the corner of his mouth twitch as he watched the ridiculous scene on the carpet in front of him. But then, she blinked, and their eyes met, and his familiar scowl was back in place.

CHAPTER 8

Killian leaped over a demon corpse and collided with the skeletal wraith that had just appeared behind it. No text scrolled across his vision. No species, category, or weakness. It was one of the first things that became clear after they defected—the Magistrate couldn't keep their lenses from functioning, but he had obviously ordered them to be disconnected from the DE database.

Killian had never been much of a reader, anyway.

He took the bony fuck to the ground and tore into it. The wraith's deafening screeches blasted his eardrums, which were even more sensitive in lion form, but he bore down, claws shining wet in the moonlight.

For Mom. And Dad. And Nandi.

Skin flew. Blood splattered his muzzle. He dug into the wraith's sternum and ripped its ribcage apart, roaring his rage into the night.

Mom, split open on the jungle floor, bones white against red flesh. Little sister, lying pale and still, her organs littering the dirt, drawing ants and flies. Dad, sprawled beside his mate, big arms wrapped around her ruined body as blood poured from his throat, slashed by his own hand, his grief too much to bear.

And Killian standing there, unable to protect them, unable to do anything but circle the drain as his world vanished.

Killian sank his teeth into the wraith's windpipe and shook it loose.

No evidence. No culprit to go after. Nothing but a lingering whiff of sulfur, a horror-struck clan, and his own wild, animal pain.

Mom. Dad. Nandi.

He'd gone for a run. A fucking run. Because his lion was riding him, and he needed some space, some air. So, he went for a run. And came back to find them dead.

Cullen wasn't even a full year older than Killian. But he became alpha that day, at twenty years old. And instead of staying by his brother's side, Killian had gone for a much longer run.

Less than a month later, he was in the big city he'd always despised, sticking a piece of tech in his eye and learning that the world was filled with more monsters than he ever imagined. And he was willing to bet that one of those monsters had taken his family from him.

He tore the wraith's spine out through its chest cavity and flung it aside.

"Ow, watch it!"

Killian's head snapped around. A small, curvy woman was silhouetted by the streetlight, fingertips glowing red in the shadows of the city park. The smell of burnt flesh wafted on the night breeze.

A quick glance around showed no other targets. No civilians, either, but Unity Park was usually deserted this time of night. Killian shifted into human form before shoving up from the pile of splintered bones. "What are you doing here?"

Jovi planted her hands on her hips. "He invited me." She pointed at Wolf, who was tearing into his own target with his trademark savagery.

"Rogan knows about this?"

Jovi's fingers sparked. "Excuse you, Rogan doesn't own me. Besides, I've been fighting these fuckers way longer than any of you."

"Yeah, but you're fighting with the squad now. And Rogan leads the squad." It had nothing to do with her being female. Rogan wasn't the type to keep his woman wrapped in bubble wrap. He was the kind of male who would want to know his female could handle herself, that she was a fighter just as ruthless as he was, able to defend herself and eviscerate an enemy. That's sure as hell what Killian would want—

He brought *that* train of thought to a screeching halt and pointed a finger at the little fire-slinger. "Whatever. Just stay away from my targets."

She shot a fireball at his bare foot.

He leaped out of the way, his naked junk dangling, and snarled at her, putting the lion into it.

"Ooh, scary."

Killian growled and melted back into lion form, stalking toward the open street, sticking to the shadows. Animal forms weren't illegal downtown, but they drew attention—exactly what they didn't want in their line of work. It was better to take the enemy out fast, in the shadows, before they latched on to an innocent civilian and someone didn't make it home for movie night.

His chest ached at the memory of last night's squad hangout. The teasing banter, the good-natured bickering, the laughter. The others' physical closeness, the easy and comfortable lean of one body against another…

It all reminded him so much of home that he could almost smell the jungle. Could almost hear his parents' low murmurs as they discussed clan business, his little sister's tiny voice begging for a ride on his shoulders.

Could almost feel the weight of their lifeless bodies in his arms, heavier than the earth, pulling him down, down, into a pit he'd barely crawled out of.

Let the others have their cuddles. Let Rogan smile at his woman and Wolf rub his naked ass on everyone. Let Cyrus hold Juno's gaze while he talked to her inside her head, offering comfort or reassurance or whatever the fuck. It was better to stick to the edges, where his heart wouldn't get flattened. Nevermind that the thing already felt like it was in a vise every time he looked at her.

Killian approached the park border on silent paws. Neon lights gleamed through the trees, highlighting the few late-night pedestrians shuffling along grimy sidewalks, food vendors closing up for the evening, and an open-collared Rafael Vasquez, helping a tousled-looking Juno out of a shiny black car.

As Killian watched, Vasquez lifted Juno's hand slowly to his lips.

Killian exploded from the trees.

Something collided with his back, taking him to the pavement. His muzzle scraped asphalt and he roared, lurching to his paws as he threw off his attacker. He spun and swiped, then swiped again, claws out, mind gone.

A gigantic white wolf leaped out of range, barely avoiding a gutting. The pink-haired woman next to it was not as lucky.

Jovi's gasp cut through the red haze of rage as Killian's claws raked her belly.

He morphed instantly back into human form. "Fuck." He reached out, but Jovi staggered back into the trees, pressing a hand to her stomach. Her palm came away wet.

Sickening guilt curdled in his gut. He took another step toward her. "Fuck. I'm sorry."

Wolf planted himself between the two of them, baring his fangs in an evil growl.

"I didn't mean to." Killian's stomach rolled. Jovi was one hell of a healer, except when it came to her own injuries. Her ability didn't work that way. As the coppery scent of blood filled the air, Killian had a moment of extreme clarity.

This was it, his last night on Earth. Rogan was going to tear his head off.

For a split second, that didn't sound so bad.

There was a noise behind him, and Juno appeared a second later. She must've heard his roar, seen their tussle from across the street. Her nostrils flared, and when she spotted Jovi, she shouldered past him to inspect the wound. Her curse cut through the quiet night.

Juno slashed a claw into her black tank top and ripped the lower half of it clean off. She pressed the cloth to Jovi's bleeding belly and looked over at Killian like he was something she'd scraped off the bottom of her boot. "What is the matter with you?"

Killian's breath pumped in his chest, his pulse pounding in his ears, head spinning with the scent of Juno's skin and Jovi's blood and the idea that he'd gutted his new squadmate because he saw some other male's mouth on his—

"I'll get her home. You—" Juno's jaw tightened. "Burn it off." She hooked an arm around Jovi's waist and led her down the path, leaving Killian and Wolf alone.

Wolf dissolved into human form and rose swiftly. For once, he wasn't mouthing off. "Dude, you're out of control. And that's *me* saying that."

Killian's breath whistled through his nose as he watched the females disappear. A pair of green eyes flashed back at him in the dark, then they were gone.

Wolf was right. He was out of control. And he had no clue what to do about it.

CHAPTER 9

"Done."

Juno watched John's smooth hands make a final pass over Jovi's belly. When the two of them showed up in the Light House library, John leaped up from his book, ordered Jovi to lay on one of the squashy old couches, and went to work without a word. Jovi told him the injury happened on patrol, but had flicked a look at Juno when John was turned away.

They both knew what really happened. Killian saw Rafael kiss her hand, and he lost his shit.

Bad. Very bad.

And worse, her cat liked it. Juno was ready to tear her hair out, but deep inside, her jaguar was purring at the show of violence, the blatant possessiveness. *Strong male.*

Fantastic.

"Thanks, Johnny." Jovi pecked John's cheek as the sound of boots marching purposefully down the hall made Juno's stomach flip. She knew that stride.

Sure enough, Rogan appeared in the door two seconds later. "There you are." He lasered in on Jovi's bloody dress. Every muscle in his body tensed. "What happened?"

"Nothing. I'm fine. Johnny fixed me."

Rogan was already in front of her, brushing her hands aside to inspect her belly while a muscle worked rapidly in his jaw. When he was satisfied that she was healed, he planted his hands on his hips and leveled his green gaze on her.

Uh oh.

"Did you go out on patrol, Jovi?"

It was fascinating to watch the woman work. A subtle shift of her stance, a softening of her curves, a melting of the lines of her body until she was gazing up at him like sex on a stick. "It really wasn't a big deal—"

"We agreed on this. You're supposed to be laying low, remember? Besides, you haven't had enough training to safely fight with a team member."

Jovi gave him a saucy smile. "You and I fought together pretty well in that cave."

The two of them had gotten stuck in a collapsed cave and been forced to fight their way through demon-infested tunnels, Rogan with a dead lens and Jovi acting as his eyes. Jovi described the ordeal as exhausting, but awesome. Rogan described it as the ultimate test of his patience. He hated not being in control, whether it came to demon hunting or the little minx who'd rocked his world.

"You threw a knife in my leg."

Her smile vanished. "Hey, that was *your* fault—"

"My point is that fighting with another person is different. You want to accidentally torch one of them?" He gestured at Juno.

Jovi huffed. "No."

Rogan tilted her chin until she met his eye. "I've put you on the training schedule. We all need to gel. We have to be a cohesive unit, no matter who we're out there with. It's too dangerous otherwise."

"I can't just sit around here waiting for Mommy Dearest to pop out of the shadows. I want to kick some ass."

Rogan brought Jovi's hands up between them. "And I want these blow torches on patrol as soon as possible. But first, we need to be safe. I won't risk anyone. Especially not you." He pressed his lips to her palm.

Jovi sighed and looped her arms around his neck with a smile. "Nash fucking Rogan."

As the two of them looked at each other like they were the only ones in the room, all Juno could do was stare.

Want.

After a cursory recheck of Jovi's healed belly, Rogan tucked her against his side and shifted his focus to Juno. There was no trace of softness when he spoke this time. "We have a problem. Magnus just called. There were attacks in Pack lands. Two dead, no evidence. I don't want to split up so soon, but I think a couple of us need to be stationed there for a bit. Check it out."

"I'll go." She couldn't get the words out fast enough. "I finished with Rafael tonight. The lawyer will be contacting Theo tomorrow." And she needed to get the hell out of here.

Rafael had changed tactics for their second date. No fancy dinner, no rehashing the past. Instead, he'd taken her into his private woods, melted into jaguar form, and nipped playfully at her fingers. They'd run together, stretching their feline muscles on the obstacle course he'd built for her all those years ago. Climbing, leaping, stalking, pouncing. Living. Breathing. Free. The man knew exactly where to point the arrow.

And then, there was the other ticking time bomb she was trying to avoid. The big, blond, bearded one. "I want to go."

Rogan's gaze narrowed on her face. "Okay. Go get packed. You'll leave first thing."

CHAPTER 10

"Killian should go."

Jovi's slanted blue eyes stared at him from beneath Rogan's beefy arm. Through the bloody, ripped fabric of her dress, Killian could see her stomach was healed. A fresh wave of relief washed over him, but it was short lived. His lion was pounding against his skull.

"I mean, Wolf can't go." There was a calculated gleam in Jovi's eye. "Magnus hates him, right?"

When he and Wolf walked through the front door and found Rogan waiting for them, he was sure he was about to meet his maker. Instead, Rogan had news—a series of mysterious attacks had occurred up in wolf territory.

Rogan glared at Wolf, who was sucking on a lollipop. "So he says. Not that he tries to remedy the situation."

Wolf grinned around his sucker, then pulled it out of his mouth with a slurp and offered it to Jovi. She reached for it eagerly, but Rogan snatched it out of the air and chucked it into a trash can with a clang, murder in his eyes. He reached into a pocket and mutely handed Jovi a mint. She took it, grinning.

Rogan gave Wolf one last venomous look. "Magnus also

hates tech." He fingered one of the many toys on his belt, his dark brows slashed. Rogan was a lethal opponent, but he relied heavily on tech weapons, and the wolf alpha was notoriously twitchy around them. "I want Cyrus here, trying to figure out how to build more lenses."

What else had Vasquez had his dirty paws on tonight? Her hair? Her waist? Her breasts? His world went yellow.

Wolf nodded. "Right. Besides, Killian could stand to get out of the city for a bit, right, bud?" He slapped Killian's shoulder.

Killian's claws sliced through his fingers. "Don't. Fucking. Touch me."

"See?"

Rogan stared at Killian long and hard, like he was debating something, but it was taking all Killian's brainpower to keep his lion inside his skin. He didn't have the bandwidth to dissect his squad leader's thoughts. "You up for it?"

Towering pines, cool mountain air, some space from all the shit he needed to get away from...

The dangerous buzzing in Killian's bones eased ever so slightly, and he nodded.

CHAPTER 11

J uno finished latching her duffle to the Light House's one and only cyberbike, stepped back, and made a face. The bike was a secondhand POS with a cracked screen and a dented fender. It was a larger, dual-seat model, but it looked about a decade old. She'd be lucky if it could even carry enough of a charge to get her to the Den.

"Got everything?"

She turned and smiled at Rogan. Freedom beckoned, just a couple hours north. "Yeah. Wish I had a spare lens, though."

"Don't we all? I want you to take these." He handed her two small, knobbly discs. "Look familiar?"

She examined them, then shook her head.

"That's what kept you from shifting in the middle of that fight in the lab." When her gaze snapped up, he nodded grimly. "Scramblers. Underground tech. Solara's still got connections in the Trident." He frowned. "We don't know these wolves. Watch your back around them. Magnus asked for help, but he's not happy about it. He knows you'll be doing nightly patrols. He also knows you might not be giving him any details about those patrols." She caught a whiff of coffee and mint as he blew out a breath. "You know he's part mage, right? I don't know anything about his abilities, but he's powerful enough even without magic. Try not to piss him off." He shook his head. "And take the scramblers, just in case. I want daily check-ins. If there's a hellmouth up there, I want you to find it ASAP. We'll call the archangels, zip it up, and get out of there."

A powerful, pissed-off alpha, a bunch of suspicious wolves, and a hellmouth to find, all on unfamiliar turf?

God, she loved her job.

Juno nodded, pocketed the scramblers, and pulled her hair elastic out of her ponytail so she could put her helmet on. As she shook her hair free, something on the Light House's front steps caught her eye.

Killian froze on the top step, a duffle hooked over each shoulder. Their eyes locked.

Fuck, fuck, *fuck*.

She'd been so eager to get away from her problems, she hadn't even considered the possibility that one of the biggest, burliest ones might follow her.

Rogan watched her. "You good?"

No. She wasn't good. This wasn't good. This was a powder keg.

Rogan waved Killian over. When he drew close, Rogan pegged them both with a hard look. "Look, you two make the most sense for this mission. And you obviously have some shit you need to work out."

Humiliation sizzled in her gut.

"We can't afford in-fighting. We already imploded once. Squad first."

Juno nodded tightly, and Killian followed suit.

"Go out there, do the job, and figure this shit—" he sliced a finger between them, "—out. Understood?"

Killian was a statue, carved from solid stone. Except his eyes. Those burned.

Hell if she would look away first. "No problem." She lifted a brow. "We'll be fine."

CHAPTER 12

er hands were on him, and his beast was roaring.

Yes. Right. Mine. More.

It was all Killian could do to focus on the road as they weaved out of the city, through the burbs and toward Pack lands. This was not part of the plan. He was supposed to be getting away from her, getting his head straight and his shit together. Instead, her thighs were parted around him, her palms were skimming his waist, and the heat of her was seeping into his back through the leather they both wore. His lion growled with pleasure, raking his claws against the inside of his skin, yearning for more.

The temperature dropped as they traveled north, leafy trees slowly giving way to evergreens and birch. They reached the border of Pack lands and were met by two sentries on the edge of a pine forest. Killian slowed the bike to a stop and removed his helmet, shaking his hair out to cool his sweating neck.

"You Rogan's people?" one of the sentries asked. At their nod, he jerked his head toward the dirt path winding into the pines. "Stay on the road."

They whirred down the dirt path, leaning into the curves

in unison, her front against his back, their bodies tight and in tune. He was so used to fighting against her. Sparring, training, battling that constant, relentless pull toward her. Moving with her was different. It made his blood hum. His lion hummed, too.

They wound their way through the sun-dappled timber until they came to a small cabin. A tall female, ice blonde with an arctic expression to match, pushed off the cabin's wall and held out a warning hand. Killian brought the bike to a stop and powered it off. He flicked the kickstand out, and both of them removed their helmets. Juno's scent washed over him.

The blonde approached them with a soldier's stride, scanning them with sharp eyes. They were a startling amethyst purple, striking against her pale skin. One side of her platinum hair was braided back from her face, and she wore leggings, boots, and a thin tank top despite the cool air.

Killian scoped her weapons. Thigh holster with several small, mean-looking daggers. Belt with what looked like a blow gun and several feather-tipped darts. Compound bow and a quiver of arrows strapped to her back. She arched a brow at the black phasers clipped to their belts, but didn't mention them.

Her nostrils flared. "Rogan sent cats?" Her low voice held a faint accent Killian couldn't place and a smirk he didn't appreciate. As she spoke, two male sentries melted into view behind her.

"Juno DeSilva," Juno offered before Killian could growl something snarky back at the female. "And Killian Diallo. Jaguar, lion." She jerked her thumb between them.

The blonde's purple eyes shifted to his face. "Diallo. Really." She scanned his body again, reassessing, no doubt wondering why the lion alpha's little brother was working for a human in the big city. Well, let her wonder. "Astrid Magnussen, second to the alpha. And sister." It was an afterthought.

Interesting. He'd met Magnus years ago at a gathering of the clans, but the wolf's sister had been too young to attend.

"Leave the bike. Grab your stuff."

They looped their bags over their shoulders and followed the wolves into the towering trees. Evergreens and aspens soared above their heads like living green skyscrapers. Sheets of vibrant blue-green moss dripped from monstrous oaks. Fat shafts of sunlight streamed through the branches, spot-lighting craggy boulders and feathery ferns, glinting off bursts of glittering purple fae. Thousands of tiny blue flowers carpeted the ground, so vivid it almost hurt to look at them.

The air was different here. Cleaner, clearer. It seemed to rush into Killian's lungs all on its own, the scent of pine and earth filling his nose. Musty and crisp, old and new. It was nothing like the hot, humid jungle he'd grown up in, but there was space here, away from the cars and lights and crowds.

The temperature dropped another couple degrees as they ventured further down the path. Killian was glad for his leather jacket. He was glad Juno wore hers, too. He risked a glance at her and wished he hadn't. Her hair was still unbound, flowing to her waist like a dark curtain, her head tilted back as she gazed at the towering trees with a smile playing around her lips.

She looked over like she felt the weight of his stare. Her smile vanished.

He refocused on the wolves in front of him. The two males flanking Astrid were tall and leanly muscled. One had a short ponytail, the other a close-cut mohawk. They slid glances over their shoulders every so often. Astrid was as tall as they were, with long legs eating up the ground and strong arms bared by her tank top. Intricate gray tattoos covered her fore-arms and shoulders. Runes. Norse, probably. A hawk feather dangled in her hair.

They walked for miles, deeper and deeper into the forest.

Killian's duffles seemed to take on even more weight as they tramped through the undergrowth. He caught Juno grimacing as she tilted her head to one side, trying to free the chunk of hair trapped under the strap of her bag.

Killian reached over and lifted her duffle off her shoulder, but before he could heft it onto his own, her grip tightened on the strap. "I got it."

He tried to tug it away. "I'm just—" When her eyes flashed and her fingers tightened on the strap, he released it. "Fine. Jesus." He dropped the bag and strode ahead, feeling stupid. The wolves flicked glances between them.

By the time they came to an early-generation security fence, its dirty, moss-covered wires blending seamlessly into the landscape, Killian's stomach was growling, and so was his lion. Juno was probably hungry, too. Had she eaten at all today? He hadn't seen her at breakfast.

Feed.

Astrid turned to face them. "Obviously, everything you see here is confidential."

"No shit."

Amethyst eyes flashed. "Glad we understand each other." Astrid gave a melodic whistle through her teeth, and the fence parted, gliding soundlessly into the trees. As they walked through the gap, Killian caught two new male scents, but he saw nothing except dense forest. It irked him.

The trees grew thicker, closing around them as they followed a narrow path. The dense boughs blocked more of the sun, and as they walked into the darkening forest, a sickening sense of dread overcame him. It crawled up his skin like a swarm of insects, wound around his throat, making his stomach turn and his breath catch. Killian stopped abruptly, and behind him, he felt Juno do the same. His claws shot out.

"Easy." Astrid flicked an amused glance over her shoulder. "Repelling ward. It'll pass."

Wards, huh? Either the wolves had partnered with a

professional security mage—which was unlikely—or Magnus's magic was a lot more powerful than they'd thought.

The sickening feeling intensified as they continued down the narrow path, and Killian was damn near crawling out of his skin by the time they reached a thick curtain of the shaggy hanging moss.

Astrid turned and pinned them with eyes that had gone wolf white. "One hundred percent confidential." She ducked under the mossy curtain, leaving them to follow.

The instant they cleared it, the feeling of dread vanished, his throat eased, and his eyes widened at the stunning landscape spread before them.

An enormous silver lake shimmered at the center of a valley. Smoke trailed from chimneys of countless A-frame cabins, their steep triangular roofs blanketed by more of the blue-green moss. The sun was a hot pink orb hovering low over the glassy water, painting the sky in shades of purple. Mountains loomed in the distance like shadowy titans, while blue faebugs darted through the trees, leaving trails of aqua glitter in their wake.

Fine, it was beautiful. But it was fucking cold.

There were wolves everywhere. Tall, lean, and pale, with hair that ranged from platinum to raven. They were all dressed thinly, apparently impervious to the chill. Sharp eyes watched their every move, young ones stopped their games to stare, and nostrils flared as they were led through the village, past a longhouse that threw out the mouthwatering scent of woodfire and roasted meat.

Astrid's sentries peeled off, and the lieutenant herself led Killian and Juno to the far edge of the village, where a small cabin stood at the edge of the woods. Astrid climbed the front steps and opened the door.

"This is your cabin. You saw the cookhouse. You can eat there if you want."

They stepped inside. Cedar plank ceilings soared over-head, coming to a high peak. The little living space contained a bathroom, a kitchenette, a couple windows overlooking the woods.

And one bed.

Any hint of chill vanished from Killian's bones. His eyes flashed to Juno's, and he saw the same *oh, shit* that was bouncing around his own skull.

"We need two beds," Juno said.

Astrid's brows knit as she glanced around the room. "I see that. We'll get another one in here tomorrow. You'll have to deal tonight." Her tone was that of a commander to her troops, expecting them to put up with discomfort like any soldier. "Dump your stuff. Magnus wants to see you."

CHAPTER 13

"Ahem. Mr. Voss is here, sir."

Magistrate Thackeray White looked up from his tablet to find his assistant, Tyrell, hovering at his office door. The Magistrate scanned his fingerprint to sign the document he'd been reviewing. Salary increases, exponential ones. But it was imperative that he retain Tallia Monroe and Raj Anand. He could find new field agents. Finding new researchers and tech engineers with the same degree of brilliance and discretion? That was a different story entirely.

Such bright, eager minds, each desperate for something. He'd given Tallia, a mage with no magic, a chance to work with the most prestigious mage on the continent. And he'd recruited Anand young, before his genius brain shriveled to nothing while making the Trident's dime-a-dozen earbuds and other useless toys.

Anand was about to get an assistant as well. A brilliant young human who had no knowledge of—or preconceptions about—the former Demon Eradication field squad.

He did love a blank slate.

He turned over his tablet, laced his fingers and smiled at Tyrell. "Show him in."

The Light House's former cook was a scrawny, sour-faced human with a shaved head and the twitchy movements of a Blitz addict. His T-shirt was grimy, his eyes bright.

"Mr. Voss. Come in. Have a seat."

Rodney Voss darted a nervous glance around the office before easing into the chair across from him. The Magistrate nodded at Tyrell, who slipped out of the office and closed the door softly behind him.

The Magistrate smiled. "Thank you for meeting me, Rodney. I understand you're no longer employed at the boarding school?"

Voss shifted, his gaze lingering over the scarred half of the Magistrate's face. "Yeah. They brought in some new cook." His mouth twisted. "I don't need that shit. I work alone."

"I see. Is she living there?"

Voss shrugged his thin shoulders. "Don't know. Probably. They all had bags."

"All? How many?"

"I don't know, man, like, five or six. Mostly guys, a couple of chicks. Hot ones," he added with a faint leer. He eyed the arcs of electricity swirling in the glass domes behind the desk. "Look, what do you want? I didn't steal nothing." He scratched at his neck.

The Magistrate kept the smile pinned to his face. "I have a proposition for you. I'd like you to watch the school for me. I'm interested in what's going on there."

Voss's brows furrowed in suspicion. "Why?"

The Magistrate shook his head and leaned forward. "No matter. Just observe. Occasionally, find a reason to go inside. Tell me what you find. I'll make it worth your time."

A calculated gleam appeared in his eyes. "I just gotta watch it and tell you what I see?"

"And what you find inside."

Voss's upper lip curled in a smile. "Let's make a deal, boss."

They worked out the specifics, and the Magistrate watched Voss lope out of his office, rubbing his palms together. He had a distinct desire to douse the room in antiseptic.

Instead, he turned over his tablet and pulled up the email he'd received earlier that morning.

The law office of Monte, Padron, and Morata had informed him that by some minute, infuriating fucking loophole, he was no longer the owner of The Light House School for Magical Youth. His own lawyers had confirmed that the play was legitimate.

His field squad, his favor with the archangels, his lab, and now the school—his future feeding source for the Demon Eradication unit—was gone.

The arcs of electricity surged behind him, exploding their glass domes.

CHAPTER 14

agnus Magnussen was even bigger than Juno expected, and she'd expected a giant.

He loomed like a titan at the head of the table in the cookhouse, his immense shoulders spanning the width of the wooden planks. Heavily muscled arms were bared by a black undershirt, exposing the long, continuous tattoo that wound up one side of his body. The tribal-style wolf was beautifully done, strong and intricate lines curling over his shoulder and up his neck to his shaved head, the wolf's fierce fangs framing his temple. A black beard matched his short mohawk and lowered brows, a striking contrast to the arctic blue eyes that watched their approach.

Chatter died as she and Killian stepped into the cookhouse, and hundreds of predator eyes locked on the two cats in the wolves' den. The food, the fire, and so many unfamiliar wolves, plus the visceral undercurrent of hostility, sent her brain into overdrive. She latched on to Killian's familiar scent and felt her nerves settle.

Great. Now, his scent was calming her.

"I invited them here," Magnus drawled in a low Norse accent. He pointed his fork around the table. "Play nice." Icy eyes landed on them. The alpha pull in them was strong, tugging at her even though she was a cat. "As long as they do." He flicked a hand, and everyone shoved down to make room.

They moved past the endless stream of watchful wolves and settled on either side of the alpha. Killian wedged next to Astrid, his shoulders crammed against hers. He shifted uncomfortably.

Silence.

"Eat," Magnus demanded impatiently, and the conversation slowly returned to the table. A plate landed unceremoniously in front of Juno, then one in front of Killian. They were piled with roasted fish, root vegetables, and some kind of berry compote.

"That's the last time anyone will bring food to you." Magnus tore into a hunk of bread and studied Killian with unnerving intensity. "You filled out, cat."

Killian grunted. "Back at you."

Juno glanced between them. "You two know each other?"

"We met once, when our fathers were alphas. We were teenagers." He spoke to Killian. "I went down to see Cullen when he took the helm, but you weren't there." When Killian just stabbed at his food, Magnus turned to Juno. "And you are?"

"Juno DeSilva, jaguar. Thanks," she added, grabbing her fork. "That was a big hike, I'm starving."

"How long have you been on Rogan's team?"

"Seven years." The fish was incredible. Moist, flaky, flavorful. She practically inhaled it.

"Mm. So, his secrets are yours."

Juno met his eyes. They were such a pale blue they were almost white, with dark rings around the irises, making him look wild. Her cat sat up straight. "Our work is confidential. But we're here to help."

Magnus ran a vast palm over his black beard, considering

her. He was handsome, if you liked that whole big, dangerous Viking thing. Power radiated from him, a mix of magic and alpha dominance and raw, potent masculinity. "Maybe someday our clans will be friendly enough to share our secrets."

Juno cocked a brow. "I'll show you mine if you show me yours."

Magnus barked a laugh. His gaze heated as it traveled over her. "Maybe, kitten."

Killian's fork hit his plate with a clatter. He snatched it up. "We need details about the attacks."

A hush fell over the table, and any hint of amusement fled Magnus's face. "One last week, the other two nights ago. We've lost two guards."

A dark-haired female stood abruptly and left the cookhouse. Another female hurried after her.

"No idea what it was?" Juno said.

Magnus tossed back half of his tankard, pain creasing his brow. As alpha, he would feel the loss of a clan member deeply, almost physically, or so Juno had been told. "No evidence. Nothing but that smell."

Let me guess…

"Sulfur. Like the hot springs in the mountains."

"Show us," Killian said.

They ate quickly, then left the cookhouse and followed Magnus and Astrid into the twilit woods. Even with his black beard and her ice blonde hair, it was obvious they were siblings. They had the same strong shoulders, the same long stride, and the same straight blade of a nose. Magnus stomped through the undergrowth, scattering an occasional cloud of tittering purple fae, until they came to a mound of artfully stacked stones. Some nearby broken limbs showed evidence of a struggle, but any whiff of sulfur was gone.

"This was the first one." Juno examined a tree missing some bark while Killian prowled the perimeter.

The siblings nodded. "Tor." Astrid stared at the stacked stones. "He was on guard duty. Fastest sentry we had. Gutted."

Magnus swept a finger gently through the air, and a blue flower uprooted from the forest floor, floating over to land atop the stones.

"DeSilva."

She followed Killian's rough voice until she reached his side. Black blood, dried and crusted on the ground. A larger puddle of it faded into a trail of droplets before disappearing.

The next site was deeper in the woods, a good mile from the main camp. There, the smell of sulfur was fresh, the copper tang of blood even fresher.

"Inga," Astrid murmured. "Just married."

Magnus's hand flexed. A tree limb cracked nearby.

What would Rogan do if Jovi died? What would she do if Cyrus, or John, or Killian…her heart gave a pang. "I'm sorry," she said, and meant it.

Two sets of wolf eyes speared her through the shadows.

Killian peered at the blood trail. "How many guards are on rotation?"

"Six, round the clock. Three shifts."

"You consider pulling them?"

Magnus's growl rumbled through the night. "Would *you*?"

If she were in Magnus's position? No way in hell. Pulling guards after multiple attacks was stupid. Weak. Magnus was neither.

But knowing what she and Killian knew? That demons were out here, invisible and deadly and picking them off one by one?

"We need comms," Juno said. "So whoever's on duty can talk to us, and vice versa."

"You'll have them tomorrow." Magnus heaved a sigh. "Now, we have a sister to send to Valhalla." The two wolves stalked away, but their heartbreak lingered in the air long after they vanished from view.

"Fuck." Killian rose from a crouch and held his watch up to his mouth. "Got me?"

His voice rumbled from her wrist. "Copy. Got me?"

"Yeah. I'll take east." He melted into the trees.

The dark forest was a completely different kind of chaos than the city she was used to patrolling. Scents bombarded her—moist earth, old trees, animal scat, and wolf, everywhere wolf. Little creatures squeaked and scampered at her silent approach as faebugs flashed bright blue against the black night.

She detected a faint whiff of sulfur here and there, but it was old. No fresh blood, no sign of demons, no hellmouth.

A flicker of flame caught her eye. She crept toward it, ducking under a veil of curling moss, and stopped short.

A wooden platform was ablaze in the center of a clearing. A vaguely human shape lay prone at its center. Silhouettes of people and wolves surrounded it, some of them wrapped in each other's arms.

Magnus's unmistakable voice boomed something foreign. The call was echoed by the group. Magnus bellowed again. The crowd echoed. Again, and again, the rough chant gained volume and speed until it ended with a ringing, guttural shout that raised the hairs on Juno's arms.

There was a moment of silence. Then, a long, lone howl pierced the night. Others joined in, one by one, until the entire clearing throbbed with raw, animal grief and the roar of crackling flames.

Throat aching, Juno backed away into the woods.

Even if they did find a hellmouth in these mountains and got the archangels to close it, what then? Would they simply tell the wolves to give them a call the next time more of their people were mysteriously slaughtered, and they'd do it all over again?

A branch rustled nearby. Juno's claws shot out of her hands, and the world went green.

A possum waddled out of the undergrowth, spotted her, and scuttled away.

She released a breath. It could've been a very different scenario. One with a wolf on guard duty, and instead of a harmless critter appearing, an invisible killing machine.

Her watch vibrated on her wrist, telling her that her shift was over. She headed back to their cabin and ducked inside to grab her phone, her belly fluttering at the sight of the single bed. She'd almost forgotten she'd be sharing quarters with a giant, growly lion.

Almost.

Rogan answered on the first ring. "Hey." Jovi's sleepy murmur sounded in the background, along with a soft rustle of sheets.

"Hey." She filled him in on the day's events and the night's fruitless patrol. "We're not enough," she finished, watching a faebug dart through the trees. "They need to be able to take care of themselves." Even as she said it, the echo of Killian's words in the gym floated back to her.

Another rustle sounded on the line, like Rogan was sitting up. Jovi mumbled something, and he murmured something unintelligible back, his voice low and soothing. When he spoke again, it was back to his usual clipped tone. "Agreed."

Juno blinked. She'd expected more resistance from the founder of the DE, the one who'd written their oath of silence. But a lot had changed. "So, what do we do?"

"Keep it under wraps for now. Work with them. Play nice, make friends. You've got a dual mission now. Find the hell-mouth, get the wolves to trust us." Another pause. "How's everything else?"

Footsteps approached, and Juno glanced over as Killian emerged from the trees, looking cranky. And muscled. "Fine."

"You two good?"

"Fine," she said through gritted teeth. "I'll check in tomorrow." She hung up.

Sweat glinted on Killian's neck. "Nothing?"

Juno shook her head. "Rogan thinks we need to loop them in pretty soon. The wolves. And probably the lions, too."

"Good luck getting any of them to stick a piece of tech in their eye."

"I know. We're supposed to make friends. Get them to trust us." She swallowed and glanced toward the cabin.

"You're kidding. How long are we supposed to stay here?"

She shrugged, acting like the same thought wasn't hammering through her head.

"This is bullshit."

Irritation flared. Yeah, being stuck with her was the worst, right? "This is the mission. Guess you'll have to try not to be a complete asshole for a while."

He shot her a glare, but she could've sworn something close to hurt sparked in those amber depths. "I need a shower. You take the bed." His warm shoulder brushed hers as he headed inside.

CHAPTER 15

He needed a cold shower. Really fucking cold.

It figured that just when he needed a good, nasty fight, the hellspawn refused to come out to play. So, after hours of creeping through the chilly woods, he'd started running instead. Then, he did a hundred pushups. Then, he climbed five trees.

She was out there in their tiny cabin, maybe undressing.

He cranked the water all the way to glacial and willed his cock to deflate. It didn't.

He had to take care of this before he walked out there at full fucking mast. Snarling, he planted one palm on the shower wall and wrapped the other around his hard length, barely stifling a groan when he made contact.

As usual, he tried to think of anyone but her. As usual, it didn't work.

He handled himself roughly, like it was his dick's fault that he wanted the one thing he couldn't have. He came in record time, his breath exploding out of him and knees locking with the force of his orgasm while he strained to stay silent.

He was so fucking pathetic.

He made sure there was no evidence left behind before stepping out of the shower into the cold bathroom. Water dripped from his hair as he scrubbed a hand over his face, scowling at his own reflection in the mirror.

A knock on the door made him jolt. "Your phone's ringing. It's Light House." Juno's muffled voice, so close while he was still naked, sent a stupid thrill through him.

Really fucking pathetic.

He looped a towel around his waist and yanked open the door. Juno handed his phone over quickly, then moved toward the bed, where she was unpacking her duffle.

He swiped to answer. "Diallo."

"Killian?" a small voice said.

"Franklin?" He stared at his phone. Christ, it was after four in the morning. How'd this kid get his cell number?

"Killian, I did it! Blaine and his friends were being mean to me, and they chased me down a hallway, and Blaine was going to use his vines on me but I turned around and *punched him in the face!*"

A barking laugh escaped him. "You break his nose?"

Juno turned from the bed, mouth twitching.

"Um, I don't know, but it bled a *lot.*"

"Good."

"And then, all his friends were scared and they ran off!" A happy sigh came through the receiver.

"Good." Killian's hand tightened on his towel as Juno came forward.

Franklin? she mouthed, and Killian managed to nod, hyper-focused on the way her tongue shaped the syllables.

"Thanks. It was awesome," the kid chattered in his ear. "I heard you're up in Pack lands."

Killian cleared his throat. "Yeah."

"With the *wolves?*"

"Yep."

"Wow. Nero says wolves are scary. But the only wolf I

know is Wolf, and *he's* not scary. I mean, he's kinda crazy, but..."

He didn't respond. Juno was bent over her duffle, giving him a spectacular view of her ass in those black leggings.

"When are you coming back?"

He ripped his gaze to the ceiling. "Don't know."

"When you come back, will you teach me to fight some more?"

Something warm tugged at the center of his chest. "Sure."

"And Juno, too?"

He glanced over at her again. "Maybe."

"That cook came back."

"Cook?" Killian said, distracted. Juno was bending over again.

"Yeah, Rodney. The guy who used to be the cook here? Before Gloria came?"

It finally registered. "What the hell did he want?"

"I dunno. Said he forgot some stuff." As Killian's instincts flared, there was some yelling on the other end of the line. "I gotta go. It's *way* past my bedtime, but Wolf said this would be the best time to call you."

"Of course he did," Killian grumbled.

"Bye!"

He hung up. "You hear that about the cook?"

Juno nodded. That sexy little frown line appeared between her brows. "Tell Rogan. He'll keep an eye on it."

He was already texting. Despite the hour, Rogan sent an immediate affirmative.

The silence was loud as a siren in the tiny cabin.

Juno moved a stack of clothes to one of the dresser drawers. "I'll take the floor. You can have the bed."

His brows lowered. "I already said I'd take the floor."

"Yeah, but it's fine. I don't mind."

"I said I'd take it."

"I'm just saying—"

"Just let me sleep on the fucking floor, DeSilva!" *Let me do something to take care of—*

She slammed the drawer. "Fine." She flicked a glance at him, her eyes raking his bare chest before she turned away.

A scent bloomed in the air. A gorgeous, spiced honey scent that triggered something very deep and very male.

It was her. Juno.

She was aroused.

Fuck.

His lion boiled to the surface, practically clawing its way out of his skin. It took everything in him to keep it contained.

He grabbed a set of sweats from his own bag and shut himself back in the bathroom in record time, his heart beating like a drum.

He gripped the sink and raised his eyes to the mirror. His lion stared back at him, big cat bones flickering beneath his skin.

WANT.

You can't have her, you dumb fuck. She's squad. And she borderline hates us.

But his lion didn't give a shit. His lion wanted her. And apparently, because there was no God, she wanted him, too.

CHAPTER 16

I t was a really long night.

Juno tossed and turned until dawn. And tried to do it silently, so she wouldn't alert the living, breathing mountain on the floor that she was too wound up to sleep.

He'd made her mouth water, flinging open that bathroom door and standing there like a wild man, dripping wet and barely covered by a towel.

She'd seen every one of her squad mates naked. Multiple times. And they'd seen her bare ass more times than she could count. Nudity wasn't a thing in the field, especially among shifters. Usually.

It had always been different with him. That spark of awareness had been there since the first time Rogan brought him to the Bunker. Juno had been in the gym, imagining Rafael's face on the punching bag she was pummeling. The breakup was still raw then, and she'd split the bag open with a vicious slash of her claws just as Rogan entered with the biggest lion shifter she'd ever seen. She'd locked eyes with Killian Diallo for the first time while sand spilled at her feet. There had been instant heat, but beneath the flash of raw attraction, there was something else. A wild, savage pain. A deep, primal rage. Her jaguar had stirred inside her, intrigued, liking the strength and brutality of him, and the little slut had stayed on high alert ever since.

Juno had slapped that awareness down, day after day, night after night, refusing to acknowledge, refusing to inspect. *If I can't see you, you can't see me.*

Tonight, when he'd flung open that bathroom door, his carved torso suddenly inches away, all those tattoos standing out against his golden skin, his wet hair dripping water down his pecs...she'd seen herself grab that wet mane and climb him like a tree.

Deep inside, her jaguar flexed her claws in agreement.

Fuck.

He got up before her, retreated quickly to the bathroom and then outside, leaving her alone in the empty cabin. She stared at the high peak of the wood ceiling, trying to ignore the low-level hum beneath her skin and wishing for maybe the first time in her life that she had a girlfriend to call.

His scent was all over the cabin. Her cat stretched and purred, wanting to roll around in it.

She snarled and vaulted out of bed before her fingers could trail down her belly and do something stupid. A quick shower, a rough scrub, and a couple layers of clothing later, she stepped into the crisp morning woods and walked to the cookhouse, her breath fogging in the air.

"You're on cleanup," a female with dark hair greeted her the second she stepped inside the noisy longhouse. A fire roared at the back, near a huge buffet table piled with platters of food.

"Everyone helps," another female said as she brushed past.

Warm welcomes all around. Juno loaded a plate from the buffet table, then turned and looked for a place to sit, feeling like the new kid in the school cafeteria. Killian was nowhere to be found.

"Hey, cat," Astrid called from the end of a long table. She jerked her chin, and Juno sat across from her, grateful for the invitation despite the chilly reception the lieutenant had given them yesterday. When Astrid raised a thick ceramic mug to her lips, a familiar scent drifted over.

"Coffee?" Shifters typically avoided caffeine since their sensitive systems didn't handle it well. But the smell reminded her of Rogan, and she'd take what little comfort she could get right about now.

Astrid shrugged. "Didn't sleep." Her amethyst eyes were full of fatigue, grief, and the hardness of a soldier, pushing through because she had to.

"We'd like to meet your patrol team today. Get comms set up, orient to the sectors." *Find a hellmouth.*

Astrid nodded, tossing back the rest of her coffee before plunking her empty mug in front of Juno. "Find me when you're done with cleanup." Amusement gleamed for a split second. "Everyone helps."

"I've heard. Happy to help." Juno gave her a tight smile. Did they think she'd be above helping out because she was an outsider, or because she was a cat? Or had they somehow found out who her father was?

They were about to meet the most helpful houseguest of their lives.

She cleared the buffet table and brought the trays into the industrial kitchen at the back of the cookhouse, where two wolves eyed her but said nothing. She figured out how to use the commercial dishwasher on her own, burned her fingers on the scalding dishes when they came out of the dryer, and wiped tables in record time. She could all too clearly imagine her father's disgust at the idea of the Silka liquor heiress bussing tables for a bunch of wolves.

"Anything else?" she asked when the surfaces gleamed. Looking mildly impressed, the wolves shook their heads.

"Cool. I'm Juno." She turned and left, barely holding back a mic drop.

She found Killian braced at the edge of the lake, his folded arms stretching his thermal shirt as he stared across the water. He glanced over at her approach. A strand of golden hair drifted across his face. Their eyes met for a moment before they both looked away.

Rogan's words echoed in her mind. *Go out there, do the job, and figure this shit out.*

"How's it going?" She mirrored his stance and took in the village in the morning light. Mist rose off the lake, chimneys smoked, purple mountains loomed in the distance. Everything seemed washed in a pale lavender glow.

"Fucking cold."

She snorted. The chill didn't bother her as much, but she wasn't raised in the jungle—not that he ever talked about his childhood. "I told Astrid we wanted to meet the team today, get comms set up, walk the perimeter."

He nodded.

The silence lengthened.

Ugh, this would be so much easier with Cyrus, or Rogan. Or anyone else, for that matter. "They sure are big on everyone helping around here." She eyed him. "Is it like that in the Pride?"

His brows lowered, and his arms tightened across his chest.

Why did she even bother? She shook her head at herself and glared at the lake.

"We're not as psycho about it."

Her gaze slid to his face. The carved cheekbones, the wide-bridged nose. Aside from his lighter hair and beard, he looked nearly identical to his older brother. Cullen lacked that raw, unhinged quality, but he radiated no less danger. It was hard to imagine either of them as young boys, grumbling about chores.

"Hey, cats!" Astrid's call echoed across the lake. She whistled through her teeth.

Killian growled, and her jaguar twitched in agreement. Being summoned like a dog didn't sit well, but they stalked around the lake to a small supply cabin, where Astrid stood with the same two male sentries that had escorted them into the village the day before. She introduced them as her betas and gestured to a table of supplies. "We've got comms for you."

The wolves' comms were the size of a stick of gum and required pressing a button to talk, like an old-fashioned walkie talkie. Juno and Killian exchanged a look as they clipped them onto their shirt collars. Comms like this were inefficient in the field, especially during an attack, but it could work to their advantage in this situation. They could communicate privately through their own comms, without the entire patrol overhearing.

They hiked all day, stopping at various checkpoints and meeting the other sentries on duty. No hellmouths, no sulfur, no scorched earth. Just a lot of immense evergreens dripping with teal moss, crystal streams tumbling over rocks, and forest fae darting between trees in flashes of purple glitter. The air was so fresh and clear, Juno kept sucking in deep lungfuls, scenting earth and animals and wide open space.

She wanted to run. Her muscles hummed with the need to be used, to feel their own power and speed. Her joints were wound tight, begging for movement.

When the village came into view again, steep triangular roofs silhouetted against a spectacular sunset, she smothered her disappointment. Her cat growled at the idea of being cooped up in a noisy cookhouse, surrounded by surly wolves—

"We're heading back out."

Killian's rough voice made her glance over in surprise. His eyes were on her, unreadable.

Astrid lifted a brow. "Thought you were on fishing duty?"

"Patrol is more important." Holding Juno's gaze, he jerked his head toward the woods, already backing away.

Glee erupted in her chest, but she kept her face serious. "Agreed." She nodded at the wolves. "We'll feed ourselves tonight. Thanks."

She caught up with him, glancing over her shoulder when she entered the trees. The wolves had already headed in the opposite direction.

Free.

She turned back to Killian in time to see him reach one hand overhead and yank off his shirt.

Heat flashed through her, and she tried to duck behind a tree without looking like she was ducking behind a tree. Like a chicken.

Yeah, it's the Maneater, devourer of enemies, scared to look at her squadmate's naked chest.

She stripped behind the trunk, tucked her clothes into a branch where she could find them later, and shifted in silence, waiting until she heard four heavy paws pad across the dirt before emerging.

Killian's enormous lion form rippled with muscle as he shook out an impressive mane and stretched his jaws. Then, he spun that heavy body around and took off into the pines.

They ran.

Juno sprinted, leaped, swung from branches, rebounded off of trees. Killian stayed grounded but kept pace, a bronze shadow beneath her. She smelled him. She smelled everything. Decaying leaves, fungus blooming on rotted logs, pine needles, and those tiny blue flowers carpeting the ground. Her muscles stretched, her lungs expanded, and her heart soared as she flew through the trees. Deep inside her animal form, she was grinning like a lunatic.

The smell of sulfur brought her to a screeching halt. She backtracked, tracing the scent to a random, nothing-special spruce. Killian followed, his deep inhalations on a lower register than hers. They scoped the area, but found nothing save for a lingering whiff of rotten eggs.

Juno hissed in frustration. Killian's snarl echoed, and they padded off, noses to the ground, lips lifted in an attempt to pick up on even the faintest trail. The forest darkened around them as they continued along the patrol route, the electric blue trails of darting faebugs the only light among the trees.

Twang!

She barely dodged the arrow that shot from the dark. The sharp metal point whizzed past her flank as she blasted forward, swiping at a tall shadow, her claws tearing into leather and flesh. Blood spilled in that split second before the scent registered.

It was a wolf—one of the sentries on patrol in human form.

Fuck. She morphed into human form, holding out her hands. "Shit, it's me, sorry."

A golden tank barreled into the sentry, taking the male to the forest floor, fangs at his throat. Massive paws pinned him to the pine needles, and the sickening snap of a bone ricocheted through the dark. The sentry hollered.

"Fall back!" Steam rose from Juno's sweating, naked skin even as goosebumps pebbled her arms and legs. She dropped to her knees beside the pair of them and shoved at Killian's furry haunches. It was like pushing a velvet-covered boulder. "Fall back, Diallo."

Killian's low growl raised the hairs on her neck, but he backed off, leaving the sentry panting on the ground. The copper tang of blood filled the air.

Juno leaned over the guy to press the button on the comm clipped to his collar. "This is DeSilva. We need a medic." She looked at the sentry. "What's your name?"

He shoved at her, grunting in pain. "Get the fuck off me."

She pressed his comm again. "This is DeSilva, come in. We need a medic, over."

An affirmative squawked over the comm, asking for their location. The wounded sentry snarled and shoved at her shoulders again, knocking her to her naked ass.

A lion's roar blasted her eardrums, and she saw Killian's claws slash through the gloom. The male let out a hoarse cry, and the smell of blood intensified.

"Fall back!" But Killian was looming over the prone male, eyeing his throat like he was anticipating his favorite meal. "Diallo!"

Killian peeled back his lips to expose lethal fangs inches from the male's face. Then, he stepped over him, slow and deliberate, making sure the guy got a good eyeful of his enormous lion dick.

Jesus Christ. Juno crossed her arms over her breasts while the wolf tried and failed to sit up. He collapsed on his back with a curse and hit his comm with his good hand.

"This is Val. The cats mauled me. Shredded arm and a broken rib, maybe two."

"Sending in your replacement. Can you make it back to base?"

Val managed to sit up, panting. "I'll make it." He let out another juicy curse and bared his teeth at Juno. "What the hell was that?"

Her cat did not like his tone. Come to think of it, neither did she. "You shot an arrow at me."

He got to his feet, cradling his arm and giving her a scathing look. "I knew this wouldn't work."

"Look, you came at me, then I came at you."

She was usually very good at keeping her cool. But when Val made a vulgar gesture, her frustration boiled over. She rose fluidly to her feet, ignoring the stinging pain in her side. "Didn't you see me? I thought dogs were supposed to have decent night vision."

Wolf eyes flashed, dangerous and predatory. "Watch it,

cat. You're outnumbered." He shot a vicious look at the lion snarling nearby, then limped stiffly into the trees, heading for the village. Killian snapped his teeth at his retreating back.

Juno swore and shifted into jaguar form for the run back. This was not good.

They located their stashed clothes and changed quickly. They were fully covered when they walked into camp, but she still felt like she should be wearing armor. A huge bonfire roared near the lake, and the wolves lounging around it had murder in their eyes as they watched Juno and Killian emerge from the forest.

Magnus's enormous silhouette stepped in front of them. "My cabin. Now."

They followed him. A warm arm bumped hers as they skirted the bonfire, and Killian's voice rumbled in her ear. "You're bleeding."

"It's fine." But her shirt was damp with blood, and her right side was hollering.

Magnus's cabin was on the opposite edge of the camp. It was larger than most, with a peaked roof, wings flaring off either side, and a wraparound porch overlooking the silvery lake. One huge Adirondack chair sat facing the water, but there was no table, no potted plant, no rug. The thick wooden door was beautifully carved with an image of a wolf howling at a full moon. It swung smoothly inward when Magnus shoved his way inside, and would've slammed shut in their faces if Killian hadn't slapped a palm to the heavy slab. His growl was lethal.

She laid a calming hand on his arm. He looked down at her fingers on his shirt, then raised his eyes to hers. She dropped her hand immediately. Her cheeks heated.

Magnus whirled in the middle of his spartan living room. "Explain."

Juno detailed the incident as impartially as possible,

though she could feel the lion next to her bristling. "We need to meet all your sentries. This can't happen again."

Magnus cursed. "It shouldn't have happened in the first place. Val is a hothead, but all of us are twitchy now." He pinned her with those icy blue eyes. "We don't like being kept in the dark."

She held his gaze and said nothing.

He grunted. "You'll start training together. I'll talk to Astrid." He stabbed a finger at Killian. "And you, lion, will keep your shit together. She attacked in self defense. You did it because you were pissed off." As they stared daggers at each other, Magnus's nostrils flared. "Who's wounded?"

"Me. It's fine." But the burning pain was growing sharper with each breath. "Sorry again." They left without looking back.

CHAPTER 17

"You need medical?"

The smell of her blood did something to Killian's lion. It was angry, pushing at his insides, demanding that he do something.

Juno cast a glance at the wolves loitering with crossed arms on the steps of the medical cabin. Most shifter clans had one member per generation who was born with healing abilities. Frida, a grizzled old female with gray hair and a pipe that seemed to be perpetually stuck in her mouth, was the wolves'. She eyed them beadily from her porch, missing nothing, offering nothing. "Not really feeling the love right now. We've got first aid stuff in the cabin. It'll be fine."

He didn't hover, didn't wrap an arm around her waist to support her, didn't scoop her up and stalk the rest of the way to their little cabin outside of camp.

And it nearly drove him out of his skull.

By the time they got inside and he kicked the door shut behind them, his hands were shaking with the effort of holding back. The sight of a second bed shoved in the corner of the room made it worse. The wolves had lived up to their promise.

And why did that realization damn near send him over the edge?

Juno pulled her shirt over her head with a pained grunt. Her sports bra was black, her skin was the color of caramel, and the slash wrapping around her ribs to her shoulder blade was a bright, shocking red.

"Shit." She twisted to examine the wound. "That arrow got me."

He wanted to break something. He could start with the asshole that shot the fucking arrow. His low growl filled the tiny room as he stalked to the wardrobe in the corner where they'd unloaded their supply duffle. He snatched up a roll of Medimend tape and a bottle of disinfectant, imagining all the ways he'd like to twist that wolf's head off his shoulders.

"Sit." He tossed the supplies on the bed.

"It's fine. I can do it."

He gestured to her wound. "How are you going to reach that?"

"It's fine—"

"Stop saying it's fucking fine!" It wasn't fine. She was hurt, and it wasn't fine.

Anger snapped in her gaze. "I really don't like it when you snarl at me, Diallo."

He leaned in. "I really don't like it when you act stupid." Her cat flashed in her eyes, but he didn't back down. "I can reach that wound and you can't. Don't be an idiot."

That did it, like he knew it would. Her chin lifted and she sat on the bed, looking powerful and prim at the same time, all sinuous strength in her black leggings and sports bra. The mattress creaked ominously as he lowered his weight beside her and lifted her arm to inspect the wound. Fairly deep, gaping slightly. Shifters healed quickly, but they still felt pain and still got infections.

"Magnus is right. You took a chunk out of that wolf even after we knew who he was."

He growled at the memory. "Yeah, and I'd do it again. He was getting aggressive."

"I can take care of myself, Diallo."

He slapped the antibacterial spray into her hand. "Spray that on your wound, then."

Her jaw tightened.

"That's what I thought." He snatched the bottle back, held her arm up with one hand, and popped the lid off with his thumb before liberally spraying her wound. Her sharp inhale wasn't a surprise—that shit burned. Instinctively, he dipped his head and blew across her skin to soothe the sting.

She went utterly still.

He froze, his mouth inches from her torso.

So close. Too close. He should pull back, shake it off, get the fuck away from her.

She cleared her throat. "So, you wanted to run, too?"

"What?" His voice could have pulverized granite.

"When we got back to the village earlier."

Sure, he'd wanted to run. But, more importantly, she had. "Yeah."

"Mm." The low noise, and the smile he could hear in it, made his cock stiffen. "It was pretty awesome. Up until the whole getting-shot-with-an-arrow thing."

What was that dog's name? Val? He'd remember that. "Yeah." He blew again, softly, and watched goosebumps appear.

The honeyed scent of female arousal bloomed in the air once more, lush and intoxicating. His lids drifted low, his thumb grazing the silken skin on the underside of her arm. He could dip his head closer, just an inch, and lick her...

Mine.

He reared back like she was on fire, chucked the spray bottle aside, and grabbed the roll of Medimend tape. The stupid stuff was all stuck to itself on the roll, and he had to drop her arm to pick at it, his blunt fingers too thick to find the edge. He snarled, ready to throw the thing.

Juno's hand appeared in front of him. He gave her the tape, and seconds later she handed it back, the sticky edge lifted. He tore off a strip with his teeth and smoothed it over her wound. Her ribs expanded with another harsh inhale, but she took the pain like the soldier she was, even when he pressed firmly to ensure a good seal and added another strip for good measure. Medimend was infused with herbs and enchanted with a healing spell—it would take care of her.

He'd taken care of her.

His lion settled inside his bones.

She cleared her throat again. "Thanks." She got up quickly, returned the supplies to the cupboard, and pulled a sweatshirt over her head. All the while, the scent of her arousal muddled his brain. "I'll report to Rogan." As she grabbed her phone, her stomach gave a mighty growl. She put a hand to her belly, irritated.

"I'll get food."

His lion surged to the forefront. *And feed you the best bites. From my hand.*

Ice shivered down his spine. A male shifter claimed a female by feeding her from his hand. By accepting it, she was accepting him as her mate.

A mate was everything to a male. Their entire universe. Their beating heart torn out of their chest and just fucking walking around outside of it, a fragile package of blood and bones and tender, breakable flesh.

If a male lost his mate, he might as well slit his own throat. Just ask his father.

Killian shot to his feet. She avoided his eyes as he left, and he avoided hers.

CHAPTER 18

Juno really, really wanted a shower. A cold shower, preferably. But like hell she was going to ruin Killian's bandage job and have to ask him to redo it.

That way lay trouble. Big trouble.

Sponge baths sucked, but scrubbing a wet, soapy washcloth over her pits and bits still felt better than going to bed covered in sweat and grime. She absolutely did not linger in certain areas, swiping the warm, wet cloth in gentle circles.

Jeez, she was hard up, wasn't she? How long had it been since she'd had a male? She thought about it as she tossed the washcloth over the towel bar. That guy from Jag, the jaguar nightclub? His apartment had smelled like cologne and stale vape, and she'd dipped back to the Bunker as soon as possible. But how long ago was that? Two months ago? Three?

She threw on the tank top and boxers she slept in and opened the bathroom door, trying to remember the timeline.

A shadow moved near the dresser.

Rat.

She leaped for the bed, snatched her phaser from the pillow, and had the safety off and the muzzle leveled in less than a second.

Rat. Thick, furry body, twitching whiskers, bald tail—
Chains. A concrete room. Fear and hunger and pain.
He didn't come.

She fired. And fired. And fired again.

The cabin door burst inward, making her jump. Her phaser was suddenly pointed at Killian's face.

He scanned the room rapidly, halting as he took in the dead rat on the floor. His eyes swung toward her, traveling from the phaser clutched in her white-knuckled hands to her bare feet planted on the bed. She dropped her arms.

Killian frowned between her and the dead rodent. "You good?"

No, she was right back there, in that concrete room, waiting for a rescue that would never come.

She flicked the safety on. "Fine."

Killian studied her a second longer before stalking inside, bending to snag the rat's disgusting hairless tail, and marching back out with the thing swinging against his thigh.

Heavy footsteps circled the perimeter of the cabin and stopped at the rear. There were some shuffling sounds, a muffled curse, then a few solid thuds that made her jump again.

Seconds later, Killian reappeared on the steps. He closed the door firmly behind him and looked at her. "Hole in the back. It's covered now."

Good. Great. She forced a swallow and gave him a nod. "Cool. Thanks."

His eyes flicked to her feet, still sinking into the mattress. "Didn't know you had a thing about rats."

She shrugged, tucked the weapon into the waistband of her boxers, and forced herself to step off the bed as she scanned every square inch of the cabin. Where there was one, there were more.

Killian squinted at her, then stalked around the room, peering into corners, opening the closet, kicking the dresser, checking behind the bathroom door. When he shut the last drawer with a snap, she released a silent breath. The scent of food registered, and she zeroed in on the plate on the little table, piled with meat and vegetables.

Her stomach rolled, memories of dark spaces and rotten food and twitching movements bombarding her until she could barely see the wooden walls of the cabin.

"I'm going for a run." Her arm brushed his as she pushed past, heading for the door.

"Thought you were hungry." He turned to watch her stride into the night. "DeSilva, you're still fucking injured."

"I'm fine." Gulping cold air, she whipped off her shirt, stripped out of her boxers, and let her cat take over.

She ran until the old scenes faded, taking the old sting of betrayal with them.

The lights were off when she tiptoed up the cabin steps several hours later. Her crumpled clothes were right on the steps where she'd left them, and she pulled them on before slinking silently inside. The arrow wound wasn't happy about her shifting to animal form before it was healed, but at least the angry red slash wasn't oozing. It'd be fine by morning.

It was freezing in the dark bedroom. Shifters ran naturally hot and could handle cold far better than others, but she was still a cat. Wasn't there a spare blanket around here some-where? Didn't these wolves ever get cold? She sat on the bed, rubbing her arms.

A lamp clicked on. Killian sat on his bed across the room, naked except for the boxers stretching over his muscular thighs, watching her.

Her brows popped. "You're up."

"You should eat."

Now that she'd run the memories out of her immediate vicinity, the idea of food didn't make her want to puke. But she was tired. She scrubbed a palm down her face. "I'm good—"

The scent of food hit her, and she opened her eyes. He stood directly in front of her, holding the plate he'd brought in earlier under her nose. Its contents were divided neatly down the middle, one half clean, the other untouched.

"Eat." He set the plate on the bed and lifted the hem of her shirt before she could protest. Growling at the wound she'd agitated, he stalked into the bathroom and emerged with the roll of Medimend. Quick and efficient, he taped her up.

When he was done, he retreated to his bed, drawing up one knee and nodding at the plate.

She ate.

The food was cold, but it tasted good. She licked her thumb and pretended she wasn't drinking in the sight of him. His bare feet were strong and golden, like the rest of him. Sitting on the sagging mattress with his head rested against the wall, he looked even bigger than usual. She was used to seeing him in the Bunker, at Light House, in the gym. Outside of those familiar places, he looked gargantuan. His quads were at least double the size of hers, and she was no string bean.

"Is it hard for you to find clothes?" She couldn't imagine Killian shopping.

"Yeah, it fucking sucks."

She grinned and forked up a mouthful of meat. "Maybe you should skip leg day every once in a while."

His snort made her look up. Was she imagining things, or was his mouth quirking?

Killian Diallo, laughing at a joke? She was strangely proud of herself.

She finished eating in silence and went to sleep, finally feeling warm.

CHAPTER 19

The wolves were not thrilled to see her the next morning.

The Medimend had done its job—her wound was healed, and it looked like Val had been patched up as well. His folded arms were unmarred when she crested the hill and found herself face to face with two dozen pissy canines in human form. Tall, lanky males and females, all of them sporting muscles and tattoos and a whole lot of sharp, shiny blades. One of them growled, and another joined in.

Juno tensed as she heard two things behind her: Killian's heavy boots on the pine needles, and the slice of his claws bursting through his skin.

"Oh, look, the kitty wants to play," one of the wolves mocked.

"Yeah, he does." Killian bared his teeth in an evil smile, like there was nothing he wanted more.

"Enough." Astrid stepped forward, dressed for training in leggings and an athletic tank. "Everyone huddle."

Nobody moved.

"Now!" Her wolf was in her voice, and there was a shuffling of feet as they all gathered around her. Tension hummed through the early morning mist, and it was all Juno could do to wrench her cat under control as she came face to face and shoulder to shoulder with the wolves.

Well, one shoulder was against a wolf. The other was crammed tight against a very big, very warm lion who was vibrating with temper. His body was throwing out scent like an air freshener, pheromones that screamed a warning.

I'm bigger than you. Don't fuck with me.

Her jaguar purred. Her body heated. Her skin tingled wherever it brushed against Killian's.

His head turned slowly toward her. Their eyes locked, only inches apart.

"We asked for their help, and they came." Astrid's sharp voice snapped her back into focus. "We're a team, for the time being. Act like it." When a growl rumbled from a burly wolf's throat, she kicked him viciously in the calf, and he shut up.

Astrid cast her gaze around the group. "Now, all of you stand there and breathe, and you plug that cat scent into your brain so no one else gets shredded. You two do the same." Pale purple eyes collided with Juno's across the huddle of seething males, and she felt the corners of her mouth lift.

She liked this chick.

They stood there and breathed. Nostrils twitched, chests rose and fell, ribcages expanded, until finally, after several long minutes, they were breathing as a unit, a huddle of bodies expanding and contracting like one giant lung.

Wolves smelled sharp. Clear and crisp, like their mountain home. Resinous, like their evergreens. Her brain whirled, processing their different scents, trying to assign them to the right person. One scent flared suddenly stronger —the wolf next to her. Their shoulders pressed together as the group breathed, and a flutter of something else tickled her nose.

Attraction. Interest.

She glanced up at the wolf beside her, a tall, muscular

male with dark hair and bright blue eyes. His lips curved in a slight smile.

"Good," Astrid said. They all shook themselves as if coming out of a trance. "Now, we run."

The energy was considerably more relaxed as they headed higher into the foothills. The wolves jostled each other, laughed, and gave each other shit. It reminded her of the squad.

She missed that. Being here with Killian was different. Even now, she could feel his looming presence humming a few feet behind her like a giant lightning rod.

"Lukas."

She looked over and found herself walking beside the smiling wolf from the huddle. She gave him a smile in return. "Juno."

"Lion?"

"Jaguar." She jerked her head over her shoulder. "He's the lion."

"Ah." Lukas cast a glance behind them, and whatever he saw made his wolf flicker across his face before he turned back to her. "So, you're a fighter in the city?"

"Wherever I'm needed."

"I've been a few times. I like the Blender."

She laughed in surprise. "You do? It's a far cry from all this." She gestured to the fairytale forest they were tromping through, the furthest thing from the crowded cacophony of downtown Concordia.

"Yeah, that's what makes it interesting. So many people. Different people. And the drinks!"

She grinned. "Which ones?"

"The enchanted ones. I like a dirty goblin. With a luck charm." His eyes gleamed.

He was cute. Really cute. "Oh, yeah? Do they make you lucky?"

"They did once. She wasn't a jaguar, though." He winked at her.

Flirt. Even as she rolled her eyes, her cat pricked her ears, intrigued.

They crested a hill and Juno sucked in a breath. An obstacle course spread before them, ropes and platforms and tunnels tucked amid the soaring evergreens. Sentries were already checking things over, testing knots and fastenings, inspecting footholds, hammering loose nails. Someone pushed over a rain barrel, sending a cascade of water over a stretch of bare dirt to create a mud pit.

Hell, yes. Holding back her whoop of delight, Juno tightened her ponytail and dropped into a series of stretches, craning to see as much of the course as possible. Memories of the Arena's course flashed across her mind—a mound of scrap metal, a series of frayed ropes, a pit filled with venomous snakes. The course Rafael built for her was huge and sprawling, but solid as a rock and about as predictable. No danger, no real challenge. No fun.

"Race you." Lukas dropped into a stretch beside her and wiggled his dark brows.

Juno eyed his long, lean limbs. He had a much longer reach than she did, and he was no doubt familiar with the course. Not the best odds. "Bring it."

Lukas grinned.

Someone tossed her a thigh holster loaded with short, sharp daggers. She strapped it on and pulled out a blade. Light as air, but sturdy. She preferred her claws, but thanks to the academy and Rogan's insistence that they excel at all forms of weaponry, she could work a knife.

Killian snarled on the other side of her, yanking at the straps of a chest holster. They were sized to fit the leaner wolves, and Killian was nowhere close to cinching the thing over his pecs.

"Here." She stepped close and loosened the straps like she

would for any teammate, trying not to dwell on the warmth and sheer size of him beneath her hands. He wore a textured thermal shirt, the golden ends of his hair contrasting with the iron gray fabric. She flicked a lock of it out of her way and instantly wanted to grab a fistful of the stuff. His chest expanded with every inhale, brushing against her knuckles. She wanted to dig her fingertips into the solid pads of muscle, grip them hard, test their strength. Sink her teeth in.

She finished and stepped away, looking anywhere but him, and found Lukas watching them.

Astrid whistled through her teeth. "Who's first?"

"I want the jaguar." Lukas was still eyeing her. He cinched his own chest holster with a practiced tug and jerked his head toward the start of the course, a vertical wall of lashed-together timbers.

"First pass, human form only. No claws, no teeth. Two blades in the bullseye before you can run back. You'll see." Astrid smirked.

Juno loosened her neck, excitement buzzing under her skin. Lukas shot her a grin as they stepped up to a line someone had dragged through the pine needles. "Watch out for the traps."

Astrid blew another piercing whistle through her teeth, and they were off.

Juno shot forward and vaulted over the timber wall, springing off the top to grab one of the hanging ropes on the other side. She swung to a platform and was nearly bowled over by Lukas, who was right on her heels. She lost her balance, windmilled her arms, and leaped off the platform, grabbing a handhold nailed into the side of a tree. There were more handholds. She scurried up the trunk, one hand over the other, only to realize it was a trick. The handholds led nowhere—she should've gone to ground. Lukas was swinging to the forest floor far below her, grabbing the dangling ropes that hung over the fresh mud pit.

Dammit. Juno's eyes flashed over the landscape. She spotted the next obstacle and sprang off the tree like a flying squirrel, crashing into another trunk for a split second before bouncing to the next, aiming lower and lower. A final leap had her landing on top of another vertical wall just as Lukas hauled himself over it. She dropped to the opposite side, barely managing to correct her course and land on one of the boulders staggered across the forest floor like massive stepping stones. She sprang from one to the next, already scoping the upcoming obstacle. The boulders were replaced by cut timbers, sunk into the earth so they stood vertically. She leaped onto the shortest one, then the next, and had to hold back her claws when she jumped for the third. It was too high, and she slid down a few feet before she managed to grip the smooth cylinder with her thighs, hauling herself up with an awkward flat-palmed grip. Lukas shimmied up the timber beside her and shot her a wicked grin as he hauled himself to the top, spun on the spot, and swan-dived. The memory of Wolf doing the same thing from the rafters only days before flashed before her eyes.

Her arms burned. She ignored them. Grunting as she mounted the flat top of the timber, she pushed herself to stand. Twenty-five feet below, Lukas was clamoring up from an enormous pile of pine needles.

She took a breath and dove, landing in a somersault and using her momentum to roll off the mound of soft green needles. She sprang to her feet and sprinted to Lukas's side, her heart pumping.

A huge, hollowed-out fallen tree formed a tunnel. Juno shot around Lukas and dove inside, cutting him off. His shouted curse made her grin, and the wolf's growl that reverberated through the tunnel afterward made her hair stand on end. His breath was hot on her ankles as she scampered through in an army crawl, scraping her elbows.

She popped out of the log, scrambled to her feet, and

immediately ducked as an arrow shot toward her. Another zipped through the air, narrowly missing her calf. She sprinted forward, darting between trees and boulders. She heard water rushing somewhere—a stream? River? There was no time to speculate. An arrow zinged her thigh, another nicked her arm, and she swore, then laughed, grinning wildly as she ran. These wolves didn't fuck around.

She *loved* it.

Lukas caught up to her on a series of mounded hills, his long legs eating up the distance between them. "Careful, kitty cat!" He reached up and grabbed an overhead net just as the ground gave way beneath Juno's foot.

Bang! One leg sank knee-deep into a hole camouflaged by sticks and debris, her boot hitting the bottom with enough force to jar her ankle and make her see stars. She planted her hands on the ground and heaved herself out, cursing.

The rough fibers of the net scraped her palms as she scuttled across the thing upside down, like a spider on a web. Lukas's tight ass was close enough to take a bite out of, and she was irritated enough to consider it, but he swung down from the net before she reached him and sprinted for a pair of ropes dangling from the limb of a giant sequoia. Juno followed, hauling herself up the rope next to his and reaching the limb just as he did.

A stunning view brought her up short. The spectacular mountain vista stretched for miles, a swath of craggy peaks spearing into a crystal blue sky while a sparkling river cut a path through the valley far below. This was not the lazy, sluggish Red River that wound through the city. This was a powerful force pummeling its way through unyielding rock. Water rushed and churned below the bough of their tree. Two tightropes stretched across the rapids, quivering in the air from the current. Lukas raised his voice over the roar of the river. "You're bleeding."

"So are you." He wasn't, but she'd let him figure that out. Juno leaped onto the tightrope closest to her, grabbing the rope that stretched overhead as a handhold, and ran for it. The ropes swayed wildly, but she was focused on the other side, where a round bullseye target was visible on the riverbank.

She lost her footing twice, body wrenching, arrow nicks stinging, but she reached the end of her rope before Lukas reached his. It was buried in a boulder, and she stood on the rock, whipping one of the daggers from her thigh holster. She chucked it at the target.

Bullseye.

She threw another one. It went wide. She saw Rogan's disapproving frown in her head and threw another dagger, pissed. Bullseye. She turned to jump back on her tightrope.

Thunk. Thunk. "Ha!"

Fuck. Lukas was a good shot.

They raced across the river, shooting glances at each other, eyes flashing with animal temper and the thrill of the chase. He gained the lead. She took it back. Their boots pounded over the forest floor as they sprinted back to the starting point, winding through trees and ducking beneath low-hanging boughs. Branches slashed at her arms and ripped stray hairs from her ponytail. The stings barely registered.

The finish line came into view. The shouts of the wolves gathered behind it were muffled by the hammering of her pulse and the rasp of Lukas's breath in her ears. His wide shoulders inched ahead.

Oh, hell no.

Her leg muscles howled. She drove them harder. Her lungs were on fire. She ignored the burn. Her heart threatened to burst, but she pushed, and pushed, leaving it all on the trail. Everything she had to give. Every last drop of her.

His bellowed curse gave her feet wings as she pulled

ahead of him, her elbows pumping, breath shredding her throat and her head ducking forward as she crossed the finish line with Lukas hot on her heels.

The crowd of shocked wolves stepped aside as she barreled through them. Her boots skidded on the pine needles, momentum carrying her straight into the gigantic male that loomed at the back of the group.

Colliding with Killian's chest was like ramming into a tree trunk—a warm one with strong hands that snapped around her arms as she bounced off his torso. An unsoldier-like yelp escaped her as his fingers clamped over the arrow graze on her upper arm, and he dropped her instantly, scanning her for injuries.

She pulled back, panting. His scent was in her nose, stronger and warmer than the two dozen wolves crowding around them. "Just a nick."

His gaze flicked to her arm, then back to her face. A slow, wicked smile curved his mouth. He looked around, radiating something that looked a lot like…pride.

Any breath she had left evaporated. She'd never seen that fierce grin on his face, those shoulders thrown back like a peacock spreading his feathers. He was beautiful.

Juno tore her gaze away, her heart somehow thumping harder, though the race was done. "Nice try, pup." She punched a panting Lukas in the shoulder. He flipped her off, still bent over. The wolves surrounding them laughed, jostling him and flicking Juno appraising glances. A few scents flared—male interest.

Astrid's sharp whistle cut through the commotion. "Next!"

Someone tossed her a bottle of water. A few of them grunted words of praise before moving off to watch the next pair. Juno ducked her head, lowering into some stretches to hide her grin. When she felt the weight of someone's gaze, she looked up.

Val watched her, unblinking.
She straightened and met his gaze head-on.
He gave her a tiny smile before turning away.

CHAPTER 20

"So, what exactly are you looking for, cat?"

Lukas's voice cut through the darkness, ringing from the wolf's comm clipped to Juno's collar. It was their first nightly patrol since the incident with Val. Running the gauntlet had smoothed things over a bit, but tension flared nevertheless when Killian and Juno reported to the guard cabin at nightfall. She was glad Lukas was one of the sentries on duty tonight.

"Don't worry about it, pup. You do you," she murmured absently, bending to inspect a trail on the forest floor.

Lukas's chuckle was suggestive. "That's getting a little old, to be honest."

She snorted, lips quirking despite herself. It was nice to be flirted with in a light, playful way. She hadn't had enough play lately. She was too busy fighting demons, making powerful enemies, and diffusing testosterone bombs.

As if on cue, Killian's rough growl came through their private comm. "I got something."

Her cat perked up. "Location?"

He started to relay coordinates, but interrupted with a curse. A scuffling sound came through the comm, followed by a lion snarl and a deep, inhuman laugh that made her hair stand on end.

Demon.

Clothes shredded as she burst into jaguar form and sprinted toward Killian's general vicinity, inhaling deeply as she darted through trees, trying to catch his scent. The landscape was a glowing green shot with the streaks of bright blue faebugs, which zoomed away as she ran. She caught a wolf's scent and heard the creak of a bowstring as she blasted past, but no arrow came firing after her. Astrid's scent exercise had been a good idea.

She heard the fight first. Snarls, hissing, Killian's short roars, the thud and smack of heavy bodies pummeling each other. The stink of sulfur came next, a trigger that sent her into kill mode. She exploded over a fallen log and saw Killian's lion form locked in combat with another cat.

The cougar was big, with a beige hide covering stocky muscle, and it smelled all wrong. Rotten eggs and infection. When Killian's claws slashed into its skin, the putrid stink of pus burned her nose.

Juno leaped onto the cougar's back, sending it into a frenzy. She clung to its flank as it bucked like a bronco. Something slashed her ear, but she ignored the burst of pain and sank her fangs into the cougar's neck, piercing fur and flesh. Its roar vibrated against her jaw as liquid corruption flooded her mouth, burning her tongue, gushing down her throat. She jerked her mouth away, and it was enough for the cougar to throw her from its back, sending her sailing into a tree.

No, not a tree. A male wolf, in human form. She knocked him over and rolled to her feet. Killian was on his hind legs, one enormous paw swiping through the air in the world's fiercest bitch slap. His claws gleamed when they sliced the cougar's throat. Black blood spurted, splattering the ferns and tiny blue flowers. The cougar staggered, gurgled, and collapsed, dead.

"What the *fuck*. What the fuck is that?" The male wolf stared at the cougar lying in a growing pool of inky black. His claws shot out with an audible *shhhk*.

Shit. That confirmed it. If the wolves could see this thing, it wasn't a demon. It was a regular animal, possessed.

Killian met her gaze before his muzzle went to his wrist, pulling a vaporizer from his watchband.

The wolf was talking into his comm in clipped tones, his scent elevated with agitation. He radioed coordinates as Juno stepped in front of him, trying to distract him, but she couldn't hide the whir and flash of light behind her.

The wolf's eyes went wide. "That's it, isn't it?" He pointed in the direction of the battle, nostrils flared. "That's what's been attacking us. I can smell it. What the fuck is it?" He didn't bat an eye as two other guards appeared behind him. Shit, those wolves were fast. Sharp eyes swept the scene, faces twitching as they caught the scent of sulfur. One of them shifted into wolf form, nose going to the ground and heading for the battle site like a torpedo—which was exactly why Killian had been so quick to dissolve the corpse with a vaporizer.

An evil canine growl reverberated through the night. Others joined in, feeding off of each other.

"What the hell was that?"

She shook her jaguar head, then jerked it toward the dark forest, trying to shoo him off.

He stabbed a finger at her. "Shift your ass into human form and talk."

Killian was at her side in an instant. His vicious growl vibrated in her eardrums.

Rogan's voice floated back to her. *Play nice. Make friends.*

As much as she wanted to join in Killian's snarl, she planted her haunches on the forest floor and shook her head.

After several long moments, the wolf snapped his jaws

and stalked into the forest. The others followed, their growls fading into the distance.

Something nudged her. She looked over to find Killian's huge, maned head bumping her shoulder. Checking in. Making sure she was good.

Surprised, she returned the nudge. He chuffed, his breath fogging in the air, and turned away.

What the hell? That was new. And almost…sweet.

Killian Diallo, sweet?

He stalked off to retrieve the vaporizer. But as his lethal fangs closed gently around the marble, all she could see was him in a school gymnasium, teaching a kid how to stand up to a bully. His big hand holding her forgotten plate of food, insisting that she eat.

Her cat purred.

Magnus was waiting for them outside their cabin. His scent was sharper than usual, and his magic was up, making Juno's blood buzz beneath her fur.

"We need to talk." Magnus stepped off the porch and turned toward the trees, giving them a modicum of privacy.

Refusing to feel awkward, Juno melted into human form and strode naked into the cabin, throwing on the first sweatshirt she found draped over a chair. It came past her ass. Even as she held out her arms to see the sleeves hanging well past her fingers, Killian's scent exploded around her.

The door creaked, and she knew without turning that he was striding inside, nude and sculpted and enormous—and noticing that she was wearing his shirt.

She yanked on a pair of leggings and turned to her dresser before whipping off his shirt and pulling on one of her own. Then, she headed outside, deliberately not looking across the cabin to where Killian was stuffing all those muscles into clothes.

"Report," Magnus demanded the moment she emerged on the stoop. When a wall of heat appeared at her back, she moved out of the way so Killian could join her on the steps. They stood side by side, arms crossed. United. Squad.

It felt good. Really good.

Juno tried to ignore the warmth buoying in her chest. "We engaged with a target and eliminated it."

"What was the target?"

"Confidential."

"What was the blast of light my sentry saw?"

"Confidential."

A low, dangerous growl reverberated through the pitch black. "These are *my fucking woods*." His accent was thicker in his anger. He slashed a hand through the air, and a tree limb cracked nearby, scattering blue faebugs. No trackband glinted on the alpha's wrist. He could deal some seriously aggressive magic without anyone knowing, and the way energy was gathering around him, he was close to doing exactly that.

Juno held her ground. "You called us here for a reason, and you knew we couldn't tell you everything."

"You haven't told me *fuck all*." His words echoed through the trees.

Killian stiffened. "Careful, wolf. We don't have to stay here."

Magnus's long legs cleared the distance between them in seconds. "You think I like having a couple of cats slinking around my land?"

Killian showed his teeth. "You called *us*."

Magnus snapped his jaws, his eyes flashing. Another tree limb cracked in half, then shot toward them like a torpedo. Magnus slapped it out of the way without breaking their gaze. The limb thunked to the ground mere feet away.

Killian's claws sliced out, and she was suddenly staring at

his broad back as he stepped in front of her, putting her behind the wall of his body.

She shouldered him aside even as Rogan's words reverberated through her brain. *Play nice.* "Stop. We're here to help. We can't tell you anything yet, but we're working on it. We're on your team. Bear with us."

Magnus's alpha stare shifted to her. Power crackled from the big male, moonlight glinting off his face until he almost appeared to glow. "Until when?"

"Until we can tell you more. There are some things we need to figure out first. And your people need to let us do our job. If they see us engaging, they need to fall back."

His arctic eyes pierced through the night. "Because this enemy is invisible to us, but not to you. Yes?"

All except the possessed ones. "Yes."

A boulder burst from the ground and smashed into a tree. It fell to the earth with a shudder and a spray of debris. Killian growled, but at least he didn't try to shove her behind him like a helpless kitten.

Magnus stabbed a thick finger in their direction. "*Teammates* don't keep secrets. Figure your shit out fast." He stalked away, disappearing into the dark.

Killian blew a breath out through his nose. "Fucking asshole."

She held the door for him as he followed her inside. "I get it."

"Yeah, I get it, too. Doesn't mean he has to be such an asshole."

She scoffed.

"What?"

She gave him a look. "You of all people are saying that?"

He tilted his head, his hair falling around his shoulders in wild, golden waves. "Are you implying *I'm* an asshole?"

Was that a glint of amusement in his eyes? Juno blinked. "Are you implying you're not?"

"Only when provoked."

She snorted and bent to rifle through the drawer for her sleep shorts. "Then, you must be provoked damn near all the time."

Silence.

She turned. He was staring at her hungrily, every inch a lion in human form. His eyes traveled over her body with unbanked heat.

"Something like that," he growled. Any hint of playfulness had vanished.

Awareness blasted through her. She shoved the drawer closed and headed for the bathroom, trying not to look like she was escaping. "Will you report to Rogan about that possessed cougar? I'm going to shower."

She closed the bathroom door behind her, heart thumping. First, the considerate moment in the woods, then the united front against Magnus and that spark of playfulness a moment ago. It had felt almost normal. The way squad should feel.

And then, the lightning bolt of sexual heat had to go and ruin it.

She pressed a hand to her flushed cheek as realization dawned. The increased sexual tension, the elevated body heat...she was touch-hungry. It wasn't in the red zone yet, but she was getting close. It had been too long since she'd had a man.

That was it. That was why he was affecting her like this.

Her cat snorted.

Shit. This was the last thing she needed, the last thing she wanted. Big, snarling, sexy-as-hell Killian Diallo, staring at her like he wanted to devour her...

The *last* thing she wanted.

She turned the shower on full blast, stepped under the spray, and held out for a full ten seconds before she touched herself.

She was already slick, already wet. He'd done that to her

with one burning look from across the room. Her fingers slipped over and around her clit, circling faster and faster, and she didn't even try to think about anything but hot yellow eyes, flexing muscles, and a low, rough growl.

A tiny sound escaped her when she exploded, shuddering against the shower wall. Her eyes flew open. He couldn't have heard that. Right?

The idea that he might have made her even wetter.

———

Later, in the black silence of their cabin, she flipped her pillow for the third time and bit back a frustrated sigh. Across the room, she heard the creak of bed springs. Something in the taut silence told her she wasn't the only one awake. "You can't sleep, either?"

A grunt.

She sighed and kicked the covers to her hips. She needed to take care of this touch-hunger soon. Could she hook up with one of the wolves without it turning into a thing?

An image of Killian's enormous naked body pumping into her flashed across her mind. The resulting bolt of heat that shot through her made her actually suck in a breath. She clamped her mouth shut.

His rough voice drifted across the cabin. "I think we need to go further outside the village. There's no hellmouth here."

Almost frantically, she focused on what he'd said. "I think you're right."

A pause. "Excuse me?"

"I said I think you're right."

"Huh. I thought I must've misheard."

She rolled her eyes. "Fuck off."

"That's more like it."

She turned onto her side and peered at the looming shape of him in the dark. Her night vision was okay, but she still couldn't make out his expression. "At least I try to be civil."

"That's right, and I'm an asshole."

Only when provoked. The memory of the heated look he'd given her earlier sent her temperature skyrocketing. Her core throbbed.

A growl rumbled across the room.

Her thighs clenched involuntarily. "Go to sleep, Diallo." She rolled over.

CHAPTER 21

He might've been raised in the jungle, but he wasn't fucking Tarzan.

Swinging through the trees, jumping from rock to rock, tiptoeing across a rope over a goddamn whitewater river? Not his thing. Give him a boxing ring. Or a car to flip.

They'd been training with the wolves every day. Target practice, tracking, sparring, trying to build camaraderie. Word about the incident with the "invisible enemy" had spread like wildfire, and a week later, the wolves were still pissed, still suspicious, and making no effort to hide it.

And it was pushing him to his limit.

Every time one of them deliberately knocked his shoulder in passing, every time they hit a little harder than necessary during sparring sessions, every time their eyes lingered a little too long on Juno's body, that dangerous buzzing was back, an ominous sizzle in his veins. He could hardly wait to burst into lion form each night and find a demon to obliterate.

The enemy was obliging. They'd come across a demon-possessed animal almost every night, and though they still hadn't found the hellmouth they were coming from, slaughtering them was helping Killian hang on to his last shred of control. That, and avoiding his squad mate as much as possible.

Train with the wolves. Do whatever chore he was assigned. Show up for their nightly demon patrol, run himself to exhaustion, and crash in his bed in their tiny shared cabin, trying not to smell her sweet, honeyed arousal.

She wanted him.

She tried to mask it, but she was getting edgier by the day, and her scent was growing stronger. Touch-hunger was sinking its claws into her, too, but it didn't stop her from being a good little soldier, stuffing down her cat's irritation and taking the shit the wolves dished out. Training hard, doing chores, reporting to Rogan each night and relaying his instructions to Killian.

Play nice. Make friends. Earn trust.

He was shit at all those things.

He was also shit at that obstacle course. No matter how many times he ran the thing, those ninja wolf motherfuckers made him look like an elephant at an aerobics class.

But Juno…Juno was better than them all.

She beat them. Every single one of those males. Wiped the smirks right off their faces until grudging respect started to replace them.

He thought his heart was going to explode each time she came flying out of those woods, ponytail streaming behind her and fierce determination on her stunning face. It was all he could do to keep from thumping his chest. Maybe he had a little Tarzan in him, after all.

It was becoming something of a challenge among the wolves. He heard them arguing for the chance to take her on, to beat her, to dominate her. Their admiring glances made his blood boil.

The lion in him wanted to gut them all. The man in him wanted to watch her kick their asses, then take her home, peel her clothes off, and lick every drop of sweat from her powerful body.

Fuck.

"DeSilva."

It was late morning, and they'd been at the gauntlet for an hour already. Astrid stood at the starting line, pale blonde hair plaited into a thick braid, amethyst eyes glinting. She tossed her bow to a nearby male and jerked her chin.

The clearing went dead still.

Every single one of these wolves had challenged—and been beaten by—the jaguar in their midst. Everyone except their fierce, formidable she-wolf lieutenant.

Juno rose fluidly from her seat on a nearby boulder and headed straight for Astrid's side. Their eyes met. Then, someone whistled sharply through their teeth and the females were off.

They were like flashes in the trees, light and dark side by side. Some of the wolves ran alongside the course, calling out commentary while Killian's heart rate skyrocketed and his nails bit into his palms.

Come on.

The wolves couldn't keep still, bouncing on their toes and climbing trees to watch the show, shouting and jostling each other like a pack of excited pups. Someone took bets. Killian hardly heard them over the pounding of his pulse. He felt like he was about to blow his optical nerve as he strained to catch a glimpse of them through the trees.

His heart nearly burst when they exploded into view. Astrid, tall and powerful and sprinting like a Viking shield-maiden through the trees, and Juno at her side, sleek and stunning and pouring every ounce of herself into the race.

She was the fiercest, most beautiful thing he'd ever seen.

They tied.

A shocked silence rang through the clearing as the females

skidded across the finish line at the exact same moment. Nobody beat Astrid. None of the males even came close.

Pride erupted in Killian's chest. He felt his teeth bare in a fierce grin. He wanted to roar it from the mountain. He wanted to call someone. Rogan. Cyrus. Then again, they wouldn't be surprised. He could just hear Rogan's dry response. *"Why do you think I recruited her?"*

The females were bent double, shoulder to shoulder, panting for breath. The wolves watched, on a knife edge of anticipation. Astrid was the alpha female, in incredible shape, and kicked all of their asses regularly. And Juno had just proven herself on the same level. Wolves were obsessed with hierarchy, and Killian could see their brains spinning, wondering what this meant.

The females straightened at the same time, looked at each other, and grinned. They clasped hands and pulled each other into a hard hug, laughing.

"Not bad, cat," Astrid said. And just like that, the tension broke, the other wolves swarmed them, and Killian watched from the outskirts as Juno was jostled and clapped on the back and showered with praise.

Camaraderie with the wolves? Check.

He wanted to join in. He wanted to shoulder his way through the throng and lift her feet off the ground and shout his pride into the forest. Then, he wanted to fill her mouth with his tongue, drive his cock into her body, and bite her neck hard enough to leave a mark, making sure everyone knew she was his.

But she wasn't. He hung back, as usual.

When Astrid called a stop to the session, he stomped back to the village on his own, trying to ignore the fact that Lukas was still hovering over Juno. And had stripped off his shirt. And was in good shape.

Killian popped his neck. So what? He was bigger. Taller. Stronger.

Fuck.

When the others peeled off toward the cookhouse, he headed straight for the shack by the lake where the fishing supplies were stored. He might be a miserable failure at that ninja crap, but he could catch a fish. He would catch all the goddamn fish.

He grabbed a couple poles, a bucket of bait, a couple nets, and found himself a nice, quiet spot on the edge of the water, far away from the cookhouse and the merrily smoking chimneys and the wolves who were suddenly acting a lot friendlier toward the jaguar in their midst.

One of the fishing poles snapped in his grip.

He tossed it aside and grabbed the other, checking the line and weights, testing the reel. When his dad was alpha, he'd insisted that everyone knew how to fish. Lions in general weren't big on eating the scaly things, but sometimes meat was scarce. Sometimes, you were away from the home fires. Sometimes, you needed to sit beside someone in silence without it being a character flaw.

He baited his hook and cast his line, stabbing the pole into the ground until it held itself upright. He chucked some more bait into the water several yards away and waited.

His eyes drifted back to the village where Juno sat on a bench, laughing at something Lukas said. Yeah, flyboy was a talker, all right. A standup comic, from the looks of it.

Killian flung out a net, waited a few minutes, and then hauled it back in, pleased to see a few wriggling silver fish caught in the rope. He tossed them in a bucket and kept going, deliberately keeping his eyes on his work, ignoring the bursts of laughter that carried across the lake. Nobody approached.

Why would they? He was an asshole.

Eventually, the smell of grilled meat wafted over, and his stomach gave a yowl of hunger. He ignored that, too. His belly could wait.

"You're good at that."

He nearly jumped out of his hide. A tiny blonde girl stood next to him, sucking on one of the honey sticks the wolf kids liked. Where the fuck had she come from? He glanced around, but they were alone.

She looked like a little elf, all rosy-cheeked and pointy-featured, three blonde braids trailing down her small back. "You caught a lot." Mossy green eyes went round at the sight of his nearly full buckets. "You must really like fishing."

Killian grunted. "Not really." He threw the net out again.

"Then, why are you still doing it?"

"I thought you wolves were big on everyone helping."

"Stick with the Pack, the Pack has your back," she recited, and resumed sucking on her honey stick.

What was that, their creepy motto? He thought briefly of Wolf and how he'd somehow gotten himself kicked out of the Den. Guess the Pack didn't have everyone's back.

"What's your name?"

He hauled the net in. "Killian."

"Mine's Elvi." She tracked the wriggling fish he dumped out of the net. "You smell funny."

"So do you."

She giggled. It sounded like tiny tinkling bells. "Do not!"

He scowled down at her. "Like a dog."

She laughed delightedly. "Nuh uh!"

He leaned down, gave an exaggerated sniff, then reared back. "A wet dog."

She dissolved into a fit of giggles. "Nuh uh!" She leaned in, returned his sniff, and pointed her honey stick dramatically at him. "Kitty litter!" she howled, doubling over with mirth.

He snorted and watched her stagger away until she collapsed to the ground, gasping for breath. "Shouldn't you be off somewhere, helping with something?"

"I'm done with chores." She wiped her eyes. "I think you got enough fish. Most of the males only get one bucket."

Was that so?

"Are you really a lion?"

"Yeah."

"Will you show me?"

"If you deserve it." He bared his fangs at her in a vicious snarl.

Those green eyes turned into saucers, and she sucked in a breath. The sharp, acrid scent of fear drifted over.

Ah, shit. He shut his mouth and winked.

Elvi's smile lit her face, then melted into a frown. "I wish I could shift. I'm layt-nent."

His stomach dropped. "Latent?"

She nodded and kicked at a few pebbles. "Everyone else can go wolf. Mama says I just need to be patient, but everyone else says layt-nent when they think I can't hear."

His chest tightened painfully. He couldn't imagine having an animal half, with all its instincts and demands, and no way to let it out. "Can you feel your wolf?"

Elvi nodded again.

Shit. "You'll be stronger than them all." When she gave him a dour look, he nodded. "Might be different, but you'll be strong."

She appeared to think about it. "I know lots more about plants and stuff. Nobody else pays attention. But there's lots of stuff you can eat around here besides meat." She launched into descriptions of roots and berries and edible mushrooms while he cast his net across the glassy water, making noises every now and then to show he was listening.

———

An hour later, Killian dropped four buckets onto the long table in the cookhouse, precisely between Juno and the group of wolves she was chatting with. They all blinked as the table shuddered under the weight. Silver fish spilled out of the buckets, flopping weakly on the smooth wood planks.

Juno's brows lifted. "I was supposed to be on fish today."

"I did it." *I provided.* "Is there food?"

"You mean besides the whole school of trout you just chucked on the table?" Lukas's words were flippant. His eyes were not. They met Killian's and held, flashing an even brighter blue.

The world went yellow.

Juno stood swiftly. "I'll show you." She walked toward the back of the cookhouse, expecting him to follow. After one curl of his lip, he did, but his lion was battering his skull as he stalked after her.

That wolf was perilously close to challenging him outright, and if it happened, shit was going to go nuclear. The sight of him sitting so close to her, the glint of provocation in his eye…

"Here." Juno handed him a plate, and he blinked the room back into focus. They were at the long buffet table at the back of the cookhouse. It was picked over. He must've missed breakfast, or lunch, or whatever it was. Blindly, he started to load his plate while Juno stood aside, her arms folded. She'd put on her favorite sweatshirt, the threadbare one with the holes around the neckline, the one that read *MLE CLASS OF 2093* and fell off of one shoulder and just begged to be pulled aside a little more, so he could bite that soft skin…

Bite. Mark. Claim. Mine.

He dumped an entire platter of something onto his plate. A chunk of whatever it was tumbled off. He grabbed a roll from the buffet table and crammed it halfway into his mouth, just to have something to sink his fangs into. She was watching him, he could feel it, could see her out of the corner of his eye, smell her, *fuck*…

The wolves at the table laughed at something Lukas said. Juno glanced over and smiled at whatever was so hilarious.

This guy just needed his own comedy special, didn't he? Killian ripped the roll from his mouth. "You having fun with your new buddies?"

Juno's brow arched. "At least one of us is attempting to make friends."

"Yeah, I'm sure Lukie over there is real interested in a new *friend*."

She stepped close and spoke through her teeth. "This is what we're supposed to be doing, Diallo. Building camaraderie, making friends. You're not even trying."

"Seems like you're making plenty of progress for both of us."

"You're right. I might as well be here by myself. Feels like I am, anyway." He must've imagined the glint of hurt in her eyes. "Why don't you just go home?"

And leave her alone with Mr. Hilarious and his wolfy entourage? Not fucking likely. "What do you want me to do, act like they're not complete assholes to me?"

"Only 'cause you're a total dick." Lukas's voice rang out from directly behind him.

Killian whirled and slammed his fist into the wolf's pretty face.

The guy recovered fast, he'd give him that. Claws swiped across Killian's pecs even as he took the male to the ground, landing on top of him in a heap of limbs, raining blows. Shouts echoed. Benches scraped. A table overturned somewhere, causing trays of food to clatter to the floor. Slashes of pain erupted along his back, his rib cage, his cheek, but he kept going, kept swinging, kept pummeling—

A scent cut through the mindless violence. A warm, spicy scent, elevated with anger. Then, his head was yanked backward and he was suddenly staring at the soot-stained ceiling.

Juno's face appeared inches from his. "Fuck's sake, Diallo." She practically threw his head to the floor, releasing the hunk of hair she'd used as a handle. He watched her powerful legs carry her out of the cookhouse, her ponytail swinging. His chest heaved.

"Hey." Lukas sprawled on the floor beside him, swiping at the blood trickling from his nose. He shook off the wolves trying to help him up. "You with her, or what?"

Suddenly, he could hear the rush of blood in the male's veins, begging to be ripped from his flesh. Could feel the snap of his bones under his grip. It would be hard to crack jokes with his jaw wired shut.

Lukas smirked despite his broken nose. "Not quite, huh?"

Killian heaved himself to his feet and stalked out, shoving an overturned bench out of his way as he went.

Juno's scent was like a beacon, leading him along a short trail to a secluded bluff overlooking the river. She was braced on the rocky edge, legs apart, hands on her hips, her hair whipping in the wind. He came to a stop just behind her, quivering, dying to get his hands on her.

Mine.

She looked over her shoulder, her eyes spitting fire. "What the hell, Diallo?"

"What?"

"You know what." She pointed toward the village. "That was humiliating."

He flung his arms wide. "What do you want me to do?" Lukas was needling him, just begging for a fight—

"I want you to get your shit together and act like a professional." She folded her arms and did that thing that drove him out of his fucking mind; she lifted her chin, cooling her eyes. "You need to take care of your touch-hunger."

That brought him to a screeching halt. "Touch-hunger."

"Yes."

"Is that what you think this is about?"

"Is it not?" She raked a glance over his body, and there it was—beneath the chilly disdain, the scent of arousal flared.

Triumph and anger and a whole lot of something he didn't want to examine loosened his tongue. "What about you, then?"

"What about me?"

"Don't bullshit me, DeSilva."

"I don't know what you're talking about."

Fine, she wanted him to call her out? He'd do it. Holding her gaze, he leaned in. "I can *smell* you."

Her claws lashed out, lightning fast. He jerked, but held his ground. Victory surged through him as he swiped at his cheek, looked at the blood on his hand, then back to her. "Looks like I'm not the only one feeling a little in the red zone."

"Fuck off, Diallo." But she was breathing hard.

He leaned in further, took a long, deliberate inhale, and this time let a purr rumble past his throat.

He dodged her claws without a centimeter to spare, backing away while blood trickled down his face and her dark eyes flashed green. He pointed at her as he neared the trees. "Don't act like it's all me." He strode into the forest before he got himself ripped to shreds.

CHAPTER 22

I can smell you.

Juno stared blindly over the cliff, her pulse hammering while she tried to get a grip on what just happened.

Killian Diallo knew she wanted him, and he'd called her out on it.

Fuck.

His scent still lingered, though he'd hightailed it out of there before she could take another chunk out of him. The memory made her groan. She *was* skirting the edge, wasn't she? Touch-hungry and on constant high alert, with no escape in sight.

How did she get herself in this situation?

Oh wait, she didn't.

Fuming, sizzling with fury and arousal and the feeling that she'd been caught red-handed, she yanked out her phone.

Wolf answered on the first ring. "Well, well. Look who's talking to me again."

"You're an asshole."

"Whatever do you mean?"

Killian's blood was sticky on her claws. With an inward curse, she wiped them off and retracted them, rubbing the webbing between her fingers. "I don't know how, but you and Jovi did this on purpose."

"I didn't do shit, toots. Rogan did. But I'm glad you're finally admitting it—"

"I'm not admitting anything," she snapped. "Except that things were tense, and you made it worse."

A snort came through the line. "And now?"

She scanned the horizon. Maybe a dip in that raging river would cool her off. "Now, it's…fucked up."

There was a loud crinkle and a ripping sound, like he was opening a bag of chips. "Why, was it not good?"

She frowned. "Was what not good?"

"You guys finally boned, right?"

She almost chucked her phone off the cliff. "Jesus! No."

An exaggerated groan. "Would you two just get it over with already? It's super annoying."

Her heart pounded. "What are you talking about? We're teammates."

He laughed, the bastard. A loud, obnoxious laugh that made her want to punch him through the receiver. "Uh huh. So, how come you don't look at *me* like you want to rip my clothes off?"

"Ew." She shook the image out of her head.

Wolf laughed again. "See? But you and Diallo get sent away *on business,* and suddenly *things are tense* and *Wolf's an asshole.*"

Shit. "We just butt heads. Everybody knows that."

A snort. "You need to *butt* something else, sweetheart. It was bad enough back here. And if you haven't taken care of it yet, it's only gonna get worse. Don't tell me none of those wolves are sniffing around."

Her eyes slid toward the village, where Lukas was no doubt mopping the blood from his face.

"Uh huh," Wolf said knowingly, crunching into the receiver. "Let me guess…Lukas."

"How did you know that?"

"Because I know the guy, and he likes things he can't have." Crunch, crunch.

Sometimes, she forgot Wolf was raised in the Den, before he did whatever it was that got him kicked out. "What's your point?"

"If the wolves are circling, the claws are gonna come out. That lion's going to stake his claim."

Goddammit. "Nobody's *claiming* me."

"Yeah, well, sooner or later, he's not going to be able to hold it back. And I'm betting on sooner." She heard him lick his fingers. "You might as well just get it out of your system. It's driving everyone nuts."

Her cheeks burned. She considered that dive into the river again. "Fuck."

"Yeah. That. Do that."

She raked her fingers through her scalp. "I didn't want any of this. I wanted to get *away* from all this. Rogan never pulled this crap with me."

Wolf snorted. "Rogan thinks of you like a sister, and besides, he ain't a shifter. You know what it's like trying to hold back your cat. Now, imagine a truckload of testosterone behind it, just *ramming into your skull*—" He punched his palm with each word, loud enough that she could hear, "—demanding that you take that female." A pause. "And it's Killian, so it's not a truckload, it's a train."

Heat rushed between her thighs. "Shit."

Cellophane rustled. "I'm just saying, if you guys don't do something about it, someone's gonna get gutted. That dude's touch-hungry like you read about. And unless you've been banging one of those males up there, I'm guessing you're getting pretty close, too."

A low groan escaped her.

"Thought so." Crunch, crunch. "I don't get what the big problem is. You guys wanna bone, so bone."

She rolled her eyes. "He's an asshole." *Most of the time.* "Besides, it would change everything."

"Oh, whatever. You're both adults. Bang it out, move on. He needs to bang *someone*, at least. Those tail-chasers he's been nailing lately ain't cutting it. Maybe a wolf would give him a better time." A pause. "Ugh, that could be one of my cousins."

Her brain was already flipping through all the female wolves, imagining them with Killian. The landscape went neon green. "Which ones are your cousins?"

"Not telling."

"What did you do, anyway? To get kicked out?"

"Not telling. I gotta go. Teaching target practice to the heathens." He hung up.

Jesus. Wolf showing those clumsy little mages how to throw knives was almost as scary as their entire conversation.

Despite herself, her brain ran down the list of all the wolf females, picturing each one in a different position with a certain lion. Spread beneath him. Pinned against a tree. Riding him like a—

She surged to her feet, pocketed her phone, and stalked toward the foothills. She was going for a run.

CHAPTER 23

That night, Killian's blood was humming with pent-up frustration, his lion was clawing at his skull, and something was off with Juno.

He felt it the second he walked into their cabin to change for their nightly patrol. He was sweaty from hiking all day, avoiding her, trying to burn off the volatile heat in his veins.

Take. Claim. MINE.

Juno looked over in the middle of zipping up her sports bra, the sharp sound like a gunshot in the tiny, silent room. The air between them snapped taut, which wasn't unusual, but there was something he couldn't pinpoint in her dark eyes.

Most of the time, he couldn't care less about magic. With her, he wished he had Cyrus's ability to read minds. "What?"

Her nostrils flared ever so slightly, like she was scenting him. "Where've you been all day?"

He whipped off his shirt and stalked to his side of the cabin, chucking the thing in the hamper on the way. "Scouting."

"Did you think to inform your teammate?"

He paused in the middle of hauling a clean shirt over his

head. He was used to her being catty, but the venom in her tone was new. And very intriguing.

He yanked the shirt down and turned to peer at her. She was pulling on her own long-sleeve thermal, and the neckline got caught on her ponytail. She tugged out the band and shook her sheet of dark hair loose, flipping her scent across the cabin. He folded his arms and waited.

She found him staring at her and tossed a hand. "Look, we're both burning it at both ends, and if you get injured out there, I need to have some idea where you are." She gathered her chocolate lengths into the elastic.

Mesmerized by her fingers in her hair, it took him a second to realize what she said. He almost snorted. "You're worried about me getting hurt?"

"Yeah, maybe."

No, this was something else. "Bullshit."

Her eyes flashed. "Fine. It's just…we're just…" She stuffed her feet into boots. "We're supposed to be a squad. Teammates."

"And?"

"And Rogan sent the two of us here to figure our shit out."

"And?"

"And I feel like I'm alone out here, dammit!" She threw an arm toward the door. "Literally surrounded by wolves, all day, every day, while my own teammate avoids me."

He imagined it again, that flicker of hurt that crossed her face. Right? "You don't seem to mind being surrounded by wolves." His lion growled in agreement, picturing handsome Lukas hovering by her shoulder, making her laugh.

"We're *supposed* to be building camaraderie. Getting them to trust us. So they'll stick a piece of tech in their eye." She slid a spare battery into her watch with a snap. "Are you even trying to make friends?"

Now, he did snort.

She glanced up. "Not at all? With anyone?"

He narrowed his eyes. She was digging. For what?

It hit him like a two-by-four.

She wanted to know if he was fucking someone.

She was *jealous*.

An evil grin stretched across his face.

She headed for the door. "Forget it."

The hell he would. He was going to bask in that shit, roll around in it, bat it around a little.

He followed her into the chilly night, watching the way her ass swayed in those leggings. She was powerfully built, all lean curves and lush muscle. He wanted to sink his teeth into her glutes. He let himself imagine it—and the ass-kicking that would no doubt follow.

His lion chuckled.

"I'll take west tonight. Unless you saw something when you were *scouting* that you wanted to check out?"

His grin grew wider. "No."

"Fine." She peeled off.

He watched her melt into the darkness before turning in the opposite direction. His lion was practically prancing, his own chest puffed so far it was leading the way through the woods.

Juno DeSilva. Jealous.

CHAPTER 24

Where the hell were the demons tonight? She wanted to punch something. She was so ready to punch something.

That smile he'd given her when she'd made an ass out of herself back at the cabin, acting like a petty, jealous...*girl.* He'd known exactly what she was asking.

Dammit. This was all Wolf's fault. Getting in her head, making her wonder.

Which female would catch Killian's eye? One of the delicate, submissive ones, no doubt.

"I'm not fucking any of the wolves."

The growl rumbled in her earpiece, and Juno froze, crouched at the base of a tree. "What?"

"That's what you wanted to know. Right?"

"I just wanted to know where my squadmate keeps disappearing to."

"Bullshit. You know I'm avoiding you."

She swallowed and scanned the dark woods, but knew she was alone. The wolf sentries on duty were miles away. "Why?"

"You know why. And I'm done tiptoeing around it."

Her pulse pounded. "Is that so?"

"Yeah. But first, I want you to admit it."

Her stomach dropped even as heat flooded her skin. "Admit what?"

"You know what."

A pale blue faebug drifted across her field of vision, but it was a blur. "I don't know what you're talking about, Diallo."

"Yes, you do. Now, say it."

"Say what?" Her brain was whirling, her heart hammering.

"You know what, and I want you to *fucking say it*."

The rough growl in her ear, the harsh demand, sent a bolt straight to her core. And raised her hackles. "Do you really?" she snapped.

"Yeah."

"Fine. We're doing this? We're doing this." She surged to stand. "You're touch-hungry, and you want me." She stabbed a finger in the air, like she was pointing at his stupid, sexy, bearded face.

"And?"

"And what?"

"*And?*"

"And what? And nothing!" Her voice bounced off of the trees. She wrenched herself under control. "You're acting like some crazy, possessive—"

"You were jealous."

Her mouth gaped, the protest getting stuck in her throat.

"You thought I ran off to fuck one of these females, and you were jealous. I want you to admit it. Because I'm sick of that look you give me, Juno, like I'm the only one in this shit. It's not just me, and we both know it, and now I want you to *say it*." His lion was in those last words, electrifying her, demanding her response.

"Fine!" she spat. "Fine. It's not just you. Happy?"

The words floated out there, into the night, into reality, where she couldn't snatch them back. Her curse followed them.

"I think that's the most honest conversation we've ever had." His voice was smug. The prick was pleased with himself.

"I think that's the most conversation we've had, period."

What just happened? Crickets chirped in the dark, and silence stretched.

Was that it? They laid it all out there, and then they were just going to leave it? Her brain whirled, but as the minutes lengthened, her pulse slowed and her head cleared.

Maybe that was it. Maybe they just needed to acknowledge the attraction, acknowledge the tension, and then let it go.

"I can't get used to these blue bugs."

The low drawl in her earpiece sent a tingle through her. She blinked. "What?"

"They're pink at home."

He never talked about the jungle. "Really?"

"And fat."

A surprised laugh escaped her as she watched the brilliant streaks of blue zooming across the landscape. "These guys don't look fat."

"The pink ones are lazy. Easy to catch."

"What's the fun in that?"

There was a pause. "You like to chase?"

She stilled. Her jaguar pricked its ears. "I'm a cat."

Another pause. "What about being caught?"

Heat shot through her. That rough voice was languid, knowing. Full of suggestion.

Was he…teasing?

Killian didn't tease. He didn't laugh. His idea of smiling

was baring his fangs. But unless she was very much mistaken, he was playing. With her.

Her heart thumped. "I never get caught."

His dark chuckle vibrated in her earpiece—and directly over her left shoulder.

She hit the dirt, somersaulting out of Killian's reach with hardly an inch to spare. He leaped after her, and Juno evaded him—barely. As he came at her again, she grabbed a tree limb, pulled up on it, and did a mid-air split, letting him barrel right between her legs. He rammed into another tree with a grunt, and she dropped to the ground, grinning.

"See?" She turned to face him. "I never—"

He took her to the forest floor like a battering ram. Her back hit the earth, her breath left her lungs, and his mouth slammed to hers.

The taste of him, wild and hot, exploded inside her. Sparks lit up in her brain, robbing her of all thought, which was probably why she gripped handfuls of his golden hair and kissed him back like her life depended on it.

He devoured her like a man starved. His hands were all over her, his big body surging against hers in a wave of pure muscle. She wrapped her legs around his hips. Her claws shot out, piercing his scalp, his shoulders, his back. He made a primal noise into her mouth. It drove her insane. God, the taste of him. The feel of him. Huge, hot, wild. She knew it would be like this—

A branch cracked nearby. Their heads whipped toward the sound, their hearts pounding against each other.

A raccoon chittered at them and waddled away.

What the hell was she doing?

She flipped him. It was like rolling a redwood, but years of sparring with him paid off. She knew what leverage to use, where to hook her foot, where to push. His back hit the dirt, and they both rolled smoothly to their feet. He uncurled to full height, eyes burning.

She was in such trouble. His scent was in her nose and his taste was in her mouth and she was screwed, screwed, screwed.

She swiped at her lips. "Never again."

His snarl raised the hair on the back of her neck.

CHAPTER 25

"Why not?" His voice was all lion. Killian dragged his tongue over his lips, tasting her.

"Come on. It would screw everything up."

"Seems like it would solve a hell of a lot to me." The words were barely comprehensible, growled through his bared teeth. Her scent was shorting out his brain, his dick hard as a sycamore in his pants.

"No. It's..." She swallowed and caught her breath. "Unprofessional."

He was up in her face in the next blink. "Unprofessional."

"Yeah."

"That's your concern."

The pulse in her throat jumped, begging for his teeth. Silence lengthened as their chests rose and fell, inches apart. That spicy, warm scent drugged him. He nearly swayed.

"We can't," she said. "We're teammates."

If she didn't stop staring at his mouth, he wouldn't be responsible for whatever he did next.

"It would fuck everything up. Squad first." She shook herself a little, refocused, lifting her eyes to his. "You need to find someone to burn it off with. Someone who's not your teammate."

Mine.

An ominous burn started in his belly. "So, what, I should just cozy up to some wolf and fuck her brains out until we're done here?"

"If that's what it takes."

"And you?"

He watched her do it—slide that mask over herself, going cold, lifting her chin. "Me, too."

A deadly, vicious snarl bubbled up from his throat, lips peeling back as his fangs punched through his gums.

Her eyes flashed, and she pointed a finger at him. "That. That, right there. I'm not yours, Diallo."

"I'm very fucking aware of that," he said over the lion roaring in his head.

"And doing this—" She gestured between them. "—would only make things worse. I'm not interested in possessive male bullshit, and I'm sure as hell not looking for a mate."

Mate.

His blood turned to ice.

Visions flashed before his eyes. His mom dead on the ground. His dad lying lifeless beside her, throat gaping from his own claw.

He straightened abruptly, heart thumping. "Don't flatter yourself, DeSilva. A mate is the last thing I want." He backed away, spreading his hands. "You know what? You're right. I'll just find someone else to bang it out with. I don't need the drama."

CHAPTER 26

She watched him like a hawk for the next few days.

Like some stupid teenage girl, she found excuses to be in his vicinity. She loitered near the lake when he was on fishing duty, hung around the tool shed when he was on sharpening duty, pretended to relax with Astrid around the big fire when she was really keeping an eye on the cookhouse because he was on cleanup. He didn't leave with any of the females, though a tiny blonde girl had apparently attached herself to him. She trailed behind as he stomped around doing his chores, and every once in a while, his gruff chuckle would echo her girlish giggles. Even now, she was chattering at him in the cookhouse, a honey stick in her hand.

It was adorable. And baffling.

"All right," Astrid said. "You and the lion."

Juno jerked her gaze to Astrid's knowing amethyst one. They were alone by the bonfire near the lake, warming their feet by the small flames they kept going during the day. "What?"

"Are you two…"

Fuck. "No."

A platinum brow lifted. "You want to be?"

"No."

"Uh huh."

The memory of his big body on top of hers during that kiss had given her a few sleepless nights. "It would screw everything up."

"Ah, the male shifter." Astrid cocked her head. "Aggressive as hell, which is fun. Possessive and overprotective…"

"Which is not."

"Which is definitely not."

They were silent for a few minutes until, unable to stand it a second longer, Juno pulled a throwing knife from her thigh holster and chucked it at a nearby tree. The blade stuck in the bark with a satisfying thunk.

Astrid considered the knife. "Are you touch-hungry?"

"Not quite to the red zone. He is, though."

"Obviously. Like a stick of dynamite, that one." Astrid threw one of her own daggers at the tree, where it sank into the bark beside Juno's. "You should just do it. Get it out of your system." When Juno scoffed, Astrid grinned. "What? He looks like he'd be a nice tree to climb."

Juno laughed, but deep down, her cat bared possessive fangs. Fantastic. "He's an ass." Her eyes drifted over to the cookhouse, where Killian was handing the little blonde girl another honey stick. "Anyway, we can't. Our squad is everything to both of us." She threw another dagger, watched it land centered above the other two. Astrid's blade followed, their knives starting to form a vertical line up the trunk. "It's already tense enough, and I hate that." *Thunk.* "He's supposed to be my teammate. He's supposed to have my back. But I can't even talk to him." It hurt to say it out loud.

Astrid muttered something foreign. "Forget it, then. It's probably weird shaped, anyway."

She'd seen Killian naked countless times. "It's not."

"Maybe it's really small."

"It is definitely not." Her eyes glazed over. What would he

look like, hard and swollen and completely erect? She practically soaked her leggings at the thought.

Astrid's chuckle snapped her out of it. "You're screwed, kitty. Or, at least you need to be. If the big lion can't handle it, why not one of our males? They don't all hate the smell of cat puss—"

Juno tackled her. They tumbled onto the ground, rolled, and had knives at each other's throat in the same instant. Astrid's grin was feral, her icy hair and gray rune tattoos making her look like something out of an ancient battlefield. She took her dagger from Juno's throat and chucked it at the tree. Juno followed suit. They both looked over.

Their blades were embedded into the tree in the shape of a giant cock.

It felt really good to laugh.

———

Glowing blue faebugs zipped through the dark forest as she suited up for patrol. Her cat liked watching them through the window. She liked that they gave her something to focus on besides her teammate changing across the room. She was still so hyper-focused on every rustle of clothing behind her that she jolted when the distress call came through the wolves' comm.

"We have a missing cub. Last seen at dinner. Six-year-old female, Elvi."

She locked eyes with Killian across the cabin and watched the blood drain from his face.

Elvi was the little girl who'd attached herself to him.

They dressed at lightning speed and hit the woods at a run, wordlessly taking opposite routes. Even as they threaded through the trees, she knew it was pointless. Wolves were better trackers, their noses far superior, and they were already out there checking the perimeter. If they hadn't found her yet…

"The river," Killian's growl rumbled across the wolves' comm. "Anyone check the river?"

"Already cleared. Why don't you stick to your secret mission, cat? We'll handle our own." It was that asshole, Val.

Silence, then Killian's rough voice rang out across their private channel. "There's a waterfall up there that she talks about. Calls it her secret spot. I don't know where it is."

"I'll meet you at the south bank." Her feet flew across the forest floor. It was a cold night, colder than usual, with only a sliver of moon in the black sky. Shifter kids had advanced senses, but they had to grow into them. It was possible Elvi couldn't see well enough in the dark and had misstepped, fallen…

Killian was already pacing the riverbank when she got there. They crossed the tightrope and fanned out on the other side.

"Check," Juno murmured into her watch.

"Check."

Her breath fogged, fingertips cold despite her sprint through the woods. She strained her ears and nose as she moved swiftly through the trees, desperate for a hint of the tiny female wolf.

"It's fucking freezing," Killian's voice muttered in her ear. "Should've brought extra clothes."

For Elvi, he meant. She might be a wolf, but she was still young, and exposure was a real threat. "She's a wolf," Juno assured him.

"She's latent."

Her heart plummeted. "What?"

"Yeah."

That little girl was out here in the mountains by herself, and she was unable to shift into wolf form? She'd be easy pickings for weather, predators, or worse.

Juno picked up the pace.

Several long minutes later, Killian's voice rumbled in her ear. "You got anything?"

"Nothing." A waterfall could be anywhere on this damn mountain. And that was assuming she'd even gone to her secret spot. "Did she say anything else about it?"

"Just called it her secret spot. Said there was a waterfall and a pool and she likes to watch the squirrels. If I'd thought it was all the way up here, I would've told her not to go alone."

They searched for another hour, traveling further along the river. Juno moved downstream while Killian moved higher into the mountains. At one point, she checked her wolf comm, and when she got no response, she realized she must be out of signal range.

"You still got me?" They could both handle themselves, but the idea of losing comms with Killian still made her uneasy. Especially when a fat drop of icy rain splattered onto her head. Followed by another. And another.

"I got you."

The low growl raised goosebumps on her neck. Or maybe that was the chill, because it was really raining now, a God awful freezing drizzle that trickled down her scalp and into her shirt and turned her fingers to ice. "My wolf comm is out."

A grunt. Obviously, he wasn't bothered by the idea. There was a pause. Then, "I do, you know. Got you."

Juno slowed as she stepped over a fallen tree.

"Even if things are fucked up with us sometimes, I've got your back."

Her throat tightened. "Same."

Something warm flooded her chest, chasing off the chill, and her mouth curved as she swooped under a curtain of hanging moss. It was amazing what a few rough words could do.

"I've got sulfur." There was a rustle, then a few excruciating seconds of silence. "Fuck!"

"Location?" Juno demanded, turning to sprint in the opposite direction, sailing over rocks and downed trees as the sounds of a fight came through the comm. "Location?"

The only response was a roar.

The forest lit up with sights, sounds, and smells as Juno burst into jaguar form. She found that one scent—the hot, wild one she couldn't seem to get out of her brain, anyway—and went after it like a bullet. The forest blurred, her lungs pumped, and her paws pounded over the earth, moving steadily higher up the steep incline of the mountain.

The sound of the fight reached her a split second before the smell. Rotten eggs and putrid flesh, acrid smoke and coppery blood. She rounded a tree and saw them—the massive golden lion locked in combat with something out of a nightmare. Horns, claws, a spiked tail, razor-tipped wings. As she launched herself into the fray, a stream of fire erupted from the demon's jaws. Her fur ignited. Pain blasted through her, and she gave a jaguar scream. The demon knocked her to her back, landing on top of her with wings outstretched and wicked tail swinging. She tore into its soft underbelly, spilling black blood and thick, slippery intestines.

The thing reared back with a hair-raising screech, and Killian collided with it, taking it to the ground and ripping out its throat with a savagery that made her cat smile. She rolled to her paws before shifting back to human form, cursing as the burns on her pelt translated to her human skin.

Killian rose from the ground, breathing hard. His eyes locked on her bubbled, blistered collarbone. "You good?"

She nodded and crossed her arms over her chest, wishing she'd stashed her clothes instead of shredding them. Stupid.

A wad of fabric hit her shoulder—Killian's enormous thermal shirt, ripped in places but still with plenty of coverage for her. She glanced up to find him pulling on his sweatpants. The sight of his thumb grazing the taut line of his lower abs made her mouth go dry.

Want.

She pulled his shirt over her head, instantly surrounded by his scent and the lingering warmth from his body. The shirt came to the top of her knees, the sleeves hanging past her fingertips. She rolled them up to her wrists and looked up to find him watching her.

She swallowed. "Thanks."

"Let's go."

They continued up the mountain, wordlessly sticking together. Her feet were tough, but she picked her way carefully across the sticks and stones and undergrowth. It was stupid to shift without stripping. Would it be worth it to backtrack for her boots?

Freezing rain pelted them, stronger by the minute, until she finally swore and came to a stop. "Diallo."

His head swung around, beard sparkling with drops of rain, hair hanging in dripping ropes around his naked shoulders. A flash of lightning lit his face, making him look like an angry thunder god.

She pushed her hair back from her face. "We need to find shelter."

He looked at the whipping trees and rivulets of water running over their bare feet, then cursed and jerked his head. "Back here."

They picked their way down the hill, slipping and sliding. That poor girl, alone in this downpour. If she was still alive at all—

A hand circled her wrist. She jerked back instinctively, but Killian had already released her, stalking toward a rocky outcropping barely visible through the sheet of rain. She followed his wide shoulders, hurrying below the rough stone ceiling and letting out a breath. Rain clattered on the roof and cascaded off the ledge like a watery curtain, but it was dry enough if they hunkered back against the rocky wall. Wordlessly, they gathered the driest wood and kindling they could find and stacked it beneath the overhang.

Too bad they didn't have a way to light the damn stuff.

"Where's Jovi when you need her?" Her voice sounded strangely loud, bouncing off the rocky shelter while the storm roared outside.

Killian reached into a pocket, pulled out a lighter, and flicked it. He lit the stacked wood in several places, then squatted to blow on the burgeoning flames until they had a crackling fire. When he looked up and found her staring at him, he shrugged. "I always have a lighter in my pocket."

She blinked. "You do?"

"My dad taught me." He brushed debris from the back of the little cave, clearing rocks and twigs. "I can't do that flint-rock shit." He stood, kicked at the space he'd cleared, then turned and stared out at the storm. An impatient sigh heaved his shoulders.

"We'll find her." She tried to put some confidence into her voice.

He didn't respond. A bolt of lightning illuminated the landscape, lighting up towering pine trees that swayed ominously in the rapidly increasing wind. It whistled through their shelter, and she shivered despite herself. This was one hell of a storm. She huddled up to the fire, holding out her hands. Her fingers felt like ice cubes, her hair a sopping, heavy mass on her back.

Killian spun and stalked back to the fire, flopping on the ground with ill grace. He glowered at the flames.

"We'll find her," she said again as a shudder racked her. As much as she tried to stifle it, the cold crept into her bones, and her body was fighting off hypothermia with no regard for her pride. She clenched her teeth to keep them from clacking together.

Killian scooted to the back wall, hissing when his bare

back hit the cold rock. He looked at her and lifted his arm, eyes blazing with the hint of a dare.

She opened her mouth to tell him she was fine.

"Don't be stupid, DeSilva."

She was shivering, her fingers and toes like ice. Refusing body heat was childish.

Want.

With an inward curse, she scooted back to ease against his bare torso, the heat of him seeping through the ripped shirt she wore. His heavy arm lowered around her shoulders, instantly enveloping her in warmth and smooth golden skin and his mouthwatering scent.

Her head spun, her entire body humming.

They watched the storm in silence while flashes of lightning revealed glimpses of the mountain vista. She tried to focus on something, anything but how incredibly delicious it felt to be against him.

"Is that so hard?"

Yes, the body surrounding her was incredibly hard. "What?"

"Letting someone help you out."

Irritation flared. "Really, Diallo?"

"Why does it grate on you so much?"

She scoffed and started to move away, but his arm clamped around her.

"See? You're already running. Is it just me, or any male?"

She shoved at him, escaping the heavy warmth of his arm and instantly shivering with the chill. "Why do you have to poke at me all the time?"

"Why do you act like you have to prove something all the time?"

"Because I do."

"To who?"

"To myself. To everyone."

"When have any of us ever doubted you?"

Images of the past seven years battered her mind. Her squadmates smiling at her, high-fiving her, clapping her on the back. Rogan sending her on dangerous patrols like any other team member. But Killian was prodding closer and closer to her deepest wound. "What about you? You're one to talk. You're a total asshole when all we've ever done is try to make you a part of this family. No wonder your own brother doesn't even want to talk to you."

His expression closed down, a door slamming shut.

Shit.

Guilt curled in her gut. Mentioning Cullen was a low blow, an easy target she didn't even understand. But Killian was so warm and he smelled so good and he was staring at her like he saw right through her, smashing through her defenses like the blunt hammer he was.

And it scared her.

"You're right. I'm an asshole." His gaze raked over her. "Enjoy the shirt."

They didn't speak another word after that.

CHAPTER 27

She woke at dawn, shivering, instinctively burrowing against the solid block of heat at her back. A band of warm steel tightened around her middle.

Her lids lifted. A craggy rock wall was inches from her nose, the earth was hard and cold beneath her, and a warm, masculine form was nestled at her back.

Any trace of sleep left her. Killian's powerful thighs were wedged beneath her bare legs, and a hand was tucked around her ribs, close enough to brush the underside of her breast.

A feather-light touch skated up the side of her neck, to the hollow behind her ear, sending a jolt of electricity through her entire body. A soft inhale told her it was his nose.

He was nuzzling her.

He did it again. Goosebumps erupted on her skin. His arm tightened around her, his chest rising and falling against her back, a solid wall of heat.

Her lids drifted shut.

Strong male. Good male. Good mate.

Her eyes flew open, and she shoved at him with an inward curse.

She leaped to her feet, swiping her hair out of her eyes as

he pushed up from the ground, shirtless and rumpled and sexy as hell.

His inner beast stared out of his eyes, locked on her with delicious intensity.

Her core went wet. Her stomach growled.

He blinked, then looked at her belly. "I'll be back."

Before she could respond, he was up and stalking away, shoulders rolling, breath fogging in his wake.

Right. Fire.

She rebuilt it as best she could, poking the embers with a stick, leaning down to blow on the coals. Was she even doing anything? She was a city cat. The last time she'd built a fire was in survival training at the academy. Why hadn't she ever thought of carrying a lighter?

She rubbed her arms and made a face at the pathetic tendril of smoke. Forget it, she could deal with the cold. At least it had stopped raining. She hit the dirt, did some push-ups and stretches to get the blood flowing.

Not that her blood wasn't already hot enough, since she couldn't shake the memory of waking up with a massive, sexy lion wrapped around her.

Said lion appeared with a handful of fat mushrooms cupped in each palm, his hair hanging in golden tangles around his shoulders and his amber gaze latched onto her.

He set one handful on a nearby rock and stepped away. Clearly, he wasn't making some stupid statement by trying to offer her food from his hand.

Good. Juno watched him toss a handful into his own mouth. "Are those safe?"

"No, I'm trying to poison us both." *Because I'm an asshole,* his eyes added.

Shit. "Sorry."

He looked away. "Elvi taught me. She's good with plants and stuff."

Her heart gave a pang. "We'll find her." She popped the

mushrooms in her mouth. They tasted like dirt and not much else. "I'll find food next time."

"Do you know anything about foraging?"

She opened her mouth, and promptly shut it again.

Killian raised a brow. "How about you let me handle it, then?"

He knew exactly how much that irritated her. "Show me."

His expression flickered. "Fine. Let's go. Maybe we can catch her scent, if the rain didn't wash it all away."

They hiked all day and found no trace of Elvi. Killian grew more and more tense as the sun lowered in the sky, but every once in a while he would point out a fruit or mushroom and tell her it was safe. He didn't know many of their names, but his easy knowledge was impressive. And sexy.

Jesus. Now, the man was sexy because he could identify fungi? She seriously needed to get laid.

When their feet ached and their eyes itched from fatigue, they found another shallow cave to hunker down in and sat around a meager fire. Killian stared broodily into the dark forest as another hard, cold rain began to fall.

"We'll find her."

Silence.

"How did she get so attached to you, anyway?"

He shrugged. "Started talking when I was fishing. She thought it was funny that I caught so many." He shut up abruptly.

The memory of him dropping those overflowing buckets onto the table in the cookhouse, his fight with Lukas afterward, and their confrontation on the cliff flashed across her mind. *I can smell you.* "Why did you?"

He met her eyes across the flickering flames.

A clicking sound made them jerk their heads toward the entrance. When the sound came again, she silently stripped out of Killian's shirt while he eased out of his pants beside her. The temptation to glance over and take in the sight of his naked body was almost overwhelming.

Click click click—

There was a flash of glistening pincers and a flurry of giant, hairy legs, and then a massive spider boiled up from the darkness.

Killian tackled it like a linebacker, and they rolled outside the cave entrance in a jumble of golden skin and long, jointed legs. Shrieks echoed off tree trunks, doubled and tripled like they were coming from multiple mouths, and the stench of sulfur and blood exploded around Juno as she gave in to her jaguar. There was a series of cracks as Killian rolled to mount his opponent, grabbed its head, and gave it a vicious twist. As the corpse flopped limply to the ground, Killian burst into lion form with a roar.

Juno dodged to avoid another huge, hairy body. There were three of them, giant arachnid demons with too many eyes and way too many legs, all of them snapping pincers and razor sharp teeth. They fell upon the enormous lion in a seething, shrieking mass while the freezing rain pounded the earth to mud beneath them.

Juno leaped onto one of them. Its screech of outrage died with the slice of her claw over its throat. As warm, foul blood gushed over her paw and satisfaction surged in her chest, a high, childlike scream echoed from the trees.

A golden blur streaked past Juno into the dark forest, leaving her to finish the last of their opponents.

She faced off with the sole demon that remained standing. When it reared back on four of its legs, she dove beneath, twisted onto her back, and clawed viciously at its underbelly, splitting flesh and holding her breath against the rain of blood and bowel. A massive weight collapsed on top of her.

Sick. She heaved and twisted until she got out from under it, shaking out her fur before following Killian's scent into the trees.

He was crouched naked by a huge boulder, murmuring in a voice that still held a lot of the lion. "Hey, hey, hey. It's me."

Juno shifted back into human form and crept closer, scanning the trees for any other threats. They were clear.

Some wet gulps came from behind Killian's broad back, followed by a long, wailing cry. Killian rose with a tiny blonde girl wrapped in his arms, one hand petting her hair.

Juno's breath caught. He looked so natural comforting the little cub, like he'd done it a million times.

Had her own father ever held her like that?

Killian raked her with a glance. "Good?"

She nodded, unable to tear her eyes away from his big hand stroking the child's head.

Splat.

A frigid raindrop snapped her back to reality. The rain fell heavily now, a freezing shower that turned the hillside to a mud slick.

Hail stung their bare skin as they hurried back to the shelter. Killian swung Elvi down to the ground, but she clung, whimpering. He gently shook her loose and tapped the underside of her chin. "You're a wolf. Be brave. What were you doing, running off in the dark, anyway?"

A sniff. "It wasn't dark when I left."

Killian grunted and added their few remaining sticks to the dwindling flames. Juno tried not to stare at his magnificent flexing ass as he stepped into what was left of his pants.

She threw his shirt over her pebbled skin, grateful for its warmth, and glanced outside. Any sticks they gathered now would be soaked with freezing rain. Cursing, she turned to find Killian sitting on the cave floor with Elvi huddled beneath one arm, tucked against his side with little hands curled into her chest.

Her heart clenched. She looked away and rubbed her arms. "DeSilva."

She glanced back. Holding her gaze, Killian lifted his free arm.

For once, she didn't argue.

Sliding under his heavy arm was like slipping under an electric blanket. They were silent for a long time, which was good, because she was having trouble hearing anything but the roll of thunder and the pounding of her heart.

"She's asleep." Killian's low murmur ruffled her hair, now hanging in damp waves over her shoulders. A few locks trailed over his bare stomach. Absently, she tried to blow them off, sending the strands dancing across his abs.

His stomach tightened, and he grunted.

Was he ticklish?

She blew again, watching the dark strands skitter over ropes of golden muscle.

Killian jerked and growled, the rumble of it vibrating against her side. She snickered, then brushed her hair off him, his skin like hot velvet beneath her fingers.

Heat flared between them. She should move. She really shouldn't be cuddling next to him like his…mate.

With that sobering thought, she eased away, feigning the need to roll her neck and stretch her shoulders. She gestured to the sleeping Elvi, still nestled under his arm. "You're good with kids." Her murmur was barely audible over the pounding hail.

"Lots of cubs in the Pride."

He was talking about home again. "As many as there are here?" It seemed like they couldn't go anywhere in the village without tripping over wolf cubs.

He nodded.

"I was never around them."

He stared at her for a while. "Your dad owns Silka."

Ex-dad. She nodded. Instantly, she was back in Silka's corporate headquarters, surrounded by sleek metals and expensive colognes and men whose smiles didn't reach their eyes.

"I'm not made for that corporate crap, either," he said.

Pride Industries built beautiful structures and had a monopoly on the major construction projects in the city. Killian's family ran the business, but he never talked about it. "Yeah, I can't really see you drawing up construction contracts."

"Cullen was always better at that boardroom bullshit."

She hesitated. "What happened between you two?"

He was silent so long she thought he wouldn't answer. "I'll tell you mine if you tell me yours."

She had a feeling she knew what he would ask. How badly did she want to know about his falling out with his brother?

Badly. Very badly.

"Fine. But you first."

He narrowed his gaze at her, then gently lifted his arm off Elvi and eased her to the ground, where she curled into a ball. Killian scooted away from the little girl, along the back wall, until his side barely brushed hers.

He smelled so fucking good.

"My lion rides me hard. Always has. I need to use it." He flicked her a glance. "You get it." It wasn't a question, and the fact that he knew she understood made her chest feel like it was going to burst. "Cullen's always had more control. And he liked the business stuff, anyway. Dad taught him. I—it doesn't matter. We were close. We ran together, sparred, hunted. Got strong." He gazed into the fire. "He could tell when my lion was riding me. He'd say, 'Let's go for a run.' And we would." He fell quiet. "And one day, we went for a run, and came back to them dead."

A twig popped in the fire, sending sparks into the air. Outside their shelter, thunder cracked. Juno hardly noticed any of it. "Who?"

"My mom. And my little sister." Long pause. "Gutted. No evidence. And my dad was next to them. He'd found his mate dead and slit his own throat."

Jesus. *Jesus.*

How did she not know this? Did any of the squad know this? "I'm sorry." What a stupid, useless thing to say. "How old was she? Your sister?"

Killian met her eyes and directed one thick thumb over his shoulder toward Elvi, asleep on the cave floor.

Juno's heart broke for him.

She laid a hand on his arm and gripped it tight. "I didn't know. I'm sorry." *For not knowing, for not asking, for not understanding your wild, animal pain.*

"I wasn't there to protect them. They meant everything to me and I wasn't there."

Her palm found his cheek, his beard rasping against her skin.

"Everything was black. All fucking black." He cleared his throat roughly, and she dropped her hand from his face. "And Cullen stepped up and started running shit like he was made for it, and I was just...nothing. Drowning." He stared into the fire, his gaze a thousand miles away. "I ran. Like a chicken shit." He tossed a twig into the fire. "And left him there alone."

She frowned. "He wasn't alone. You were."

"He wouldn't see it that way."

Unable to stop herself, she stroked a hand down his heavy arm, offering wordless comfort, wanting to give him a tether to the here and now, to keep him from drowning in memories.

"And then, like some twisted joke, I ended up fighting the things that killed them, and I can't even tell him. Not that he wants to talk to me, anyway." His brows slashed downward, and he shook himself before pinning her with his amber stare. "Your turn."

Though her stomach squirmed, she eased back and nodded.

Killian didn't hesitate. "Vasquez."

She pulled Killian's shirt over her knees, trying to tuck her bare feet into the fabric. "What about him?"

"How'd he fuck it up?"

His chest looked enormous in the firelight, rising and falling steadily, the wild lengths of his hair tangling over his shoulders in a riot of gold and bronze. So different from dark, sleek, contained Rafael. "He tried to put me in a cage."

"How?"

It was her turn to throw a twig into the fire. "Always wanted to *keep me safe*."

"Is that so bad?"

"Wanting to keep someone safe and wanting to turn them into someone else are two very different things," she snapped, shooting him a look.

His eyes glittered in the firelight.

"You're right, I do get it. I need to use my cat, too. She *needs* to be used. But it's more than that. *I* want to be used. I want to run, I want to be strong, I want to be physical. It's who I am." She rolled her shoulders, feeling the urge to stretch her muscles even now. "Rafael knew that about me. He saw me fight in the Arena how many times?"

Killian's focus sharpened on her face. "You fought in the Arena?"

"You didn't know that?" A dangerous smile curved her lips, memories flickering like the flames behind him. "They thought I'd be a novelty match, something to lighten things up between the real fights."

Killian scoffed, and the sound warmed her more than the fire.

"I almost killed that first male. They had to reattach his arm. After that, they booked me for real fights. I made a little money, got a shitty apartment. Started to make a name for myself in the Arena. They called me the Maneater."

"You're the Maneater?" His stunned expression was almost comical. "People were still talking about The Maneater when I fought there." He scanned her body as if seeing her for the first time. A dark, sexual grin spread slowly across his face.

Heat speared through her. A smiling Killian was infinitely more dangerous than one baring his fangs. "Anyway, Rafael liked that I was strong and physical. I think he liked the idea that he tamed the Maneater, but he never said it that way." Her brow pinched. "After I stopped fighting in the Arena, I went back to running around the city. Rooftops, scaffolding..." She shrugged. "Whatever was the most challenging. The most fun." Her brief smile fell. "Raf didn't like that. He was worried I might get hurt, especially since I liked to run at night." Old anger bubbled in her belly. "He never asked me not to. But he'd plan things when he knew I was itching for a run. Events, vacations, fancy dinners." If her dad had still been around at that point, he would've loved Rafael. Would've loved his lucrative business ventures even more.

Juno glanced at the bearded, tattooed lion lounging beside her and almost laughed at what Juan DeSilva would think of him. "He built me a course. A big, beautiful obstacle course on his private grounds so I wouldn't have to leave. So I could go for my runs and he could keep tabs on me, make sure I was safe."

A low growl rumbled out of Killian's chest, almost beyond hearing.

"I saw it for what it was. But I loved him." The words tasted bitter in her mouth. "I loved him, and he loved me, and he wanted me to be safe, and he built me this beautiful place so I could do the thing I loved, and how could I be mad about that? How could I be ungrateful about that?" It poured out of her like the torrential rain beyond their shelter, hard and battering. In the far corner, Elvi stirred in her sleep.

With an effort, Juno dropped her voice. "So, I tried to stuff it all down and cinch it all up, parade around on his arm and be content." She shook her head. "I was shriveling."

"What a fucking waste."

Her heart bloomed a little at that, but her smile was sour. "I thought MLE was my perfect solution. I'd get to be useful, chase down magical thugs, catch the bad guys. Raf didn't love the idea. He tried to talk me out of it. But I told him it was important to me, and he finally agreed. *Agreed*. Like it was his decision." She shook her head at her former self, answering to some male, waiting for his approval. "I was so excited." Lead settled in her belly. "And then, I found out he tried to pull my application. Made some calls. He has powerful friends."

Sparks popped in the fire again. The dancing flames became Rafael's handsome, alarmed face. The wind howling outside their shelter became his placating words, his pleas for understanding. "So, I left. And I told myself I would never put myself in that position again." She met Killian's eyes. "I'm never going to be some tame little female sitting at home. That's not who I am."

"No, you're not." It was practically a purr.

She focused on the glowing coals. A blast of frigid wind swept a strand of hair across her face. She swiped at it irritably, trying to tuck her toes further under the hem of Killian's shirt.

"That male is a fucking moron."

She shot him a smile. "Hey, look at that. You and I agree on something."

The corner of his mouth lifted ever so slightly. God, he was fucking sexy.

Killian's nostrils flared.

I can smell you.

She should move away, break their eye contact. Interrupt this flickering firelight confessional. Stop looking at his mouth.

"You're cold."

There was nothing cold about the look he gave her. He lifted his arm again, looking like some enormous sculpted statue any woman would be a fool to ignore.

She didn't move.

"There's a cub here, Juno." *We're not going to fuck each other with a kid sleeping next to us,* his expression finished, with a glint of humor.

Now, he was teasing again? God help her.

She scooted under his arm before she could talk herself out of it. They stared out at the raging storm.

"Did you find someone to…" She couldn't finish. Her heart pounded into the lengthening silence.

"No." Thunder rumbled. "Did you?"

She thought her heart was pounding before? "No."

His thumb grazed her shoulder, once, twice. And the tempest on the mountain was suddenly nothing compared to the one raging beneath her skin. Every nerve ending lit up like the lightning flashing in the distance.

They sat there, watching the storm, while the scents of their arousal swirled around them.

CHAPTER 28

Elvi's mother, a fierce female with sharp eyes and a muscular frame, fell to her knees when they walked into the village the next afternoon. Killian swung the little girl off of his bare shoulders, where she'd been riding for the last leg of the trip, and watched her fly into her parents' arms. Shouts of relief echoed around camp, and Astrid grinned as Killian and Juno approached, Killian in his ripped pants and Juno in his torn shirt, her thighs bared to the crisp morning air. They'd found the remains of her clothes on the mountainside, but nothing was salvageable except her boots.

He loved seeing her in his shirt.

Elvi's father came forward to clap Juno into a hard hug. "Thank you."

He held a hand out to Killian, but once their palms met, he hauled him into a rough embrace. Startled, Killian stood there like an idiot, his arms hanging limp. He tried to swallow the lump in his throat. It wouldn't budge.

Astrid was barking into her comm, alerting the search party that Elvi had been found, when an enormous black wolf loped out of the woods and morphed into a gigantic, naked

Magnus Magnussen. He strode into the gathered crowd, teeth bared in a gleaming grin.

"Gave us a scare, cub." He bent to grasp Elvi's chin and gave her an alpha stare. Power hummed from him. Killian's lion twitched. "What did you learn?"

"Don't go out alone."

"Not until you're ready. And when you are?"

Elvi blinked, mouth open. She was clearly at a loss.

"Know your boundaries," Killian and Magnus said in unison. They slid each other a look before Magnus straightened.

"I think this calls for a celebration!" A cheer went up from the gathered crowd, and several wolves slapped Juno on the back. "Get the mead. We start at sundown." He gave Killian and Juno an approving nod before stalking away.

———

These wolves could drink.

Killian stood in the packed longhouse later that night, ears ringing with the drunken laughter of some of the most lethal predators in the world. The air was thick with the aromas of smoke, sweat, charred meat, and sweet honey mead. The kids had long since gone to bed, some of them curled up in corners or in their parent's arms. Their peaceful sleeping faces made his heart lurch.

Safe.

Someone jostled him, splashing mead onto his sleeve with a slurred apology and a clap on the shoulder. They'd scored major points with Elvi's rescue, and even Killian was being treated like one of the Pack.

It was nice.

It was also loud as fuck, but that didn't keep him from hearing Juno's throaty laugh from across the longhouse. A crowd had gathered around one of the tables near the entrance, watching a drinking game that was apparently just chugging your entire mug and issuing some sort of challenge for your opponent to beat. Wolves were tall, but Killian was taller than most of them, so he could still see her entire body lean back from her seat on the bench, her stomach clenching beneath her tight thermal shirt. Her nose scrunched with a wide smile as she righted herself and threw some snappy insult at one of the wolves. Whatever the wolf said in response made Juno slap the table with another peal of laughter. A few strands had come loose from her ponytail. She twisted her mouth to blow them out of her eye, drank her entire refilled tankard, then caught her tongue between her teeth as she shook a leather-bound cup vigorously before dumping it onto the table and spilling several carved dice.

A raucous cry rang through the longhouse. Juno leaped to her feet with a shout of victory, arms raised and shirt hiking up to reveal a peek of tawny abs. Then, she spun around, shaking her ass and wiggling her fingers before ending with double deuces and lapping up the feigned outrage of her competitors. Bowls of snacks littered the tabletop—shelled nuts, some sort of dried meat, a pile of plump wild strawberries. She popped a few berries into her mouth, grinning as she chewed, and motioned to her opponent.

Killian loved seeing her like this. No cool facade, no hard mask. Laughing and teasing, radiating warmth and wit. She was like that with the others in the squad most of the time. It never ceased to amaze him how she could flip the switch from relaxed, laughing female to lethal killer. It was sexy as hell, knowing she could reach over the mead-sticky table and snap her opponent's neck in the blink of an eye.

Her teeth sank into another red berry before her full lips wrapped around it, sucking at the juice and giving him all kinds of filthy ideas. He'd make her bite it, then he'd run the juicy end all over her nipples, down her stomach, into her sweet pussy, just so he could follow the trail with his tongue.

As if she felt his eyes boring a hole in her face, her gaze snapped toward him. His dick swelled up tight behind his zipper, but he didn't look away.

She grinned.

Grinned. At him.

Her opponent dribbled mead down his shirt while he chugged his entire mug. He gave a massive belch that earned him a round of applause. "Top that, jaguar!"

Playful determination danced across Juno's face before she swung her legs over the bench, then stepped onto it so she was a head above the crowd.

Killian squinted across the smoky room. Did she sway ever so slightly?

Her throat bobbed as she drained her tankard again. Lowering her mug with a gasp, Juno threw her arms wide and let out the loudest, most obnoxious belch Killian had ever heard in his goddamn life.

He felt his jaw drop as the longhouse erupted into laughter and cheers. Juno wiped the corner of her mouth with an elegant finger, then hopped off the bench, her boots hitting the floor with a bit less than her usual grace.

Killian couldn't keep the grin off his face as he swigged his own mead. This stuff was pretty good. No wonder the wolves liked it so much.

Juno plunked onto the bench, eagerly awaiting the next challenge. Her eyes slid to Killian's again, and her mouth twitched before she refocused on her competitor.

After some whispered words from the buddy hanging on his shoulder, the wolf staggered to his feet, drained his refilled tankard, and launched into song.

"When the colors fill the sky
And your female gives the eye
Aoooo, boys, watch your tails
She-wolves got more balls than males!"

The longhouse boomed along with the last line. Killian's

ears rang with wolf howls and laughter. Juno clapped gamely for her opponent as tankards clinked all around. Her own mug was refilled. She knocked it back.

He wanted to bite the slender column of her throat. Lick it, suck it, encircle it with his fingers. Not to hurt her. Never to hurt her. To make her feel his strength, so she'd know he could take her, protect her, handle everything she could give him—

The heavy ceramic bottom of Juno's empty tankard hit the table before she shoved up from the bench. She definitely swayed that time.

Killian squeezed his way closer to the table. How much mead had she had? He drank absently from his own mug, which someone had apparently topped up. Helpful bastards, these wolves.

Juno swallowed hard and pinned her gaze on the wolf across from her.

"A loyal dog will never fail
To fetch a bone and wag a tail
But if you want your female wetter
A pussy always does it better."

Killian's eardrums practically burst. Groaning in defeat, Juno's opponent stumbled from the bench, turned, and clumsily stripped naked before streaking into the night. Apparently, that was the agreed-upon punishment for the loser. Boots stomped, tankards sloshed, and raucous laughter bounced off the ceiling beams, Killian's included.

"What do you think, lion, is she right?" Someone slurred from behind him.

"Damn right she is." He couldn't keep his eyes off her.

Her sparkling gaze met his from across the smoky room. She leveled a finger at him. "Diallo."

A deep "Ohhhhhh…" traveled through the longhouse. Eager gazes flicked between the two of them.

She was challenging him. She wanted to play...with him.

And maybe that honey mead was stronger than he thought, because he found himself winding through the tables toward her as she placed another strawberry into her mouth. The room swam with scent—smoke, meat, mead, wolf —but hers speared straight through it all.

She watched his approach. The shiny red berry disappeared between her lips. She flicked away the stem like a cigarette butt, her pink tongue darting out to swipe juice from her lips.

Fuck. He stopped directly across from her. Silence fell.

Slowly, holding her gaze, he stepped over the bench and sat.

Another cry erupted from the crowd. Wolves were suddenly at his shoulder and in his ear, hissing suggestions for challenges, sloshing mead. A hush fell over them when he tossed back his drink and snatched the cup of dice.

"Loser does what?" someone questioned.

Sits on my face. "Should I make you strip naked, too?"

"In your dreams, Diallo."

Got that right. "Wheelbarrow to the big fire and back."

Juno frowned. "What's a wheelbarrow?"

"You've never done a wheelbarrow?" Lukas said incredulously. Of course the twat would be hovering close by. He gestured to his buddy, who promptly dropped to a push-up position, then kicked his feet up until Lukas caught them. Lukas started running, and his buddy yelped and swore, trying to move his hands fast enough to keep up. They careened out of the longhouse with shouts and laughter following them.

Juno grinned. "Top or bottom?"

He leaned forward. "Whatever you want." He'd never meant anything more in his life.

Her eyes heated before she jerked her chin at the cup.

Killian put his palm over the top and shook the thing before dumping it on the table. The dice were carved with symbols that apparently represented the type of game to be played. Boots shuffled as everyone leaned in for a closer look.

"Personal trivia!" someone shouted. "You ask, they answer. They get it wrong, you have to give the correct answer. Two wrong guesses and you lose."

Killian leaned back and folded his arms with a smirk. His head felt light, the vise around his chest loosening with booze and camaraderie and the fact that he was going to win this thing without even trying. He'd studied Juno DeSilva like she was his college fucking major.

Juno squinted at him suspiciously. "My favorite color," she fired off.

"Purple."

After a startled blink, she nodded.

Cries erupted.

He smiled. "My squat record."

"Fourteen hundred."

He felt his eyes pop. How the hell did she know that?

A little smile quirked her mouth. "My pet peeve."

"Being told you can't do something."

Her expression faltered for a split second. "Wrong. People who say *ain't.*"

Bullshit, he told her with his eyes.

The tiny crease appeared between her brows.

"One down!" someone called.

It was his turn. "My favorite food." She'd never guess.

Her frown told him he was right. "Gloria's roast beef."

He shook his head, grinning, before abruptly realizing he had to spill the truth. He folded his arms.

"Well? What is it?" someone asked.

Fuck. "Pinkfruit."

Snorts and sniggering sounded behind him. *"What the hell is pinkfruit?"*

"He means pussy."

"Ah, yeah, then that's my favorite, too."

Suggestive whistles and laughter surrounded him. His cheeks felt hot.

"I've had pinkfruit." Magnus's voice boomed over the din. "From the jungle. Very sweet. *Very* juicy." Black brows wiggled over the rim of his tankard.

Juno narrowed her eyes at him. They were even.

"My drink of choice." He rarely drank at home, she'd never—

"Whisky."

Dammit. "Lucky guess."

She grinned and popped another of those ripe red berries in her mouth. "My middle name."

"Andréa." He even said it with an accent.

Her smile fell.

Smug and tipsy, his next question slipped out without thought. "My worst fear."

Oh, shit. She knew his worst fear. She remembered his little campfire story about losing damn near everyone he loved; he could see it all over her face. And she was going to blurt it out in front of all these wolves—

Her eyes held his. "Snakes."

She was covering for him so he could keep his tender bits shielded. His heart squeezed, and he nodded, ignoring the jocular teasing that the big, bad lion was afraid of snakes.

"My favorite movie," she said.

He knew what it was. He might sit on the floor by himself during their squad movie nights, but his ears worked just fine. "*Pretty Woman.*"

She burst out laughing. "Wrong! You lose!"

The bystanders were too drunk to notice that she hadn't revealed the correct answer, but Killian let it slide and shoved up from the bench. Juno mirrored him. Killian snagged his tankard, tossed back the entire thing, and slammed it down, wiping his beard. "Top or bottom, DeSilva?"

Her tipsy gaze flared. "Top."

"Why am I not surprised?" His low murmur was for her ears alone.

Wolves parted for him as he rounded the table. Juno positioned herself behind him, and when he dropped to the ground and donkey-kicked his feet toward her without warning, whoops and shouts almost drowned out her curse. Almost.

"Ding ding," she said, and they barreled into the night.

"Fuck!" His hands pedaled wildly to keep up with her psychotic pace, scrabbling along the dirt while she shoved at his legs. All the tankards of mead he'd slugged sloshed in his stomach as she ran him around like a drunken lawnmower. Echoes of the crowd in the longhouse receded. They raced over the dirt, heading for the big bonfire blazing by the lake. He stumbled, swore, and barely righted himself on his palms. Her laughter rang over his curses, distracting him—

His hand slipped. A guttural squawk burst out of him as the ground rushed up to meet him. His nose and chin scraped dirt, bringing them to an abrupt halt. Juno rammed into his ass, and they tumbled to the ground in a tangle of limbs. The sloppy grappling session that followed would've made Rogan scowl, but he couldn't bring himself to care. Not with Juno's laughter in his ears and her thighs straddling his chest as she slammed his back to the ground, pinning him there with a forearm. The night was black behind her, dotted with thousands of sparkling stars. The nearby fire threw shadows over her face, but he could see her smile clear as day, her chest pumping with her rapid breaths.

"*Terminator 2*," he panted.

She yanked him up by the shirt and crushed her mouth to his.

Tongues slipped. Lips slid. Was that his heart hammering against his ribs, or hers?

Her hands dove into his hair and pulled tight. "How do you know that?" She bit his lip.

He dug his fingers into the lush globes of her ass. "What?"

"The movie."

He scoffed. "I pay attention."

She cursed and came back for more.

He groaned into her mouth. "You taste like fucking strawberries."

Their kiss went nuclear. She squirmed and undulated on top of him, like she was trying to crawl inside his skin. Like she couldn't get close enough. He knew the feeling. He was seconds away from throwing her onto her back and tearing her leggings off right then and there—

A peal of laughter made them freeze. Silhouettes stumbled across the clearing, arms draped over each other.

"Shit." Juno clambered to her feet and offered him a hand, swaying slightly. They clasped forearms and she helped haul him to a stand. He loomed over her. Maybe he swayed a little, too.

She stepped back and wagged a finger. "Drinking around you is a bad idea, Diallo. A very bad idea." She shook her head, trying to clear it. "Whoa."

His protective instincts flared. "Let's go get some water and hit the sack. My sack. I mean, you hit your sack and I'll hit mine." He shook his head, too. Were the stars moving? "Not that sack. I'm not going to be hitting my sac."

Juno hunched over with a surge of giggles, ending with a little snort.

He stared at her, blinking hard to clear his vision. "Did you just snort?"

"Shut up, I'm drunk."

"Yeah, you are." He was loving every second of it.

"So are you!" She swiped at her hair.

"Not as drunk as you, sweetheart." He could watch this all night. "Let's go."

By the time they climbed their cabin steps, everything was swimming. He wrenched open the door and let her go first, mostly because he wanted to take a deep, shameless inhale as she brushed past. Which he did.

A lock of her ponytail caught in the door hinge, yanking her backward. She collided with his chest. They both grunted and stumbled in the open doorframe. Killian managed to steady her shoulders and get his own feet under him at the same time, which he thought was pretty damn impressive at the moment.

"Stupid hair." She pulled at it.

"Stop, you'll rip it." He batted her hands away and took over. Were his fingers really this fat? They felt fat, fumbling with the tangled strands.

"I know I shouldn't have it this long, anyway. I should just cut it all off." She scowled, weaving slightly in her boots.

"Your hair?"

"Yeah."

"Well, that would be a fucking crime. It's beautiful."

Juno blinked at him, lips parting in surprise. "You think so?"

Wedged into the doorframe as they were, her face was close enough for him to see the tiny flecks of copper in her dark eyes. "A blind man would think so."

That little line formed between her brows. "No, I should be more practical. I'm a fighter."

His finger was apparently just as drunk as the rest of him, because it came up to trace her frown line all on its own. "You're a woman, too." He went back to untangling her hair.

She huffed a laugh. "I spend so much time trying to get people to look past that, sometimes I forget it."

His eyes rolled so far back in his head he almost saw the inside of his own skull. "I'd give my left nut to forget it."

"What?"

"I'd love to forget that you're a beautiful woman." He picked moodily at her hair. "It'd make my life a hell of a lot easier."

Seconds ticked by in the throbbing silence.

"You think I'm a beautiful woman?" It was a husky whisper.

A more sober male would've kept his eyes on his task. Killian swung his head around to take in the bones of her face, the tawny color of her skin. The beauty mark by the corner of her mouth that was begging for his lips. "I think you're the most beautiful woman I've ever seen in my life."

Shock slackened her expression.

"And one of the scariest fighters." He pointed a finger at her. "You can be both, you know. You don't have to give up one for the other." He was very wise in his sodden state.

She was quiet as he picked at her knotted hair until it finally came free. "There." When he tucked the slightly mangled strands over her shoulder to join the rest of her ponytail, his fingers grazed the side of her neck.

Electricity zinged through him at that simple touch. *Warning, warning!* He took a hurried step backward and rammed his spine into the doorframe. The twinge of pain barely registered—he was too busy watching goosebumps appear on Juno's silky skin, radiating from the point where his fingertips had brushed her neck.

It took everything he had to keep his back pressed against the door. His entire body was demanding that he lick that spot. Drag her against him and wrap that luscious hair around his fist, hold her in place so he could feel her pebbled flesh against his tongue.

She spun away with a muttered thanks and headed for her bed, where she collapsed onto her stomach. The gorgeous globes of her ass were a gift and a torture device all at once. The mattress bounced. His dick bounced, too.

"Water," he croaked. If he sounded like a man dying of thirst, and it wasn't far from the truth.

Juno made a questioning noise into her pillow. Despite the steel rod in his pants, Killian grinned.

The Maneater was cute when she was drunk.

He made sure she drank three glasses of water before falling face first onto her bed again. He tugged off her boots and left them on the floor before shuffling to his side of the room and collapsing onto his back on his own mattress, which squeaked wildly. His legs sprawled.

Muffled, unintelligible words floated across the room.

He lifted his heavy skull. "Huh?"

Juno flipped her head around on her pillow. Dark eyes focused fuzzily on him. "What's pinkfruit like?"

He grinned at the gently spinning ceiling. The lamp on her nightstand cast little light over the room, leaving most of it in shadow. "Little sweet, little tart. Really juicy." His mouth watered.

Her mattress creaked as she rolled onto her side to face him. There was a pause. "How juicy?"

The amount of sex poured into those two words should've been illegal. His dick tented his sweatpants.

"How juicy, Diallo?"

His dick swelled even more. He could practically see the thing under his waistband. He slid his teammate a look. "Stop flirting with me, DeSilva."

Her mouth curved. "Why?"

Jesus, his head was already fuzzy, and if she kept looking at him with those heavy-lidded eyes... "Because I'm about to do something about it."

All the air left the room. His heart hammered in his ears. He was drunk, he needed to keep his mouth shut—

The scent of her arousal bloomed in the silence. "Like what?"

Oh, fuck.

His mead-muddled brain swirled with dark, filthy images. Fantasies. Things he really, really shouldn't say out loud. "Like bend you over that bed."

Their gazes locked across the shadowed room. Her pulse jumped in her neck.

"What if I didn't want to be bent over?"

"Then, I'd yank you to the edge of it." His cock surged behind his pants. Her eyes held him hostage. "Drop to my knees. Run my hands all over your gorgeous fucking body."

Slowly, she lifted a hand to her breast, kneaded once, then slid her palm over her ribs, to the curve of her waist, across her flat stomach. Heading south.

His heart thundered. "I'd spread your knees apart."

Chocolate eyes burned into his. Then, with excruciating slowness, she rolled to her back, keeping her head turned to face him, and raised one knee. Her hand rested on her lower abs, rising and falling faster.

His mouth was dry. His dick was already weeping for her. "Wider, Juno."

For the first time in her life, she did what he told her.

Fuck. Fuck. His fuzzy brain shorted out entirely. "Then, I'd touch you."

She waited.

"I'd run my finger down, down, all the way down." He watched her hand disappear beneath the waistband of her leggings. "I'd dip inside and feel how wet you were."

Holding his gaze, she moved her hand, the black fabric of her leggings stretching, hiding everything and masking nothing. She sucked in a breath.

"Are you wet for me?"

She nodded.

Fuck me. "Of course you are."

She narrowed her eyes, but she didn't sass him, didn't take her hand out of her pants, didn't put a stop to this thing, and fuck if he was in any shape to be a hero.

His voice was rough as rock in the dim room. "I'd drag that wetness all over everything, making it all slick. Especially your clit."

Her hand moved ever so slightly beneath her leggings. Her lips parted.

He practically swallowed his tongue, his cock straining. "Is your clit slippery?"

She nodded, her mouth opening further.

He groaned and gave up, sliding his own hand under his pants. When he gripped his raging erection, another groan tumbled out of him, loud and long in the silent cabin. He wrenched his eyes open to find Juno staring at his hand beneath his waistband. Her own hand moved quickly under her leggings.

"I'd circle your clit faster and faster." When a hard breath fluttered past her lips, he gave his dick a long, firm stroke and groaned again. His head was still blurry, but he saw her with laser clarity, breasts heaving under her shirt, finger circling rapidly. He stroked himself again, starting up a rhythm, dragging the wetness from the tip all over his length. Imagining himself drawing his dick across her slick center, coating himself in her. "And when that little bud swelled up..." Her lids drifted shut. His hand squeezed and stroked, building pace. "When it swelled, and I knew it was close to blowing..." He pumped himself harder, faster, drowning in her scent, thick and honeyed in the air between them. "I'd lick it."

A little sound escaped her. Her free hand came up to squeeze her breast while her fingers moved under the fabric.

Fuck, he was going to lose it. "I'd lick it, and lick it, I'd bury my face in that pussy, I'd rub my tongue all over that clit until you fucking *scream*—"

Her cry rang through the shadowed room, bursting out of her while her body clenched up tight, mouth falling open, eyes squeezing shut as her hand moved feverishly under her leggings.

Her scent surged, and Killian was gone.

He came with a shout, working himself with hard, frenzied strokes. Pleasure exploded behind his eyeballs, blinding him to everything but the feel of his slick hand and the scent of her arousal tunneling into his brain. His lion roared inside, wanting more. Wanting everything.

When he came back down to earth, it was to the faint sound of Juno's heavy breath from across the room. He opened his eyes and stared at the wood planks above him. His brain was even more muddled now, spinning with mead and pleasure and some tiny, flickering feeling that he'd royally fucked up.

He chanced a glance at her. She stared at the ceiling with the same shocked realization on her face. Without looking, she reached over and turned off the lamp, plunging them into darkness.

CHAPTER 29

orning dawned all too soon, along with the cold light of reality.

What did they do?

Juno pressed a hand to her pounding eyeballs. Her fingers carried a lingering trace of her own sex. She dropped her hand like it was on fire.

A groan floated from the other side of the room.

Squinting one-eyed, she watched Killian lurch upright, his hair even more tangled than usual. "Fuck me." His voice could've ground glass.

I feel like I almost did.

What the hell was she thinking? Getting wasted, making out with her squadmate, then *mutually masturbating to completion?*

Touch-hunger, that's what it was. She really needed to get laid. And stay far away from the mead. She sat up and clutched her throbbing head. "Oh, my God."

"You gonna hurl?"

"No, but my head's going to explode." Gripping her hair to keep her skull from rolling off her neck, she took him in. "You don't look as bad as I feel."

"Trust me, I'm feeling pretty fucking rough."

Their bleary gazes met. She snorted, then snickered. He gave a weak chuckle.

I think you're the most beautiful woman I've ever seen in my life.

Their smiles died, and suddenly all she could think about was his rough voice floating across the room while her fingers slipped and slid—

"We should check the perimeter." Get outside, get some fresh air, get the blood moving. Back to the job and away from temptation.

You don't have to give up one for the other.

"Yeah. Right. I'll take west."

"Cool."

They dressed in silence, moving carefully. For more reasons than one.

The wolves were not done partying. They made it very clear that the celebration would continue at nightfall. Apparently, they didn't suffer hangovers from their own mead because all of them were chipper as ever, going about their chores as usual and teasing Juno goodnaturedly about her performance during the drinking game. Rescuing a wolf kid, belching, and reciting a dirty poem were apparently the way to the Pack's collective heart.

It had been fun. Really fun. Even playing with Killian had been fun, though he'd shocked the hell out of her by knowing all that stuff about her.

They'd swept the perimeter that morning and found nothing. Which was a good thing. She totally was not hoping for some vicious demon attacks to take her mind off of how mind-blowingly sexy her squadmate was.

He'd been splitting wood at the edge of the village that

afternoon, shirt off and sweat gleaming on acres of muscle. She'd busied herself elsewhere. Maybe it really was time to proposition one of the wolves. Could Lukas keep it chill?

Her belly squirmed at the thought.

The central bonfire roared like a blazing mountain that night, bigger and brighter than Juno had ever seen it. Torches flickered along the lake, glowing paper lanterns floated on the glassy water, shouts and laughter bounced off of trees and cabins. Someone played a raucous fiddle, another pounded on a drum, and the notes of a penny whistle floated on the crisp breeze, which carried the mouthwatering scents of berry pies and sweet honey mead.

A bit of that liquid sloshed out of the tankard someone shoved into Juno's empty hand, and she leaped back, laughing. "I'm pacing myself tonight!"

"Oh, kitty can't hold her liquor? They must water it down in the big city!"

She gave them a scathing retort, but her amusement faded as she pictured the Pyramid's stunning crystal decanters filled with shimmering golden liquid. Her father would never allow Silka to be diluted. It was written into every distribution contract.

"*A thing of such beauty should never be cut,*" he would say, swirling a glass beneath his nose.

Funny, he never seemed to have a problem cutting *her* down.

Someone stepped on her toe, jolting her out of her brooding thoughts. People were dancing, silhouettes writhing like black wraiths against the roaring bonfire.

Part of her twitched at the idea that there could be real wraiths out there, creeping through the forest while the wolves partied. But she and Killian had agreed on one more night off from patrol. They'd gained a massive step toward camaraderie, there weren't any other signs of looming attacks, and the second part of their mission was just as important: Build trust, make friends.

But no drinking games tonight. And certainly no other games back in their cabin.

She couldn't keep her gaze from sliding over to Killian's enormous frame near the mead barrels, where he stood flanked by a pair of jocular sentries. She could guess what kind of stories those sentries were trading based on their occasional bursts of laughter and bro-shoving, not to mention the way they eyed any female who sauntered past. Killian stood stoically between them, his arms crossed.

A blonde female stopped in front of them, no doubt tossing out a saucy response to the sentry's appreciative whistle. But it wasn't the sentry that held her interest. She cocked her head in that wolfish way, bluntly scanning Killian's muscled frame.

A scraping sound made Juno's ears ring. Her claws had shot out, dragging against the metal tankard she held in a death grip.

You were jealous. Admit it.

Killian's face was in shadow, so she couldn't see his expression as the blonde eased closer. But he didn't back away.

Her cat hissed.

Say it.

She tipped her head back and drained her entire mug of mead. Sweet and somehow earthy, it slid down her throat and warmed her belly. Maybe it would drown the green monster that had taken root there.

"Impressive."

She lowered her empty mug to find Lukas watching her. His dark hair was tousled, and she caught the flash of his teeth as he grinned.

"Remind me not to challenge you to a chugging contest."

"Challenge me to anything you want." That female was easing closer, and Killian still wasn't backing away.

"All right, then. A dance." Lukas's hand appeared before her.

Right. Touch-hunger. Here was her opportunity to get rid of it.

She set her empty mug on a nearby stump and put her palm into his.

His expression was wicked and playful as he backed toward the bonfire, tugging her along. Without warning, he swung her into a wide circle, and she stifled a shriek as her boots nearly left the earth. Lukas laughed, spinning and twirling her until she was dizzy, shouting when she bumped into other dancers, all of them bouncing off of each other like pinballs. He yanked her close and then sent her out again, tethered by his strong, sure grip. When he grabbed both her wrists and spun her in another wide arc, she let her head fall back and marveled at the streaks of brilliant color in the night sky. Ice blue, electric green, turquoise and cerulean and teal, all undulating like enormous neon ribbons among a thousand sparkling stars.

Lukas eased to a stop, his chest pumping. His scent was crisp and clean, with a masculine edge beneath it as he tugged her away from the roaring fire. "Come on, you can see them better in the dark."

Juno's eyes slid toward the mead barrels. Killian and the blonde were gone.

Smothering the burning sensation in her stomach, she let Lukas lead her along the lakeshore and around a bend. The aurora danced overhead, crystal clear and so breathtaking that all Juno could do was tilt her head back and stare.

"There's a story about them." Lukas's deep voice rumbled beside her, his shoulder warm against hers. "In the beginning, the father wolf roamed the skies, all alone. He didn't know what loneliness was, but he knew he was searching for something. And how do wolves search? We dig." He nodded toward the looming mountains. "The lakes and valleys are his holes. The mountains are the dirt left behind." Juno smiled at that, and she caught his answering grin out of the corner of her eye. "So, he prowled the earth, searching, digging. And finally, he got so lonely he sat down and howled his despair to the sky." He lifted his chin and did exactly that, a melodious wolf's howl thrumming from his human throat, floating into the night. A couple distant calls answered. He lowered his head to twinkle at her. "His song painted the sky with huge swaths of color. And the mother wolf, who was wandering the other end of the earth in her own loneliness, followed the lights to him." His voice dropped to a murmur. "The stars are their children. And the ones that fall become…us."

Something in her chest ached a little. "That's very beautiful."

"Yes, it is." He wasn't looking at the sky.

You're a woman, too. A very beautiful woman.

She turned to face him. His hand slid around to cup her head. When his mouth lowered to hers, she didn't pull away. There was absolutely no reason she shouldn't kiss him. She needed this touch, needed to take the edge off this hunger so she wasn't tempted to do stupid shit with her squadmate. And Lukas was attractive, charming, and uncomplicated.

Just what she wanted.

Her lips parted beneath his, and he changed his angle, his tongue sweeping into her mouth like silk. Her cat stirred at the feel of it, so incredibly smooth, like hot, wet satin stroking hers. She'd never kissed a wolf. He tasted crisp and earthy, with a hint of tartness, like biting into a juniper berry. She ran her hands along his torso, up his chest. A pleasant hum built in her veins…

And went nowhere.

Deep inside, her cat stretched, yawned, and sat back on its

haunches. And her mind replayed a rough voice floating across a dim cabin.

Is your clit slippery?

Lukas lifted his head. "You're not into this."

She bit back a curse. "It's not you."

"Oh, I know that." His smirk was cocky, but disappointment shimmered in his eyes as he eased back. "Is it the lion?"

"It's my problem, that's what it is."

"Meow."

"Fuck off." But she huffed a laugh. "You remind me of Wolf." And now, she felt slightly gross about kissing him.

"Who?"

"Wolf. Fennimore?" When he only frowned, she raised her brows. "The guy Magnus kicked out of here a while back?"

But Lukas's easy vibe had vanished. "Do you mean Fennimore Magnussen?"

She frowned. "Magnussen…"

His tone was urgent. "Have you seen Fenn?"

Her cat pricked its ears, wary and alert. She stepped back, instinct telling her to tread carefully. "Wolf Fennimore is my squadmate."

Lukas shook his head, crowding her space again. "I've never heard of any Wolf Fennimore. But Fennimore Magnussen is Magnus's cousin, and he went missing five years ago."

A block of ice settled in the pit of her stomach. Any trace of honey mead evaporated from her brain. "What?"

"Do you have a picture of him? Your squadmate?"

She took another step back. "No."

"Yes, you do." He came forward urgently, his scent sharp. The world flashed green. He gripped her elbow, scanning her body as if looking for a stash of photos. "Come on, Juno—"

As her claws pricked through her skin, a crunch of pebbles sounded nearby, and Killian strode around the bend. He lasered in on Lukas's hand on her arm.

She didn't know he could move so fast.

Killian's fist slammed into Lukas's nose. The crunch of bone echoed by the quiet lake, and Lukas's feral snarl answered a second before he threw a right hook into Killian's temple. The metallic smell of blood rose in the night air, along with the elevated scents of both men—Lukas, sharp and crisp, and Killian, hot, musky…and just underneath, a layer of something feminine.

Juno's claws shot out, and she didn't bother sheathing them as she reached into the tangle of muscle to wrench the males apart. "For fuck's sake!" Her cat was in her voice, wild enough to draw their attention, giving her the split second she needed to plant a hand on each taut chest and shove. They parted, breaths whistling through flared nostrils, animalistic eyes flashing.

"Keep your fucking hands off her." Killian's growl was all lion.

"I'll tell him if I want him to keep his hands off me." She wanted to rip her squadmate's head off and chuck it in the lake. Maybe it would wash off the delicate scent clinging to his hair. "Diallo, we need to talk. Lukas, go back to the party." Without giving either of them a chance to dive back into the brawl, she strode away along the lakeshore, quivering with fury.

The instant she felt Killian's hot breath on her neck, she spun, spraying pebbles, and pointed in the general direction of the scuffle. "That was some bullshit."

"Damn right it was."

She rolled her eyes. "I meant you going ballistic. I can handle a wolf."

"He was handling *you*."

Her temper flared. "Maybe I wanted him handling me. You smell like you've been handling someone yourself." She folded her arms. "So, who was it?" She waved it off like she wasn't *this close* to gutting every female in the entire village and smelling them later. "Never mind. Whatever. We have bigger issues—"

"Bigger issues than what?"

Her brain stuttered. "What? Nothing. Never mind—"

"You have an issue with me being with one of these females?" His big chest pumped.

"No." It just made her want to punch someone's throat. "We both need to burn it off, like we said." But even as the words left her mouth, she realized the feminine scent wasn't deep enough on his skin. If they'd had sex, it would be a lot stronger.

Her eyes lifted to his. She felt suddenly short of breath. "But you didn't."

He stepped close. When he leaned down, she didn't shove him back. His beard rasped against the shell of her ear as he took a long, slow inhale. "You, either."

The heat of him was doing something to her brain. "My cat didn't want him."

"Mine didn't want her."

They stared at each other for a long, throbbing moment, as all the oxygen vanished from the earth.

She leaped on him.

Their mouths collided, hot and angry and desperate. She fisted his hair. His fingers dug into her ass, hiking her up so her legs could wrap around him, his tongue sweeping against hers. His erection was a rod of steel between them, pressing against the laughable barrier of her leggings as he stumbled blindly away from the distant bonfire and sounds of the raucous celebration, his growl vibrating against her all the while.

Her back hit a tree, and she opened her eyes long enough to realize he'd walked them into the woods before he leaned his hips against her, and her eyes rolled back in her head. He was enormous, hard as iron, and pressing against her in just the right spot. She wrapped her legs tighter around his hips and ground herself into him. They both swore.

One hand left her ass to slide up her ribcage, palming her breast and squeezing, kneading. His hands were so big, so warm. She yanked his hair, hard, knowing he could take it, knowing he would like it—

His growl turned into a snarl, and she felt the sting of his teeth at the hollow of her neck. Her body went electric. She sucked in a breath and felt the hot, wet glide of his tongue on her skin.

Some distant part of her brain stirred enough to make her pull on his hair again until he looked at her. His cheekbones stood out in the moonlight, carved and dangerous. "Just sex."

"No shit." He dragged his tongue up her throat, his hips surging against her in a relentless, powerful wave.

Oh, God… "Just once. And—"

It was her turn to have her hair gripped, her head pulled back. "Shut. *Up.*"

His mouth covered hers, his tongue invaded her mouth, and the last shred of her common sense was obliterated. His palm slid under her shirt, calluses rasping against her bare skin. He jerked at the front zip of her bra. There was the faint snapping sound of the zipper breaking, and then the bra split in half and his hand was on her and she was panting into his mouth. He rolled his erection against her and brought his other palm up to knead both of her breasts with hot, strong hands. The rough bark of the tree scraped her back through her rucked-up shirt, little flashes of pain lighting up her nerve endings.

She shoved her hands under his shirt, marveling at the ridges of clenching muscle. "Fuck, Diallo." He was incredible.

He tore his mouth from hers and leaned back just enough to whip off his shirt, keeping her pinned to the tree with his hips, the undulating movement of his sculpted torso making her mouth go dry. He was beautiful. She'd been against this body countless times, sparring, training, but now, she let herself run her hands over him slowly. He was suede over steel, his smell earthy and wild around her. She was already soaked.

Her hand slid between them to grip his shaft through his pants. He made a feral sound, head tilted to the sky, tendons standing out in his corded throat. Then, he grabbed the neckline of her shirt and ripped it in two.

Their naked torsos crashed together, and the rough golden hair on his chest grazed her nipples, wrenching another groan from her even as his mouth covered hers once more. She gave his shaft a firm stroke, her core gushing at the feel of him, huge and hard and hot.

He pulled her legs from his hips. Her boots hit the pine needles. There was a swift tug, then a rush of cool air on her bare ass, and then her leggings were around her knees and his hand was between her legs and one hard, thick finger slipped through her soaked folds to slide deep inside.

A groan escaped her as her eyelids drifted shut. Killian made his own desperate noise, then his finger was thrusting deep, stroking her inner walls until he hit the spot that made her cry out. With a growl of satisfaction, another finger joined the first, and he worked her hard, stroking that spot ruthlessly while his naked chest pinned her to the tree and his tongue flicked the hollow of her neck.

She exploded around his fingers, drenching them, a cry wrenching from her open mouth as fireworks flashed behind her eyes. His teeth closed around the tendon in her neck, his growl vibrating against her throat, his fingers driving her up, up, up, giving her no reprieve. She came again, gushing into his hand.

His breath was hot against her neck, his heart thundering against hers. "Fuck." He slipped his fingers from her sheath while she reached for his waistband. Her eyes flared as she freed his erection. He was enormous, magnificently thick and arrowed straight at her, his plump head glistening with a crystal drop. She wrapped her hand around him and groaned at the feel of him in her palm. He let his head fall back again, revealing his thick throat, and she rose on tiptoe, leggings around her knees, wetness dripping down her thighs, to lick the trickle of sweat that rolled toward his collarbone.

He took her to the ground.

Strong male. Powerful male.

Her back hit the pine needles, and then he was yanking her boots from her feet, ripping off her leggings, tossing them aside. His face was fierce, those rawboned features standing out starkly in his passion, his hair a wild mane around his shoulders as he shoved his pants down his hips.

Wariness flared to life. She rolled them, landing on top and pinning him to the ground with a hand on his chest.

Better. She was on top. She was in control.

Their eyes met as she split her thighs wide over his hips, wrapped her hand around his thick length, and impaled herself with one quick, deep thrust.

Stars exploded in her body, in her brain, in her blood. Her jaw dropped as she clutched his shoulders and stared down at him.

That was…this was…

"Holy fuck," he rasped, the same shock reflected in his eyes.

And then, he let loose.

His fingers dug into her ass, pulling her into each pounding thrust with a savagery that made her shout with pleasure, his thick cock hitting the perfect spot over and over until she was one endless, buzzing orgasm, a rolling electric current.

He surged upright and wrapped a big arm around her as if he was about to flip them. She planted a hand on his pec to stop him. Their eyes met. He tensed again, ready to spin her to the ground. She shoved at his chest, shaking her head.

"No. Like this."

His eyes narrowed before he fell to his back and jacked his knees up, knocking her forward. Her hands landed next to his head, one breast inches from his lips, and he opened his mouth over the tip before thrusting into her again.

She swore. He was solid as rock and driving into her like he wasn't holding anything back. She pushed upright, her nipple slipping from his lips with a wet pop, and rode him hard, squeezing her eyes shut, hearing the slick slap of their bodies pounding into each other, smelling forest and sex and *him*—

"Look at me." A harsh demand.

Defiance flared, and she ignored his command, riding him faster.

There was a hard yank on her ponytail. She wrenched it free and glared down at him, even as she ran wetter.

His claws pricked her thighs. Their eyes locked, bodies still.

"Now."

He drove into her, and she came instantly.

With a growl of pure male triumph, he pounded into her faster, wilder, all control gone. Her claws raked his chest. He threw back his head, his neck straining as he roared his own release into the night.

Then, he reared up and bit her.

CHAPTER 30

Mate.

Oh fuck. What had he done?

Killion's lion roared its approval as he stared blindly over Juno's shoulder, trying to keep his heart from beating out of his ribcage. Her silky core clenched his cock like a hot, wet fist. His brain whirled, trying to latch on to anything but the scent of her, the feel of her, the sense of his entire world sliding into place.

Mate.

Oh, God, no.

His teeth were still in her flesh, right in that gorgeous curve where her neck met her shoulder. Marking her.

MATE. MINE. PERFECT. MORE.

He pulled his mouth away on a harsh inhale, lifted her off his protesting cock, and scrambled to his feet. Pine needles stuck to his bare ass as he stood, stumbling over a stick or a rock or who the hell knew…

All he did know was that she was sprawled naked on the dirt, and she'd felt better than anything in his entire life, and he was so, so fucked.

MATE. MINE.

No, no, no.

He stared at her, his heart racing, and she stared back, looking almost as stunned as he felt.

He had to get out of here. Now.

"I'm going up the mountain," he blurted, jacking up his pants and looking anywhere but her. "To see if I can find anything."

"What—"

He took off, his dick still twitching and his lion clawing his insides to shreds.

CHAPTER 31

N o, he didn't.

Juno stared at the enormous back stomping away into the darkness, each heavy footstep hitting her like a slap.

No, he *fucking* didn't.

Killian Diallo just fucked her and left her.

Killian Diallo just gave her the hottest sex of her *life*, then left her bare ass in the dirt.

She looked around for her leggings, yanked them on, then snatched her bra from the ground, only to find its zipper busted and hanging from a few pathetic threads.

She picked up her shirt. Well, she picked up half of her shirt. The other half lay a few yards away.

Hottest. Sex. Of her life.

Killian's shirt lay wadded on the ground. Cursing, she pulled it on, instantly surrounded by his scent and the lingering warmth of his body. She stuffed her feet into her boots, sizzling with fury. And the tingling aftershocks of the *hottest sex of her life*.

She stalked back toward the village, holding on to every

last ounce of control. It was either that or she'd start scream-ing. Or murdering. Or something a lot worse.

The Maneater did not cry. Certainly not because of some moronic male.

The party was still in full swing when she rounded the bend of the lake, but Lukas's expression was anything but jovial as he stood with folded arms at the edge of camp.

"Magnus wants to see you." His eyes raked over her, and his nose twitched, but he just turned and strode toward the alpha's cabin. With a vicious inward curse, Juno followed.

Magnus stopped pacing his living room the second she entered. He cast a glance over her, drowning in Killian's shirt, her hair mussed, the bite mark still stinging on her neck. And her teammate conspicuously absent.

Humiliation threatened. She beat it back.

Magnus pinned her with his freaky arctic gaze. "I hear you have something of mine, female."

This was the wrong time to pull alpha male bullshit. Juno squared off, ticking her chin up. "I have a squadmate named Wolf Fennimore."

"Where did you find him?"

"He found us. He'd been trailing us for months, showing up on our patrols." Watching them fight invisible enemies. "He finally convinced Rogan to let him join." She folded her arms and shrugged, Killian's shirt hanging around her like a blanket, making her feel small. She hated feeling small. "All we knew was that he was a crazy lone wolf who wanted a job. He said he got kicked out of the Pack and couldn't go back."

Magnus muttered something foreign.

"He's your cousin?"

"Our fathers were brothers." Magnus wiped a palm over his black beard, making the jaws of the wolf tattoo flex around his temple. "They both died in the accident."

Juno vaguely remembered hearing something about a

mountain logging catastrophe in her early adulthood, but she hadn't paid much attention. Lots of wolves had died, she remembered that much.

"He was always such a wild little shit. Never listened to anyone, wouldn't follow rules."

That sounded like Wolf, all right. "Is that why you kicked him out?"

Arctic eyes flashed. "I didn't kick him out. The *drittsekk* disappeared. When the trail went cold, we thought he was..." Something besides anger flickered across his face. "Do you have a picture?"

The space around her suddenly felt vast as a canyon, with her standing in the center, painfully alone. *Dammit, Diallo.*

Juno pulled out her phone and scrolled through its photo reel before landing on a picture from last summer. She showed it to Magnus, who swore.

The cabin door swung open, and Astrid's blonde head appeared, followed by a blast of laughter and wild music. Her grin fell instantly. "What is it?" She shut the door firmly behind her.

Magnus gestured to Juno. "Show her."

Juno handed over her phone, pulled up to a selfie of her and Wolf. His long arm was outstretched to get the right angle, tongue sticking out of his mouth while she pretended to punch him in the face.

Astrid went white as a sheet. Her purple eyes snagged Juno's.

"He's our teammate," Juno said. Rogan was going to shit a brick.

"The idiot told them I kicked him out." Magnus's beast flashed under his skin, feral wolf beneath human bones. She'd seen the same thing countless times with other shifters, but something about Magnus's wolf made the hairs on Juno's arms stand up. "And gave them a fake name, like a fucking coward." The coffee table trembled violently. He looked at Juno. "I want to talk to him."

Holding his gaze was not easy. "I'll ask."

"*Ask?*"

"Yes. I'll ask if he wants to talk to you."

"You would keep me from one of my own?" His low tone suggested it was a very, very stupid thing to do.

"He's one of ours, now. We'll tell him you want to talk. If he wants to, he will. If not..." She lifted a shoulder.

Power crackled from the alpha. His upper lip peeled back. "Careful, cat."

A thrill of alarm shivered down her spine. She'd faced a lot of opponents in the Arena, but Magnus was his own kind of scary. And she was outnumbered. And alone.

Because her teammate left her in the woods like a piece of trash.

Yeah, definitely the wrong time to try to intimidate her. "Sounds like he left of his own free will. In our squad, we don't force anyone to do anything. I'll let him know you want to talk."

His eyes flashed. "Just when I thought we were becoming friends."

Tension snapped to life, filling the cabin with a thrum of danger that put her cat on high alert. *Threat.*

"I'll let you know if Wolf wants to talk." Meeting each of their predatory stares, she backed out the door, then sped across the raging party toward her cabin, vibrating from anger and shock and something perilously close to heartache.

She was going to kill them both.

CHAPTER 32

One of the wolves knocked into Juno's shoulder as they passed, making her fumble the stack of dishes she was carrying. Her curse was lost under the cacophony of plates clattering to the floor. A few people glanced over, but nobody offered to lend a hand. Surprise, surprise.

Word traveled fast in the Den.

Any points they'd scored with Elvi's rescue were obliterated by the news that her squad had been sheltering the missing Pack member they'd all considered as good as dead. Well, it wasn't so much the sheltering that pissed them off, it was more the fact that the squad wasn't forcing his return.

Rogan was stunned when she'd relayed the news, but days later, he still stood by Wolf's refusal to talk to Magnus. "Squad first. I don't know what the hell happened, but he doesn't want to talk, and I'm not getting in the middle of that shit."

Which meant *she* was in the middle of it.

Gritting her teeth, she gathered the plates from the floor and dumped them in the commercial dishwasher, ignoring the icy glares of the other wolves on kitchen duty that day.

Sweat dampened her brow, and she wiped the back of her hand across her forehead, focusing on the one thing that had kept her sane the past few days.

All the ways she was going to make Killian Diallo pay.

What was he doing, up there on the mountain? Frolicking in the flowers? Warming his feet by the fire? Blowing off steam with some demon fights while she was stuck here doing bitch work, getting knocked around by the same people she was here to protect?

She'd start with a punch to his throat…

Another wolf jostled her as she left the cookhouse, heading for the obstacle course. "Go home, cat."

She couldn't go home. Rogan wouldn't let her. "I need you two to stay put. Forget about the Wolf thing, just figure out where these attacks are coming from. I have a bad feeling about them." A pause. "A bad feeling about a lot of stuff."

They'd found more drones hovering around Light House and had beefed up their security tech as best they could, but legally removing the boarding school from the Magistrate also meant removing it from his money. The squad members each brought their own savings with them when they defected, but funds were dwindling fast. Plus, they were apparently getting harassed by MLE officers on the streets.

"He's spreading shit about us." Rogan's voice had been clipped, but Juno knew he had to be in pain. Having a father figure turn on you would do that. "And we're not finding anything on our patrols. Maybe Inara's pulled her minions back, but that doesn't explain the rest. It's like the demons are all biding their time, waiting for something. I don't like it." A pause, then a tight sigh. "You two good?"

Ha. "Fine."

"Good. Hang in there. Find that hellmouth so you can come home. And try to make nice, if you can. We can't afford to make enemies of the Pack."

Oh, sure, fine. Easy. She'd just protect the village, smooth over an epic extended-family feud, and solve a multiple-murder mystery all by herself. While her teammate was off doing fuck knew what, fuck knew where.

Punch to the throat, then knee to the balls, she thought, stomping through the woods toward the training run. Then, maybe she'd grab a fistful of that hair and give it a brutal pull, yanking his head backward, exposing that thick throat so she could jump up and sink her teeth into it.

Her blood heated at the thought.

The obstacle course was empty. She sighed in relief, rolling her neck at the starting line. Birds chirped, and a couple of faebugs drifted past, little black blobs in the daylight.

She set a punishing pace for herself, running the course like she had a big, invisible competitor chomping at her heels. What she wouldn't give to whoop Diallo's ass on this course. But he didn't give two shits about it, and he'd only snorted when Astrid challenged him to race against one of the sentries, like he didn't care what they thought of him. Must be nice.

She pictured him marching around on that mountain, stomping through the glowing undergrowth, swiping at branches. Was his touch-hunger back? Was he edgy, agitated, running hot? She was, and it had only been a few days.

Fucking Diallo.

It felt good to run. She let everything else fall away, diving deep into her physical body. Muscle, breath, heartbeat. Wind on her skin. Sweat in her hair. Air in her lungs. Sweet, blessed relief from all the shit swirling in her brain.

She burst out of the trees and sprinted for the finish line, only to find a familiar face smirking at her.

She skidded to a halt, trying to pretend she wasn't winded.

Val smiled at her. "You're fast."

Her nose flared with her breaths, and his scent flooded her nostrils, hard and biting, with a metallic edge that set her on high alert. That sharp, scraping note reminded her of some of the opponents she'd faced in the Arena. The crazy ones.

"Where's your lion?" Val continued.

"Scouting."

"Hmm. Been gone a while."

She didn't like the glint in his eye. "We're trying to figure out where these attacks are coming from."

Something flashed across his expression, but was quickly smothered. "Ah. Yeah. Almost forgot that's why you're here. Seems like you've been doing more dishes than anything."

Keep your claws in.

"You do get back to your cabin late, though."

A chill went through her.

"What are you doing in the forest all night, city cat?" His tongue rubbed his lower lip.

"What are you doing watching my cabin?" She allowed her claws to pierce her skin, extending them slowly, letting him see.

It didn't escape his notice. He smiled again. "Just looking out for mine. What's left of it, anyway." His smile fell, his face contorting. "I don't know why Magnus lets you stay. You're hiding something. Our people are in danger, and you're hiding something." His eyes went wolf. "He still says you're hands-off, though."

She held his gaze. "Smart of him."

He smirked.

Anger boiled up inside her. This wolf had no clue who she was, what she'd seen, what she was capable of. How thin the thread of her self-control was, growing more and more fragile by the minute. Her fangs extended. The world went green. Her eyes flicked to Val's midsection, taut with muscle but still soft, still vulnerable. It took every last ounce of restraint to hold herself back.

Was this how Killian felt all the time?

The thought of him made her snarl. Val answered with his own.

The thread snapped.

They collided in a flurry of muscle and bone, claws and teeth, fury and fangs. Pain lit up her shoulder blade, her lower back, her glute. He was viciously fast, slicing through her thermal shirt with a speed she hadn't expected.

Which, naturally, pissed her off even more.

She was failing her mission, her squad was in trouble, she was surrounded by angry wolves who treated her like crap, and she'd let this asshole get close enough to take a slice out of her.

And Killian Diallo fucked me and left me in the dirt.

She went off like a bomb.

She tore into cloth and flesh, spilling blood, smelling it, tasting it as she sank her fangs into whatever she could reach. Everything was a blur—pain, rage, and triumph blending together in a green haze of fury. Visions of dead wolves, an angry alpha, a hard, golden body flashed across her mind while she tore into her opponent with the kind of brutality that had made her a name in the seedy underbelly of the city.

Maneater. Maneater.

And then, suddenly, she was flying backward through the air.

Her spine hit a tree trunk, knocking the wind out of her and clearing her head as she fell to the ground.

Magnus stood between her and a bloody, savaged body lying immobile on the ground.

Oh, shit.

The alpha's enormous frame swelled, his muscles expanding, the wolf tattoo writhing over his torso like it was alive. Veins lit up beneath his skin, pale blue and humming with a kind of power that sent primal fear spearing through her.

"Get *OUT!*" he roared.

The Maneater fucking ran.

Trees uprooted as she sprinted past. Towering sequoias and redwoods fell like massive dominoes around her, shaking the earth, the boom of their falls battering her eardrums as she dodged and leaped and ran, ran, ran.

She burst into jaguar form and tore through the forest, Magnus Magnussen's bellow of rage giving her paws otherworldly speed.

CHAPTER 33

Killian was going out of his goddamn mind.

He stomped through another crystal clear brook. Frigid water seeped into his boots. He'd brought a stack of clothes with him and stashed them in a cave halfway up the mountain, but hadn't thought to bring a change of shoes. His feet were frozen. He marched on, leaving wet footprints on the ground. The cold barely registered, anyway. All he could think about was her.

Mate. Take mate. Claim mate. NOW.

She's not our mate. Never will be. Get it out of your head.

His lion took a swipe at him deep inside.

Even if he wanted to, he couldn't just claim her as his mate. The bond was a two-way street. Both of them had to want it, accept it, open themselves up to it. Juno DeSilva would never do that.

Would she?

Jesus fucking Christ. He shoved that terrifying thought out of his brain and kept walking, sucking in oxygen-rich air, breathing in the scent of the pines and the fragrant blue flowers that carpeted the ground. Every step crushed them beneath his boot, releasing a sweet perfume that trailed behind him like a cloud.

Nothing overrode the warm, spicy scent that had embedded itself into his brain. Even the thunderous storms that raged across the mountain each night didn't wash it away. He was ready to grab a fistful of these flowers and scrub his face with them, shove them up his nose, anything to escape.

Take mate.

Fuck.

The image of her sprawled on the ground, wet pussy gleaming in the moonlight, naked breasts still pumping, was seared onto the inside of his skull. A scar. A brand.

He was either the strongest male on the face of the planet, or the stupidest. Either way, he'd cemented his asshole status by fucking her like an animal, then running for the hills before his dick quit kicking.

Was she okay? Was she eating? Was she cozying up to Lukas now that his sorry ass was gone?

He ripped a curtain of lush hanging moss aside with a snarl.

His patrols yielded a demon or two each night, but still no hellmouth. Good thing this mountain was big enough to keep him busy for a few weeks, scouring every inch of the strangely lush landscape. Cold, yes. Pounding hail storms every night, yes. But the babbling brooks were full and clear, teeming with fat fish, and evergreens towered like richly colored skyscrapers far above what should've been their natural treeline. Mushrooms and wild strawberries littered the undergrowth while blankets of hanging moss glowed blue-green in the night. Even the faebugs seemed more vivid up here. It was like everything was bigger, brighter, enhanced. Maybe that was why he couldn't drag his thoughts away from her. Maybe that was why she was all he could see, all he could think about, all he could smell...

He froze mid-step. His head swiveled, staring into the twilit woods as if pulled by an invisible thread. That wasn't a memory of her scent. That was the actual thing, somewhere nearby.

Along with the foul, earthy smell of sulfur.

His brain clicked off. His body took over, turning back the way he'd come, sprinting through the trees, leaping over rocks and fallen logs. Her presence pulled him. Yanked him forward, as if the end of a zipline was buried in her chest, and he was riding the cable, helpless to stop the inevitable crash. A jaguar scream pierced the dark. Glowing moss blurred with his speed.

Juno's sleek feline body battled three enormous demons that had her cornered against a huge granite boulder. She was lightning fast. Powerful. Vicious.

Losing.

Blood poured from a deep wound on her pelt, right above her left hip, and from another on her foreleg. One of the demons landed a blow to her head, and she staggered.

Killian exploded into lion form with a roar of fury.

The demons turned as one, but they were too slow. Anything would've been too slow to escape him in that moment. They had her cornered. They'd hurt her.

KILL. END. DESTROY.

For once, he didn't argue with his beast.

He eviscerated them in seconds and reveled in their shrieks of pain. When he looked up, a jaguar was ripping out one of their throats with a snarl that made his chest puff with pride.

Fierce female. Strong female.

Glowing green eyes met his, and then Juno melted into human form, panting and bleeding and glaring at him like she wanted to tear out his throat, too.

She spat black blood. "Nice of you to fucking show up."

CHAPTER 34

Juno's head throbbed. The gashes across her forearm and hip burned. She spat again, unsure if her stomach was churning from hellspawn blood or from the pain. The demon had nailed her right across the temple, and she was still seeing little birdies circling above her head. If she had a concussion, she was in trouble.

She was already in trouble. Her clothes were gone, her wounds were deep, and Killian Diallo had just saved her ass.

He shifted to human form and rose naked from all fours. He always looked massive, but right now, he seemed even bigger, black tattoos standing out against his golden skin, marred by an assortment of bleeding cuts. His hair was a wild tangle around his shoulders, his eyes still glowing yellow.

"What are you doing here?" His nose flared with his breaths.

Her cat yowled, reaching for him. "Magnus threw me out."

"What do you mean, threw you out?"

Why did that rough voice have to sound so sexy? "He's pissed about Wolf." She took immense satisfaction in his confused frown. "Oh, that's right, you don't know. Didn't stick around for that."

"For what?"

For anything. For a word, a compliment, an acknowledgement. For my goddamn orgasm to finish. Juno folded her arms over her bare breasts. "Wolf is Magnus's cousin. And his name isn't Wolf, it's Fennimore. And he didn't get kicked out, he ran away." The world flashed green, memories of their firelight confessional blazing across her mind. Killian had run away, too. "Like a chicken shit."

He glared at her, hearing the insult loud and clear. "Why would he lie about all that?"

Goosebumps pebbled her skin. She wrapped her arms tighter around herself, grimacing when the gash on her forearm screamed in protest. "Apparently, he screwed up and got some people killed." Her stomach twisted, both for the pain her friend must have felt, and from the rolling nausea caused by her wounds. "Everyone thought he was dead."

Killian was suddenly close, grabbing her wrist to examine her arm. His fingers on her skin were like electricity. She yanked out of his grip, and he scowled at her. "Does Rogan know?"

"Yeah, *I* filled him in. And dealt with all the bullshit afterward."

"What bullshit?"

"Wolf doesn't want to talk to Magnus, and Rogan's not forcing him to. You think Magnus is happy about that?" Her words practically sparked in the cold air. She had a sudden vision of the dangerous glitter that flickered over Jovi's skin when she was angry. She wouldn't mind a little fire magic right now. It would be very satisfying to light this stupid lion's hair on fire. "You think *any* of them are happy about that?"

His gaze pinned her to the spot. "Have those wolves been fucking with you?"

"Of course they have. They're pissed. All the trust we built is gone."

The words landed between them with a double meaning. The two of them had started to build some trust, hadn't they? And now…

He stared at her. "Fuck."

"Yeah. Val finally came at me today."

Claws erupted from between his fingers. "*What?*"

A thrill shot through her at the violence of his response. "Does that bother you?" She couldn't keep the venom from her words. "You didn't seem to have a problem leaving me to fend for myself."

"Dammit, Juno, I—"

"You told me you had my back." She stabbed a finger toward him to cover up the pang in her heart. "Have you been having fun up here, playing on the mountain? Find any hellmouths? No?" Her usual control was nowhere to be found, obliterated by pain and fury. "No problem, I'll handle that by myself, too." She stalked past him, holding her breath against his delicious scent. "Don't follow me."

"Dammit, Juno, wait. You're injured."

She flipped him off, stalking through the trees.

Even his snarl seemed louder up here. "Don't be stupid, DeSilva."

She whirled, strode up to him, and backhanded him across the face.

His head snapped to the side, a bright blotch of pink emerging on his cheek.

She leaned in. "Don't you *dare* call me stupid."

Yellow eyes flashed. "You're being so stupid right now I can't even grasp it." He looked at the gaping slash on her arm, and the other one oozing blood down her thigh. "You're about to march off, buck naked and injured, across a freezing fucking mountain. Does that sound smart to you?"

They glared at each other, breath whistling through their

noses, teeth gnashing. The air around them felt charged, practically crackling with energy, like their anger was seeping into the atmosphere. "I can take care of myself. Been doing it a long time."

"Oh, for fuck's sake—fine!" Killian flung a hand toward the trees. "Go freeze to death, or get infected, or whatever the hell you want."

Pain, anger, humiliation, and that horrifying little heartache speared through her. She pointed at him as she backed away, the slice on her hip burning with every step. "Stay away from me. Shouldn't be too hard for you, right?"

His curse followed her into the trees. She didn't know which pissed her off more, the fact that he didn't come after her, or the fact that she wanted him to.

CHAPTER 35

ine, he was right. She was being stupid. But it was his
fault.

Killian Diallo made her stupid.

Fucking him was stupid. Letting Val push her over the edge was stupid. Taking off for the mountain without any spare clothes was stupid.

Still wanting him was the stupidest thing of all.

Juno stayed in jaguar form as long as she dared, her thick pelt oblivious to the cold. But the smell of him, the draw toward him, was so much stronger in cat form that she shifted back and forth almost every hour, trying to keep from tracking him.

Which was exhausting. And exacerbating her wounds.

Stupid.

She'd dozed for a few hours, sheltered in one of the shallow caves that dotted the mountainside, and woke up freezing, but at least the sleep had helped her injuries heal. She ate a few mushrooms, scowling because the only reason she knew they were edible was because he'd taught her.

She couldn't get his scent out of her nose. It lingered like a hot, brooding presence as she stalked through the trees, hungry and pissed and fighting that *pull* toward him, like he had a rope around her rib cage and was hauling her in, hand over hand, while she dug in her heels.

It hurt.

Dusk drenched the mountain in purple shadows. She ducked under a sheet of hanging blue moss, the plush, soft ends glowing with a faint inner light. Everything was so lush. Shouldn't everything be scrubby and sparse up this high?

A screech echoed through the trees. Her head snapped around. Finally, a nice fight to take the edge off—

A lion's roar blasted her eardrums, and her feet were moving before her next blink.

She bolted through the trees, bursting into animal form mid-stride. The landscape erupted into a riot of scents, but one blazed to the forefront. She followed it at lightning speed, her paws light and sure on the forest floor. The sound of rushing water reached her a second before she flew out of the trees.

Killian's lion form battled two enormous winged demons by the edge of a raging river. One of the demons belched a stream of flame, catching Killian's mane. His russet fur lit up, the scent of burnt hair and sulfur overpowering anything else.

Roll, you idiot! She wanted to shout at him. He was being stupid, tearing into the hellspawn and ignoring the flaming ruff around his neck. Juno took one of the winged demons to the ground and let her claws loose on its belly. A blast of fire caught the side of her neck. She couldn't hold back her feline scream.

Tuck, roll, put out your flaming fur, and get back in the game. Pelt smoking, she launched herself at the demon once again. The thing was stumbling to its feet while its intestines spilled like slippery black ropes. The slash of her claw nearly severed its head. Blood poured from its gaping throat as the demon thudded to its knees, giving her a clear view of the riverbank.

The second demon struggled in the grip of a lion's paws, writhing and contorting, throwing them both off balance. They careened wildly into a tree at the river's edge and bounced off, locked in a vicious dance.

Even as Juno sprinted toward them, she knew she would be too late.

They tumbled off the bank, wrapped in each other's claws. There was a demonic bellow, a burst of flame, and a snarl as Killian tore out his enemy's throat.

Then, a sickening crack as the lion's head hit a tree limb hanging over the water.

His body reverted to human form and hit the water's surface like a corpse.

No.

She leaped off the bank, sailing over the dead demon floating facedown, spilling blood like an oil slick. The river churned, a deadly current of icy water, broken tree limbs, and jagged rocks.

An obstacle course.

She landed on the tip of a boulder, her paws scrambling for purchase on the slippery surface. She didn't dare take her eyes off the big, naked body being swept down river. He was face up, thank God.

The river was cacophonous. Water rushed around her forelegs as she sprang to the next surface, a tangle of fallen trees sweeping along with the current. Leaves slapped at her as she barreled through the wall of branches, but she gripped the trunk with her claws and forced herself into position.

Riding the tree like a surfboard, she measured the distance and sprang to another tree shooting down the river. The current dragged against her legs like a thousand icy hands. Her muscles tightened against the pull. Wet bark crumbled under the grip of her claws. She jumped again and again, bounding across rapids, sailing over jagged trees, closer and closer...

Killian's head dipped beneath the surface, then reemerged. Water shone on his closed lids.

The second she was close enough, she leaped on him. Her weight took them both under, but she dug her claws in tight until they breached the surface. Then, she wrapped her jaws around his wrist and held on.

Jaguars were strong. Very strong. They had the strongest bite force of any big cat, and she used every ounce of it, tasting the iron tang of Killian's blood in the rush of water that filled her mouth. Her paws worked furiously, churning toward shore, dragging her squadmate behind her. He got snagged on something. She tugged, fighting against the current and tasting fresh blood. She pulled harder, got him free, and kept going.

We're fine. We're fine.

Tendons twitched against her teeth. Her heart leaped. *Wake up.* She wanted to scream inside his head, snap him out of it, bring him back to her…

Something slammed into her back with the force of a truck.

Killian's wrist slipped from her jaws as she was driven down, down, down, hitting the river bottom with a soundless thud, an enormous weight pinning her jaguar's back leg into the muck.

Frigid water churned overhead as she twisted her feline body, trying to wrench free. Something in her ankle snapped.

Pain rocketed through her, white hot and blinding, shocking enough to jolt her cat into retreat. Suddenly, her naked human form was the one pinned beneath the trunk of a tree, her human ankle the one searing with agony, and her human lungs screaming for air.

She shoved at the tree with every ounce of her strength. It shifted an inch. Victory surged through her even as her lungs burned and pain shot through her leg. She shoved again. Water churned overhead, like she was trapped at the bottom of a freezing jacuzzi. The tree rolled, squeezing her broken ankle beneath it, and her eyes bulged as she gasped in a lungful of river water.

Panic threatened.

Do not panic. You cannot afford to panic.

She yanked at her leg, but it didn't budge. She clawed upward, as if she could reach the surface by sheer will.

Think, DeSilva. You've obliterated far worse enemies than a fucking tree.

There was nothing to pry her leg free, nothing to pound against the tree limb that trapped her. Lungs screaming, she heaved at it again.

Nothing.

Darkness flickered around the edges of her vision.

No.

She shoved again, weaker this time. Her eyelids took on weight.

You're going to get yourself into trouble one day, her father's voice echoed from the past.

Everything was heavy. Her fingers, stretching toward the surface, weighed as much as the earth. Her lungs were on fire. Her head pounded.

No.

She couldn't keep her eyes open.

Blackness.

CHAPTER 36

She blinked awake. Slowly.

There was cold ground beneath her cheek, a throbbing pain in her leg, a low, flickering fire…and a huge, masculine shadow seated behind it.

Alarm shot through her. She jolted upright before she caught a hot, wild scent.

She sagged. Alive. He was alive. They were both alive.

The sleeves of a thermal shirt pooled around her hands. Killian's shirt. Her head was a lead weight on her shoulders as she looked around. They were in a shallow cave. Small logs were piled against one wall, along with a wad of shredded clothing.

Her ankle pounded. She looked down the length of her bare leg to find it neatly splinted with branches and strips of torn fabric.

Her sinuses felt like they'd been hollowed out by sandpaper, but she still caught the metallic tang of blood in the air. It wasn't hers. She couldn't see Killian's wrist. Had she torn him up that badly?

She swallowed through a throat full of cotton. "Killian?"

Yellow eyes glittered at her in the dark.

She blinked hard. Some of the fuzz cleared from her brain. "Killian?"

"You almost died. Again."

The rough words sent a little jolt through her. "I'm surprised you came after me."

There was a sharp silence. "Are you joking?"

She scrubbed her face, trying to untangle the past from the present. Anger and pain, fear and confusion, their argument on the mountain, her father's disdain. *You're going to get yourself into trouble one day. And I will not bail you out.* "We were really mad at each other."

"So?"

Old, bitter memories swirled in her brain, churning like the river that had nearly drowned them both. "So, I'm just surprised you came after me, is all."

"Because we were fucking *mad* at each other?"

She should've kept her mouth shut. "Forget it. Never mind." The flickering flames made shadows dance over his naked torso, playing over the ridges of muscle and bold lines of his tattoos. She traced the designs with her eyes, desperate to root herself in the here and now.

"Who left you hanging?"

Her eyes jerked to meet his. "What?"

"Who left you hanging because they were mad at you? Vasquez?" Even from across the dark cave, she saw his lion flash under his skin.

"No."

"Then who?"

"Just forget it—"

"Bullshit. Who?"

Anger sparked, her brain too soggy and her body too raw to hold back the words. "My dad, okay?"

The fire popped. Something in his eyes held her fast, refusing to let her look away. "What happened?"

"I was never who he wanted me to be." The old, familiar

ache flared into sharp pain. She focused on her ankle, picking at the bindings. "He wanted me to be contained and controlled, and I wanted to run. I told you I've always been physical. He wanted me to be physical in a different way. Use my looks to string men along, make them think they could have something if they did business with my dad. Play the part." She raised her eyes again and found herself pinned by a lion's stare. "I told him I didn't want to do that. I wanted to learn martial arts, I wanted to run, I wanted to be useful. He told me as long as I was under his roof, I'd behave like a DeSilva, not some wild beast. I was already secretly fighting in the Arena. I finally made enough money to get an apartment and get out from under his roof." Her fierce pride at the memory faded quickly. "Eventually, someone recognized me and started writing stories about the princess of Silka tearing out men's throats for money." Any trace of a smile left her. "My dad and I had a huge fight. He told me DeSilvas were better than that. He said if I was going to put myself in those kinds of situations, he wasn't going to bail me out. He was humiliated. At least, that's what it said in the letter."

"What letter?"

"I got a letter in the mail. Voluntary termination of parental rights." She raised a humorless brow at the look on his face. "You didn't know you could do that? It's easy if you have the money."

"Are you fucking kidding me?"

"Nope." She watched a pulse jump in his neck. "I was an embarrassment. *Mentally unstable.*" She bit that one out. "A threat to his business's reputation, and therefore his livelihood. I'm actually not his biological daughter—my mom was pregnant with me when they met. But he's the only dad I've ever known, and legally, I've always been his." She shook herself. "Anyway, I was seventeen, already living on my own." She lifted a shoulder. "Honestly, it didn't change much. Except that I won't inherit millions." Her sarcastic smile wasn't returned. She looked away and tried to swallow the lump that had wedged itself in her throat. "There were a couple times I could've used his help. I reached out, but he didn't answer."

"Like when?"

She shook her head. "I don't want to talk about it."

He stared at her.

She tossed up her hands. "Fine, like the time I lost a fight really badly and ended up in the hospital. I didn't have enough money or anybody to take care of me while I recovered. He didn't come. Or when a guy who worked at the Arena threw a bag over my head and tossed me in a storage unit, hoping for ransom."

She caught the glint of his fangs punching through his gums.

"My dad didn't come. Rats did, though." She tried to say it flippantly, but she couldn't completely repress a shudder. Tied up in that concrete box, hands and ankles bound, jerking away from twitching noses and heavy rodent bodies... "I finally managed to cut my ropes. Then, I cut the asshole who put them on me." She'd never forget the wide-eyed shock on his face when he'd hauled open the storage unit door to find her waiting for him. "He was my first kill."

"Good."

His dark, deadly growl made her lips curve. Most males, her father included, would be horrified by the admission. "He had my dad's response to his ransom letter in his pocket." The neat, slanted scrawl was burned into her memories. "*Juan DeSilva has no daughter.*" She blinked the cave back into focus, trying to smother the howling ache in her chest. "Anyway."

She needed to end this conversation. The memories, the near drowning, the pain in her ankle—she was too raw. She pressed her cool palms against her lids, breathing past the phantom weight suddenly crushing her lungs.

There was a rustle, then a pair of strong arms around her, lifting her into the cradle of a hard, warm lap.

Her heart skipped. "What—"

"Shut up." Killian tucked her closer, settled her against him, holding tight. "You need this."

No, no, no, she did not need this. She needed to be alone until she got herself under control. "Seriously, I'm—"

His head swung down, bringing their noses an inch apart. "If you tell me you're fine right now, I'm going to lose my fucking mind."

She swallowed, unable to tear her gaze away. The warmth of him seeped into her, easing the chill.

And then, to her horror, she started to tremble.

Killian's brows knit together. He tucked her head into the curve of his neck and wrapped his arms tighter around her, bringing his knees up so she was completely supported, completely surrounded by warm muscle and bronze skin and that scent that turned her brain to absolute mush.

Trembles turned into shakes. Memories swamped her, battering her like a thousand unrelenting fists. She pushed at him instinctively, desperate to escape.

His arms tightened around her.

And so, instead of pushing Killian Diallo away, she grabbed whatever part of him she could reach, and hung on.

He held her for a long time. Eventually, the shakes subsided, and a long breath escaped her. Her body went limp against him, his heart beating steadily against her side.

It had been a really long time since she'd been held like this.

One thumb brushed over her elbow. Electricity arced through her at that simple touch. Her lids lifted—they'd drifted shut at some point, but now, she found herself staring at the pulse thumping in his neck, only a breath from her mouth. A tendril of golden hair tickled the hollow of his throat, the ends still slightly damp.

"Thank you," she murmured. When there was only silence, she lifted her head.

Molten yellow eyes pinned her to the spot. "I will always come for you."

Something tugged at the center of her chest.

"I don't care how mad we are. I don't care if you think you're on your own. I will *always* come for you. Do you understand me?" He pointed at himself. "*This* backup will always show. Got it?"

Stunned, she could only nod.

His gaze dropped to her mouth. Her heart ticked up. Yes, she needed his mouth on hers, needed that rush of physical sensation to stop the mad swirling of her thoughts...

He eased her head to his shoulder and tucked her close.

Her eyes went wet. After a few seconds of pulling her shit together, she cleared her aching throat, watching that strong pulse jump in his neck again. "You're pretty good at this *taking care of people* stuff."

His grunt rumbled against her ribs, and she felt a smile tug at her mouth. Then, a big hand stroked her hair, drifting slowly down her back. Petting her. Soothing her. A vivid memory of him doing the same thing to Elvi flashed across her mind, and her throat tightened again.

She had to get herself under control. She should pull away, get off his damn lap. *In a few minutes. Just a few minutes more.* She'd almost drowned, for God's sake.

Stroke. Stroke.

She sighed. Her nose brushed his neck. He smelled *so* good. Why did he smell so good? Her cat was stretching luxuriously, basking in his scent.

She opened her eyes, admiring the bronze of his skin. What would he taste like, right there in the hollow of his throat?

She hesitated for a split second before dragging the tip of her tongue over that jumping pulse.

He stiffened. Something stirred beneath her, hardening against her ass.

Warmth infused her entire body. She licked him again.

He squeezed. "No."

The word shot through her like a bullet. All the warm fuzzies evaporated, and she tensed, but he held her firmly in place.

"You're injured. Just—" He bit off the rest, threading his blunt fingers through her loose hair while her brain whirled. "Relax. Recover."

"I'm fi—"

The fingers tightened into a fist, gripping her hair and bringing them nose to nose.

She was used to seeing him angry. The barely leashed rage in his eyes was on a different level altogether. "Don't you dare." He tucked her head against his neck again, wrapping her up, hitching his legs up higher to cradle her. She blinked into the curve of his throat while he practically simmered around her.

Okay… "What—"

"Shh." It was sharp. "Just let me—" He cut himself off. "Just…"

When she pulled back to frown at him, she caught a glimpse of his mangled wrist.

"Oh, my God." She pushed up from his chest and held up his arm.

She'd almost ripped his hand off. His wrist was a mass of raw, exposed flesh, a chunk missing here, a tendon exposed there. Her stomach turned. Shapeshifters healed fast, but they could still be permanently injured if the trauma was bad enough.

He tried to tug his arm out of her grasp. "It's fine."

"*Fine?*" Her gaze shot to his just in time to catch the tiniest spark of humor. Words fled her.

Killian's amber eyes gleamed. "See how irritating that is?"

She tried to find a response and failed.

He considered his mutilated wrist. "You did tear the shit out of it, though." He looked back at her, and any humor was gone. "Thank you for saving my ass, *even when you were mad at me.*"

Yeah, she had been pissed at him. Beyond pissed. But here, now, after the rescuing, and the spilling of her guts, and the cuddle session..."Gotta admit, I was a little nervous there for a second."

"You scared the hell out of me, DeSilva."

Hesitantly, she cupped his cheek. His beard rasped against her palm, rough and soft at the same time. She laughed a little at the thought. "Like you."

"What?"

"Nothing." Something big was bubbling up inside her. Her breath was coming faster, and the bulge pressing into her ass was growing bigger, and her core was getting wet, but it was the pressure in her chest that worried her.

"I'm sorry." His rough growl cut through the pounding of her pulse. "For leaving you like that after we..." His gaze met hers, both of them remembering that night in the woods. "I was scared shitless."

She swallowed. "Why?"

"Do you really want to know?"

She should say no. Instead, she nodded.

"Because the second it was over, I knew it wasn't enough."

The fire popped, but neither of them looked away. Her heart hammered against her ribcage. "So, your cat isn't done with me yet?"

He shook his head slowly. "Not even fucking close."

Her blood went molten. "Mine, either."

The air between them throbbed. "You want more?"

Her fingers had found their way into his hair. "Just sex. Just until it's out of our systems. Deal?"

Something unreadable flickered across his expression before he nodded.

She yanked his head toward her, but his big hand gripped her hair, holding them apart at the last second.

Slowly, he lowered his mouth to hers.

It was gentle, and it was tender, and for the second time that night, she nearly drowned.

His tongue glided against hers, his lips sipping softly while his hands caressed her in long, strong strokes. The bulge in his pants grew harder against her, and he groaned before adjusting his hold to lay her back on the cave floor, careful with her ankle.

He knelt over her, hands slipping under his shirt she wore. Rough fingertips grazed her skin, molding her curves like he was committing them to memory.

She went for his zipper, needing him to fill her, needing him strong and solid inside her, needing him *now*. His hand clamped over hers. Her gaze shot to his face, but he was already working down her body, pressing hot, open kisses to her neck, peeling up the hem of her shirt to brush his lips over her stomach, heading lower.

Her breath caught, and she clutched at his shoulder. Not that, not right now. She was already too vulnerable, too soft—

He looked up at her from the juncture of her thighs and planted a hand on her abs. "Stay."

She opened her mouth to protest, though the sight of those tattooed shoulders wedged between her legs made her entire body throb.

"No." The word cracked like a whip in the dark. "You're going to lay there, DeSilva, and you're going to let me lick you."

He lowered his head and dragged his tongue up her center.

CHAPTER 37

This.

This was everything. This was all of it, all Killian needed, the only sustenance he required. He groaned against her pussy, opened his mouth wider, took another long lick, tasting her folds and her opening and the silken wetness that flowed out of her. She made the sexiest sound in the world, something feminine and soft and so unlike Juno DeSilva he could've roared in triumph if his mouth wasn't busy. Very, very busy. He dipped his tongue inside and would've fallen to his knees if he wasn't already on his belly between her thighs. The taste of her, the hot satin feel of her…

"Perfect," he rasped. Another one of those breathy sounds escaped her, and his dick hardened painfully. His fingers dug into her thighs. Her hand wrapped around his head and tugged upward, and he followed eagerly, lapping at her wet flesh until he reached the hard bud of her clit.

Her gasp set him ablaze. He pried his hands off her legs to pull back her pussy, exposing every perfect inch of her, swirling his tongue around and around, his head moving with his motions, her claws pricking his scalp, her little gasps spurring him on. Those noises, those fucking noises, those soft, high, feminine sounds coming out of his tough-as-nails female…he groaned against her again, flicking faster. She tensed, every muscle going tight beneath him, her clit swelling in his mouth.

She erupted with a keening cry, shuddering so hard she almost jostled him out of place. He held her down and kept working her while she clutched his face to her beautiful, dripping core.

Fucking hell, he suddenly got why Blitz addicts would lie, steal, starve for their fix.

She pulled at his shoulders, practically dragging him up her lush, panting body. "You," she demanded, going for his pants.

Together, they shoved them down to his knees, but before he could plunge inside her, she rolled them, putting herself on top. Frustration threatened to snap out of him, but then she grabbed his dick and guided him to her soaked entrance. He slipped inside her hot, silky sheath, and any protest died on his lips.

Click.

His breath caught. Hers did, too. She stared down at him, dark eyes wide. "Do you feel that?"

Lost in her, he nodded.

She laced their fingers and leaned into his palms. He held tight, loving the way she let him hold her up even as her shoulders flexed with her own considerable strength. They moved together, eyes locked and hands locked and something else trying to lock together deep inside them, a key skittering over its hole.

"You are so fucking beautiful," he whispered.

The soft tips of her breasts brushed his pecs as she leaned down and ran her tongue up his throat, hips rolling and grinding, her body moving in the world's sexiest wave above him. He muttered a curse when her teeth sank into the side of his neck. He shoved up into her harder, deeper, needing to feel her clench tight around him so he could let go.

When her pussy gripped him and she cried out, he erupted with a roar.

Mine.

She sagged into their joined palms for a second, then eased upright. Instinctively, he grabbed her hips before she could slip off, wanting to keep them together for just a few more seconds. Minutes. Hours. An eternity.

Her core pulsed around him. Her lids flickered, like it felt exquisite.

"What was that?" he asked, watching her face.

She slanted him a look. "Aftershocks."

He felt a slow grin stretch his cheeks. "Really."

"Don't flatter yourself, Diallo. It's totally normal."

"Oh yeah?" He tensed his pelvic muscles, making his cock twitch inside her, and grinned wider at the expression on her face. "That normal, too?"

"I'd be more impressed if you were ready to go again." Her dark brow quirked in challenge.

His eyes traveled over her taut breasts, her abs, her strong legs split over him, the ends of her hair tickling her nipples. "Give me thirty fucking seconds."

She laughed, and he felt it around his dick. He knocked her hands from the ground, making her fall to his chest with a whoop. He rolled them the opposite way, careful of her ankle, but she was already flipping them again. They tumbled across the cave floor, a jumble of naked limbs and sinuous muscle and the teasing prick of claws.

The smell of burnt hair reached his nose seconds before the heat at his back registered.

"Your hair!" Juno flipped them again, away from the fire they'd damn near rolled into, landing on top and pounding the flaming tips of his hair into the dirt to extinguish them.

"Fuck." He looked up from the smoking ends of his

charred strands to meet her eyes. They were wide and sparkling, and she wore an incredulous grin on her face as she straddled him. She was naked and perfect and laughing, her curtain of dark hair falling around her shoulders like silk.

He didn't believe in reincarnation, but he was pretty sure he'd just been reborn.

Killian couldn't speak. He just looked at her, searching those chocolate eyes for regrets, for anger, for the cool indifference that drove him out of his skull. He didn't find any of it.

When she slipped off of him, it took everything he had to let her go. The chilly air on his wet length was shocking compared to her warmth. He wanted to wear her like a damn blanket.

He closed his eyes. If he looked at her a second longer, he'd undoubtedly say something stupid. She might have shown him something tender, but knowing Juno, she'd be zipping it all up, stuffing it all in, and pretending those soft moments didn't happen.

A warm, silky body slid against him. His eyes flew open, and he lifted his arm to see Juno snuggling up to his side, easing one lean, muscular leg over his thigh and draping an arm over his chest. Her heart pattered against his ribs.

He slowly lowered his arm around her, giving her every chance to pull away, like a wild animal.

Her nose nuzzled his bare skin, and she shifted her leg higher on his, getting closer.

The ache in his chest intensified until he couldn't breathe. He rested his hand on her arm, light and easy. She sighed deeply, her breath feathering across his bare chest.

Holy fuck.

He traced his thumb over her smooth skin, slowly, waiting for her to bolt. She didn't.

The fire sparked. Wind howled through the trees. It was storming again—what was it, monsoon season on the mountain?—but he couldn't bring himself to care. Happy little fucking butterflies fluttered behind his sternum as he stroked her shoulder, her arm, the gorgeous curve of her strong back...

"You're purring."

He froze. Oh, shit. That fluttering behind his rib cage was real, and audible. He cut it off abruptly.

Her soft laugh sent a puff of air across his pecs. "No, I like it."

Well, damn if he didn't start rumbling like a freight train. She chuckled. Her short nails skimmed the outline of his ribs. She was petting him. Petting *him*.

He stared down his body, mesmerized by the darker tone of her skin against the gold of his. Her fingers trailed up his torso, light as feathers. His nipple pebbled when she grazed it, and the little minx did it again, drawing circles around it while his cock hardened under her thigh.

She gave another low, satisfied laugh. "Already?"

If she only knew. "Always, for you."

Her fingers halted.

He cleared his throat roughly. "How's the ankle?"

She glanced down their bodies and extended her leg with a dancer's grace. Her ankle was still bound with his makeshift splint. She flexed and rolled it as much as she could, appearing satisfied.

"Fine." She shot him a playful look even as he glared down at her. "It really is fine, so don't get all pissy with me."

The sight of her beautiful naked body draped over his, the smile on her face and the sparkle of amusement in her dark eyes, stole his breath. His bite mark was a red smudge in the curve of her shoulder, already starting to bruise. Satisfaction rushed through him as he traced the outline of it and watched goosebumps appear.

She sighed contentedly and dropped her head to his chest. He trailed his finger down to brush her dusky nipple. It rose to attention. He wanted it in his mouth, but hell if he was going to move an inch, not when he'd been gifted with a naked, satisfied Juno DeSilva cuddled up against him.

Cuddling. Juno. The Maneater. He shook his head vaguely.

Her stomach growled.

He eased his arm from beneath her and was on his feet in an instant, brushing dirt from his ass. "I'll get food."

Lightning flashed. Juno raised a brow at the thrashing storm outside their little shelter. "It's pouring out there."

"I saw some berries outside." He stopped just inside the cave entrance and spun to meet her heavy-lidded gaze. "I will be *right* back."

CHAPTER 38

n other words, *I'm not screwing you and ditching you again.* Juno sat up and scooted to the cave wall, unable to keep the smile off her face as she watched him disappear into the night. His muffled curses floated from beyond the entrance, barely audible over the storm.

He emerged from the dark a couple minutes later, ducking inside with dripping hair and a scowl on his face. "Fucking hail." One cupped palm overflowed with the plump wild strawberries that grew all over the mountainside. He settled beside her, cold water trickling over his bare skin.

Blunt fingers brought a berry to his mouth. The sight of his lips wrapped around the wet red flesh sent a hot tingle through her.

Staring into the flames, jaw flexing as he chewed, Killian offered her the handful.

Dancing firelight turned his skin a burnished bronze and the rain-soaked berries a deep, glossy scarlet. Ripe. Ready. Dripping. Temptation itself.

It wasn't like he was putting the food directly into her mouth. This wasn't him claiming her.

Pulse hammering, Juno selected a berry from his hand and

lifted it to her lips. Tension throbbed in the cool air. She took a bite.

One bronze fingertip twitched.

And as sweet, flavorful juice burst on her tongue, something else threatened to burst deep inside.

He wasn't feeding her. Not technically.

After an audible swallow, Kilian took another berry. So did she. They shared the rest in silence, watching the fire.

CHAPTER 39

An earthquake jolted Juno awake.

She sprang to her feet as the ground shuddered beneath her and debris rained from overhead, belatedly remembering she had a broken ankle. It was healing fast, but pain still shot through her, making her suck in a breath. Before she could utter a word, she was scooped off the earth and clutched against Killian's hard, warm chest. And then, they were flying out of the cave and through the trees, being slapped by spiny evergreen branches while an ominous rumble grew louder at their back.

She looked over Killian's shoulder and felt her eyes go wide.

The entire mountainside was barreling toward them, a waterfall of dirt and rock and uprooted trees tumbling down the hillside.

She clung to his neck and wrapped her legs around his torso, gritting her teeth when she locked her ankles together at his back. She could deal with the pain of it. They needed to move.

Killian was a tank, not a torpedo, but he flew through the trees at a pace that made her eyes water. When he leaped over fallen logs and ducked beneath limbs, she squeezed around him like a monkey. They'd thrown his clothes on again in the middle of the night, thank God—at least only his top half was naked as he bolted through the forest. Her legs were still bare, her core pressed tight against his abs, his big shirt rucking up to expose her ass to the chilly air. She held her breath against a cloud of dirt that surged up from behind them. The roar of the landslide was deafening. Killian's feet scrabbled for balance on the undulating earth. A rolling log took his legs out from under him, and then they were spinning through the air, tumbling, flipping, squeezing each other tight. Her back slammed into the ground, knocking the wind from her lungs even before the gigantic man landed on top of her. There was a thunderous rumble, the smell of earth, and a smack of pebbles and hard dirt against her skin.

Darkness.

Silence.

Her heart pounded in her ears. Killian panted against her neck. His body was plastered over her like a sheet, forearms braced on either side of her head to allow a pocket of breathing room. He had quick reflexes, she'd give him that. Her head was tucked down, her nose mashed into his chest.

"You good?" they said in unison.

Killian took a gathering breath, then his forearms flexed by her head, and he pushed upright. Earth rained down around them. Weak morning sunlight speared through the cloud of dust, and Juno squinted as Killian heaved the load of dirt off his back, his massive arms bulging, rising to his knees above her like a god emerging from the underworld.

Her mind went blank.

Dirt tumbled off him as he stood and held out a hand. They clasped forearms, and he hauled her to her feet.

Together, they looked toward the mountaintop. A hole gaped near the summit, like someone had shot a giant bullet through the peak.

Something was crawling out of it.

"Is that a snake?" It sure as hell looked like a slow, serpentine body was slithering its way out of the dark hole at the top of the mountain. If they could see it from this far, it had to be huge. As they watched, the monstrous flesh-colored thing poked its head out, swaying side to side before retreating slowly into its cavern.

Killian eyed the creature with distaste. "Think we've found our hellmouth?"

"Only one way to find out." She narrowed her gaze on the mountaintop. It was a long, long way up. She took a step forward, only to suck in a breath as pain shot through her ankle.

Killian's hand was under her elbow in an instant, supporting her until she balanced on her good foot. He squatted in front of her to prod at her ankle. The yelp that escaped her was not good for her image.

"It's fine," she snapped automatically as Killian looked up at her. When he glowered, she couldn't help but laugh. "Okay, it's not fine. But it will be. Just go on ahead, I'll catch up."

He rose slowly from her feet to tower over her. "Are you kidding me?"

"No, seriously, go ahead. I'll follow your trail." It would take her forever, but she'd do it.

His glower turned deadly. He gestured to the ruined landscape. "Look around. I'm not leaving you out here with a serious injury, in the middle of a fucking mountain, after a goddamn landslide, in nothing but my *fucking shirt*!" He was yelling by the end of it, quivering with anger, his lion flashing across his face.

Maybe it was because of everything she'd shared with him the night before. Maybe it was because of the way he'd held her, comforting her even when she wanted to run away. Maybe it was because he was right. Whatever the reason, instead of raising her hackles, the fierce, incredulous, totally Killian outburst made her grin.

That smile must've shocked Killian almost as much as it surprised her, because he blinked a few times, then shook his head like he couldn't begin to understand her. He stripped off his pants and shoved them at her. "Hold these. And for once, Juno, don't argue with me."

She held the pants as he burst into cat form. Lion eyes met hers, then he tossed his head toward his back as if to say—

Her stomach dropped. "No."

He growled.

She eyed his golden back, long and strong and covered in soft fur. Shifters did not allow others to ride their animal form. It was degrading and humiliating.

He snapped his teeth and tossed his mane toward his back again.

She swept a glance across the landscape and heaved a sigh. "Fine." Feeling like a fool, she tied the legs of his pants around her waist and stepped gingerly to his side. Bracing a hand on his flank and cursing the river and landslide and her own bones for betraying her, she eased her ass onto his back and swung her leg over to straddle him.

He didn't give her a chance to change her mind, just took off at a speed that had her clutching the coarse bronze hair of his mane and leaning forward to keep her balance. His shirt rode high on her thighs. Her bare core pressed against his hard, fur-covered spine, rocking with his speeding gait.

Oh God.

Tingles flared to life as her clit rubbed against his back. She shifted around, but every tilt, every adjustment, only brought her into closer contact.

Oh, this was *so* not happening. No.

He loped across the landscape, his muscles bunching under her thighs as her fingers gripped his mane and her calves gripped his flank and she tried to get a fucking grip on her libido. What was the matter with her? Not only was she *riding* her squadmate's back like a circus pony, she was *getting off* on it?

She adjusted her position again, but it was no use. His speed increased, and they hit an incline, pressing her even more firmly into his spine, bringing the fur-covered ridge right up against her swollen, tingling clit.

He broke into a run, found a smooth, relentless rhythm, and, oh God, she was rocking faster on top of him, and the tingles were building, and shit, she was going to—

Sensation overtook her. Her eyes squeezed shut and she fisted his mane, holding on for dear life as blissful electricity rocketed through her veins. The lion slowed to a stop. Powerful flanks expanded with his long, deep inhale.

Mortified, Juno released her death grip on his mane and slid rather unsteadily from his back, barely remembering to keep her bad foot off the ground as she struggled to act like nothing had happened. "What?"

The lion dissolved into a muscled male kneeling in the dirt. He raised up on his knees. A wicked smile stretched his face. "Did you just *come on my back*, DeSilva?"

His nostrils flared with another deep inhale. Triumph and heat flashed in his eyes. "You did."

He came toward her on his knees.

She backed away.

He followed, grinning. "I didn't even have to try."

Her spine hit a tree. She opened her mouth, but her protests and denials died at the sight of him kneeling before her, looping first her bad leg, then her good one over his massive shoulders. He wedged himself between her thighs, cupped her ass in his big hands, and sucked her into his mouth.

A shuddering gasp escaped her. His tongue on her clit felt incredible, lapping at her sensitive bud while his fingers kneaded her glutes and his growl reverberated against her core.

"Fuck, Diallo!" It was both praise and curse as she gave in, grabbed a fistful of golden hair, and rode his tongue, pressing her back against the tree for more leverage. In a massive rush and violent explosion, she came in his mouth, grinding herself against him while she cried out.

He surged to his feet, lifted her by the ass, and thrust home. His hands slid to the backs of her knees, spreading her wide as he pounded his hard, thick length into her.

They came together, their shouts echoing in the trees, startling a couple of birds.

They panted against each other. Finally, he guided her feet gently to the ground and stepped back, wiping a palm over his mouth. Amber eyes gleamed.

She tugged the hem of his shirt down. "Fuck, Diallo."

"Yeah, you said that." His grin was evil. Christ, he was handsome. He looked a lot like his brother when he smiled, but somehow, she doubted she would've orgasmed just from sitting on Cullen Diallo's back.

What the hell was she doing? She scrubbed her face.

Killian's low chuckle was suddenly very close, and when she opened her eyes, he was standing inches away, the picture of a smug, satisfied male.

She mustered up a glare. "Don't look so pleased with yourself."

"Gotta say I'm *pretty* damn pleased with myself."

She shoved at him, and he let himself lazily stumble back a few paces. His dark blond beard glistened with her juices, which was hot as hell and embarrassing at the same time.

She lifted a brow. "What can I say, I'm a spine girl."

His laugh boomed through the trees. "I'll remember that."

She stared. That was, she was pretty sure, the first time she'd heard him really laugh. All the years of living together, working together, eating together, and she'd never heard him issue more than a rough scoff.

She tried to think of something witty to say and failed, especially when he sucked his bottom lip between his teeth.

"We should try to get further today. Unless your clit can't handle it." Wicked humor danced in his eyes.

Killian Diallo was teasing her. Laughing. Smiling. Hell had frozen over. "Don't flatter yourself." She tightened the legs of his pants, still tied absurdly around her waist, and strutted forward as best she could with a limp.

Instead of morphing into lion form, he snagged an arm around her waist and yanked her against him. "I'd offer to let you ride me like this, but I've got a great spine in human form, too."

She shoved out from under his arm as he laughed again. "I could make you come with my pinkie toe, Diallo."

"Can't wait."

CHAPTER 40

Killian kept his nose open as they continued up the mountain, hoping to catch the mouthwatering scent of her coming on his spine again, but apparently that was a one-time miracle. The higher they traveled, the more lush the scenery got—fleshy mushrooms, blooming wildflowers, evergreens with huge, soft needles and branches heavy with fat berries. All around, a faint hum of magic tingled in his nose.

They came across a rushing waterfall just as dusk fell. The wide pool at its base sparkled aqua blue, and he padded to the edge of it, feeling Juno's thighs grip his back. He shifted into human form without warning, grinning at her surprised gasp when she suddenly found herself riding a naked man instead of a lion. He could feel her skin in this form, and the heat of her core pressing against his bare back had him thinking all kinds of things. Not that he hadn't been thinking about them all day. All week. All six years he'd known her.

Her curse floated down to him as he knelt in the dirt, and his grin widened. Catching Juno DeSilva by surprise was no easy feat—

A smack on his bare ass made him jump as her weight left him, and a satisfied snicker reached his ears.

He spun on all fours and swiped at her, but she danced out of reach, barely favoring her ankle. It must be almost back to normal. She shot him a smug look and shoved up the sleeves of his shirt. It was huge on her, the hem reaching almost to her knees, and he fucking *loved* seeing her in it, knowing she'd be covered in his scent.

He rose slowly. "Did you just *spank* me, DeSilva?" He came at her fast. She evaded his grab with an arm block, but he countered and managed to whip his arms around her. She threw her weight, making them both stumble, and their joint curses echoed around the clearing as they tumbled into the pool.

Icy water nearly stole his breath, and he released her so they could both sputter to the top. His head broke the surface —only to get a face full of frigid water, sent his way by an expert swipe of her palm.

His eyes popped open to find Juno already gearing up to splash him again. He went under, wrapped his arms around her hips, and yanked her down. She broke his hold and kicked up. This time, he breached the surface cautiously, squinting through one eye.

She was breathing hard, hair plastered to her skull and a wild grin on her face. His heart skipped. He wasn't used to being the recipient of that radiant smile. He'd seen it directed at the others, watched her laugh and play and shed her armor, but never with him.

She was lowering her walls. Letting him see her. The beauty of it, of her, was staggering.

Her teeth chattered.

Play time was over. "Come on. It's freezing."

It was, though not nearly as cold as it should have been halfway up a damn mountain. They heaved themselves out of the pool and headed for the small cave near the base of the waterfall. A possum scuttled out when they approached, and they kicked its scat and leaf bedding out before collecting sticks for a fire. After stripping their soaked clothes and wringing the water from them, they laid them out to dry on the cave floor. Juno knelt to arrange the sticks for the fire, stuffing pine needles and leaves into the little teepee, shivering ever so slightly.

Killian snagged his lighter from his pants pocket, praying the sodden thing still worked, and tossed it over as she looked up. She snatched it smoothly, flicked it a few times, then put the little flame to the kindling. When it caught, she tossed it back to him. He snagged it from the air and slipped it back into his pocket.

Stupid, that something like that should warm him so much.

They'd been squadmates for years—of course they'd work together well. But that seamless, wordless exchange felt different somehow. They were working together without any of that sizzling animosity, that underlying tension that set his teeth on edge. This was smooth, effortless…easy.

She knelt by the growing flames, rubbing her arms. Her dark hair hung in dripping ropes around her shoulders. She grimaced and gathered the mass in her hands, twisting to wring the water from it.

He knelt next to her and put his hands on top of hers to help her squeeze. Water trickled over their knuckles. His lion settled, knowing he was taking care of her—

She leaned away. "I got it."

"I'm almost done."

"I got it." She eased out of his grasp.

Abruptly, her words echoed in his ears. *Just sex. Just until it's out of our systems.*

He rose quickly. He needed to reel in these stupid instincts before he made an even bigger fool of himself. But instead of shutting up like any self-preserving male would, more ridiculous words tumbled out of him, sharp and biting. "Just curious. Would you let Rogan help you dry your hair? Or Cyrus? Or John, or Wolf?"

"They wouldn't try."

He tossed his hands. "And somehow, I'm still the asshole."

Something flickered across her face. Sympathy? She opened her mouth.

"Forget it. I'll see if there's food. Unless you need to get your own." The warmth he'd just been basking in had vanished, leaving him cold to the bone as he stalked to the edge of the pool. He welcomed the bite of the frigid water around his calves, the rough stone beneath his feet. He obviously needed something to shock him back to his senses.

Just sex. Just until it's out of our systems.

Somehow, among all the laughing and teasing and sex and snuggling, he'd forgotten that.

A fat moon was reflected on the water's shimmering surface. It had been a full moon when his dad taught him to fish this way, standing in the water until the fish decided he was just another rock or branch and got close enough for him to catch with his bare hands. They'd stood there forever in the Red River while jungle birds called around them, their shoulders brushing. His dad was broad, so broad, with arms like tree trunks and a booming voice that resonated even in a whisper.

"They're like females, son. You have to let them come to you. And when they get close, that's when you grab on and don't let go." An amber wink, then a lightning-fast snatch into the water to emerge with a wriggling trout clutched in his claws.

A sigh sounded from behind him. "I'm sorry."

He stared at the moon's quivering reflection.

"You were trying to do something nice and it freaked me out."

"Why?"

"Because I liked it."

That brought his head around.

Her face scrunched up. "I didn't mean to say that." She glared at the moon, like it was to blame for loosening her tongue, and folded her arms over her naked breasts.

He could see the goosebumps on her skin from here, but managed to keep his hands to himself. "I get it." She'd given everything up, fought fang and claw to get where she was today. Arena champion. Warrior female. Respected squad member. "The soft shit is hard for you." He dragged his focus back to the water.

In the long silence that followed, tiny snowflakes started to fall, drifting through the night to vanish on the surface of the pool.

"The soft shit always comes back to bite me," Juno murmured.

"Not with me, it wouldn't." The words fell out of his mouth. Just before his lids lowered in disbelief at his own stupidity, he saw her head snap over.

What the fuck was wrong with him? Why couldn't he keep his mouth shut on this mountain? Heart hammering, he tried to come up with a way to smooth it over, to play it off like he hadn't just told her he wanted more.

He didn't want more.

Mate.

"Killian—"

His eyes popped open. He nodded at the water. "You want to learn?" When she didn't speak, he forced himself to look at her. Snowflakes floated between them, fragile and silent, like all the things he wasn't saying.

A single flake landed on her hair, its intricate lace pattern standing out against the dark lengths for a split second before it disappeared. "Killi—"

"I'll show you." He jerked his head toward the pool and focused blindly on the glossy waves.

Feed. Provide.

The heat of her body called to him like a siren as she eased into the water. He held his breath against her scent, but it was no use. It was in his nose, in his lungs, in his brain. "Stand still. Let them come to you."

Juno was a natural, of course, catching a silver trout on her first try and whooping in victory. They caught another, gutted both with their claws, and roasted them over the fire back in the cave. He had to practically sit on his goddamn hands to keep from offering her bite after flaky bite, to keep from petting her bare skin as it pebbled in the chill. It was warm in their little den by the fire, but their clothes were still damp, and they were still naked.

Claim.

When they were finished, he wanted nothing more than to haul her into his lap and warm her chilled skin, but she didn't ask, and he didn't offer. Instead, he dug out his pocket knife and sharpened it on a rock, trying not to compare the *shhhh-hik, shhhhhik* to the little slices tearing up his insides.

Just sex.

"I want to teach *you* something."

He couldn't bear to glance up and see the firelight teasing her naked curves, so he kept his eyes on his knife. "Oh yeah?" *Shhhhhik.* "What could a city cat like you teach me?"

"Hey." Something hit his shoulder—a pinecone. His lips twitched. "I know a lot that you don't."

He didn't doubt it. "Like what?"

"Like...Rogan's coffee order."

"Why would I care about Rogan's coffee order?"

"Because it's an enchanted one."

That made him look up. "No."

She nodded, smirking. "Triple shot of espresso with a double luck potion."

He snorted. Rogan was always burning it at both ends,

trying to give himself an edge, but buying enchantments? He shook his head.

"And Cyrus has a thing for Solara."

The half-breed mechmage? "Then, why's he boning everything with a slit?"

"Good question." Her tone had some bite to it.

"Maybe he doesn't want to have a thing for her." *Maybe he knows it's way more than a thing, and that scares the piss out of him.*

Their eyes met for a taut moment before they both looked away. An owl hooted in the distance, melodic and haunting.

"Wolf volunteers at a nursing home."

He couldn't help but swing his gaze back to her. "You're kidding."

A smile played around her mouth. "I know, right? Can you imagine him pushing old people around in wheelchairs?"

Yeah, he could, one in each hand, racing down bleach-scented hallways with a diabolical grin and a maniacal laugh. "Jesus."

"And John has a stash of Moon Cakes in his room, enough to outlast the apocalypse."

Moon Cakes? Those nasty, synthetic snack cakes that tasted like chemicals and vegetable fat? He made a face.

Her smile faded. "These are things you learn when you don't completely shut everyone out."

He scowled at his knife. "Weren't we just talking about how the soft shit is tough for you?"

"Yeah, well, I'm working on it," she snapped, then tucked her knees up and wrapped her arms around them. "Squad is safe."

He didn't know if she was saying it to herself or to him, but for a second, he let himself imagine it. Spending time with the team when he wasn't on duty. Sitting on the couch instead of on the floor. Laughing, joking, being a real part of it. His heart squeezed. His jaw clenched. He slid his blade against the rock with gusto.

"I've learned some things about you, too, Killian Diallo."

"Like how I've got a great spine?" He meant for it to be flippant. It came out bitter.

"Like how you're good with kids. And good at taking care of people. Even when they're bitchy about it."

Sparks flew from his blade as he swiped it against the rock.

"And that you like to play."

His heart panged.

"And that you're not really an asshole at all."

As he glared at his knife, his throat started to ache.

There was a rustle, and then suddenly, the fiercest female he'd ever known was parting his hands and climbing into his lap. The blade and stone thudded to the cave floor, and his arms wrapped around her automatically, palms rubbing over her goosebumped skin. Her round ass settled on his junk, and he grunted, adjusted, then jerked to attention when she cupped his face.

Chocolate eyes held him hostage. "I like this Killian. I think the other guys would like him, too. And I think you might even like to be liked."

The scent of her, the feel of her body on his, was clouding his senses. "What's the point?"

"Of being liked?"

"Of getting close."

Mom and Dad, smiling and touching. Little Nandi, laughing on Cullen's shoulders. The three of them dead on the jungle floor. Cullen's white face staring at him in shock—

"Because it feels better than being alone. And it's more fun. And like I said, I've discovered you actually like to have fun."

He gave her a grudging look.

"I think *this* Killian should come home when this is all over. Not the asshole one."

If she kept looking at him like that, he was going to say all kinds of stupid shit he couldn't take back. "No guarantees."

That made her lips curve, and he felt his own do the same.

She shivered. "Brr, it's cold." When she moved off his lap, he felt the loss of her warmth like a blow. He watched her pat the clothes they'd spread out to dry on the floor. Apparently, they were suitable, because she stretched out on them, met his gaze, and crooked her finger.

Because he was a goddamn glutton for punishment, he crawled over and lay on his side behind her, feeling the heat of her from inches away.

When the Maneater reached back to pull his arm around her, snuggling close against his torso, he thought he might suffocate from the pressure around his heart.

"Your tattoos are cool." She traced a bold black line along his bicep.

He could watch her finger trail on his skin forever. "They don't mean anything."

"No?"

He shook his head, enjoyed the way it made his lips rub against her hair, and did it again. "I got them done right when I got to the city. Right after—" He swallowed. *Right after I lost everything.* "I wanted to mark myself up. Be someone different." It both helped and hurt to see himself in the mirror those first few months, his skin streaked with harsh black lines.

She squeezed his arm.

He cleared his throat. "Besides, Cullen hates tattoos."

She snorted, tracing another line. "Probably thinks it would be a crime to mess up his pretty skin."

Jealousy simmered to life. "Yeah, he's pretty, all right. And he knows it."

"You're way hotter than he is."

Disbelief was quickly followed by a rush of male pride. "You think so?"

"Maybe." Her sly tone made his dick jump. She ran her fingertip along another line, leaving a tingling trail. "Do you like them?"

He shrugged.

Her fingernail tickled the sensitive inside of his elbow. "I think they're sexy as hell."

Did she now? He was suddenly a hell of a lot more fond of them. He nuzzled her neck, unable to help himself, then stopped short. "Does Vasquez have any?"

"Tattoos?"

"Yeah."

"Why?"

"Just wondering if he was sexy as hell, too." He trailed his tongue up her neck, waiting for her response.

"Yeah, he was."

His tongue stilled in the hollow behind her ear.

"Still is, actually. No tattoos, though."

Fucking Vasquez. His fingers dug into her hip bone.

She chuckled.

Minx. He dug in harder, nipped her ear. "Are you *trying* to piss me off?"

"It's so easy."

He bit down on her lobe. Her little gasp morphed into a smug laugh, like she'd gotten exactly what she wanted. "Careful, female. I just might know how to push *your* buttons."

"Promises, promises." There was a sultry smile in her tone, but he could tell she was getting tired. She sighed, nuzzling his bicep. "Why do you smell so good?"

He felt her drift off, but didn't dare close his eyes. Miss a single second of this? Not on his fucking life.

CHAPTER 41

Her feet were freezing.

Juno cracked an eyelid. Outside their little cave shelter, dawn painted the mountainside a pale blue. The waterfall pounded nearby, mist rising from the pool at its base. She lay on her side, the hard, cold ground beneath her and a furnace at her back.

She opened both eyes and stared at the strong arm extending out from under her head that she was using as a pillow. Another arm was draped around her middle, and a heavy thigh was thrown over her legs, wrapping her in a living, breathing blanket that warmed her in more ways than one.

Except her feet. She tucked them under a heavy male calf, digging in, seeking heat.

A grunt rumbled against her back, and his legs shifted, but instead of jerking away from her frigid toes, he sandwiched them between his legs, instantly warming them. His palm lifted to cover her shoulder, rubbing down her arm.

God, he was *sweet*. Killian Diallo was sweet.

She breathed deeply against his golden skin. He smelled good. He felt good. This felt good.

The soft stuff always comes back to bite me.

Not with me, it wouldn't.

"Good morning, beautiful savage." Killian's deep voice vibrated against her back.

Searing lust and a deep, tender ache shot through her. Who would have thought that Killian Diallo would purr something so perfect in her ear? *Beautiful savage.* His rough growl rang with reverence, his words spearing straight to the very heart of who she was. How she longed to be seen.

Blood pumping in anticipation, she reached back and stroked his hard cock. His deep groan sent a bolt of heat through her. Then, quickly enough to make her suck in a breath, he rolled her to her stomach, pinned her to the ground, and nudged her thighs apart with his knees.

Slowly, he fisted her hair and gently pulled, arching her neck.

Sleepiness vanished. She was naked, pinned, and bent backward with her throat exposed. Few positions were more dangerous for a fighter or a female. She'd never allowed this, in the Arena or in bed.

Here, now, with him, a primal thrill shot through her. *Strong male. Strong protector.*

Killian leaned down and took a long, slow sniff of her arched neck. A hot tongue dragged up her throat. His grip tightened in her hair, just enough.

"What do you want?" he growled directly into her ear.

Even when he could take whatever he wanted, he asked.

"You." The word floated out in a breathless whisper, but it felt heavy. Resonant. A dark truth spilling from some deep, soft part of her. "I want you."

His big body went still. He pulled her upright until they were both kneeling, her back to his front. One arm slipped around her waist, clasping her against him. The other slid up her torso to grip her chin, softly caging her throat.

Not a threat—a promise. He was in control. He was holding her, supporting her, and he wasn't letting go.

For the first time in a long time, she didn't want him to.

Holding her tight, he sank his cock inside her one delicious inch at a time. They both moaned. He felt incredible inside her. Behind her. All around her. An iron cocoon wrapped in warm satin, cradling every inch of her.

"You are so beautiful." His lips grazed her neck.

Tears pricked behind her eyes. Her whole life, men had commented on her beauty. There was always an edge to it. An unspoken promise of pursuit, a desire to possess, to own. A threat.

With Killian, there was only admiration.

He moved in her, slow and deep. Pleasure sparked in her veins. She shuddered in his hold. Her body longed to give in to the sizzling sensations rolling through her. It was all she could do to hold herself upright.

"I've got you." His breath was hot in her ear. "Let go."

Heart pounding, she relaxed against him, giving herself over to his strength. Firm, gentle fingers around her throat and jaw. Hard, warm arm around her body. Strong thighs and torso behind her. She was surrounded by his power, his warmth, his rock solid presence.

"Yes." His whisper was laced with triumph as she softened in his hold. His muscles tightened around her, absorbing her weight as his strokes deepened, hips rolling against her in a dizzying rhythm.

Every long, slow pump was pure pleasure. A hot flush swept across her skin. Her moans thrummed against his hand encircling her throat. His own echoed against her back. His hand slid up her ribcage to knead her breast, his thumb teasing her nipple while he pressed open-mouthed kisses to the sensitive hollow of her neck.

"So strong. So beautiful. Juno..." There was desperation

and yearning in his hushed words, in the groan that followed. "Come for me."

The force of her climax bowed her spine. As her shout echoed into the dawn, Killian's arm clamped around her, and his thrusts grew harder, pummeling the source of her pleasure until stars danced before her eyes. She reached back and raked her claws deep into his thigh. *Mine.*

His answering bite in the curve of her neck made her core seize again. This time, he came with her, every muscle tightening as he growled against her skin.

They panted against each other, both of them kneeling upright, his belly on her spine. Slowly, he released her chin and slid his hand down her throat, between her breasts, to rest on the curve of her waist. He kissed his bite mark. Her heart lurched. His breath ruffled her hair.

The stars in her eyes finally cleared, bringing the cold cave back into focus. Killian's abs pressed into her back with every deep breath.

"Made you come on my back," she said, unable to resist.

He chuckled and eased out of her, running an appreciative palm down the curve of her spine. She arched into the stroke like the cat she was.

She turned to face him. He sat back on his heels, golden-skinned and hugely muscled and giving her a sated grin with his hair spilling around his shoulders. If she wasn't already breathless, he would've stolen all the air from her lungs. "You're gorgeous, Diallo."

His smile faded. "I'm a goddamn ogre compared to you."

Rough and soft at the same time. She shook her head in mock disappointment. "Gorgeous, but not very bright."

He lobbed a pinecone at her. She blocked it, snagged her own, and whipped it at him. He dodged, then dove for her.

Their laughter echoed in the trees, startling birds into the morning sun. They ate fish. She insisted on catching it herself, feeling a rush of pride when she snagged two wriggling trout in under ten minutes. Killian smiled, roasted them over the fire, and very deliberately gestured for her to take hers from the flames when it was done.

Which was good. She didn't want him to feed her from his hand. Didn't want to be claimed.

"Want to ride me again?" Killian asked after they'd kicked dirt over their fire, ready to continue up the mountain. His amber gaze sparkled.

This teasing, playful side of him did things to her. A lot about him did things to her. "No…" It didn't come out quite as decisive as she meant it to.

He lifted a brow at her feet. "Rough ground for bare feet."

"My feet will be fine. I'm shifting."

He shrugged. "Your loss." He shucked his pants and gestured to his shirt she wore. "Tie them to me." He burst into lion form.

She made a bundle of the clothes and tied them around his huge neck, her fingers lingering in his coarse mane and stroking his flank.

Vibration under her fingertips made her chuckle. "You're purring again."

The lion tossed her a glare and took off. Laughing, she melted into cat form and raced to catch up.

They jostled each other, nipped playfully, ran and chased and teased. She silently jumped onto a tree limb and waited for him to realize she was missing. It didn't take long. Seconds after she lowered her belly to the branch, gripping tight with her claws, he stopped, whipped his big feline body around, and scented the air. If she was in human form, she would've had to stifle a giggle.

He prowled closer, his great muscles flexing under golden fur, and stopped under her tree. She waited for him to look up, ready to pounce on his face the moment he did. But instead, he rammed his enormous lion forehead into the tree trunk. Her perch shuddered. She gripped tighter, her tail whipping—

There was a sharp yank on the end, and her haunches dipped off the branch.

Did that dick just pull her tail?

She leaped to the ground and sprinted, threading through trees, his hot breath on her heels. He growled. Deep inside her jaguar form, the woman grinned. She was faster than him, and more nimble. She just needed to find the right time to spin and take him by surprise—

He slammed into her shoulder, knocking her to the ground—and out of the path of a winged demon swooping toward her with a hair-raising screech. Killian swatted it to the ground and pounced. Bones snapped. Its shrieks were cut off abruptly.

Juno leaped for the second pterodactyl-like demon rocketing toward her face. Sulfur stench, flapping wings…

How had she missed them?

They dispatched it quickly, but not before it opened its toothy beak and belched a stream of something green at her. She spun enough to avoid a faceful, but the stuff landed on her left hip. She tore out the thing's throat an instant before the wet feeling turned to something that felt like fire. She gave a jaguar scream and craned her neck to watch a hole burn through her fur.

Fuck. She changed back to human form with a guttural cry. The acidic spit had been stuck in her pelt, only just grazing the skin beneath, and if she could wipe it off, she'd be fine…

There was a rough curse, a warm hand on her lower back, and then a swipe over the burning spot on her hip. She yelled in protest, but it was too late. Killian's cry of pain meant he'd done exactly what he shouldn't have, and wiped the stuff off with his own hand.

Sure enough, he was rubbing his palm vigorously against the ground, pine needles sticking to the goo that lingered on his skin. Every grunt of pain hit her with a pang. When a quick glance around confirmed they were again alone, she grabbed a fistful of dry leaves and took his wrist, wiping the last bits of flesh-eating demon spit off his wide, calloused palm. They were both breathing heavily when she was done.

He frowned fiercely at her blistered skin, not even glancing at his own hand, which she knew had to feel like he'd slid down a flaming rope. When he met her gaze, his uninjured hand stroked her loose hair. "You good?"

Her stupid heart melted, and a horrible realization slid into the pit of her stomach.

This was more than a couple shifters easing their touch-hunger. A lot more.

Alarm flashed across his face. "You hit somewhere else?" He dropped his hand to her shoulder, raking a glance over her naked skin.

She shook her head, unable to speak.

His grip tightened on her shoulder. "DeSilva." He grimaced, shaking out his injured hand, though his gaze never left hers. "What?"

She eased away from his hold. "That could've been bad. Really bad."

"No shit. Good thing it wasn't."

Her pulse hammered. "I didn't even notice them."

"Yeah, they came up fast."

"I would've been hit if you hadn't knocked me out of the way."

His amber eyes sharpened on her face. "Good thing I did, then." When she just stared at him with dread curling in her gut, he pointed a finger at her. "Don't."

She'd been distracted, too busy focusing on her sexy squadmate and their stupid game to notice the enemy.

"Your teammate had your back, Juno. That's what we do. You pulled my sorry ass from the river, remember?" A shaft of sunlight made his hair shimmer like spun gold.

Right. He was right. That's why they never patrolled alone. "Yeah. Okay. Thanks." She nodded, and he did the same. The ugly feeling simmering in her belly eased.

Killian squinted at her burned hip. "That looks pretty bad. Better let me give you a ride."

She chucked a pebble at him, laughing. He was right. Teammates had each other's back. The alarm bells going off in her head were a kneejerk reaction to being taken by surprise, that was all. She'd just have to pay better attention.

Yeah. This was fine.

CHAPTER 42

The terrain got tougher as they headed for the summit. Still strangely luminous and full of vibrancy, but as the moss grew thicker and the blue flowers even more fragrant, the craggy ground grew rougher, and the incline steeper. Storms rolled in every night, each one more severe than the last, soaking them with freezing rain and hail until they found shelter.

Juno didn't give a shit. She hadn't had this much fun in a long time.

Three days after he'd taught her to catch fish with her bare hands, Killian Diallo had shown her how to make a slingshot, tie flower stems together to make a crown, and whistle into an acorn cap. He'd lost the hard edge that had always lingered around his eyes, he'd laughed more than she'd heard in six years, and he slept curled around her like a housecat until morning. A big, growly housecat who purred in his sleep.

Each night, after he'd tugged her into the warm embrace of his body, she'd stayed awake, waiting for the rumble of his purr against her back. Then, she'd drifted off with a smile on her face.

What the hell was happening on this mountain?

They hadn't had a demon sighting since the venom-spitting birds. The big snake hadn't even peeked out of the hole at the summit. Not that they'd seen, anyway.

They might have been slightly distracted.

She couldn't get enough of him. And if the amount of sex they were having was anything to go by, he felt the same. Thank God her fertile window was still months away.

All he had to do was look at her. Laugh. Smirk. Wink. Yeah, Killian Diallo winked at her, and it made her lose her damn mind. Once he discovered that, he used it ruthlessly.

He was smarter than she'd ever known. Sweeter than she'd ever known. Sexier than—well, she'd always known he was sexy as hell, but here, on the mountain, just the two of them? She felt like she was really seeing him for the first time.

She lobbed an acorn in his direction, pinging him in the forehead. He whirled around, golden hair flying, and spotted her at the top of the bluff above the sparkling pond they'd discovered.

"Careful, female," he growled, and a thrill shot through her. Aqua faebugs zipped through the encroaching twilight, streaking around him like sparkling laser beams.

"Come up here. It's gorgeous." The valley was a wash of purples and deep blues, the river glittering far below. The threads of smoke from the village were barely visible, the silvery lake at its center hardly more than a mercurial spec. Mountains rose like towering violet pyramids all around them. The sun was a magenta orb sinking slowly into the shadows between their peaks.

Killian's gaze heated as he stared up at her. "I like the view right here."

"I'm serious, come here."

Her pulse sped as he leaped from rock to rock, hauling himself up the bluff before finally springing over the edge in an impressive feat of power that made his massive arms flex.

She watched him through lowered lids as he rose, sauntered forward, and hauled her against him for a slow, filthy kiss. When he pulled away, she yanked him back for more.

He chuckled against her mouth. "Still not sick of me yet?"

Her head spun, her whole body humming. "Hmm?" When he chuckled again, she blinked, his words registering. Nerves shot through her. "Why do you ask?"

"Just making sure you haven't gotten me out of your system."

Just sex. Just until it's out of our systems.

"Why? Have you?" Her heart thudded.

"Not even fucking close."

She managed to hold back the sigh of relief. "Good."

"Yeah?"

This close, his eyes were like pools of dark, rich honey. "Yeah."

He nuzzled her before giving her a soft, gentle kiss.

And just like that, whatever was left of that hard, frozen ring around her heart disappeared. Gone. Evaporated. He'd been melting it for days, for weeks, and now, with a tender press of his lips, it was just...gone.

He pulled back and tucked her against his side so they could look out at the twilit landscape. She didn't see it. She was too busy staring at his fierce, rawboned face.

His gaze slid toward her. "What?"

"Nothing."

Bullshit, his eyes said, but he looked back at the view and tugged her closer, the heat and scent of him surrounding her. "Wonder how it's going down there."

Some of her glow vanished as she considered the tiny village far below. Had there been more attacks? Were the wolves down there scrambling, suffering, wounded or worse, while she and Killian were up here cuddling and fucking and falling in—

She sucked in a breath.

He frowned down at her. "What?"

Oh, fuck. Oh, fuck.

Pulse pounding, she forced herself to look up at him.

Mate, her cat purred.

His brows slashed, and he turned to face her, gripping her elbows. "What is it?"

Oh, fuck.

Realization flickered across his expression as he searched her eyes, and when he spoke again, it was a rough, knowing whisper. "What, Juno?"

Somewhere between six years of snarling and climbing a mountain together, she'd fallen for Killian Diallo.

CHAPTER 43

The way she was looking at him made him feel like his heart was going to explode. Hell, everything about her made him feel like his heart was going to explode. These past few days had been like a waking dream. The slightest touch felt like a thousand feathers trailing over his skin. The rich color of her skin, the depthless chocolate of her eyes, and the shine on her dark hair seemed amplified. The twist of her lips hit him like a sledgehammer. The sound of her laugh lit him up like a light bulb. His dick was at permanent attention.

The previous night, they'd found a hot spring bubbling in a clearing. The mist rising off of it smelled slightly like sulfur, but they'd lounged in the hot water for hours, watching the vibrant colors of the aurora undulate overhead, larger than life and vivid as neon lights. They were nothing compared to the electricity of Juno's dripping finger tracing the tattoos on his chest.

"They seem brighter up here," she'd murmured, gazing at the lights.

Everything was brighter, here at the top of the world with her.

Now, he tucked a strand of silken hair behind her ear, loving that she'd run out of hair elastics, that he was the only one who got to see it loose and flowing around her strong shoulders. Loving and fearing the shell-shocked expression on her face, like she'd just realized something monumental.

"What?" he whispered again.

"What happens when we go home?"

He managed to keep his voice steady. "What do you want to happen?"

Those dark eyes stared into his, shimmering with all kinds of things he'd never hoped to see and wanted with every fiber of his being. "You first."

He huffed a laugh. "Hell, no." His thumbs skimmed her elbows. He couldn't stop touching her.

That little crease appeared between her brows. "I don't know. Everything's different here. We're different here."

His heart was in his throat. "Do you like how we are here?"

She gave him a flat look. "Of course I do. It's just..." She shook her head. "I don't know how we can be like this at home."

Fuck. "So, you want to go back to the way things were?"

"No, I'd like you to not be an asshole when we go home."

A block of ice dropped into his gut. "Is that all?"

She didn't say anything.

"Is that all? I come home all nice and tame, and we both go back to fucking other people?"

There was a burning slice of pain along each arm. He looked down to see that her claws had shot out where she gripped him above the elbows.

"You fuck another female and I'll gut her. Then, I'll come for you." Her claws sank in a little more before she released him to rub her face, her curse floating into the dusk. "This wasn't supposed to get complicated. I was just supposed to bang you out of my system and then go back to being me."

"What the hell does that mean? Do you not feel like yourself when you're with me?"

He waited, fists clenched, while she warred with herself, deciding whether to be soft or throw up her blocks. "I feel like...all of me."

MATE.

"And the last time I let myself feel like that..."

The mere hint of Vasquez made his blood boil. "Would you stop comparing me to him? This is different."

She looked at him so long, he thought he might burst. "Let's find some shelter." She started back down the bluff while he stood there with his heart threatening to beat out of his body.

She turned. "Coming?"

Always.

CHAPTER 44

They reached the summit the next day. He'd woken to Juno's mouth on his cock and had barely managed to hold his load before hauling her up his body and plunging inside her. It was more than the sensation of her tongue and lips and the wet slide of her mouth around his shaft. It was the fact that the strongest female he'd ever known was kneeling at his feet, offering him something purely for his pleasure. It had taken every shred of control to refuse his lion's pounding, relentless demand.

CLAIM MATE.

The word still sent a blast of fear through him, but the warning bell was growing more and more distant with each night he spent curled around her, with each day they spent laughing and running together, wild and free.

The sight of the summit made his stomach drop. When they found the hellmouth, they'd call the others, have the archangels seal it up, and their mission would be over. It would be time to go home.

He didn't want to go home.

The scent reached him first. He slowed, flanks heaving from the pace they'd set, and inhaled, long and deep.

What the fuck was that?

Sulfur, magic, and something else. An animal he'd never smelled before.

At his side, the black jaguar scented the air and chuffed. He growled in agreement. They crept forward. There was no smoke, no charred patch of earth that would signal a hellmouth, but every instinct screamed that a threat was nearby.

Protect mate.

She can handle herself.

It was true, and it eased some of the knot in his chest. Some of it.

Beside him, Juno sank low on her paws, focused on a spot just over the rise of the hill. Killian followed suit, swept the scene, and felt his blood run cold.

There at the summit's peak was the giant hole they'd seen after the landslide, gaping like a yawning black maw. A scraping sound rang from inside, like flesh dragging over stone, and a head emerged from the darkness.

A monstrous worm the size of a goddamn bus, with rough, pale skin that looked hard as armor, slunk into view. It had no eyes, just a grotesquely oversized mouth ringed with row after row of long, pointed teeth. The stench coming off of it was unbelievable—sulfur and earth and rot, and a punch of magic that was strong enough to make Killian's head hurt.

KILL.

For the first time since they'd defected, Killian wished his lens was still linked to the DE database. Sure would be nice to know what this thing was and the best way to kill it. He had a feeling their claws would be no match for its armored skin.

Slowly, the giant worm slid backward, and was gone.

He and Juno exchanged a glance. They crept forward, eyes and ears peeled, trained human soldiers with predator instincts and animal senses. When they reached the hole, the worm was nowhere to be found, but the scent of it poured from the opening like water from a hose.

Another shared glance, a silent agreement. Together, they stepped inside.

His cat eyes adapted instantly. Juno's would, too.

The sense of something Other hummed in the air, tingling along his nerve endings until he wanted to shake out his mane. He bit at the air instead, tasting a hint of whatever it was. It made his hair stand on end. He glanced at Juno, wondering if she felt it, too.

The floor buckled beneath his paws.

He went down, scrabbling at the air as the earth fell out from under him. There was nothing to grab, nothing to dig his claws into—

Pain sliced through his foreleg. Juno's claws bit deep into his flesh, her back feet skidding as his weight dragged her toward the hole. Then, lightning fast, she reared forward and sank her powerful jaws into his foreleg.

The pain nearly blinded him, but he wasn't about to complain. The strongest jaws in the big cat kingdom were dragging his ass to safety, hauling him to the edge of the collapsed spot and flinging him to solid ground.

Their eyes met.

The floor dropped out from under them, and they both plummeted into darkness.

Air rushed past as they fell, clawing at nothing, desperate to grab hold of something. He grazed something soft—shit, Juno—his tail whipping wildly, trying to stay upright.

His ass hit something rock hard and freezing cold. A startled roar burst from his throat, echoing all around, and Juno landed on top of him as he began to slide.

They jostled against each other in a jumble of feline limbs. Ice—this was a chute of ice, and they were flying down it like a bobsled team on Blitz.

By sheer force of will, he stayed in cat form, though every instinct screamed at him to get his human arms around her, wrap her up, and take the brunt of the impact as they bashed into the icy walls. His cat form could handle it a lot better than his fragile human skin, and so could hers.

The frozen surface beneath him vanished, and his stomach floated up to his throat as they sailed into space.

He dug his claws into whatever part of Juno he could reach and held on tight.

They landed with a brutal crunch. Pain shot through his tail, but he was distracted by the lights.

Veins of electric blue lit the walls, growing thicker and thicker until the two of them were shooting down a glowing tunnel that hummed with hair-raising energy.

Little bursts of pain lit up his feline torso—Juno had dug her claws into him, too. They held on tight to each other, a couple of big cats rocketing down the world's biggest luge. It might've been funny if he wasn't so focused on protecting his female.

The tunnel opened up, and they shot into a vast, rocky cavern lit by the striations of electric blue. Rotten egg stench exploded in his nose, his lion eyes peeled wide, and Juno's claws bit deeper into his flesh as images passed in a blur—icy stalactites spearing from the ceiling, blue-streaked walls, and enormous, worm-sized tunnels leading in every direction.

Down, down, down they fell.

He saw the water a second before they plunged into it, the frigid surface hitting like cement, knocking Juno from his side and stealing the air from his lungs. Bubbles exploded in his wake as he slammed into the sandy bottom of a vast, freezing pool.

His lion was a shit swimmer. He shifted to human form and instantly regretted it. The shock of the glacial water nearly made him suck in a fatal breath, but by some miracle, he kept his shit together.

Where was she?

There, already pawing toward the surface. Her sleek jaguar form was a black blur beneath the water and a far stronger swimmer than his lion. Even as he planted his feet and shoved off the bottom, her feline head swiveled to check on him.

That small action gave his human muscles the strength of a thousand lions. He broke the surface with a gasp that shredded his throat, lungs on fire and head pounding. Before he even wiped the water from his eyes, he was looking for her.

She was treading water at his side in human form, her hair plastered to her skull and eyes wide with shock.

"You good?" they said in unison.

He let out a shaky breath, shivering with cold and relief.

Together, they glanced at the vast shoreline, where tendrils of smoke curled from chimneys and the scent of roasted meat wafted from a long cookhouse.

"No fucking way," Juno gritted out.

They swam to shore, stroke for stroke.

CHAPTER 45

They didn't run into anyone between the lake and their cabin, which was fine with Juno. She was half-drowned, half-frozen, and trying to figure out what the hell they'd just seen.

Killian cranked on the shower as soon as they got back, pulling her into the tiny bathroom and shutting the door. While they waited for the water to run hot, he rubbed his big palms briskly over her arms even as he shuddered violently.

"This fucking thing takes forever to heat up." He scowled at the shower head, haphazardly squeezed the water from his hair onto the bathroom floor, then reached for hers. His hands wrapped around her soaking wet locks before he halted.

Their eyes met. Shivering, heart pattering, Juno reached up to gather his still-dripping hair in her own hands, squeezing hard. Water trickled over her knuckles, but she hardly felt the cold. Not when Killian Diallo was looking at her like that.

He slowly worked his way down her mass of hair, keeping the freezing lengths off her back while icy water ran down his thick forearms.

"Thank you," she whispered.

Wordlessly, he tugged her into the shower, positioned her under the hot water, and wrapped his arms around her for a long, long time.

She smiled against his pecs. "I'm good, you know. Not even banged up."

"I know."

She pulled back to examine his arm. Her jaguar's bite marks were deep, his flesh slightly torn, but it was healing. "I gotta stop jerking you around with my fangs."

A purr rumbled from his chest. "I like your fangs in me. Especially when they saved my ass. Again. Kind of," he amended. "I still fell down a fucking worm hole."

She nodded. "We need to tell Rogan."

"Food first."

Her stomach growled. "Yes, food first."

They dressed quickly. It felt strange to step into a fresh pair of leggings. She'd gotten used to wearing nothing but his enormous shirt. She almost missed it.

He watched her hungrily. "I think I like you better in nothing but my shirt."

She arched a brow. "I think I like your mouth better between my legs."

His eyes went volcanic. "You eat first. Then, I'll eat you."

Jesus, this male.

Nerves kicked in as they walked toward the cookhouse. It had been a week, but she wasn't sure Magnus had cooled off enough to welcome her back into the village. Not to mention Val. She wondered if she'd done any lasting damage to the wolf. He'd looked bad when she'd left. She couldn't dredge up much remorse.

The village was deserted when they emerged from the forest. Chimneys smoked and the smell of cookfires wafted on the air, but none of the wolves were at their usual posts. Nobody sharpened weapons at the long table, nobody wrestled by the lake, and no kids chased each other around the big bonfire.

She and Killian exchanged a glance and picked up the pace, finally coming across a frightened looking female emerging from one of the cabins.

Juno's instincts flared to life. "What happened?"

"Cave-in at the mine." The female pressed the heel of a hand to her sternum. "Everyone's there except us. We stayed back with the kids."

They took off without another word.

CHAPTER 46

The quarry was a vast ring of rock tucked between two foothills. Timberland Materials was the city's major supplier of timber, stone, and steel, and the Pack's major source of income. When Killian's dad had been alive and at the helm of Pride Construction, he'd often grumbled about the Pack's strict quantity limitations on timber purchases, but there'd been respect alongside his frustration. The lions loved and protected their land, as well.

The wolves still guarded their resources as viciously as he remembered. Killian and Juno had only been shown the quarry and lumberyard at their insistence, and had been forbidden to go there without a Pack escort.

A cloud of dust hung over the site, muting the sunlight and coating several of the wolves who paced in human form. As they drew close, a dismayed shout rang from the mine entrance, where a couple of people were carefully hauling away chunks of stone, trying to make an opening. They'd created one, all right, and apparently, what they saw inside was dire.

Magnus loomed like a thundercloud near the collapsed rubble. The air around him practically throbbed. Black brows drew menacingly low as he watched Killian and Juno's approach. "I thought I told you to get out."

Killian didn't like the male's tone, but Juno only craned her neck to see around the alpha's enormous shoulders. "I did. Now, I'm back. How many are in there?"

"Two," one of the dusty wolves answered, his eyes haunted. "We made it out, but Sten and Bas are still in there."

Another wolf with a sandy ponytail peered through the hole at the blocked entrance. "It's a mess, Magnus. I'm worried we'll be too heavy."

"Let me see." As Juno stepped up to the wall of rubble and looked through the opening, Killian's heart started to race.

She stepped back and looked Magnus straight in the eye. "That's an obstacle course."

Oh, shit.

Protect mate.

A dangerous hum filled Killian's ears, like his terror had taken the form of a thousand hornets swarming inside his skull.

Protect mate.

Magnus peered into the entrance, cursed, and flung out a hand, sending a nearby block of stone whipping into a piece of machinery. His thick fingers flexed.

Juno's chin ticked up. "I can do that."

PROTECT MATE.

"It's jacked up in there, but I can do it. I can see my way."

No.

Magnus's upper lip curled. "Why would you risk yourself for my people? You already nearly killed one of them."

"I've been risking myself for your people since I got here. It's my job." She pointed at the mine. "And I can do that."

"She was better than all of us at the course, alpha." The sandy-haired wolf wiped a palm over his face. "I can't fit. There's no way you could fit."

Killian's breath quickened. The hornets were so loud he could hardly hear what the others were saying, but he got the fucking gist, and he could picture it all too clearly. Broken beams, jagged rebar, a quivering stone ceiling on the verge of further collapse...and his female, sleek and powerful and determined as fuck, threading her way through a death trap the wolves wouldn't even attempt.

And him, standing outside like a giant useless pile of shit, unable to talk to her. Not knowing if she was injured. Not knowing if she needed him. Not knowing if she was coming back.

She was already rolling out her neck, stretching her shoulders, eyeing the small opening in the rubble like a marksman. She shot him a grin.

She was excited.

"You're just going to let her go in there alone?" Killian demanded over the buzzing between his ears.

Magnus slid him a glance. "Do you have another suggestion?"

Let those fuckers die in there while I take my female home and wrap myself around her like a bulletproof vest. "Why don't you do it?"

"Diallo." Juno's sharp warning barely registered.

Magnus's eyes flashed. "Because I can't fucking fit, *drittsek*. And she's already proven she's better than any of my people at this kind of thing, as much as it pains me to admit."

"What about Astrid?" he croaked, desperation bubbling up inside him even as he felt Juno's eyes drilling a hole into his temple.

"Supply run in the city." Magnus's expression softened infinitesimally. "Your female is the best option."

"No." It slipped out of his mouth and landed like a ticking bomb.

They all stared at him, but he couldn't stop. His lion was

in a frenzy behind his skin, shoving at his muscles, demanding he do something.

PROTECT MATE.

"I know she can do it, but not alone. Not without backup." His claws shot out.

"Diallo."

He flung an arm toward the collapsed mine and practically shouted at Magnus. "You won't even send your own people in there. Shore it up, tunnel in from behind, do something—"

"*Diallo!*"

Panic seized his lungs. He spun around. "It's too fucking dangerous, Juno."

"I can see exactly where I need to go. I got this—"

"That is a fucking death trap." His brain whirled, his lion pounding at his skull.

PROTECT MATE.

"This is what we do, Killian."

What if he couldn't get to her?

"I've got it, I promise."

What if she needed him and he didn't even fucking know it?

"I'll be fine—"

"*NO, JUNO!*"

His roar echoed around the silent quarry.

And just like that, he broke them.

CHAPTER 47

The world rushed back to him with his own bellowed words ringing in his ears.

He felt it before he even looked at her—the hammer coming down on the beautiful thing they'd built over the last few weeks.

Suddenly, he knew the sound of her heart cracking. He knew what heartbreak looked like in her eyes.

Fuck. "Just—"

But she slid that mask over her expression, shutting him out. And that was the most terrifying of all.

She turned to Magnus. "Let's do this. I'm ready."

Panic was a wild thing inside him, cornered and desperate, ready to eat him alive. "Juno—"

She tightened her ponytail and left him in the dust.

———

Killian had a long, continuous heart attack until the first dust-covered head emerged from the collapsed tunnel. His chest eased ever so slightly as a second wolf tumbled out, quickly supported and carried away by his comrades, but he didn't take a full fucking breath until a jaguar slid out of the gap, its black pelt gray with dust. She moved gingerly, but melted into human form and only took a few breaths before rising to stand, pulling on her clothes that had been held by a female wolf who stood nearby.

Killian started toward her, relief threatening to take him to his knees.

She turned her head and gave him a look that froze him in his tracks. *Come near me,* the look said, *and I'll gut you.*

She and the rescued wolves were loaded onto a four-wheeler and carted toward the village while the rest of the wolves laughed in relief and clapped each other on the back and the entire fucking world crumbled at Killian's feet.

He'd done exactly what Vasquez had done. Undermined her abilities, tried to keep her from doing her job, and treated her like a fragile possession instead of the terrifying, capable fighter she was.

He'd tried to cage her.

He made record time back to their cabin, heart in his throat. When he palmed his way inside, she was standing at the dresser, obviously fresh from a shower, her wet hair leaving damp spots on her thermal shirt. She didn't look at him.

"I fucked up." Desperation made his voice louder than he intended.

She pulled on one sock, then the other.

"I fucked up," he repeated.

"You did exactly what I expected you to do." Her voice was tired. She shook her head. "I don't know why I'm surprised."

His heart thundered. "Because you know I'm not the same as that fool."

"No?" She slammed a drawer and gestured out the window. "What was that, then?"

"That was me trying to keep you from doing something

stupid." When pain flickered in those chocolate depths, he felt it in his own body. "Fuck, I didn't mean that—"

Pain turned to anger. "You did. You meant it now, and you meant it back there when you said no, like it was *your fucking decision to make*." Her eyes flashed. "This is exactly why I don't do this shit."

The words sliced through his chest, stealing his breath. He barely managed to speak. "I screwed up. I'll figure it out, I just—"

She tossed her hands. "What are you going to do, Killian, have a meltdown every time I go on patrol? Tell Rogan we can only go on duty together, so you can protect me?" The anger left her eyes, replaced with something else. "This is who I am. This is what I do. This is what I *want* to do. I thought you actually got that. I thought you—" She cut herself off, shaking her head again.

"I do get it. I just saw that fucking death trap and couldn't —my lion..." He swallowed past the lump in his throat. "I'll do better. I'll figure my shit out."

She stared at him. "How?"

He didn't have an answer. Because she was right—the idea of Juno putting herself in danger with no way to talk to him made his brain explode, and he had no clue what to do about it.

MATE. TAKE. CLAIM.

The sadness in her eyes cut him in two. "I can't do this. We can't do this."

His heart fell to his feet. "Don't."

She shook her head, pain knitting her dark brows. "This has to be done."

He shook his own head, desperate.

Her whisper carried across the cabin like a scream. "We're done."

CHAPTER 48

He was going to have to leave the squad.

It had been almost a week since they'd rocketed down the core of a mountain into the bottom of a lake. A week since Juno put a stop to their…thing. She'd reported to Rogan, and apparently, there was some shit going down in the city that needed the squad's attention more. He couldn't get the team into wolf territory for a few days yet.

They'd found a couple more demons prowling around the village. Nobody was hurt, because he and Juno caught the hellspawn in time. But because there had been more sightings, Rogan told them to stay put.

And Killian was going out of his skull.

He was a ticking bomb. A festering boil ready to pop. A volcano. Touch-hunger had roared back to life, angrier and more volatile than before. Night after night, he shared her space, the cabin floor stretching between them like a chasm. She tried to stay silent, but he heard every rustle of her sheets as she flipped over, adjusted her pillow, and bit back another frustrated sigh.

Sleep eluded him. Visions kept flashing across his mind— her triumphant grin when she caught her first fish by hand.

The glint in her eye when she teased him. Her fingers tracing the lines of his tattoos. Her strong legs opening to him like the gates to heaven.

How was he going to go back to the city when this was all over? How was he going to live a few doors down from her, eat at the same table, use the same goddamn bathroom? What would he do when he had to sit in the same room during their stupid movie nights, knowing what she felt like curled in his arms? What she looked like when she came? What sounds she made? What she fucking felt like *inside*?

He'd almost forgotten what it felt like to ache all over. To move through a fog, to have a constant headache from wearing a permanent scowl. They'd gotten back into the wolves' good graces thanks to Juno's mine rescue, but it did little for Killian's social life.

He'd gotten into a few fights.

A lot of fights.

Fucking Lukas and his snide remarks, baiting him around the cookhouse, flirting with Juno whenever he was in sight. She didn't flirt back, but he apparently couldn't take a hint.

The male in question stepped out of the weapons hut as Killian stalked by on his way to chop some wood, or uproot a tree, or anything to take the edge off. "Yo, lion. You know what I've noticed?" He was flipping a knife, and the handle landed in his palm with a slap. "Ever since you two got back from your little trip up the mountain?" *Flip, slap.* "She doesn't smell like you anymore."

Rage boiled beneath Killian's skin, but by some miracle, he kept walking.

"Wonder why that is."

Just. Keep. Fucking. Walking.

"Maybe she needs a male who can show her how it's really d—"

His fist connected with the male's face. Bone cracked, blood flew, shouts echoed. He got the fucker on his back and wailed, and wailed, and wailed, his fists flying, the red haze of fury taking him over—

Pain tore through his scalp as he was yanked back by the hair. He didn't care. His arms kept swinging.

Suddenly, he was nose to nose with a gigantic bearded Viking. Killian showed him his teeth. Magnus bared his own, then shoved him toward the trees. "*Go.*"

Killian stalked off, steaming, with Magnus's heavy footsteps on his heels. When they reached a clearing, he felt another hard shove in his back, and he spun, snarling.

Magnus was ready for him. "Let's go."

They collided like a pair of titans. Magnus's fists were hard as boulders, but Killian barely noticed the blows raining on his ribs, his cheekbone, across his jaw. All he felt was rage.

"Claws," Magnus barked, and unsheathed his monstrous talons before taking a swipe at Killian's face. Killian reared back, escaping by millimeters, then barreled into the male's stomach, taking him to the ground as hot slashes of pain erupted across his back. They rolled and grappled, landing more punishing blows until they finally shoved apart and lurched to their feet, breathing heavily.

"Take another female," Magnus snapped.

Killian spat blood. "I can't."

"Why not?"

"My lion won't."

"Bullshit. The man won't."

"Fuck you." He dove at the Viking, ramming him into a tree before pummeling his abdomen in a flurry of fists.

Magnus shoved him away with a roar, adding a punishing kick to his quad for good measure. Pain radiated down his femur. Magnus wiped his bleeding nose and swept a look of disgust over Killian, muttering one of his foreign curses. "May the Gods save me from the mating call."

Killian spun, shaking his head. Wild, blind, he slammed

his fist into a tree. Agony exploded in his hand. He hit it again and again, desperate for the physical pain.

When his hand hung limp and bloody from his wrist and shards of white pierced through the flesh, he tilted his head back and roared his anguish into the sky.

Want. Want our female.

Enormous palms sandwiched his mutilated hand. Killian saw stars. The world spun, and he vomited into the undergrowth, trying to tug his hand away.

"Stay still."

Killian held on to consciousness by a thread as a prickling sensation started beneath his skin. It ran from his elbow to his raw, ripped fingertips, so faint he thought he might've imagined it. Magnus cursed and dropped his hand, which fell like a throbbing cinderblock to his side.

"Bah. I'm shit at healing. Better at throwing things." A chunk of fallen tree sailed across the clearing and thudded to the ground in demonstration.

Killian's breath whistled through his nose as he concentrated on keeping down what was left of his lunch.

Magnus watched him. "I met your parents once. They had a good mating, no?"

Focus on the pulsing agony of splintered bones and ravaged flesh. Not on the ache in your heart at the thought of your parents, always touching, smiling...

"You don't think you and the jaguar would be good together?"

Killian swayed at the images that bombarded him, of him and Juno together, really together, laughing, pushing each other's buttons until one of them snapped, then making up in the best possible way. He gripped the tree with his good hand and dug his claws in.

"Ah. You *do* think you'd be good together, and it scares the piss out of you."

Killian stared blindly into the woods. *Focus on the pain.*

"My parents had a good mating, too." Magnus's voice was a low rumble. "She died giving birth to Astrid. It nearly killed him."

"What do you think I'm trying to avoid?" Killian burst out, pain loosening his tongue.

Magnus laughed. The bastard actually *laughed* at him. "You fool. You're already there."

Fear clenched his heart, so visceral he pressed his good palm against his chest. He nearly whimpered. "Fuck."

A meaty hand slapped his shoulder and squeezed hard. "Yeah." Magnus tugged him toward the path. "Let's get you to Frida."

Half an hour later, he was flat on his back with tingles rushing through his hand and a grumpy old female bent over him, a pipe clenched between her teeth. The door to the healer's cabin swung inward, and Juno's dark head appeared. Her eyes flashed to his battered hand. She didn't even ask what happened, just looked at him like she somehow knew he'd used a sycamore as a punching bag.

He stared at the ceiling, his heart lurching.

You're already there.

"How long do you think this'll take? Rogan wants a call."

"An hour, maybe. He shattered most of this, stupid pup." Frida's lids were closed, her hands hovering over Killian's ruined flesh.

There was a pause. Juno's scent drifted across the room, warm and spicy and killing him.

"I'll be in the cabin."

He released a breath when the door closed after her.

"Why are you fighting it?"

He cracked an eyelid at the healer's gruff voice. "What?"

She swatted him upside the head. "The mating call. It's howling so loud in here I can hardly concentrate." When he only stared at her, she gave him a stern look. "It's dangerous to ignore it for so long."

He refocused on the ceiling. "It's more dangerous to listen."

Frida snorted and moved her hands to hover over a different part of his fingers. They twitched at the prickling sensation. "Most people can't wait for their mate. The bond is a gift. It's also one of the best ways to keep an eye on them."

"What do you mean?"

She gave him a withering look. "Don't they teach you cats anything? You can feel your mate through the bond. Their emotions, even their thoughts, if the bond is strong enough. It's how I knew my Anders was in trouble when he fell into the ravine." She muttered something that sounded a lot like *dumb skull.*

Killian swallowed past his dry throat. "Did you… was he—"

Her iron-gray eyes softened ever so slightly when she looked at him. "We found him in time. If we hadn't bonded…" She shook her head. Her pipe wagged. A puff of sweet-smelling smoke drifted toward the ceiling.

He'd heard mated pairs talk about the bond, but never in this kind of detail. He knew there was a connection, but he never thought…never knew…

In a rush, he imagined being able to feel Juno deep inside, to have an internal siren that would go off if she was ever in danger. She could call him if she was in trouble. He would always know she was safe, and if she wasn't safe, he would know where to find her.

Joyous, sweeping relief filled his chest, like he'd cracked open his ribcage and filled it with sunlight. His lungs eased, his shoulders drooping as if the ligaments had been cut.

"Ah." Frida granted him a small smile. "You see now?"

It was stupid to even think about. He didn't want a mate. She didn't want a mate. They'd both made that very fucking clear.

He couldn't stop picturing it.

They were silent a long while after that, Frida humming softly under her breath while he lay there reeling. Finally, she picked up his hand, examining it with knitted brows. "That'll do." She released it to his abdomen, then gave the tip of his nose a sharp flick. He jerked at the unexpected sting, but she stared him down, her wolf in her eyes. "Now, stop being a damned fool. A mate is this world's greatest blessing. Don't waste it."

"She doesn't want it." It was a croak.

"Ah. She's a fierce female, no? Doesn't want to be tied down."

"I don't want to tie her down." He just wanted to know she was safe, to know where to find her if she needed him.

"So, prove it."

His heart rammed against his sternum. He shouldn't be talking about this. Shouldn't even be considering it. "How?"

She laughed. "Tell her. Then, show her." She shrugged like it was the simplest thing in the world.

He left the healer's house in a daze, hardly seeing anything as he crossed the village. His pulse raced as he neared their cabin. A thin stream of smoke curled from the chimney, warm and welcoming. For a second, he was back in the jungle, staring up at the warm glow of lights in the tree-house windows, hearing laughter float down from above.

He pushed open the door and stopped short. Juno was stretching on the floor, her legs spread wide, torso lying flat on the hardwood planks and round ass pointed directly at him. He nearly swallowed his tongue. "Jesus Christ."

She sat upright, graceful as a ballerina and a thousand times more deadly. Her gaze flicked to his hand. "Was that about me?"

There was no point in lying. "Yeah."

Her scent washed over him as she got to her feet, stepped close, and lifted his hand to inspect the damage. Every brush of her fingers sent electricity along his nerve endings.

She shook her head and went to release him, but he gripped her wrist. Her eyes lifted to his.

He yanked her against him and slammed his mouth to hers. His arms whipped around her, clutching her as tight as he could, as if his muscles knew it could be the last time he'd hold her. His groan tunneled past her lips into her mouth, and he wanted it to go further, down her throat into her gut, absorb into her system so he was always there, running through her veins.

She met him there, in the inferno, in the frustration boiling over, climbing him until her ankles locked around his waist and her hands tangled in his hair and all he could feel, smell, taste was her.

He spun toward the nearest wall and flattened her against it before dragging his tongue up her neck.

She made a desperate noise. "This has to stop. You're a mess, I'm not sleeping…" She cursed when he sucked her earlobe into his mouth. "Your scent drives me so fucking crazy I can't breathe." She gripped him tight and pulled his head to the side so she could bury her nose in his neck.

His heart clenched. "I miss you."

She whimpered, yanked his head back, and kissed him like the world was ending.

Yes. This. Her. Only her.

She wrenched her lips away and shoved at his shoulders with a curse. He managed to release her, watching her walk away while his breath shuddered past his lips.

She spun and stared at him achingly from across the room. "Why couldn't you have stayed an asshole?"

His feet carried him back to her. They always seemed to carry him back to her. He gave her every chance to slip away, but she didn't, just watched as he eased up against her, taking in every beautiful detail.

She shook her head. "Why'd you have to be more?"

He cupped her face. "It's *always* been more with you."

He'd never seen Juno DeSilva look so fucking sad. It killed him. Her lids lowered, and she turned her face away before wrenching it back to nuzzle his palm, like she felt the same magnetic pull toward him that he felt toward her.

"Bonded mates can talk to each other," he blurted.

Her chocolate eyes flitted to meet his. "What?"

"They can talk in their heads. Telepathically or whatever. Check in."

Her heart rate kicked up, her pulse fluttering in the hollow of her neck.

His own heart was going to beat out of his chest. "I'm sorry I fucked up." He swallowed hard. "I don't want to change you. I don't want to cage you."

"You already tried."

"Never again. I swear it."

She stared at him. "What are you saying, Diallo?"

He couldn't say it out loud, so he put it all in his eyes, letting the last shreds of his internal shield fall away, laying himself bare.

And she recognized it, because hope and pain glimmered in her own gaze. "I thought you didn't want a mate."

"I didn't."

"So, what's changed?"

"I don't think I have a choice." He wanted to kiss her again. He always wanted to kiss her. "And now that I know about the bond, I don't think I would go so crazy if you could talk to me inside my head, you know? Like, 'Hey, Killian, I'm stuck under a tree at the bottom of a fucking river, come help me out.'"

A glint of wry humor flickered across her face.

Hope surged through him. "I know you can take care of yourself. You're fucking terrifying." When that earned him a little smile, he rushed on. "I just need to know you're safe when you're out there. Check in, keep tabs."

Her smile faded. "Keep tabs."

Fuck. "Not like that."

But she was shutting down. He could see it in the lines of her face, the stiffening of her body. She started shaking her head. "I've been here before."

"You know I don't mean it like that."

"How do you mean it, then? How is it different? Because he just wanted to make sure I was safe, too. And he wound up suffocating me. And going behind my back to make sure *my life* was as safe as *he* wanted it to be. It's my decision to make."

"I'm not trying to take anything from you. It's just...the shit we do is so dangerous—"

"Then, why aren't you asking to *keep tabs* on anyone else on the squad?"

"Because I'm not in love with anyone else on the fucking squad!"

It burst out of him in a roar. A myriad of expressions crossed her face—shock, joy, pain, resolve—all washed in the yellow of his lion's gaze.

Silence rang while he fought to keep his beast inside his skin.

TAKE. MATE. MINE.

The wetness shimmering in her eyes destroyed him. "I can't do this again."

She turned and strode through the door, into the woods, out of his grasp.

He watched her leave, his lion roaring in his skull and his heart shattering at his feet.

CHAPTER 49

Rogan still wouldn't let her come home.

"I want you two to stay there in case that fucking hole opens up." He sounded even more tense than usual, huffing a breath through the receiver. "We're being watched. Drones, surveillance, agents *I trained* harassing us on the street. Why are you so eager to come home?" Rogan's voice sharpened. "You two good?"

"Fine," Juno said, maybe a hair too quickly. "We're fine."

She was not fine. She was one big, throbbing wound.

Killian had barely spoken to her in days, and when he did, his words were sparse and clipped. They were back to the way things were, except now she knew how he felt inside her, wrapped around her, knew his smiles and his laughter and his complete and utter sweetness.

Bonded mates can talk to each other. Check in. Keep tabs.

Rafael had wanted to keep tabs, too. Just so he knew she was safe. Then, he wanted her to run on the obstacle course he built for her instead of out on the city streets. Then, he wanted her to reconsider applying for the academy. Then, he wanted to prevent her from attending without her finding out.

The strong lion is different.

Some deep part of her thought her jaguar might be right.

"Lion. Got a job for you."

Juno looked up from the pile of arrows she'd been repairing at the weapons table. Lukas stood near the big bonfire with another sentinel, each sporting a small pack over one shoulder. Neither of them looked thrilled to be facing Killian, who was chopping wood with fierce swings of an ax. Every crack had been like a blow to Juno's chest, and she couldn't keep her eyes from sliding across the village every five seconds to watch the sweat drip down his spine.

Lukas jerked his head toward the woods. "A couple of bridge cables need repairing. Everyone else is on a training run."

Killian's broad shoulders flared with heavy breaths. Even across the clearing, she could hear his rough voice like he was whispering in her ear. "Bridge cables? You need someone who can climb."

"You can climb, can't you?" The sneer was audible.

"Not as good as Juno."

Her hand froze on the arrow shaft.

"It's over the rapids. Dangerous. We need someone strong." The mocking tone had left Lukas's voice.

"Yeah, you need someone strong who can shimmy up a fucking pole. She can do it." Killian turned back to his log and flipped his ax into his grip, dismissing them.

Holy shit. He'd just given up a mission. A dangerous mission. Because she was a better fit. Because he believed she could do it.

Her heart soared. The arrow in her hand clattered to the table and rolled off the edge, forgotten.

Good male. Strong male.

Lukas glanced over from across the camp, but it wasn't his gaze she was suddenly desperate to catch. Killian's powerful back arched with another swing of the ax. The crack of the blade splitting wood snapped Juno back into focus just as Lukas and the other sentinel approached.

"We hear you're the right person for a job, kitty cat."

She tightened her ponytail, smiling for the first time in days.

———

The bridge repair went off without issue, though her stomach swooped once or twice when she was at the top of the support pole, clinging with her thighs while fastening the heavy cable to the eye hook with the river raging far below. It had taken all her strength to keep her balance and heft the cable into place, fighting against the wind. The triumph that surged through her when she slid to her feet once more had half as much to do with a job well done as it did with the one who'd recommended her for the task.

She wanted to thank him. Not for *letting* her do a dangerous job, but for telling others she was better suited for it than he was. For knowing she could handle it, even though it probably took everything in him to hold back his lion.

He was trying.

She made sure to catch his eye when she came back to the village, giving him a nod and ignoring the clap on the back from Lukas. Killian raked a yellow gaze over her and went back to chopping firewood.

Some of her satisfaction deflated. She watched his muscles flex with another swing of his blade, fighting the very real urge to yank the tool from his hands, toss it into the forest, and leap on him.

Chest tight, she checked the time and headed around the edge of the shoreline. The two of them were splitting watch between the lake and the mountain, making sure they kept eyes on each site. They hadn't seen another glimpse of the giant worm, and there hadn't been any more demon sightings around the village. Maybe the hellmouth, wherever it was, had sealed itself shut.

For once, she wouldn't mind leaving a mission incomplete. She was so ready to get out of here, back to the city and away from a tiny cabin covered in his scent. Back to normal.

Yeah, right.

She gripped a tree limb and counted chin-ups, her ankles hooked together. She'd just tested her muscles at the top of the bridge, but it still felt good to use them, to feel strong and capable. Especially when she felt so fucking tender on the inside.

She was strong. She was the Maneater.

Too bad it felt like she was the one being eaten alive.

The silvery lake shimmered in the purple dusk, bobbing in and out of view as she raised and lowered herself with slow, steady control.

I'm not in love with anyone else on the fucking squad.

Her cat yowled. Her heart ached. Going back to Light House, to the squad, to the way things used to be, was going to be hell.

Arms burning, she pumped out another set.

Gravel crunched under boots, quiet enough she could've missed it. But a scent registered soon after, one that brought her brows low.

"You're strong." Val emerged from the shadow of a tree, arms folded, watching her. "But I already knew that." Apparently, he'd spent a lot of time in the healer's cabin after their fight in the woods.

Pull up, lower down. "I'm a soldier." She dropped to her feet and faced him.

His lips lifted. "Yeah, you are. Still haven't figured out what kind, though. It's not like there's a bunch of bloody fights in the big city, right?"

"You'd be surprised."

"Oh, yeah? What do the city kitties fight over?" He grinned. "Parking spots?"

There was a sinister edge to that smile, and she wasn't in the fucking mood. She allowed her claws to prick her skin, extending a few deliberate inches.

Val's eyes tracked the movement. "Ooh. Touched a nerve. Sorry." He stepped forward, easing out of the trees. "Just never met a female quite like you."

"Your females are strong."

He shook his head, easing ever closer. "Mm. You're right. My sister was a sentinel. But there's still something different about you."

Her claws elongated further. Blood dripped to the forest floor. "Back off, Val."

Another step, another smile.

"I'm telling you to back the fuck off, and I suggest you listen."

"Why?"

"Because Magnus told me to play nice, but I'm having trouble with that right now."

"No, why do you suggest I listen?"

Ice shivered down her spine.

"I mean, what will you do? There's no one out here. Your lion's back at camp." He spoke easily, conversationally, and then his arm moved, quick as a flash. Something whined past her ear. She jerked aside, but a tiny lick of pain stung her neck. Her hand whipped to the spot and ripped out a single feather-tipped dart.

Oh, hell no.

She leaped at him, tearing into every inch of skin she could reach. Swiping at his throat, but only grazing it. Lashing at his face even as she stumbled off balance. He swore, then barreled into her, taking her to the ground. She flipped them.

Or tried.

His blood dripped onto her face as she jerked sluggishly under his weight.

His smile went blurry.

CHAPTER 50

Scrape. Scrape.

Juno pried her eyelids apart. She was lying on her side on a cold dirt floor, there was a foul, medicinal taste in her mouth, and her lashes felt glued together.

She twitched, trying to move her feet. They wouldn't separate.

She blinked hard and craned her neck to look toward her feet, her cheek scraping dirt.

Tied. Her feet were tied together. Thick rope was knotted around her ankles, and when she tried to jerk her hands apart, she felt the bite of rope around her wrists.

Not this. Not again.

"You're awake."

Her eyes snapped toward the voice. A male figure was ducking inside the entrance to what appeared to be a small cave. There was the sound of something dropping to the ground, then a scuffing of boots.

Val appeared, sinking to a crouch with a smile.

A jolt of fear blasted through her, instantly followed by burning rage. The cave flickered green, her cat ready to burst to the forefront.

Blinding pain speared into her brain, wrenching a startled cry from her. Deep inside, her jaguar writhed in agony. Her fingers and gums prickled, but her claws didn't split her skin, and her fangs didn't punch into her mouth. There was only an excruciating feeling of being squeezed, crushed like she was in the grasp of a vicious python.

"Ah, ah," Val admonished, wiggling a knife in her view. He cocked his head as she dragged air through her nose, her eyes wide against the sensation of pain and suffocation. "No going jaguar on me. You're a mean one." A deep slash on his cheek glinted in the light as he held up a small, knobbly object. A tiny green light shone in the gloom.

One of the scramblers Rogan had given them.

Her stomach dropped. "Where did you get that?" Her voice was rough. Whatever tranquilizer he'd used on her was powerful. How long had she been out?

"Found it in your cabin. It took me a while to figure out what it does."

Fully clothed. She was still fully clothed, thank God. If he'd touched her…

An image of Killian's devastating, primal fury flashed across her mind. If he'd touched her, Killian would burn the world down.

I'm not in love with anyone else on the fucking squad.

Val squinted at her. "I knew you were different. You and the lion." He tapped the knife absently against his palm. "What is it you do in the city? Because my own alpha doesn't seem to know, but he still brought you in when our people started mysteriously dying. Why is that?"

"What do you want, Val?" *Keep him talking.* Her bonds were tight. Too tight.

"What do I want? I want some fucking answers." His pleasant tone set her hair on end. "I want to know what killed my sister. My baby sister. She was younger than me, but she was strong. A soldier, like you." His eyes traveled over her body.

Shit. "Inga was your sister."

He slapped her, hard. Pain blossomed in her cheek. "You don't say her name." The pleasant tone was gone. "Have you ever seen the organs of someone you love? I saw her intestines. I saw her lungs." Tears shimmered in his eyes, but his face was a mask of hatred. "And *you* know what fucking did it, and *you're going to tell me.*"

A knife was suddenly pressed to her throat, the hard steel cold against her delicate flesh. She went very still.

Meeting Val's glittering stare without spitting in his face was a true test of her will. "I'll tell you."

He cocked his head. "Yeah?" The blade pressed more firmly against her throat.

A drop of blood ran down her neck. "Yes. Put the knife away."

An ugly expression crawled across his face. He placed the point of the knife on her collarbone and sliced diagonally across her chest. Fire followed the trail of his blade. Juno barely held back the gasp of pain. "This isn't a negotiation, and you're not in charge." He dug the knife into her chest again, making a long cut from the other side, crossing the other line before examining his work. "X marks the spot."

She'd defeated a lot of crazy people in the Arena. But they were alone, in the middle of nowhere, she was tied, and she couldn't shift.

Bonded mates can talk to each other.

She was a fool.

"I'm part of a secret team." Pain burned across her chest as warm blood trickled over her breasts, soaking into her thermal shirt.

"Go on."

She was an idiot who was too proud to let a strong male

stand at her side, ready to back her up at a moment's notice. "We fight enemies you can't see."

The hungry look in his eye made the hair on her neck stand up. "What kind of enemy?"

"The kind that killed your sister. But even if I tell you what they are, it won't do you any good. *You* can't see them, Val. You can't hunt them—"

He punched her in the temple. Everything went black.

CHAPTER 51

Pain. Pounding, throbbing pain.

Juno lifted eyelids that felt like they weighed a thousand pounds. Val sat across the fire, his back against the opposite cave wall. She licked her dry lips and pulled her knees up, trying to gather them beneath her. If she could sit up—

The second she attempted it, pain sledgehammered through her brain, her stomach lurched, and she vomited on the floor.

Shit. She spat, wriggling away from the puddle of sick. Everything was swimming. If she had a concussion, she was more screwed than she thought.

"Don't fuck with me, cat." *Scrape, scrape.* Val was sharpening his knife again, the blade gleaming in the firelight with every stroke against the whetting stone. "Talk."

Bile burned in her throat. Anger smoldered in her belly, the kind that led to some of her most brutal takedowns. The kind that earned her her nickname. "If you need me to talk, you might want to rethink your tactics, wolf."

He kicked out, sharp and vicious, and a spray of ash and hot sparks flew into her face. She recoiled, coughing, and bit back the nasty curse she was dying to let fly. The sour scent of her vomit burned in her nose, the taste of it lingering on her tongue.

Her hands and feet were bound. Her brain and body were sluggish from drugs. No claws, no animal strength. He had the upper hand. Much as she wanted to eviscerate him, she had to play the game until she figured a way out of this.

A large part of her screamed that she might not find a way out of this alone.

I'm not in love with anyone else on the fucking squad.

She should've said it back.

Heart aching, she met Val's gaze. "Fine. You want to know?"

His knife stilled.

"Demons."

Insects chirped far outside the cave. "What?"

"You heard me. That's what we fight. That's our enemy. That's what you can't see."

There was a pregnant pause. "Are you fucking kidding me?"

"I'm not really in a joking mood."

He kicked dirt at her again, and this time, some of it got in her mouth. "Bullshit."

She spat and used her tongue to swipe grit from her teeth. At least now she tasted earth instead of puke. "Why would I bullshit you right now?" A spark landed on her shirt, glowing brighter as it caught on the fabric. She swore and rolled onto her front, crushing it.

A hard hand grabbed her shoulder and shoved her onto her back. All her intentions of keeping her cool and playing the game vanished as Val straddled her roughly, pinning her to the ground. She fought like the bound, bruised, bloodied wildcat she was, bucking at him, wrenching her torso, twisting. Curses flew out of her mouth, all the names she'd wanted to call him, and one name she didn't mean to shout, but that tore from her throat as she struggled beneath Val's iron grip. *"Killian!"*

"You're going to regret bullshitting me, you fucking bitch," Val panted. "You're going to regret it all."

She headbutted him. Pain exploded in her forehead, and darkness overtook her.

———

A sharp slap dragged her back to consciousness. She blinked up into Val's face, twisted with wrath and madness. He was still straddling her. She didn't feel any erection against her belly, but she did feel the cold metal of his knife at her throat.

"Demons, huh?"

His weight on her hips was revolting. The only male she wanted on top of her was a big, growly lion.

She should've said it back. She should've bonded with him.

NEED MATE.

"And nobody can see them but you guys, huh? Why?"

Every bone in her body ached to destroy him. She measured the darkening bruise on his forehead against the pounding of her own. Could she withstand another headbutt? "We have special contact lenses."

"Contact lenses."

"Yes. Underground tech. Like those scramblers."

He thought for a long moment, then leaned forward, his weight shifting on her pelvis. Anger and revulsion coursed through her. He was all lean, solid muscle, fast as a snake, and the sharp edge to his scent was a screaming warning that something was very, very wrong. The rational part of her knew she could not afford to push him further.

Val leaned closer to peer into her eyes. "Which one?"

Her blood went cold even as her jaguar screamed, shoving at her insides. "Which what?"

"Which eye has the contact lens in it?" The tip of his knife glinted inches from her face. "Or is it both?"

Panic took over. She thrashed, but he was heavy, and he bore down, a forearm over her throat and sharp, burning pain near her left eye. Her brain went blank. She was pure instinct, pure terror, pure agony as an incredible pressure built below her socket. A harsh, high gasp tore from her throat. Pressure, pain, fear, fury—

She bucked his weight with all her might and sent him tumbling into the flames. Before he could scramble up, she threw herself onto his legs, pinning him to the ground with every ounce of her strength. His upper body caught fire even as he writhed like a worm, screaming.

She screamed back.

She held him down and screamed, one half of her vision red with blood, the other filling with smoke and sparks and the blaze of the wolf going up in flames.

CHAPTER 52

Killian raced through the undergrowth, leaping over fallen logs and ducking beneath low-hanging limbs. He let his lion take the lead, wanting its nose, its senses, its instincts.

She'd been missing for twelve hours, and he was losing his fucking mind.

He'd been avoiding her, but she hadn't been at lunch, or at dinner, and when he finally gave in and stalked around the edge of the lake, he didn't find her patrolling. He found drops of blood and two scents—hers, and *his.*

His paws skidded over fallen pine needles as he spun, his mane tangling in tree branches. His nose burned with the cold, sharp smell of the wolf that had raised his hackles from day one.

He crested a hill. There, in the distance, a flicker of flame.

He flew over the earth like a bullet. *Go. GO,* he urged his lion, putting forth a burst of speed and ignoring the stabs of pain as he landed on a sharp rock here, a spiny thorn there. The fire was drawing closer, and the cold scent was getting stronger, and another one beneath it—

A duet of screams pierced the night.

He sailed over a bern. The mouth of a small cave opened like a black hole, lit by the dancing light of a small fire. He thundered inside, spraying dirt and debris over the entire scene; a charred body twitching weakly in the fire and his female plastered over its legs, her mouth open wide while her roar of fury ricocheted off the stone walls.

Killian detonated.

He leaped over the fire and knocked Juno aside. Flame singed his fur. He didn't give a shit. He threw the body across the cave in a haze of sparks and smoke and was on it before it landed, pouncing on its chest and reveling in the crack of bone beneath his weight.

Val's face might have been charred to a crisp, but Killian caught his scent even over the stench of burnt flesh.

He roared into the mask of blackened meat. Then, he unleashed.

Flesh under his teeth. Hot, metallic blood in his mouth. His fangs closed around the fragile human neck. Sinews snapped. Tendons ruptured. The spinal column broke with the most satisfying crack he'd ever heard in his whole fucking life as he used his teeth to rip the fucker's charred head off his worthless fucking body and throw it across the cave. With a roar, he dove back for more, ripping off hunks of crispy neck, spitting out windpipe, cutting his gums on sharp white bone and spitting it all on the dirt where it belonged while the iron tang of blood filled the air.

HURT MATE. TOOK MATE. THREATENED MATE. KILL, KILL, KILL—

"Killian."

Her voice was the only thing in the galaxy that could've snapped him out of it. He glanced up from the pile of flesh to find Juno's face inches from his. She was straddling the headless body, tucking first a knife, then a small, knobbly object into her pocket. A deep slash oozed under her eye. A blood-crusted X was sliced into her heaving chest.

Killian shifted to human form, hauled Juno into his arms, and tore out of the hellish cave with her feet dangling against his shins. He pulled her legs around his waist, holding one thigh with a hand while the other gripped her head, their hearts thudding against each other as he headed for the other cave he'd passed on the way.

When they reached it, he didn't peel her off him, didn't bother to make a fire, just slammed his back against the far wall and sank to his naked ass, holding her tight against him. His arms weren't big enough. He wanted to cover her, blanket her, encase her in a suit of fucking armor made from his limbs.

Her arms tightened around his neck. Her cold nose brushed against his throat. He clutched the back of her head. They sat there and breathed for a long time, their hearts slowing together.

Finally, she spoke into his neck. "You came."

His chest clenched. "*Always.*"

When she only sighed, he stroked a hand down her back, over her hip, along her thigh. All her clothes were intact, but he still had to know. Dread curdled his gut. "Did he touch you?" His voice was all lion.

Her head shook against his neck, and relief made him sag. He wanted to take her far, far away from where this had happened. The city. The jungle. Anywhere.

"Inga was his sister, the one who got killed in one of the first attacks. He didn't know what killed her, and he knew we were lying about it, and it made him crazy. He stole my scrambler from the cabin…"

Her breath feathered against his throat, and he tightened his arms around her even more, inhaling her scent. She was here. She was alive. Here. Alive. Untouched.

Well, not entirely untouched. He pulled back to examine her. The deep cut at the corner of her eye was close. Way too close. A shudder wracked him as his gaze traced the clotting wound, traveling over a nasty bruise on her cheekbone, down her blood-splattered neck to the X slashing her thermal shirt.

He peeled off her shirt. The X across her beautiful chest was a bright, angry pink against her tawny skin.

Her palms cupped his face. She lowered her forehead to his. "I'm okay."

"*I'm* not fucking okay." His hands found her bare back, his fingers digging into her strong flank.

Her shuddering breath feathered across his lips. "Me, neither. Just hold me."

His heart lurched. His beautiful, savage female wasn't pushing him away and telling him she was fine. She was asking him to hold her. He banded his arms around her, adjusting his legs so she fell between them and he could wrap those around her, too. If he'd been even a few seconds later…

Terror blasted through him again. His arms clenched around her, as if he could pull her inside the shelter of his bones if he tried hard enough. "I knew you'd hang on. I knew you would. I knew you would."

He repeated it over and over. Maybe if he said it enough, it would finally get through to his beast.

CHAPTER 53

*S*afe.

Wrapped in Killian's big, warm body, Juno felt safe. Shocked and trembling, but safe. "I kept wishing I could talk to you."

"Would've saved me a thousand heart attacks."

"I know." Her heart thudded into the long silence. "Thank you."

He shook his head. "Always, Juno."

Emotion surged through her, and this time, she didn't hold it back. She didn't want to hold it back. "I miss you."

He went very still.

She pulled back to look at him. "I miss us." She stroked his smooth muscles, watching his chest rise and fall under her hands. "I can't stop wanting you."

His whisper was pure gravel. "I am *never* going to stop wanting you."

She saw it all there in his face, in his amber stare. He meant it. Really meant it. Forever kind of meant it.

Her heart fluttered. "I'm still me. This shit doesn't change that. I'm not going to stop fighting. It's my job, it's my life, it's who I am."

He framed her face with his hands, his blazing gaze holding her hostage. "Juno fucking DeSilva. I don't want to *tame* you. I want to *claim* you. So I know you're *mine*. So no other male can touch you. So I know you're okay." His lids closed, and he lowered his forehead to hers once more. "You think it's easy? Having my fucking heart just walking around outside my chest?" His eyes opened abruptly, spearing into hers, and he gave her shoulders a little shake. "I love that you're a fighter. I love that you can rip a man to shreds. I love knowing that you can take care of yourself out there." His voice dropped to a harsh whisper. "I *have* to know you can take care of yourself out there. Juno…" He nuzzled her, slow and drugging. "I don't want some fragile fucking flower. I want you. My beautiful savage. I've always wanted you."

Love erupted in every cell of her body.

This man. This man knew her, saw her, all of her, and wanted every inch. And she wanted every ounce of him—the growly, sullen parts, the soft, tender parts, the enormous heart behind the thorny wall. Her teammate. Her partner. The sexiest male on the planet. The one who would be there always, giving her the backup she didn't know she needed.

She wound her arms around his neck, grabbing handfuls of golden hair. "You want all of me? For real? For good?"

His breath caught. A thousand emotions flashed across his face. Shock and relief, desperation and yearning. He nodded.

"And you won't try to put me in a safe little bubble?"

He gripped her face, hard. "I will only ever want to watch you *tear this world apart*."

Her heart soared. "Swear it."

His claws unsheathed with a snap, and he raked them across his chest, deep and brutal, holding her gaze like a knight pledging to his queen. "I swear to you."

Yes. This man.

She'd jumped off of buildings her entire life. This time, she couldn't catch herself. This time, she had to trust that he would be there to break her fall.

Staring into his eyes, she opened herself up, freefalling into the abyss as the world dropped out from under her.

CHAPTER 54

A white-hot fist slammed into her rib cage, gripped her heart, and squeezed it tight, stealing her breath.

Juno watched Killian's eyes go wide, his jaw dropping silently, and knew he felt the same. She couldn't breathe. His hands crushed her shoulders, and she clutched him, her pulse pounding into empty lungs as the fist clenched harder around her heart...

Something was wrong. This wasn't right, couldn't be right, she was suffocating—

And then, suddenly, there he was.

The fist released, and she sucked in a ragged lungful of air as her heart bloomed inside her chest, filling with life and blood and a huge, hot presence she would recognize anywhere. Killian's essence shoved its way inside her, taking up space like it was flexing enormous muscles.

Click.

Deep inside, a tether snapped into place, and a distinctly male sense of triumph roared across it. And her entire body exploded with ecstasy.

Then, his lips were on hers and his tongue was in her mouth and he was kissing her with everything he had, and she was devouring him and feeling him inside, outside, everywhere.

A surge of emotion rushed through her, throbbing and overwhelming, coursing along the invisible current that now stretched between them. It was *his* emotion, as vast and raw as he was. The force of it staggered her.

Jesus, he felt so *much*.

"Oh my God," she whispered, every nerve and vein humming with life and electricity and *him*.

"You feel..." His big shoulders rose and fell with his breath. "So fucking *fierce*." His arms came around her like a vise. "Thank fuck." Relief coursed across the bond. He cursed, tucking her head under his chin and holding her so tight she felt her spine pop. His swallow was loud against her ear.

She pulled back, grinning. "Did you expect anything but?"

A glint of humor flickered across his face, and he shook his head.

Her throat tightened. "Good. I would hope my mate would be smarter than that."

He cupped her face. "My *mate*..." His lids dropped as another rush of emotion surged through the bond. "...is the strongest..." He pressed his lips to hers. "...sexiest..." He did it again. "...most savage fucking female I've ever known." He waited until she met his eyes. "And she's *mine*."

WANT.

She jerked back in time to catch his glower. "Was that..."

"Yeah. See how fucking irritating he is?"

"Oh my God. Make him talk again." She prodded his chest, unable to stop smiling. Was she giddy? She was giddy.

"Trust me, he fucking will—"

TAKE FEMALE. TAKE. WANT. TAKE. CLAIM. MINE.

His lion's voice in her head was rough as rock and fiercely primal. "That's what you've been dealing with?"

He lowered his chin, giving her a dark look that was devastatingly sexy. "Six. Fucking. Years."

Her heart was apparently turning to pure liquid. "Really?"

His fingers tightened in her hair. "Every fucking second." He kissed her, hot and open. "Of every fucking day." Another kiss. "Since the day we met."

She managed to speak through the dizzying sensation of his lips on hers. "That must've been so annoying."

"You have no idea."

She laughed, and he gave her another panty-melting grin as he lowered her to the floor. She lifted a hand to his face, stroking the dark gold of his beard. Soft and rough at the same time. "I love you."

His eyes flared as he loomed over her. "Good, because you're not getting rid of me now."

She shoved at his shoulder. "You're supposed to say it back."

He gripped her chin, utterly serious. "I have loved you every second of every day for six fucking years."

She kissed him with everything she had. He gave it all back to her, yanking off her leggings and tossing them aside. The second she was bared to him, he thrust deep, deep inside.

Click.

They both froze, staring into each others' eyes as their cats roared inside their heads. Her entire body sang, as if she was filled with the world's most beautiful voices all singing in perfect, ringing harmony. And she knew Killian felt the same because she could *feel* his pleasure like a distant echo, thrumming down the thread that bound them.

Jesus fucking Christ. His rough voice sounded in her head.

Her eyes went even wider. *Holy shit.*

They stared at each other, joined on every level imaginable.

Move, she demanded.

He plunged deep inside, wrenching a groan from them both.

Again.

Another deep thrust, another burst of pleasure in her body, in her mind, in her soul. They were in a room of mirrors, every thought, feeling, and sensation reflected back at them a thousandfold.

More. More.

He started pumping inside her with deep, thorough strokes that made her eyes roll back in her head. His thoughts, scattered as her own, broke through the whirlwind in her mind.

You on top.

She flipped her big, heavy mate onto his back and rode him with hard, fluid motions, feeling charged. Buzzing. Electrified. She leaned her head back, laughing in joy and wonder. This was incredible. This was…

A gift. A fucking gift. Killian's pleasure speared through her, making her own body light up in response. *Claim me, Juno. Take me. I'm yours.*

She rode them into another burst of ecstasy, their cries echoing into the night.

He pulled her down for a deep, passionate kiss. Their tongues darted and danced, slipped and stroked. Her head spun. When his deep purr rumbled against her sternum, she smiled against his lips.

Her stomach growled.

He pulled back instantly. "You're hungry." Before she could protest, he'd lifted her off of him, set her on the ground, and leaped to his feet. She laughed as he strode out of the cave, his naked, flexing ass disappearing into the night.

Mere seconds later, he ducked back into the cave and dropped to his knees before her, holding a ripe wild strawberry in his fingers.

The last time a male tried to feed her from his hand, she

practically ran for the hills. Now, her heart fluttered, and her lips curved. "That's not going to make much of a dent." Her stomach growled again.

"I'll kill something for you later." He gazed at her intently, holding the berry up, letting her make the final move. Not forcing, not demanding.

She grabbed his wrist, brought the berry slowly to her mouth, and took a bite.

His cock jumped, but his gaze didn't waver. It was the sweetest, most flavorful strawberry she'd ever tasted in her life. Maybe it had something to do with the male looking at her like she was a goddess come to earth.

"More." It was a rough command.

The soft flesh of the berry burst on her tongue as she took another bite. Juice filled her mouth.

"*More.*"

She took her time with the third bite, savoring the flavor and the meaning and the look on Killian Diallo's face. Desire and demand, love and lust, triumph and awe. A drop of sweet liquid escaped from the corner of her mouth. Hot yellow eyes latched onto it, and with a groan that sent a shiver down her spine, he grabbed the back of her head and kissed her with abandon, swiping his tongue over her lips, licking up the juice, delving into her mouth.

Before she completely lost her head, Juno pulled away, grabbed the half-eaten berry by the stem, and put it to his lips.

Killian took the entire thing in his mouth along with her fingertips. She laughed even as his tongue swirled around her fingers, snagging the fruit from her grasp and pulling her hand from his mouth while lowering her to her back.

"I thought you were going to get more food," she teased, though her body was already humming for him.

He tossed the stem aside. "Later."

CHAPTER 55

This had to be a dream.

Killian glanced down at his female—his *mate*— as they walked into the village side by side. He was naked, since he'd sprinted into the woods in lion form to find her. He didn't care. Juno thrummed under his skin, a constant, silken presence in his bones, her fierce spirit tucked deep inside, a part of him.

How did an asshole like him get so lucky?

I told you, you're not really an asshole, you just act like one.

He pinched her ass. She swatted his hand away, sliding him a sharp look that made his dick twitch. The scent of roasted meat drifted from the village. He couldn't wait to feed her again. Would she let him do it in front of everybody?

A shrill cry brought his gaze around as a tiny blonde girl raced across the village and into his arms. He scooped her up without breaking stride, his heart swelling even as he scowled at Elvi. "Cats don't like loud noises, pup."

She gave a delighted, high-pitched howl that almost burst his eardrums, making Juno wince and laugh at the same time. Elvi howled again, enjoying her audience.

"Enough of that." He gave her an admonishing squeeze before setting her on her feet. "Go on now."

But Elvi turned to stare between the two of them, her nose lifting as she scented the air. "You smell different."

He and Juno shared a glance. He grinned like an idiot.

"You mixed." Elvi's face scrunched in confusion.

"They bonded."

Magnus strode toward them with a cluster of his sentries, Astrid included. She tossed Killian a pair of sweats. "Finally. Your dynamic was fucking with my pack."

"It was fucking with ours a lot more," Killian grumbled, stepping into the pants.

But Magnus's black brows had lowered, his nostrils flaring. "Is that Val's blood?" Eyes raked over Juno's blood-stained clothes, the healing gash under her eye, the X slashed into her shirt.

Fury coursed through the bond—his and hers, hot and visceral. "Yeah, it's his," Killian growled. "You'll find his body in a cave up the mountain somewhere. His head, too."

Snarls reverberated around the little group. "You killed him?"

"Val drugged me and brought me to a cave to interrogate me about our mission. He tied me up, assaulted me, and almost cut out my eye before I killed him. Unless the Pack has different laws than other shifter clans, I was well within my rights to take him out." Juno's anger zinged along the bond. Her face, however, was cool as ice. How did she do that?

Ice-cold upbringing and lots of practice, babe.

Christ, he loved her voice in his head.

Magnus jerked his head at a couple sentries, and they instantly peeled off toward the mountains, no doubt to track down their comrade's worthless corpse. "You killed one of my people."

"He left me no choice. Losing his sister broke him."

Magnus's upper lip curled back from his teeth. Anger and

something else radiated from his enormous frame, that strange otherworldly power Killian had never been able to put his finger on. He tensed, and beside him, Juno did the same.

Magnus leaned in, his eyes completely wolf. "Whether or not you were within your rights, I'm done with you. Get the fuck off my land."

Yeah, they were done here, too.

It didn't take long to pack their shit in the cabin. Killian couldn't say he was sad to leave, but his gut twisted at the thought of what waited for them back home. They had a lot of explaining to do.

"I know."

He glanced over his shoulder to where Juno was zipping up a duffel.

She met his eyes. "I'm nervous, too."

His heart plummeted. He didn't know what he would do if she had regrets, if she wanted to back out and sever the bond. Was that even possible? He had no clue, hadn't even considered it. Shit, he was such an idiot—

"Hey." She crossed the cabin, dropped her duffle to the floor with a heavy thunk, and cupped his face. His stomach swooped. The fact that she was touching him like this, looking up at him with eyes full of something he didn't deserve…

"*Hey.*" She gave him a long, hard kiss, and he clung to her as she pulled back. "I don't have any regrets, Diallo. Don't *make* me have any regrets." Humor glinted in those chocolate depths, then died into seriousness. "We'll figure it out. It's not like the squad can go out and recruit any random person off the sidewalk, right?"

"I'd give it up," he blurted. "I'd give it up, let you stay on the squad, if it came to that." He'd figure something out. Work security or some shit. Be a bouncer at a club, maybe even get back into the fights at the Arena.

There were suddenly arms around his neck, legs around his waist, and a luscious ass in his palms as he caught her. He blinked into Juno's sultry, smiling face.

"You're so fucking sweet." She kissed him, hard and hot. "We're both staying on the team. Rogan can deal. They can all deal. We'll figure it out." There was a firm, loving stroke down the bond, like she ran a hand down his middle, and he arched, a rumble vibrating his chest.

Her full lips curved. That sexy smile was going to be the death of him. He brought their mouths together, needing to get his tongue inside her, digging his fingers into the round globes of her delicious glutes.

"Well, that explains it."

They jerked apart to find John standing in the middle of the room, staring at them in shock. The crow on his shoulder fluttered her wings, ruffling his sheet of black hair. "I knew the web felt different." He shook his head, refocusing. "We have to go. Attack in Pride lands. Cullen's asking for help." His fathomless dark eyes were pained. "The jungle's burning."

CHAPTER 56

Smoke clouded Killian's vision as he materialized into the hot, humid air of his childhood. His stomach rolled, and not just from the aftereffects of teleporting with John.

It looked like a bomb had gone off. Smoke and ash, flickering flame, screams and roars, the stench of sulfur and burning flesh...

John gave him a shove the second they solidified. "Go. I'll get her."

Instinct screamed at him to wait for his mate. *Can you hear me?*

I got you. I'm coming. Go.

Relief flooded him. Even a world apart, she was still there, in his head, in his gut, in his heart. He burst into lion form and charged into the jungle, sprinting past males and females he knew by scent, though the smoke was thick enough to hide them from view. He squinted into the gloom, looking for a hellmouth or a pack of demons or—

A pink-haired succubus wearing a dozen candy necklaces, throwing whips of fire around the goddamn jungle.

Unfucking*believable.*

He charged toward Jovi, who was whirling her flaming lassos while the surrounding foliage dripped with flame. Lions gathered nearby, biting and swiping at the air, struggling to see what she was trying to wrangle with her fiery ropes.

Killian could see it.

Juno, get here now.

I'm here, I'm coming.

He leaped over a fallen log and skidded to a stop as a blinding flash of light lit the clearing and Alistor appeared like a towering idol, one huge hand clamped on Cyrus's head, the other on Wolf's, like he was palming two basketballs. A bruise was already forming on one high cheekbone. Black brows knit as he took in the scene, and he dropped Cyrus and Wolf instantly, reaching toward his belt for a sword that wasn't there.

The angel's bellow of fury shook the trees, and Jovi yelled something, but Killian was too busy avoiding tentacles to pay much attention.

The beast in the clearing was straight from a nightmare. Its body was like an enormous, writhing centipede, but instead of stubby little legs, this thing had tentacles. A hundred of them. Long, thick appendages glinting with razor sharp spines, whistling as they flailed through the air. A forked tongue unfurled past rows of pointed teeth as the creature gave a long, deafening shriek.

As Killian charged into the battle, one of the tentacles latched on to a watching male lion, wrapped around his thick golden torso, and swung him high in the air before slamming him into its jaws. Teeth gnashed. Roars echoed around the clearing, and the scent of blood mixed with that of smoke and sulfur and frightened, enraged animals.

The whir of a phaser zinged past his ears as he ducked and dodged, heading for the beast's soft body. A blast of light hit the monster directly between its eyes, leaving a smoking hole and a trail of black blood. Rogan had arrived.

The beast screamed. Tentacles whipped madly. One of them grazed Killian's back, and he couldn't hold back the roar of pain. It felt like fire. Or maybe one of Jovi's whips got him? He didn't know, didn't have time to figure it out. He needed to get to this thing's body and tear it apart—

Get down! Juno barked in his head.

He hit the dirt without a second thought. A sleek black body landed next to him, flattening to the ground as a tentacle whistled over their heads. There were shouts—Rogan and Cyrus—and another cacophony of lion roars as a female, still in human form, was snatched off her feet and tossed into the beast's mouth.

Screams sounded all around, followed by the crack of bone.

Soft spot on the head, Juno said.

Killian ducked, smelled burnt fur as his mane was singed, and when Jovi's flaming whips wrapped around a group of tentacles and pinned them to the ground, he saw it—a green-ish, pulsing spot on top of the beast's head.

Get me up there, his mate growled.

He crouched, waited for Juno's paws to land on his back, and shoved upright with all his strength, giving her the boost she needed to fly. Fear and pride gripped his heart as she landed on its flailing body, claws sinking in, muscles standing out starkly in her gleaming black flanks as she held on for the ride. *Get it!*

She sank her jaws—those terrifying, strong jaws that had dragged his ass from a raging river and out of a mountain sinkhole—into the pulsing spot on the monster's head. A geyser of black filth erupted into the air while the beast roared and screamed, its tentacles whipping wildly as Jovi fought to lasso them to the earth. The beast staggered and fell to the ground in a shuddering, writhing mass, and the jaguar rode it to its death, her fangs never leaving their target.

I am so damn proud you're mine.

FIERCE MATE.

The jaguar lifted her head from the corpse, spat, and gave him a catlike smirk. She leaped gracefully to the ground, and he was right there to meet her, butting his big head against her shoulder, rubbing his mane against her.

A woof brought their heads around. Wolf, his enormous white pelt streaked with inky blood, stared at them with very clear surprise on his canine face. He sniffed the air between them, then dissolved into human form, his lanky body sprawled naked in the dirt as he pointed between them. "No way! No fucking *way*." He stared at Juno. "You want to bone *this dude* forever? Like, *forever*—"

"Wolf. Not now." Rogan's bark was sharp enough to rival any shifter's. His green eyes flicked between the two of them and landed on Killian. "Cullen's hurt."

CHAPTER 57

The alpha's hut had been severed in half, the beautiful hexagon of artfully charred wood hanging open like a dollhouse.

Killian stared down at his brother, who lay unconscious on a pile of blankets. Cullen still looked larger than life, even on death's doorstep. A bloody bandage covered half of his head and one eye. His auburn hair was tangled and stiff with dried blood. Burns blistered his bronze skin from shoulder to hip, a long slash of torn flesh providing evidence of the swipe of a razor-spined tentacle.

As fear sliced through him, Cullen's visible eye opened and lasered right at him, like he knew Killian was there.

A huge breath filled Killian's chest, and relief pulsed through the bond as Juno took a breath beside him.

Cullen stared at him, hurt and accusation practically pulsing from his muscular form. The last time they'd spoken, they'd nearly come to blows in the middle of hyena territory.

Talk to him. Juno's fingers brushed his before she turned and descended the wood-and-rope steps hanging from what was left of the platform deck.

Cullen's one eye never left him.

He opened his mouth to say something—he didn't know what. "Demons."

Cullen's one eye blinked.

Fuck it. He'd already said it, and it was too late to take it back. "It was demons." He sounded strangled. He felt strangled. "It was all demons. The hyenas, Mom and Nandi, this…" He gestured weakly around the ruined alpha hut. "It's demons. That's what I fight. What we fight. I couldn't tell you. You can't see them. Nobody can see them." He was babbling. "We have special tech. Lenses." He gestured stupidly to his eye.

His brother's nose flared, trying to scent a lie. Killian opened himself up completely, baring himself to his brother's —his alpha's—scrutiny.

Shock dawned in the one eye before it shifted toward the steps Juno had descended moments before. "You bonded with the *jaguar*?"

The voice was barely a rasp. But the arrogant tone was so familiar, so Cullen, that Killian was suddenly crushed beneath the weight of a million different memories. Joy and grief. Love and devastation. Boyish youth and grown men's bitterness. Laughter. Secrets. The sound of his own feet stomping out of the jungle, leaving his big brother behind.

Killian dropped his face into his hands, sucking in ragged gasps of air. "I'm sorry."

"Is it that bad already?"

That wrung a hoarse laugh out of him, and he let his hands fall to his lap. "No. She's…everything." He shook his head. "I'm sorry I left."

Old, unhealed pain, and *very* unhealed anger, glinted in Cullen's eye. "Didn't act like it."

"I couldn't handle it. I couldn't deal. They were gone and you were alpha—"

"Yeah, they were gone, and I was alpha, and then *you fucking left.*" Cullen struggled to sit up, his breath hitching, but he smacked away Killian's outstretched hand and levered himself upright. He looked like hell. He also looked like he could maybe still kick his ass. "And I had to deal with this shit all on my own."

Killian's chest felt like it was cracking open.

There was a stroke along the bond. *You're fine.*

He sent a snort back to her.

A glint of humor. *Talk to him.*

Juno's calm, reassuring presence in his mind, in his soul, gave him the strength to continue. "I know. You've always been better than me at dealing with shit, you know that. I couldn't handle it. I was so fucking lost." He lifted his burning eyes to his brother. "I'm sorry, Cullen. I'm sorry."

Cullen stared at him for a long, long time. Finally, his good eye raked over Killian's bare torso. "I hate your tattoos."

He blinked before a choked laugh escaped him. "You're just jealous 'cause you're too pretty to pull them off."

A tiny smile curled the corner of Cullen's wide mouth, then fell. "Where did you go?"

Killian swallowed past a tight throat. "The Arena. That's where Rogan found me."

"And Rogan fights demons." Disbelief rang clear in his brother's deep voice.

He nodded. "We all do."

Long silence. "I call bullshit."

"You can *smell* me."

"Still don't believe it."

Stubborn asshole, as always. Killian took a deep breath and spoke to his mate inside his mind. *I need you to bring me a piece of it.*

Long silence. *Okay. But I think we need to loop the team in on this.*

He met his brother's intense alpha stare. *Yeah. It's time.*

CHAPTER 58

"Ew, don't you want to, like, wash that?"

"How do you expect them to wash a contact lens?"

"Don't you guys have fluid or something?"

"Do we look like we have fucking fluid on us?"

Jovi smacked Wolf's arm, and he bared his teeth. She rolled her eyes.

"Enough," Rogan snapped. He was intensely focused on the lion alpha sitting on a pile of blankets in his ruined home, staring at the clear silicon lens on the tip of his finger like it was a bomb about to blow. The squad had gathered while the lions tended to their wounded and mourned the dead. Smoke hung heavy and acrid in the air, but the jungle was eerily silent. No calling birds, no shouts of Pride members, no cubs laughing.

Cullen's good eye shifted to Killian. "So, I just…stick it in there?"

Wolf and Jovi snickered like he'd made a dirty joke. Rogan shot them an incredulous look.

Killian demonstrated peeling his eyelids apart and placing the lens on his eye. "Go easy. Blink it into place."

His brother glanced around suspiciously before complying, jerking when the silicon hit his eyeball, scrunching up his face with a distaste that would've been funny if Killian wasn't so beyond humor at the moment. After a few seconds of rapid blinking, Cullen opened his eye and looked around.

The entire team held its breath.

He knew the moment Cullen saw the chunk of razor-spined tentacle that lay oozing on his floor. He couldn't see the thing himself anymore, since Cullen was wearing his lens, but he watched his brother's eye widen, then his nostrils flare, then his claws shoot out. Cullen tried to move to all fours, grunted in pain, and stayed put. Finally, he raised his gaze to Rogan. "Show me the rest."

"Let them heal you first." Rogan jerked his chin toward John and Alistor, who stood watching from a corner.

Cullen glanced at Jovi. "Why not the firebug? She does a hell of a job, from what I remember." He managed to put some sex into it despite a bandage covering half his face.

Rogan's jaw hardened until it looked like it could cut stone. "Because I don't want her hands on you, that's why."

Jovi twirled her hair, gazing at Rogan with starry eyes.

"She's also one of them." Rogan gestured at the floor, where the chunk of demon corpse presumably oozed.

Her starry eyes went murderous. "Hey!"

Rogan shifted guiltily. "It's not *untrue*."

"It's *half* true, dick, and you're just saying it to make him think I'm gross!"

"She's one of them?" Cullen stared Jovi up and down. "Is that what that smell is?"

Jovi's jaw dropped in outrage. "I am not one of them. Sick. I'm a succubus. Half succubus." She saw the need to clarify. "Half succubus, half angel. Fallen angel. His." She gestured to Alistor.

Rogan pinched his nose. "Jesus Christ."

Jovi tossed up her hands. "What, it's okay to out me, but not him?"

"She's got you there." Cyrus smirked before his pale blue gaze drifted back to Juno. It had been doing that a lot since the team arrived.

Killian didn't like it. *Is Cyrus talking to you?*

Yeah.

She must've heard his lion's internal growl because her mouth quirked. *He's checking in. Making sure I'm good.*

Pretty sure that's my job.

Juno's dark gaze slid to his. *Watch it, Diallo. He's been talking inside my head way longer than you have, and nothing's going to change that. He's my brother.*

It didn't make him feel better.

But I mated you.

That made him feel slightly better.

Exactly. Save the growling for the bedroom.

"We need to discuss these things before we blast them all over the place," Rogan was saying through his teeth. He gestured to Alistor. "Yes, he's an angel. A great healer, too. That's where she gets it." He raised his brows at Alistor and gestured to Cullen. "Would you mind? John needs to recover."

"I'm good," John said.

"You've got limited reserves. Alistor doesn't. Recover."

John folded his arms. Tika rustled on his shoulder.

The angel crouched beside Cullen. "It has been many centuries since I healed a shapeshifter." He held up his hands. "You will not claw me." It was a command, and Cullen stiffened before jerking his chin in affirmative.

The angel's palms landed on Cullen's chest, and a second later, a flare of golden light swept beneath his skin, rushing to the wounds like a magnet. Alistor's whole body didn't glow like his daughter's did when she used her healing abilities— only his enormous hands, which looked like they were dipped in sunlight. As his shredded skin knit together, Cullen relaxed bit by bit, eventually giving a quiet sigh.

When the angel removed his hands, Cullen tugged the bandage from his head and shook out the mane of auburn hair that always drove the females crazy. He stroked a palm over his healed chest, rolled his neck, then cocked a brow at Jovi. "He's better than you, firebug."

"Apparently you think so." Jovi smirked at Cullen's lap—and the enormous erection pitching a tent under his blanket.

A chorus of shouts erupted. Wolf pointed and laughed. Rogan turned away, muttering. Cullen covered himself and glared at Alistor.

The angel looked uncomfortable. "I did not mean to arouse you."

"You didn't arouse me," Cullen snapped. "I'm just feeling good. Really good."

Jovi snorted. "Obviously."

Rogan pointed at her. "You are absolutely not healing him anymore."

"I'm sure he'd rather have an archangel boner, anyway."

Rogan's phone rang over renewed laughter and Cullen's muffled curse. As Rogan turned to take the call, Cullen eyed the spot where the chunk of demon tentacle lay on the floor, then met Killian's gaze. "Is this shit for real?"

He nodded.

"Mom and Nandi?"

He nodded again, all traces of humor gone.

Cullen's jaw ticked. "Does Magnus know about this?"

"Not yet."

"We need to go. Now." Rogan loaded another cartridge into his phaser. "The Pack is under attack."

CHAPTER 59

They landed in the middle of a war zone. Juno had to admit, riding with Alistor was a lot more comfortable than being transported by John—more of a warm tingle than the hot, fizzing sensation she always had to grit her teeth through.

Any comfort fled the second she and Killian materialized. Cabins blazed like torches while wolves in human form worked to douse the flames. Smoke billowed. Wolves darted around, vicious and lethal and completely, hopelessly blind.

Demons. Demons everywhere.

Jesus.

Rogan appeared at their side a second later, John's hand on his shoulder. He swept the scene with one piercing glance, turned to John, and said, "Go get Cullen. Give him your lens."

John looked as though he'd been slapped. With a sharp nod, he vanished.

She and Killian shifted, and they all dove in.

Juno jumped onto the back of a demon who was blowing a stream of flame at the cookhouse. Shouts and high yelps rang out before dozens of young wolves burst from the shadows, both in wolf form and human, followed by females who herded them toward the alpha hut. A pup tripped over its too-big paws, stumbled, fell, and was turned to cinders a second later, incinerated by a blast of demon fire.

Horrified cries echoed. Juno barely heard them over her own jaguar scream, tearing out the throat of her target before leaping to the one who'd just turned that baby—that *baby*—to ashes. Killian's roar echoed through the smoke and down their bond.

They weren't enough.

Another roar—Cullen. His distinctive red mane flashed through the battle, knocking demons over like bowling pins while a huge golden counterpart ravaged the enemy at his side. Brothers united once again.

Juno battled her way past the now-burning cookhouse, the supply cabin with its doors ripped off, and the medical cabin, where Frida ushered in more frantic, yelping pups.

Something exploded. Juno skidded to a halt to watch a geyser burst from the middle of the silvery lake.

More shocked cries echoed around the village, but the civilians couldn't see the real danger. A cluster of demons rode the column of water high into the air, their bodies writhing and flailing before plummeting back to the lake. Hope flared within her as bodies smacked the surface like bags of cement. Maybe the impact would be enough to kill them.

But the water churned as one by one, demons began paddling rapidly to shore.

Cyrus! She found him already near the water, along with Alistor and Magnus in his enormous wolf form. *They're coming from the lake.*

This whole time, they'd been coming from the lake.

The hell you think I can do about that? Cyrus's dark face

dripped with sweat as his phaser fired rapidly from one hand, the other directing boulders into groups of demons.

Can you set up a perimeter?

Not that big.

She growled as a blast of fire singed her tail, then whipped around, tackled the demon, and snapped its neck. *Maybe Magnus can help.* Her gaze landed on the giant black wolf tearing into a demon with brutal savagery, his claws and fangs no more than a blur.

Wait, how could he see the enemy?

Cyrus shouted and pointed at the lake. The next moment, the black wolf was gone and the tattooed Viking stood naked by the silver water. When Cyrus gave a sharp whistle, John appeared beside him. The two of them dematerialized to the opposite side of the lake, and then, John vanished once again.

Magnus bellowed a single foreign word. The force of the shout rippled over the earth and across the water, ringing in Juno's ears, vibrating in her bones. The alpha clapped his massive hands together and pulled them apart in a wide arc. On the opposite shore, Cyrus did the same. A shimmering bubble formed over the water, following the sweep of their hands.

John reappeared at her side, gripping a struggling Wolf.

"No, no, no…" Wolf froze in John's grasp, his eyes growing wide at the scene before him. He locked gazes with Magnus, and all the color leached from his face.

Magnus pointed one thick finger from across the lake. *"Fennimore Magnussen!"*

She'd never seen true fear in Wolf, but apparently, there was something that scared him after all. He whirled toward a pale John, grabbed his arm, and whispered, "Please."

After a moment's hesitation, John clamped onto Wolf's free arm, and the two of them vanished.

The mountains trembled with Magnus's roar of fury.

Disbelief rooted her to the spot. He'd bailed on them. Wolf

had looked around at all this, at his own home burning, his people bleeding, his squad fighting for their lives, and abandoned them.

She shoved the shock and pain aside and skidded beneath the shield bubble just before it struck the ground, sealing the lake off from the village.

You good? Killian's rough voice demanded in her head.

She sped into the water, her pelt shielding her from the shock of the icy cold. *I'm going in.*

Be safe.

She sent a stroke down the bond and dove deep.

She'd spent her entire life making sure she was strong enough, confident enough, to face anything. But the second she laid eyes on the bottom of that lake, she turned and swam for the surface as fast as her paws could carry her.

You good?

Fear thumped through her as she climbed ashore and headed for the closest demon she could find, tearing into it even as Killian roared in her head.

Answer me, Juno!

Found our hellmouth.

Are you good?

We need backup. She snarled as a demon slashed at her shoulder, pain burning down her foreleg like the thing's talons were tipped with acid. *Fuck. Find Alistor. We need ARC.*

Are you good?

Dodge, swipe, bite.

Tell me you're fucking okay, goddammit!

PROTECT MATE.

Great, now his lion was screaming at her, too. *I'm fine! A little busy here.* She rolled, narrowly dodging a swipe, and shifted into human form to talk into her watch. The chill of the air barely registered on her naked skin. "John. Get Theo, now."

Alistor appeared at her side. A bruise darkened his

cheekbone. Blood ran from a cut on his forehead. He fired his phaser, missed, cursed, and punched an oncoming demon instead, snapping its neck and letting it drop like a stone.

He whirled to Juno, his trenchcoat flaring and his perfect face twisted with rage. *"I want my SWORD!"* He kicked another demon with the sole of his enormous boot, sending it flying to the middle of the lake.

She snatched his phaser to fire at the trio of demons clambering out of the water. "Call ARC. The hellmouth's down there."

A look of trepidation crossed the angel's face, but after surveying the scene inside and out of the protective shield, he pulled his archangel medallion from beneath his shirt. The second he pressed it to his heart, it glowed like a star going supernova, and Alistor's deep voice intoned, "Come."

Flashes of light streaked through the sky, arrowing straight for Alistor—only to crash into the shield surrounding the lake. White-robed archangels slid down the bubble with looks of furious astonishment.

It would probably be funny later. Right now, she was busy trying to stay alive. "Drop the shield!"

The second the shield evaporated, archangels hurtled to their side like shooting stars. The air beside her shimmered, and John appeared with a disheveled Theo. Her scarlet hair was loose over a green silk kimono, and her vape pen smoked between her fingers. John weaved on his feet. Tika flapped around his head, cawing in alarm.

Theo ducked as Cyrus sent a boulder flying with his telekinesis. "What the—"

Juno unsheathed her claws and tore out a demon's trachea. "The lake, Theo. Part the lake!"

Alistor kicked another demon, which latched onto his boot. He pinned it to the ground and crushed its skull like a bug. "She cannot see them, jaguar."

"She doesn't need to see them." Dodge, swipe. "Do it, Theo!"

She could feel the aquamage's baffled anger, but Theo tossed her vape pen, took a deep breath, and clapped her hands together before drawing them slowly apart. As she did, the water parted.

The lake split down the middle as if parted by an invisible blade. Colossal walls of water rose on either side, swirling with weeds and fish, glinting silver like Theo's eyes as she worked her magic. And at the very center of the empty lake, standing tall and regal in the silt, was a stunning woman.

She was achingly beautiful, all lean curves and exquisite bones, blood red hair falling to her hips in a satiny sheet. But her luminous white skin was marred. Dark circles shadowed her eyes, and an ugly, blackened wound puckered her skin at the juncture of her shoulder. Streaks of black radiated from the spot, creeping up her neck to graze her delicate jaw, slithering down her arm toward her elbow, as if corroded oil flowed through her veins.

Juno's blood ran cold. Even if the woman hadn't looked like a taller, more sinister version of Jovi, the sword wound in her shoulder would've given her away. She was Inara, Jovi's mother and the succubus who caused Alistor's fall.

Inara's crimson brows slashed as she took in the mountains, the burning village, the towering walls of water held apart by Theo's shaking hands. When her sharklike eyes landed on Alistor and the archangels racing toward her, she peeled back bloodless lips to bare perfect white teeth.

Alistor roared something in a foreign tongue.

The angels charged into the silt at the center of the lake, their white linens trailing in the mud.

Inara vanished in a cloud of swirling black smoke.

Alistor's bellow of rage was drowned by the ringing of five divine swords being drawn at once. The archangels stabbed their blades into the muck.

The impact shook the earth, the blast wave knocking Juno off her feet as the hellmouth sucked in on itself. From the corner of her eye, she saw Theo fall to the ground, but the female kept her straining arms apart, teeth clenched, holding the water with every last ounce of strength. Demons screamed and scrambled for purchase as the earth swallowed them whole in a rush of squelching mud and bottom-rotted trees.

Theo's arms collapsed.

Massive walls of water thundered to the earth with a deafening crash. Pain shot through Juno's ear. A giant wave rolled toward shore, refilling the lake in a rush and drenching them with a spray of water as they stood there, panting.

She felt Killian's hot presence at her side before she even glanced over. He looked beat to shit and sexy as hell. When she rose to stand, he scowled and thumbed away the blood trickling from her ear.

Rogan, Jovi, Cullen, and Cyrus fell in beside them, all battered and bleeding. Jovi had a streak of soot on her cheek, and her slender throat was bare—she must've used all her candy necklaces in the battle. She headed straight for the unconscious Theo, but was held back by Rogan, who pulled a sugar straw out of his pocket, ripped the paper top off with his teeth, and tipped the whole thing into Jovi's waiting mouth, his fingers gentle on her jaw. The look Jovi gave him made Juno's heart swell. Sugar replenished, Jovi knelt at Theo's side. Alistor met her there.

Rogan glanced back at the village, blinking blood out of his eye from the nasty gash dripping down his forehead. "Clear."

The archangels strode toward them at the same moment Magnus stalked up from the opposite side. The wolf tattoo wrapped around his muscular frame seemed to glow, the black ink faintly luminous, as if lit from within. "You have some fucking explaining to do, Rogan." He looked at the archangels looming beside them. "And you." He locked eyes with the archangel, Michael. "I told you, I can handle my mountain."

Michael, blond and stunningly beautiful even when covered in muck, raised a brow. "Apparently not, *vulfkin*."

CHAPTER 60

'm not putting that in my eye." Astrid stared at the lens floating in a glass of water on the alpha's dining table.

"Don't be a fool, Astrid." Magnus wiped a huge palm over his face. They'd all gathered in the alpha cabin while the wolves worked to heal their wounded, put out the lingering embers in the village, and prepare to mourn their dead. Alistor and Jovi had already done what they could to help, and the archangels had vanished, leaving them to deal on their own. Then again, Magnus hadn't exactly invited them to stay. Apparently, they knew each other. Because the Magnussens were immortal.

"Cocky *drittstøvel*," Magnus had muttered into the flashes of light as they disappeared.

They'd made introductions over a bottle of honey whiskey. Magnus's suspicious gaze had lingered on a revived Theo, who told him in no uncertain terms that she wasn't going anywhere.

"This is the second time I've been pulled into battle for this shit, and these people are living under my goddamn roof," she'd snapped, tossing back her whiskey and smacking her glass on the table. "I'm staying."

Now, Killian's shoulder brushed against Juno's, the warmth of him seeping through their borrowed sweats. They stood side by side, their folded arms grazing each other with every breath. And just that, the simplest contact, was enough to settle both Juno and her jaguar.

A demon carcass lay black and bony on the wood floor. Magnus pointed to it. "Can you see that?"

Astrid's jaw clenched. "No." Her shoulder was red and blistered, and blood seeped into the sweats she'd thrown on, a dark spot growing near her hip. She'd refused to be healed. Her eyes were shiny with pain, grief, and anger. At the moment, anger was at the forefront.

"So, why can you see it and she can't?" Jovi sucked a lollipop, glancing between the siblings.

A huge sigh heaved Magnus's chest. "Because she's not alpha. When she's alpha, her full *vulfkin* powers will manifest. That includes being able to see the bottom-dwellers." He shook his head. "If only I would've seen them before."

"They were in the lake. Or gone by the time you found the bodies." Juno wanted to lift some of the despair that shadowed the Viking's proud face. The simmering animosity between them had vanished, leaving only a sense of grim camaraderie.

"Still. The High Ones told me when I took the helm that the hellspawn were always seeking the surface. I should've guessed."

"They've never come before," Astrid murmured. "Not in our lifetime."

There was another silence before Jovi broke in. "Sorry, but she won't become alpha unless you die, right?"

Magnus nodded.

"And you can't die?"

A spark of arrogance glinted in his arctic eyes. "Not very easily, firebug."

"But your dad and uncle died in the accident." Cullen

stared at Magnus like he was putting puzzle pieces together. His back was straight, his shoulders broad as always, but the weight of the day's events hung heavily on his handsome face. He'd lost people today, too.

"Decapitated. It's the only way. The cable broke when the mine collapsed." Magnus's expression darkened. "Supports were weak. Fenn was supposed to repair them."

Oh, shit. "That's why he left the Pack."

Old wounds shone in the alpha's eyes. "The immortal line runs on our fathers' side. My father was alpha. When he died, it passed to me. Astrid is next in line."

"And Wolf is third."

"Fenn is third." He scoffed. "*Wolf.* Where is the *drittsekk*, anyway? Still hiding?"

Rogan checked his phone. His jaw ticked. "Still not answering."

John hadn't reappeared, either, but it wasn't surprising. He'd been nearly dead on his feet after all the teleporting during the battle. Hopefully he'd flashed himself and Wolf back to Light House where he could safely pass out from exhaustion.

John's absence was understandable. Wolf's still felt like a betrayal.

Jovi raised a hand. "So, just to be clear, Wolf is immortal, too?"

Magnus and Astrid exchanged glances before nodding.

Lots of brows raised. Cyrus muttered, "That explains a lot."

"Our family are the *vulfkin*. We've guarded the mountain for centuries," Magnus said. "It's our duty and our honor."

"Why does the mountain need guarding?" Theo asked.

Magnus considered her shrewdly before sighing, resigned. "The auka." When the group only stared at him, he ran a huge palm over his shaved head. "The auka is a compound.

An ore. It has powers, and its veins run through the mountain."

It was Juno and Killian's turn to share a look. "Is it blue? Shimmery?"

"How do you know that?"

They told them about the huge worm, their slide down the mountain, all the tunnels burrowed into its core, and the streaks of shining blue they'd passed on their way to the lake. When they were finished, Magnus and Astrid swore in unison, and Magnus poured them both another drink.

"What does it do?" Rogan asked.

Magnus tossed back his whiskey. "It enhances."

"Enhances what?"

"Everything." Magnus braced his big palms on the table. "I can't believe I'm telling you this." He straightened. "The auka amplifies anything it comes into contact with. Anything nearby." His gaze shifted to Killian and Juno. "Did you notice anything interesting while you were up on that mountain so long?"

A sick feeling twisted her stomach. "Everything was stronger. Brighter, more vibrant. Just...more."

What if this thing with Killian was all because of this auka? What if a stupid rock was the reason he fell for her?

You were driving me out of my skull long before we set foot on that mountain, Killian's voice growled in her head.

The knot in her belly relaxed slightly.

The only thing that rock enhanced was the strength of my tongue. He quirked a brow. *Or did it?*

Her doubts evaporated.

"When people find out about the auka, they tend to lose their heads. Warriors want to become stronger. Leaders want more influence. Mages want more power. There was war, long ago. The High Ones fought alongside my people to protect the auka." He glanced at the fallen archangel looming in the corner, arms crossed. "Were you there?"

Alistor nodded.

"Legend says the *vulfkin* were made of the mountain. We're bound to protect it. When the war was won, the *vulfkin* and the High Ones agreed that we would guard the mountain and keep its secrets safe. My father only told me and Astrid about the auka when we were in our late teens. The rest of the Pack know nothing."

In the stunned silence that followed, noises from the village floated through the cabin windows. Wood being stacked. Shouts for assistance. Frida's gruff voice barking at someone to *sit down before you fall down.*

"So, um, that worm thing?" Jovi spoke around her lollipop. "Did it have a big, round mouth with lots of pointy teeth? And no eyes?"

Killian and Juno nodded.

"Shit." Jovi pulled the sucker from her cheek, color draining from her face. "It's the Mouth."

Rogan's hand twitched on his phaser. "What the hell is the Mouth?"

"One of my mom's pets." Jovi sounded close to vomiting. "It eats. Eats through anything. Everything. She used it to… punish." Tendons jumped in Jovi's neck, her eyes haunted. "But it's smart, so she might be using it for other things. Like, trying to tunnel up to the surface." She looked at Killian and Juno. "How big did you say it was?"

"City bus?" Juno estimated.

Jovi's sucker thunked to the floor. "Oh, fuck."

"How big was it before?"

Jovi swallowed. "Chihuahua?"

Juno's stomach dropped. *Oh, fuck is right.*

"Even then, it could still eat through rock. And bone. And spit venom. Its teeth…" The horror on her face sent a bolt of fear through Juno. "And if it's been tunneling through that auka stuff…"

Magnus frowned. "Who is your mother?"

Rogan swore.

————

Well, all the family secrets were coming out tonight. After Magnus and Astrid listened to the shortened version of Jovi's story, which included Alistor's story, which led to the story of how they'd all defected from MLE and ended up at Light House, the liquor bottle came out again. This time, everyone took a slug.

Magnus sprawled in his chair, fatigue etching deep lines on his face. "I have to admit, I had no idea you were so interesting, Rogan."

"Back at you," Rogan muttered from where he stood against a wall, Jovi's back resting against his front.

The sound of distant hammering filled the silence. The wolves were building their funeral pyres. Juno swallowed hard.

"So, is Astrid going to put that lens in her eye, or what? Because if she isn't, I am." Theo was also propped against a wall, her green kimono stained brown with mud. The circles under her eyes didn't make her any less intimidating. "I kind of feel like I'm ahead of her in line, anyway." She gave Rogan a deadly look.

Magnus eyed her trackband. "What kind of mage are you, Ms. Donnovan?"

"Did you miss the whole parting-the-lake thing?"

"Theo's an aquamage," Rogan cut in. "She's been a friend for a long time."

"Yeah, and Rogan's been keeping me in the dark for a long time."

Rogan sighed. "Theo—"

"No. You've been keeping secrets from me long enough."

"You know why I couldn't tell you."

"Yeah, well, now I know, and I deserve to see it. You've

brought me and my people into this shit multiple times. I'm done being blind."

"Theo—"

"Wait a second." Jovi narrowed her eyes, gesturing between them. "Did you guys used to *bone*?"

When Rogan muttered a curse to the ceiling, Juno barely kept her jaw off the floor.

Did you know that? Killian's voice echoed in her head.

Uh, no, that's definitely news to me.

That's way better than knowing his coffee order.

"Relax." Theo held out a placating hand to Jovi, whose fingers were literally shooting steam. "It wasn't even a thing. And it was over long before you came around. It's *irrelevant* right now." She raised crimson brows at Astrid, who was once again staring at the contact lens in the glass like it might explode. "Are you going to put it in or what?"

With a grimace, Astrid placed the lens into her eye.

The team was silent. Juno had a feeling each of them was remembering the first time they wore a lens and saw a demon in the flesh, realizing the enemy, the mission, and the oath of silence were very, very real.

"Gods," Astrid whispered, staring at the demon corpse in shock.

"Yeah, it's a real kick in the ass, isn't it?" Cullen raked a hand through his auburn mane.

Astrid's fierce purple gaze swung to Rogan. "We need these."

Rogan's jaw ticked. "I know. That's the problem."

CHAPTER 61

hey were going to split up.

The squad—minus John and Wolf, who still hadn't shown—gathered at the far edge of the lake later that night. A dark cloud hung over the village as the wolves cleaned up and made repairs. Several of them walked around weeping.

Killian had been relieved to learn that the pup who'd been incinerated wasn't Elvi. Then, he'd felt like an asshole for being glad some other kid was burned to a crisp.

"We can't leave any of the bases unprotected." Rogan watched a pair of wolf children hauling sticks for funeral pyres across camp. The tear tracks cutting through the grime on their young faces were visible even from a distance. "Agreed?"

They all nodded. It was strange to think that, suddenly, they had multiple home bases—Light House, the Den, and the jungle. Cullen and Magnus might not have liked the idea of needing someone else's protection, but the fact was that they didn't have enough lenses to go around. And though Inara hadn't looked so hot when she appeared at the center of the hellmouth, she was obviously still targeting shifters.

Plus, a giant razor-toothed worm was eating its way through a mountain of magical ore, growing stronger by the day. Because they didn't have enough problems.

"We'll all regroup at Light House first, get some R&R. Then, I want us to rotate in teams. I'll leave Wolf in the city for now, assuming he's there when we get back." He shook his head. "Cyrus, I want you back there, too. Maybe you and Solara can put your brains together and figure out these lenses." He dragged a hand over his hair before his pale green stare flipped to Killian and Juno. "I'm assuming the two of you want to stick together?"

Jovi gasped in delight. "Oh, are we talking about that now?"

Killian folded his arms, braced for an argument. He glanced over at Juno and saw her in the exact same stance.

Her chin ticked up. "We mated."

"I gathered as much. Not exactly what I had in mind when I told you two to figure your shit out, but..." Rogan studied each of their faces in turn. "You seem good. Better." A small smile curved his mouth.

"We are. And it won't affect us on duty."

"The hell it won't." Rogan's gaze lingered on his woman. "We don't turn a blind eye. We pivot, learn this new dynamic, acknowledge its strengths and weaknesses, and adjust accordingly."

"We can talk inside each other's heads." It slipped out of Killian like a boast. And so what if it was?

That got Rogan's attention. "Really?"

Juno's playfulness zipped along the bond as she turned to Cyrus and tapped her temple. "Give me something for him to do, and I'll tell him."

The devilish expression on Cyrus's face did not bode well. Killian gave him an evil glare. A few seconds later, Juno's lips twitched, and she relayed the cerebromage's instructions inside Killian's head.

Killian flipped Cyrus off. Cyrus grinned.

Do it, Diallo. Juno's eyes gleamed.

You'll pay for this later. Then, he turned around, shoved his sweatpants to his knees, and bent over, wiggling his bare ass at the group.

"Ah, ah," Cyrus chastised while Jovi and Juno shouted with laughter. "What did you forget?"

He shot a glare over his shoulder. "Fuck you."

Cyrus cupped a hand to his ear, grinning.

Killian turned around with a growl and wiggled his ass in time. "I'm a little teapot, tall and black. My squadmate's gonna kick my ass—" He yanked up his pants and lunged for Cyrus, who darted away with a whoop, using his telekinesis to put objects in Killian's path.

He chased the asshole to the edge of the lake and tackled him to the ground. They rolled, then shoved apart, both breathing hard.

"I don't have to tell you to treat her right." The humor had left Cyrus's eyes, replaced with the hard, deadly edge most people didn't see until it was too late.

"No, you don't." Instead of holding it back, he let it out. "She's everything to me."

Cyrus nodded, watching him.

"And if I fuck up, she'll kill me herself." He felt a slow smile stretch across his face.

Cyrus grinned, nodded, and clapped him on the shoulder. For once, it didn't make Killian feel like he was going to explode. "Exactly." They hauled each other to their feet and started walking back toward the group. "I always knew you were smarter than you looked."

CHAPTER 62

"You're purring again."

Sunlight slanted through the blinds, turning a strip of Killian's arm a brighter gold. Juno stroked the spot, loving the feel of his hard forearm, the soft hairs dusting his skin, the rumble of his purr against her back.

"Sorry." His nose nuzzled her neck before he placed his mouth directly over her ear and growled, raising goosebumps all over her body. "You like that better, don't you?"

Tingles rushed over her skin. "I like them both."

"Yeah, but only one of them makes you wet."

Jesus. Her core responded instantly, like he'd commanded it.

His low chuckle told her he knew exactly what he'd done. Cocky, wasn't he? He'd pay for that. *Get down!*

They rolled apart, diving off opposite sides of the bed to land in a crouch on the cold concrete floor.

"Fuck, DeSilva." Killian rose irritably, cupping his enormous erection. "I crunched my dick."

She snorted with laughter, crawling back on the mattress while he watched, catching his bottom lip between his teeth. "The enemy doesn't care about your dick." Her gaze traveled over every hard, delicious inch of him. "Even if it is magnificent."

They'd run this drill several times over the last couple days. They might be newly mated and enjoying some mandatory R&R, but it didn't mean they could let themselves get soft. Even if they had moved into one of the big rooms at the end of the hall and spent more time petting each other than anything else.

Killian planted his palms on the bed and prowled toward her, snagging her ankle and flipping her onto her back so he could yank her to the edge of the mattress. Her heart kicked up a notch when he sank to his knees and spread her legs. His growl thrummed through the room. "Does the enemy care about me licking you 'til you come?" His hot yellow eyes flipped to meet hers.

She stared down at him past her own pumping chest. "I don't think they'd interrupt that."

"No?" He lowered his head, one corner of his mouth lifting.

She swallowed. "No. Definitely not."

His breath was hot on her core. "And why is that?"

"Oh, you know…" Her flippant response flew out of her head at the first drag of his tongue. "Oh God."

Another long, slow lick followed. "You were saying, DeSilva?" A flick, then a soft, wet circle.

Her breath hitched as electricity shot through her. "What?"

His tongue lapped at her. "Why wouldn't the enemy interrupt this?" His lips wrapped around her clit and sucked.

Her hips arched off the bed. She pressed the back of his head, keeping him in place. "Because I'd fucking kill them."

His pleased hum vibrated against her core. "That's my woman."

His woman. His female. His mate. She still couldn't believe it, and yet nothing had ever felt so perfect. *Faster.*

No.

Faster!

No.

Give me a finger, then.

A hard, thick warmth slipped inside her, and she groaned as he slid his finger in and out while his tongue teased her clit. *Flick my spot.*

He obeyed.

Noises were escaping her, and she didn't care. *Touch my breast.*

A big, warm hand slid up her body to palm her breast, kneading and rolling, pinching her nipple.

Oh God. *Faster. More tongue. Oh God…*

She exploded with a guttural noise, then a keening cry when he sucked her again, unrelenting. His fierce male satisfaction roared across the bond, magnifying everything, sending her pleasure into the stratosphere.

"Mmm." His rumble vibrated against her wet center. "Pinkfruit."

She dragged him up her body, her core throbbing. "Get in me."

He plunged deep, wringing hoarse cries from them both, then planted one knee on the bed and pounded harder, deeper, his eyes locked on hers. She gripped his hair. He gripped hers. She gripped his heart. He gripped hers.

Come for me, Diallo.

Always.

ACKNOWLEDGMENTS

Raise your hand if you're a girl who grew up playing superhero games with the boys. Me, too! We used to run around pretending to be Ninja Turtles or X-Men, and while I loved dressing up and feeling pretty (still do), I always wanted to be just as powerful and physical as my brothers. Juno is a tribute to all the girls who feel that way. We are beautiful and we are savage. We don't have to give up one for the other. If I could instill one thing into the hearts of little girls everywhere, it would be that.

To everyone who loved my first book and cheered me on as I wrote this one, thank you. You're making my biggest dream come true. I appreciate every single one of you more than you know!

To my parents, thank you for always loving and accepting your quirky girl who marches to her own beat. It means everything.

To my team at Harbor Lane, my circle of author friends, and my incredible beta readers, I can't thank you enough for your encouragement, enthusiasm, and endless patience!

To the Les Mills fitness community and on-demand fitness app: You've truly changed my life. In many ways, you inspired Juno, who is the epic personification of my late-blooming inner athlete. Because of Les Mills, I understand the burning need to use my body and unleash my inner warrior. You allowed me to channel Juno's energy every single day while working out in my home gym. Thank you!

To my self-proclaimed superfans who tell all their friends

about my books, get this series into indie bookstores, and leave Hellbound quotes all over my house, I don't deserve you. You keep me going.

To my husband, my dragon keeper, my mate. I fall more in love with you every single day. You feed me, you make me cocktails, you help me talk through plot problems, you shout your pride from the rooftops. You are my strong male lead. I'm the luckiest dragon alive.

Thank you all for coming on this adventure with me!

(As always, if these characters said/did anything to offend you, take it up with them. I just write the incident reports.)

Join me on Facebook and Instagram for funny memes, bookish ramblings, author updates, and more!

xoxo,

Gin

ABOUT THE AUTHOR

The real world is boring. Gin prefers the realm of fantasy, where heroes smolder, heroines kick ass, magic is real, and love conquers all.

When she's not writing paranormal romance, she's usually reading it. Otherwise, you can find her singing in her retro band, Vandello, enjoying good food and cocktails, or training to be a superhero in her home gym.

She lives in the midwestern woods with her golden retriever and her husband, who has a sexy beard he's forbidden to shave.

Favorite things include: funky music, tart drinks, strong candles, and big, goofy dogs.

ABOUT THE PUBLISHER

Harbor Lane Books, LLC is a US-based independent digital publisher of commercial fiction, non-fiction, and poetry.

Connect with Harbor Lane Books on their website www.harborlanebooks.com, TikTok, Instagram, Facebook, X, and Pinterest @harborlanebooks.

ALSO BY GIN GRIFFITH